FOR A GOOD TIME,
Call...

ANNE TENINO
E.J. RUSSELL

A BLUEWATER BAY STORY

I0563574

RIPTIDE
PUBLISHING

Riptide Publishing
PO Box 1537
Burnsville, NC 28714
www.riptidepublishing.com

For a Good Time, Call...

Cover art: L.C. Chase, lcchase.com/design.htm
Editor: May Peterson, maypetersonbooks.com
Layout: L.C. Chase, lcchase.com/design.htm

ISBN: 978-1-62649-593-7

First edition
April, 2017

Also available in ebook:
ISBN: 978-1-62649-592-0

FOR A GOOD TIME, Call...

ANNE TENINO
E.J. RUSSELL

A BLUEWATER BAY STORY

RIPTIDE
PUBLISHING

TABLE OF CONTENTS

*I*t's just a theater, not a torture chamber. You're here to consult, as a favor to a friend, nothing more.

No matter how many times Nate Albano had repeated that to himself in the last few hours, his palms were still sweaty as he entered the Bluewater Bay Theater lobby. *Chill. Focus on the task at hand—or on the building itself, not what it stands for in your own pathetic life.*

From his research into town history, Nate knew that the theater had started life as a vaudeville house in the early twenties, but had hosted barely six months' worth of acts before it closed, a victim of the rise of the nickelodeon and the difficulty of luring quality performers to the Olympic Peninsula. It'd had a second life as a first-run movie house in Hollywood's golden era, but had closed again with the rise of the multiplex and a downturn in the local economy.

Now, it was experiencing another revival—in more ways than one. The vintage movie posters lining the lobby were a little yellowed with age, but now they were encased in glass and high-end frames. The carpet, still dotted with random crimson tufts where the installers had been sloppy with the vacuum, hadn't lost the odor of newness. No doubt about it—the playhouse had benefited from its association with Levi Pritchard.

Nate could relate. He had Levi to thank for his own presence in Bluewater Bay. In the aftermath of Jorge walking out on their six-year relationship, Nate had burned so many bridges in Hollywood that he hadn't worked for over a year. Then he'd gotten that call out of the blue—Levi had recommended Nate for a spot on the special effects crew of *Wolf's Landing* on the strength of his work on the SFX crews of Levi's indie films. So what if setting foot in a theater again knotted his belly and sent his pulse into overdrive? Levi had asked for his help on his latest community theater production—and Levi could pretty much ask him to do anything, short of taking a flying leap off the edge of Sandy Bluff, and Nate would follow through.

When he slipped into the auditorium, Levi was standing at the edge of the stage, flanked by a woman wearing a headset and a man scribbling notes on a clipboard. Nate knew the drill all too well—he'd logged enough hours in darkened theaters to identify the defeated slump of the crew's shoulders and the tension fairly vibrating off Levi. *Welcome to tech week.*

Nate started down the aisle as Levi cursed under his breath.

"The set looks great, Jack, don't get me wrong. But the vibe for this scene—Darla, can we do something with the lights to make this look more like a luxury hotel gone to seed and less like the Transylvania Holiday Inn?"

The woman muttered into her mic, and the lights bathing the stage dimmed and took on a bluish cast.

"Yeah, that's it. Can we get more of the moonlight effect through the window? And what about— Nate." Levi beckoned him over. "Thank God. Come meet everyone."

When Nate reached the front of the house, Levi clapped him on the shoulder. "Folks, this is Nate Albano, who's on the special effects crew for *Wolf's Landing.* Darla's our lighting designer." She nodded but turned away to continue her conversation. Levi turned to the man with the clipboard, a thirtysomething guy with sandy hair and a determined chin. "And Jack's my technical director. He's done miracles with our limited budgets."

Nate shook hands, nodding at the set, with its dark wainscoting and realistic plaster walls. "I can tell. You must have a killer fly system to be able to cap the walls with the ceiling that way."

"Yeah." Jack shrugged. "Thanks to Levi. He ponied up half the cost for the upgrade a couple years back."

"Don't give me more credit than I'm due," Levi said. "Guy Parker was the real hero there. Between his fundraising campaign and his own donations—"

Jack leaned toward Nate and spoke out of the side of his mouth. "Only because he didn't want the scenery to fall on his wife's head."

FOR A GOOD TIME, CALL . .

Levi chuckled. "Elle Parker is one of our regular actors—she's playing Elizabeth. Hey, Elle," he called. "Come on out and meet the man who's facilitating your murder."

A willowy blonde woman poked her head out of the wings. "You bellowed, oh fearless leader?" She walked out onto the apron, her long rehearsal skirt setting the residual construction dust swirling. A thin, nervous-looking man in a business suit followed her, squinting in the lights.

"Elle, meet Nate." Levi nodded at the man. "That's her husband, Guy." Guy raised a hand in greeting but didn't come closer.

Elle leaned over to shake Nate's hand. "Pleased to meet you. I make it a practice to be on good terms with all my killers."

"Don't think of me as a killer. I'm more a serial enabler."

"That's right," a deep voice boomed. "Don't encroach on my territory." A huge guy—made even huger by boots with stacked soles and a shirt with some serious shoulder padding—stomped onstage. His face was seamed with scars and distorted by some convincing prosthetics.

Holy— Ty, the cook at Flat Earth, was intimidating enough just wielding his long-handled pizza peel. But now? "*You're* playing the Creature, Ty? Wow. Talk about typecasting."

"Watch it, Albano," Ty growled, "or I'll slip jalapeños under the mushrooms on your next combo pie." Then he grinned, offering Nate a fist bump.

"Elle, Ty, can you run through the blocking for this scene for Nate? I want him to see what we're trying *not* to do."

"Sure thing, Levi." Ty lumbered off stage right, while Guy sidled over to stand next to Nate and Levi.

Elle took her place in the middle of the set and began to pace, glancing at the camelback clock over the fireplace, peering out the window as if waiting for someone to return.

Something thumped stage right outside the door. Elle spun around as the door swung open slowly, revealing Ty looming outside, filling the doorframe. He growled low in his throat, took a step forward . . . and banged his head on the lintel.

"Ow!"

Elle burst into giggles as Ty rubbed his forehead.

3

Levi sighed. "Ty, we talked about this. You need to slam the door open. Try it again, and this time, really whale on it."

"Got it." He exited, closing the door gingerly.

The actors started the scene again, and on cue, Ty flung the door open so hard that it bounced off the wall and creaked closed in his face. This time, even Levi laughed—although he also pinched the bridge of his nose.

"See why I called you? This is a climactic scene. If we were doing *Young Frankenstein* instead of just *Frankenstein*, that would have been golden."

Nate's cell phone shrilled from his jacket pocket. "Shit. Sorry, Levi. Should have silenced it before I came in." His mother would have murdered him for disrupting a rehearsal with a cell phone call. He pulled the phone out—*speak of the she-devil*—and took great pleasure in turning the damn thing off when he saw his mother's name on the caller ID.

Levi cleared his throat. "Didn't mean to invade your privacy, but Iris Bedrosian, Nate? *The* Iris Bedrosian?" His eyebrows snapped together. "You're not leaving *Wolf's Landing* for Broadway, are you?"

"Trust me. There's zero chance of that."

"Then why— I mean, sorry if I'm intruding, but it seems odd she'd call you if it wasn't about a job."

"Well . . ." Nate rubbed the back of his neck. "She's my mother."

"You're kidding. We've known each other how long, and you never thought to mention it?"

"Not exactly something I advertise. I didn't speak to her for over fourteen years."

Levi nodded. "Mom issues. I get it. Been down that road myself."

"Yeah? Did yours lie to you the way mine did to me?"

"Actually, it was the other way around. I lied to her and my father about being bisexual."

"We didn't have that issue, but—" Nate shook his head. "Hey. We're not here to talk about motherly love or lack of it. I take it you want to beef up the impact of this scene."

"You think?"

"So . . ." Nate squinted at the coffered ceiling on the hotel room set. "How would you feel about an audience-shits-their-pants moment?"

Levi grinned. "I'd kill for one. Think you can deliver?"
With this set and a competent TD? "Yeah, I can do that."
"That's why I love working with you. What have you got?"
Nate pointed to the ceiling. "We can take full advantage of the
current design. All we have to do is—"
"Levi?" Carter Samuels called from halfway down the aisle. "Are
you ready to go?"
Levi's smile bloomed as he gazed at his husband. "Hey, babe.
What—" He winced. "C.J.'s party. Damn. I forgot. But it's tech
week—"
"Yeah, and your actors and crew have other jobs." Carter sauntered
over. When he gave Levi a kiss, the expression on both their faces was
one of total adoration. *Just like I thought I had once.* "Come on, you
slave driver. Let everyone go."
"You're right." He turned to the stage. "That's it for tonight,
everyone. Tomorrow night, same time." He grabbed Nate's elbow.
"Not you, though. You can fill me in on your ideas at the party."
"I . . . uh . . . wasn't planning to go."
Levi frowned. "How long have you been in this town? Six
months? Seven?"
"Eight and a half, actually."
"Eight and a half, then, and you haven't gone out with us once."
"I have. A couple of times."
"Only because you were forced. This'll be an easy one. It's just over
at Ma Cougar's, nothing too fancy, everyone welcome." Levi lowered
his voice, let go of Nate's elbow, and squeezed his shoulder instead.
"It's been three years since he left. Isn't it time to get out there again?"
What was it about people who were stupid in love? Why did
they think everyone else burned to be in the same state? Nate was
managing just fine on his own. He had his job, his dog, his hobbies.
If he was lonely from time to time, so what? Better that than a futile
search for a soul mate, someone who *got* him. *I've had that. Twice.*
Can't expect lightning to strike a third time.
"I'm good, Levi. Really."
"Even so, you're coming along tonight. Have a drink or two and
tell me about your ideas, because we've only got a week to implement
them. Jack? Can you join us?"

"Sure. Soon as I lock up."

"See you there." Levi slung his arm across Carter's shoulders. "Let's get going—the sooner we make our appearance, the sooner we can leave."

Nate sighed and followed the couple up the aisle. What the hell—it wasn't as if he had to meet anyone's socializing expectations. *It's just a drink.* For Levi, surely he could survive one evening out.

CHAPTER TWO

On Sunday morning when Seth Larson went to his grandmother's house to steal coffee, he found her lying in wait for him. "I'm absolutely certain there are squirrels in the attic," she said in greeting after he'd let himself in the kitchen door.

"Grandma." That was totally a whiny voice. *You're thirty, shape up.* "Let me at least finish one cup first."

Peering at him over the top of her newspaper, she nodded. He'd been his grandmother's de facto handyman long enough—twelve years, on and off—to read her unspoken message. This was part of her plan to get the Sentinel House—the Larson family manse—in shape to sell.

He couldn't crush her dream of getting rid of this albatross and moving into Bluewater Bay Senior Estates. So, he spent the next eight hours hunting for squirrels in all the hidey-holes and crawl spaces his great-great-grandfather had had built into the place.

It took all day, and he never found a single squirrel. He did run across a total of five mummified rodent corpses. Thank God for work gloves, because when he planted his hand right in the remains of the first one and it crunched flat under his weight, he nearly shrieked. He managed to contain it to a yelp. Yet another reason for Grandma to sell the damn place. If only they could convince the rest of the family.

Finally done, he had to rush back to his studio apartment over the garage. He had barely a half hour to clean up and make it to Ma Cougar's to meet Lucas Wilder. Even though he was looking forward to going out tonight, Seth debated with himself about it while he was in the shower. Grandma had seemed unnaturally melancholy. Maybe leaving her alone wasn't a good idea. But he wanted to get out, even needed it. Since his grandmother had decided to get the house sale-ready, she'd been having him do more chores than normal around the place. He'd hardly seen anyone under fifty all week other than at work.

What am I going to do when Grandma moves?

Well, there was something he hadn't thought of.

Huh. Realizing he was doing nothing but standing in a spray of warm water, staring at droplets forming and then running down the glass door, Seth shook himself from his thoughts and finished washing up.

It only took him a few more minutes to fix his hair and trim his beard with the clippers in order to keep it just the length he liked. He was only meeting Lucas after all, this wasn't a date in either Grandma's sense or his own. He hadn't gotten "social" in a while, but he had high hopes that Lucas would make a good wingman.

Maybe "high" hopes was a bit of an exaggeration.

Ma Cougar's was less than a block away. The hip new gastropub had been built on the site of the town's first lumber mill, which in turn had been built by none other than his own great-great-grandfather.

Interesting how his father and uncle were okay with selling off the mill land, but couldn't bear to part with a house neither even wanted to live in. He filed that thought away for future use, when the sale of Sentinel House became a family "discussion."

Light met him at the double doors that opened on the restaurant side, and warmth blasted his face the second he walked in. For some reason, when he wasn't working he preferred entering this way. Like going in the front door instead of the servants' entrance.

"Hey, Diana." He smiled at the assistant manager as he passed the hostess stand. She smiled back and waved before continuing what she'd been saying to the new hostess under training.

He found Lucas at a table in the narrow passage between the bar and dining room areas.

He and Lucas should have been friends in high school. They were in the same grade, were each descended from pioneer families that had settled the area and—most importantly in Seth's mind back then—they were both gay. They hadn't been friends though, because Lucas had been a douche.

Except Seth had an inkling that if things had been reversed and Lucas had been the accidentally outed gay boy while Seth had been the closeted one desperately trying to appear straight, he might have avoided Lucas like the plague much the same way Lucas had avoided him.

Even back then, Seth was pretty sure he'd been the more butch one of the two of them. An impression he only confirmed for himself as he watched the dude sipping a fruity drink through a straw while waiting for him. Or maybe not—Lucas jerked his head back from the glass after a sip and grimaced at it, as if it had personally offended him. His expression was still one of distaste when he caught sight of Seth and lifted a hand half-heartedly.

Did *no one* want to see him tonight? *Buck up.* Diana had been busy, and Lucas was being, well, Lucas. Not all of the dude's douchebaggery had been left back in his teen years. The difference was now he apologized if it was pointed out to him, and he seemed truly repentant. It was the only reason Seth socialized with him.

Well, that and the need he seemed to have to make Lucas like him. *There* was something he wished he'd left back in twelfth grade.

"This is *disgusting*," the man in question said once Seth was within hearing range. "I hope when you start tending bar you don't force shit like this on me."

"Someone forced you to order an orange drink with a pineapple and a little parasol?" Seth shrugged his jacket off and hung it on the little hook at the end of the booth. As he turned to sit, he found Lucas had stood and was kissing him on the cheek before plopping down again.

Seth snorted as he slid into the booth. "Sometimes you make it really hard to forget you haven't lived here since you were eighteen."

"No kissing friends hello, then, huh?" Lucas rolled his eyes before leaning forward to take his straw back into his mouth, biting it and shaking his head with his teeth bared. Apparently that was his opinion of social customs in Bluewater Bay.

"Kiss me if you want." Seth shrugged. "I'm just saying people don't see two guys greeting each other that way around here often."

"Why did I move back again?"

"Gabe," they both said at the same moment, and Lucas's dissatisfied expression melted away as he went dreamy-eyed. There was no other word for it. Lucas sighed and sipped his drink, which apparently killed his mood all over again.

"Yuck. Screw this." He shoved the glass toward the end of the table. "I can't do it. I'll have that beer I usually order." Leave it to him to assume Seth would know what he meant. "The light caramel one, you know? Just a skosh bitter?"

Of course, Seth *did* know. Lucas ordered it every time he came in, as soon as someone reminded him what it was. "Local Logger Lager." How hard was that to remember? "How'd you end up with—" he squinted at the pear-shaped cocktail on their table, trying to place it. *Got it.* "—a zombie, anyway?"

Lucas bobbed his head toward the wall next to them, and the glossy, picture-laden specialty cocktails menu that was posted there. "I couldn't resist the name. You should come up with some classier mixed drinks."

"I'm only a lowly bartender, I'm not in charge of that stuff," Seth reminded him as he flagged down Zoe. "Plus, I technically don't start the new job until tomorrow." Ma Cougar's seemed extra busy tonight, and Zoe looked extra flustered as she headed their way, carrying a fully laden bar tray. "Hey, hi." He gave her his most winning smile as she lurched to a stop next to their booth.

"You guys want something else?"

"A couple of Local Loggers?" He hated asking her when the place was packed. "Or I could go get them myself."

"Nah," she said over her shoulder as she started off again. "Let me, it's your last night before starting the new job."

Lucas spent the first half hour catching Seth up on his life. It was mostly about some gallery show Lucas was making a lot of work for, and everything Gabe had been doing regarding his tree farm. To hear Lucas tell it, it sounded as if Savage Tree Farm was quickly turning into a marijuana operation. Seth didn't need all the updates—his regular customers kept him current on just about everything and everyone in Bluewater Bay—but he took a sip every time Lucas said his boyfriend's name. He'd finished his first beer and nodded at Zoe for another before Lucas asked, "So, what's up with you?"

"Nothing, really." He shrugged. "You already know about my promotion, and otherwise it's same old, same old." Mentally debating whether it was a good idea to tell Lucas about sprucing up Grandma's house to sell, he busied himself with spinning a beer coaster on its side. Until Lucas slapped it flat, killing all motion. "So no one new?" he asked pleasantly, in complete contrast to how aggressive his coaster offense had been. "Seeing anyone regularly?"

Seth raised his brow and pointedly eyed Lucas's hand, still palm down on the table in front of him.

"Sorry," Lucas sighed, withdrawing his arm. He grimaced apologetically and picked up his beer—still nearly full—sipping it while he watched Seth over the rim.

Ever since Lucas Wilder and Gabe Savage had gotten together, Lucas had been cajoling Seth into finding a "one true love." In keeping with his preferred lack of making an effort, Lucas did so by asking a lot of questions about who Seth had been messing around with, and what kind of "future" they might have as a couple.

The guy was motivated by his own guilt, and his desire to get rid of it. Guilt over being a dick to Seth in high school and over "stealing" Gabe. Probably mostly over the stealing of Gabe, which was all in the dude's head. Seth and Gabe had been fuck buddies and friends, nothing more. He still had half of that, and it wasn't very difficult to find someone to hook up with in this town, not since *Wolf's Landing* had started filming here.

Right now, talking about Grandma's house seemed like a better topic, even if he *was* trying to keep gossip from getting around until after the rest of the family had agreed to the sale. Lucas wasn't likely to tell anyone, anyway. He wasn't likely to remember it past tonight. The guy gave new meaning to "self-absorbed."

Maybe I still have issues with him . . . Whatever.

Seth's thinking silence had consequences. "I haven't seen you around much, lately," Lucas continued as he set his beer down. "I thought maybe you and—"

"I'm helping Grandma get her house ready to sell." He wasn't throwing her under the bus by telling. Not really. "She wants to move into the Bluewater Bay Senior Estates."

"Oooh!" Lucas's eyes lit up, which seemed a pretty damned odd reaction. "Gramma—Gabe's grandmother—would move there in half a second if she thought she could."

Crazy. Even talk of Gabe's family affected the dude. Or he really liked Gabe's grandmother. Not impossible to believe—Seth really liked *his* grandmother. "That so? Huh."

"I think she wants to be closer to the gossip." Lucas squinted. "And her friends."

"Why doesn't she move?"

Lucas shrugged. "She feels like she needs to stay with her family. Gabe's mom would be all alone in the house if she left. I mean, Jane tells her it would be fine, but Gramma doesn't believe it, I guess."

Jane was Ms. Savage's first name? He'd never known that. Lucas must be pretty close to Gabe's family. Of course, the couple lived in an apartment that Gabe had built years ago in the horse barn, while Gabe's grandmother and mother lived in the "big house." It was a lot like Seth's own situation, minus his mother and a live-in partner. Oh, and his apartment was much smaller.

"Listen, don't tell anyone about the house, we're trying to keep it secret. Although she might already have a buyer—Charley Sykes and his wife want to turn it into a B&B." They were locals, about ten years older than Seth and Lucas were, but their kids were already off to college. People started young in small towns. Some people.

He could tell by the way Lucas squinted and stared at the ceiling that he had no clue who that was. Lucas didn't ask though. "So once your grandma sells the house, are you leaving Bluewater Bay?"

The question startled Seth so much he could only blink for a second. But Lucas didn't jump in and continue, instead he waited with what looked like true interest. "Um, I wasn't planning on leaving, no." Not that he'd made a plan to stay. Or any plans at all. Why had this whole issue only occurred to him tonight?

"Really?" Lucas screwed up his brows. "If it wasn't for Gabe, I wouldn't stay here."

As if Seth didn't know Lucas was only here now because Gabe was tied to his family's tree farm? *Oh, cool it.* Getting prickly with Lucas because of his own questions about what he was going to do and why he was even still here in this town was stupid.

Still, he didn't feel like revealing any of his internal quandary to Lucas, no matter how civilized the dude had become. "Why would I want to leave? This is the farthest north you can go in the continental United States and still regularly bang TV stars."

Lucas laughed, and Zoe came by just then, giving them a work-mode smile that Seth knew well. "So, are you guys planning on ordering any food, tonight? Because—"

"We can move to the bar, no problem." Seth was already scooting to the edge of the booth and grabbing his jacket. When he reached back for his beer, he caught Lucas's frown. Darn it, was the guy going to cause problems? Did he think his butt was too important to make room for a more lucrative customer's?

"I didn't even think of that," was all Lucas said, though. "It *is* really crowded in here, huh?"

"It's Prime Rib night," Seth explained, then tried to decide the fastest way to get Lucas to cooperate.

Except he didn't need to because Lucas had already stood and taken his own glass, contradicting all Seth's assumptions about the guy's self-centeredness.

Shit, he really was still holding a few grudges about Lucas, wasn't he?

With the chaos of the party swirling around their corner table, Nate had to almost shout so Jack and Levi could hear him. "See what I mean? We'll only have to deal with this little section . . ." He scribbled a few final notes under his sketch and passed the paper to Jack. "It'll be easy to replace for each performance."

Jack nodded, a smile finally dawning on his face after a solid hour of scowling into his beer. "Yeah. Yeah, that'll be a snap."

"This is *outstanding*." Levi threw back his head and laughed, causing everyone in the bar to look their way—Levi wasn't normally a gut-laugh kind of guy. "I owe you. Big time."

"The least I could do. Besides, design is the easy part. Jack has the tough job—he'll have to prep the new sections and rebuild the lab table in a week."

Levi slapped Jack on the shoulder. "No fear there. This guy can work miracles. Sometimes I think he actually lives in an alternate dimension where time runs at a different pace."

For a dour guy, Jack blushed like a teenager. "It's nothing. Just doing my job." He stood up. "Thanks for the drink, Levi. And Nate? These designs—well, I hope I do them justice." He lifted a hand and threaded his way through the crowd of *Wolf's Landing* cast and crew, stopping near the door to exchange a couple of words with Carter.

Levi's gaze lingered on his husband for a moment before returning to Nate. "Seriously, I can't thank you enough."

"No thanks necessary, man. After you went to bat for me—"

"No hardship there—in fact, Anna practically genuflects to me every time you pull off another effect that supports her anti-CGI position. And if you keep the actors safe . . ." His gaze wandered again, to where Carter was chatting with C.J. and Ginsberg.

Yeah, it's not "actors" in general that he's protective of. But Nate didn't begrudge them their happiness—much. Well, *begrudge* wasn't the word precisely. *Envy. Yearn. Crave.* Those were words he could get behind, when he was honest with himself, because it was obvious how connected the two men were, regardless of what went on in the bedroom.

That was what he missed, what he had little hope of finding again—someone who knew him so well that they'd meet his eyes across a room and their smile would be enough to ground him at the same time it lifted him up. A promise that no matter what crap life threw at the two of them, they were in it together.

A movement beyond Carter's shoulder caught his eye. Over at the bar, a blond guy with a neat jawline beard stood up, turning a knockout smile on the waitress.

That's the kind of smile I wish was waiting for me at the end of every day. But how likely was that? Given how few people understood the nuances of his orientation, the odds were astronomical. He'd beaten the odds twice—for a little while at least—but he'd given up on hitting the kind of jackpot Levi had with Carter. And given how gutted he'd been when both his previous relationships had ended, he was better off not gambling on another one, not with his lousy luck.

Much safer that way. Lonely, but safer. *Although*—he couldn'l help stealing another glance at the smiling blond—*it would sure be nice to beat the odds for good.*

CHAPTER THREE

The bar was unusually crowded for a Sunday—sometimes that happened for no rhyme or reason—so Seth led the way from the booth toward the barstools, which were probably their best shot at getting an actual seat. The very moment he stepped out of the dining room proper, the air grew staticky. Maybe it was because the area was so crowded—at least a third of the patrons were standing, unable to find seats. Maybe occupancy in excess of the fire marshal's limit created electricity.

"Guy!"

Did Lucas feel that strange atmosphere too? Seth screwed his head around to catch a glimpse of Lucas out of the corner of his eye. "What guy?"

He turned back the way he was going just in time to avoid walking into another pillar. Except this pillar was a person.

Oh, *Guy*. "Hey there." Seth smiled at Guy automatically. He was good people. "Come have a drink with us?"

A sharp, shoe-sized object kicked him in the ankle from behind. *Lucas doesn't like Guy?* The dude was a total geek, even in his thirties, but perfectly agreeable. Maybe a bit overly eager to be accepted, but he'd always been that way.

Be nice, it's good for you, he thought at Lucas while nodding Guy toward the bar area. "Behave," he hissed over his shoulder once Guy turned to lead the way to a stool that was opening up at that moment.

Guy reached it, then waved Lucas's butt onto it as if he were landing Air Force One, ignoring the other plane lined up to land. Namely, Seth. He'd just managed to drape his jacket on the stool's backrest before Lucas had completely claimed it.

Okay, that might be annoying. But it was Lucas's bad luck to be one of those people that others were desperate to have like him. Seth couldn't claim he had a lot of sympathy.

After five minutes of experiencing Guy in "schmooze" mode, he had *all* the sympathy. Guy was downright obsequious toward Lucas. First he insisted on buying them drinks, even though theirs were nearly full, then he peppered Lucas with inane questions about his work and his life before Lucas had moved back to Bluewater Bay, with heavy emphasis on what kind of "presence" he intended to create in the community.

Well, you had to give Guy points for caring about the town.

Regardless of Seth's attempts to find this side of Guy tolerable, Guy didn't ask him a damned thing. Which was sort of expected—Seth saw Guy frequently, usually as his waiter, and Elle, Guy's wife, was the one who usually chatted with him—but he couldn't say he liked being ignored in favor of someone deemed more important.

"So, you're flying solo tonight?" he asked once Guy had taken a break from flinging questions at Lucas.

"Um." Guy finally looked away from Lucas. "No."

"I meant," Seth said, as Guy continued to frown at him, "Is Elle with you?" Then *he'd* have someone to talk to.

"Oh, got it." The parts of Guy Seth actually liked shone through at mention of his wife. He perched his elbow on the bar top and leaned his weight on it, smiling less maniacally than before but much more believably. "No, she didn't come. She had to go home after rehearsal to finish prepping for tomorrow. She's a teacher, you know." He directed the last part at Lucas. "I came with some of the theater crowd. You know, from the Bluewater Bay *Playhouse*. Used to be the Theater Company, but we're rebranding." His eyes lit up as he leaned closer to Seth to stage-whisper, "*Levi Pritchard* invited me. Hey," he continued in a normal voice, gaze flicking between them. "You guys want to meet him?"

"Who's Levi Pritchard?" Lucas asked guilelessly. But the split second of side-eye he shared with Seth showed the lie—Lucas knew who the actor was.

Predictably though, Guy bought it, deflating instantly. "You don't watch *Wolf's Landing*? I thought everyone did."

FOR A GOOD TIME, CALL . .

Perhaps sensing that he was about to be forced to listen to Guy's explanation of the show and the relative importance of everyone in it, Lucas waved a careless hand. "Oh, *that* Levi Pritchard. I've met him."

He couldn't have disappointed Guy any more if they'd stolen his pocket abacus. But the man didn't stay down for long. He turned eager eyes on Seth. "Have you met him?"

"Um, well, I mean, he and Carter come in to the restaurant sometimes, so I *know* them." That had to qualify. "I haven't been formally introduced, *per se.*"

"Oh, well, c'mon, then." Making a looping-arm motion, Guy took a couple of steps backward, watching them expectantly.

Seth didn't do more than shift his weight, and Lucas's butt stayed firmly on the barstool. "Are you sure they want to be bothered?" For the first time, Seth looked around, trying to find the "theater crowd." The only crowd he could see was from the TV show—he recognized them from serving them, and could match most of the faces with their usual orders. Then Derrick Richards moved out of the way, revealing the guy sitting next to Levi Pritchard and—

"Whoa." *How the hell did I miss* him? He was one of the most gut-wrenchingly attractive men Seth had ever seen in his life, hitting everything on Seth's checklist for hot: black hair, square jaw, perfect yet pronounced nose. Not that it mattered, because it was really about how the elements were put together, and this man's face was the perfect balance of strength and shadows.

"Whoa, what?" Lucas's voice rang with all the interest he hadn't shown for the last half hour.

"Just . . ." Seth shook his head, turning back. If Lucas saw the dude, it could lead to more speculation on Seth's love life, when all Seth wanted to speculate on was his immediate sexual future. "Dizzy spell." He winced internally. *Bad save.*

"That guy?" Lucas jerked his chin toward Levi's table. "With the curly hair and a touch of silver in his whiskers?" Just his luck that this was the one time Lucas would be paying actual attention. "We definitely go for the same type."

Well, duh. Gabe kind of proved that. He managed to not confirm or deny anything until Guy started asking, "Which one? Are you checking someone out? I could introduce you." He was nearly panting with eagerness, like a dog with his tongue lolling out, dying to sniff someone's butt.

"What are the chances he's even gay?" Seth answered without really answering.

"It's the theater crowd—I'd guess they're better than average." Lucas scooted to the edge of his stool and craned his neck. "That dude?" He helpfully pointed the gorgeous one out to Guy. "Sitting with Levi?"

Squinting, Guy nodded. "Nate. Just met him tonight, but he's single—I heard him say something earlier. His last relationship was with a 'he,' so that would make him gay, right?"

"Or bi."

"Or open-minded," Lucas offered, nudging him.

"This is ridiculous," Seth muttered. But if Guy was so desperate to make himself useful . . . He sighed and set his empty glass on the bar. "Lead on." He pointed at Lucas. "You stay here."

To Seth's surprise, Lucas did, but the set of his mouth was very smug. He'd be able to watch Seth get shot down just fine from this vantage point. *Excellent.*

When approaching a man, Seth's usual method was to assume success until he'd been given reason to think otherwise, but tonight his characteristic confidence failed him as he followed Guy across Ma Cougar's. He knew he was attractive enough to score more often than not, but he wasn't in this Nate person's league. Nate could have just stepped out of the pages of *GQ*—the Italian edition, judging by his swarthiness.

Another thing, did Seth really trust Guy to know if Nate was actually some shade of gay? And what did it say about *him* that he was being introduced by the town's nerdiest actuary?

Don't be an asshole. And you've been with guys who were way out of your league before. He'd long ago found that attitude and persistence counted for much more than general attractiveness or social status. It was the only thing that had gotten him through high school.

In the nick of time—Guy was already lifting his hand in an attention-getting wave—Seth's normal demeanor reasserted itself, dispelling (or maybe quashing) his uncharacteristic nervousness.

"Hey, Nate," Guy began. "Got someone here who you should meet."

Not that he didn't have some residual nerves as he stepped out from behind Guy and got his first up-close look at this evening's potential "date." Nate was more drool-inducing here than he'd been across the room. Not model-perfect, as Seth had thought, but better because he looked like a real person, not an airbrushed icon. A guy with acres of sun-darkened skin that Seth would love to inspect for tiny freckles.

"This is Seth," Guy was saying as Nate pushed back in his chair, turning just enough to face their direction.

Nate stood up, turning a pair of beautiful gray eyes on Seth. He stepped away from the table and held out his hand. "Hi. Nate Albano."

Seth was sure his smile was lighting up the bar, he put so much enthusiasm into it. "Hello there."

Nate had sculpted hands, warm and rough to the touch, that gave the overall impression of being square. Square fingers and knuckles just knotty enough. Even his grip was secure and well-built, if that made any sense. "Seth Larson." He didn't need to repeat his name, but it gave him another second to feel Nate's hand wrapped around his.

Nate didn't let go after that. He held on, lips parting as he stared. "Larson? You're not related to Finn Larson, are you?"

That bastard. "Oh, no." Seth waved him off with the back of his free hand and then extended his pinky in the most posh manner, knowing he was overdoing it but unable to stop himself from hamming it up for this guy. "I'm from the *Bluewater Bay* Larsons, don't you know. We practically *built* this town."

The sarcasm was clearly lost on Nate, because his very attractive brow wrinkled up while Guy chortled. "But they did, didn't they? It was Fennimore Larson who established the old town around the mill. I mean, this bar—it's standing on the original mill site, right?" Slowly, as if he, too, were reluctant to lose physical contact, Nate loosened his grip and let his hand slip away. Was it Seth's imagination that he took a few too many moments to let go? His palm had pressed against Seth's in an explicitly intimate way, hadn't it?

Seth chose to believe that was all intentional. But then Nate's questions sunk in.

Shit. "Why the hell would you know that?" That didn't sound as rude aloud as it had in his head, did it? "I mean, it's kind of obscure." Although his uncle Kirk would be thrilled to know his efforts to make the local historical society a major attraction were apparently working on this one person. Of course, that depended on how much and what exactly Nate *knew* about Fennimore Larson.

Nate broke into a small, somewhat sheepish smile, flashing his straight, white teeth. Everything about this guy was stellar, wasn't it? "I'm . . . ah . . . kind of a history and genealogy buff."

That abashed little grin was darling. With that and the genealogy line, he'd have all the self-centered boys eating out of his hand. Of course, where Nate was concerned, nearly anything would work.

"It just so happens I'm well-versed on the founding of the town." Or certain parts of it anyway.

"Wait—*Seth* Larson? Holy shit, I've got you on the Larson family tree. Fennimore was your great-great-grandfather, right? It's so great to meet you. I've checked out the land grants at the state level, but I've been dying to talk with someone in the family about the founding of the town."

He's got me on a family tree? Seth wasn't sure if that was really flattering or really creepy. "I've never met a nonlocal who's interested in hearing about it, actually." Seth knew enough about it to keep them here a few hours.

But land grant and deed records were one of the exact things his family most wanted people to forget—how to suppress them was the main topic of conversation during family holiday mealtimes. Besides, he didn't want to bore the dude, he wanted to keep him talking about himself, or at least his interests. "What led you to digging up my ancestor?" So to speak.

"Whenever I move to a new place, I always research the town. It's a hobby—although Morgan—" he pointed to a tall black woman who was smiling at Derrick "—calls it an obsession, especially when I get involved in chasing down something interesting and forget I'm supposed to meet her for dinner." He grinned sheepishly. "Fennimore cuts a pretty wide swath in Bluewater Bay history. He's pretty major."

Seth laughed shortly, unable to help himself. "Well, my father and uncle would like to think so." He stepped a little closer, near enough for the conversation to seem private. "My family has some excess pride in their ancestry. If you're really into it, I'd be happy to tell you all about my history." Seth just stopped himself from winking. Nate brought out the cheese in him, clearly. He'd have to watch it, because he didn't want to overplay this.

"That'd be great." Nate glanced back at the three-top. Levi and Jack had vacated at the same time as Nate, but it had already been claimed by someone else. He shrugged. "I guess we stand, if that's okay."

Perfect for my purposes. Seth took a small, unobtrusive breath through his nose in an attempt to clear his head. Make sure what he was about to say wasn't too much too soon.

Nope, sounds fine to me, his libido offered. "Maybe we should go someplace a little"—*more intimate*—"less busy to talk. I mean, if you want to know all about the Larsons."

Bad call! his higher brain was screaming in alarm before Seth even finished. *What about the woman Nate "forgets" to meet for dinner?* The one he was exchanging speaking glances with right this minute in the kind of communication that only long-established friends would use.

Or a couple. *Could he be bi?*

It doesn't matter what his preferences are if he's with someone else.

Fucking Guy. Why had he believed what a straight man said about another man's sexual preferences? Stupid mistake. Seth's chest began to tighten up—with his luck, he'd not only made a very obvious overture to a straight guy but he'd done it very publicly.

Run away! Run away! He swallowed, straightened his shoulders, and prepared to salvage some pride, damn it, by not waiting to be shot down in front of an audience that included half the town and his coworkers. His extensive experience with public humiliation had taught him that a dignified exit was the best way to escape complete disgrace.

Before he could babble out anything about needing to go find his friend, Nate glowered in the direction of the front door. "I'd be *happy* to get out of here. Stomping Grounds okay with you?"

Wait, what? Seth's libido had already switched gears and said, "Great, let me get my jacket," turned him around, and marched him off toward Lucas before the rest of him caught up to the unexpected situation change. Thank God for his libido's quick thinking, though, because he wasn't halfway to the bar before he realized he'd nearly fucked up the best thing that had happened to him in months. Well, from a sex point of view.

"I'm outta here," he said as soon as he was close enough to speak to Lucas without shouting. Knuckling the guy's back, he nudged him to move so he could get his jacket off the back of the barstool.

"Nice work." Lucas smiled smugly, then glanced down at his phone, where he'd clearly been texting someone. Probably his boyfriend. "I'm outta here in a second too, as soon as Gabe shows up."

So definitely texting Gabe.

It wasn't a sure thing, by any means, but Seth threw caution to the wind, potentially jinxing his evening. Grinning at Lucas as he took a couple steps backward, about to turn, he saluted the guy. "Looks like we're both gonna get some tonight."

CHAPTER FOUR

*W*ith Seth off grabbing his coat, Nate edged toward a gaggle of *Wolf's Landing* grips, pretending to be part of their conversation. It never paid to be obviously unoccupied when Finn was on the prowl, and the last thing Nate wanted right now was to get sucked into one of Finn's never-ending budget rants—not tonight, when he had something so much better to look forward to.

Seth had been . . . unexpected. The look on his face when Nate had been telling him about his embarrassingly unhip hobby—blue eyes wide, blond eyebrows lifted, smile just curving his lips. Hell, even his trendy haircut looked interested in Nate's story. *Curiosity.* Most guys Seth's age—he had to be at least ten years younger than Nate's thirty-seven—based their image on knowing everything already. Blasé post-college pseudo-expertise on everything from movies to technology to sports. If they ran into something they *didn't* know about, they either pretended knowledge, dismissed it as stupid, or changed the subject.

Nate peered through the crowd to track Seth's progress—he had stopped and was exchanging a few words with a dark-haired guy sitting at the bar. Both of them looked over at Nate, and Seth flashed that killer smile.

Then Nate's view was blocked by six feet of zaftig badass. Morgan—his coworker and best friend—tucked a stray dark curl under her African-print headband as she glanced over her shoulder in Seth's direction. "Careful, Nate. Your rep as an ice-cold mofo is skating on the edge with the way you're checking that boy out."

"I'm not 'checking him out.'" Nate widened his stance and crossed his arms. "For your information, we were chatting about town history—he's descended from the founder—and he was totally into it. Now that the Prince of Darkness has joined this party, we're heading over to Stomping Grounds to grab a cup of coffee. To *talk*. I know you find it hard to believe, but other people think history and genealogy are cool too."

"Other old, *boring* people." She took a sip of her beer and watched Seth disappear through the door behind the bar. "Trust me, that boy is not thinking about ancestors and descendants—unless it's how to get your pants to *descend* to the floor."

Nate scowled. "Cut it out. You know I'm not into that."

"At the moment, sure. But you have been—more than once— and maybe you will be again. Besides, just because *you're* not into it, doesn't mean *he's* not."

"Morgan—"

"Just sayin'. You haven't exactly circulated the Nate-is-grace memo."

"It's nobody's business but mine."

"I know. Sorry, baby. Have a good time talking about *ancestors*."

She planted a kiss on his cheek before wandering over to talk to a cluster of stunt performers. They greeted her with grins and hugs—but so did everyone. Morgan might be fierce, no-nonsense, and straight-talking, but as long as you weren't an asshole, she was totally approachable and gave the best hugs on the planet. Nate had reason to know—Morgan's hugs were all that kept him sane some days, when his need for a little human touch outweighed his sense of self-preservation.

Seth reappeared next to Nate with a tan canvas jacket slung over one shoulder. He squinted at Morgan's back for a minute before he turned to Nate. "You . . . uh . . . still want to take off?"

Since Finn was still at large somewhere in the pub, that was an easy answer. "Hell yeah." He grabbed his own coat, scanning the crowd for Levi.

Shit! Finn was threading his way through the crowd, angling to get past Mount Derrick, Ginsberg's giant boyfriend. Levi would just have to forgive him for not saying good-bye. He took Seth's elbow to steer him away from the danger zone, but released him once they'd gotten safely out the door.

"Sorry for the, you know, manhandling. But, God, I hate that guy."

"Finn? Yeah, you and everyone else in town, whether they work on the show or not. I mean, *all* the waitresses hate him. They have regular support groups—I think it involves a drinking game. One shot for every time Finn called one of them 'honey,' 'sweetheart,' or 'darling'—in the last three days. Extra points if he hollered for coffee as soon as he walked in the door."

"Sounds like Finn." Nate stuffed his hands in his pockets as they walked down the street. The breeze held the scent of the ocean and a hint of coming rain. Yeah, summer was definitely over.

"Does your girlfriend," Seth jerked his thumb back toward Ma Cougar's, "feel the same way?"

"Girlfriend? Who—" Nate barked a laugh. "You mean Morgan? God, she'd bust a gut if she heard you say that."

"Really? You seemed . . . friendly." Seth's tone was a little on the chilly side.

"We are. She's probably my best friend in town." Not that he had many. "She's on the effects crew with me. She does handhelds—you know, knives, guns, china that can shatter without slicing the cast to ribbons—while I do the bigger set pieces, like windows and furniture."

"So you're into *big things*? Intriguing."

Nate chuckled. "What can I say? If Hunter Easton didn't have poor Gabriel getting the shit beat out of him every third scene, my job would be a lot more boring. Not that it's all that thrilling for someone who isn't into SFX. No one wants to hear about how tricky it is to build something that looks real enough to be a threat but won't maim the actors and stunt performers. Do you know how many stuntmen were killed in the early days of silent films? There were no safety protocols, no—" He ran a hand through his hair. "Ah, shit. Sorry. I get a little carried away when I talk about history."

"Hey, no complaints here. I could listen to you all night long."

"Not all night, maybe, but long enough, right?" They walked past Stomping Grounds' plate-glass window, and Nate opened the door to let Seth enter. Warm air, heavy with the aroma of coffee and cinnamon, surrounded them. "Whew. Now suddenly I'm hot."

"I'll say," Seth murmured.

Nate stripped off his jacket and slung it over his arm. "What'll it be? It's a little late for coffee, eh? Maybe something else warm?"

"Definitely."

"What do you like?"

"Mmm. I prefer mine tall, dark, and sweet, with a hint of spice."

Nate grinned. "I know just the thing. Grab a table and I'll come as soon as I collect our supplies."

Seth opened his mouth as if he was about to say something, but then he shook his head and headed for a table in the far corner.

Nate walked up to the counter. "Hey, Buck. How you doing? Can you give me two tall spice tea lattes?"

The big barista grinned. "You got it, Nate. Want a couple of pastries too? We need to move them before closing."

"Sure. Give me two of those pecan twists for here and toss another four in a bag to go."

Buck raised his eyebrows. "Expecting company for breakfast?"

"Me? Nah. But it never hurts to show up at work with extra, you know what I mean? Besides, I wouldn't want you to be forced to take them all home to Ari. We need him to keep that svelte figure, or else the costume shop'll have to rebuild all his breakaway shirts."

"I think his metabolism runs on carbs," Buck said over the hiss of the milk steamer. "You should see how many doughnuts he can put away at one sitting."

"Some guys just win the genetic lottery, I guess. Now me—I'll pay for these with an extra half hour out running with Tarkus."

He chuckled. "You'll be lucky to get away with half an hour. Your dog has more stamina than any three guys."

"Tell me about it. I don't need a personal trainer when I've got him."

Buck arranged the order on a tray. "That'll be twenty-three fifty. By the way, I see you're here with Seth Larson." His voice rose slightly at the end of the sentence, making it almost a question.

"Yeah." Nate handed over his debit card. "Just met him tonight. I'll bet you know him though, since you're both townies."

He didn't meet Nate's eyes as he ran the card through the reader. "He's a few years older, so we never ran in the same crowd."

Nate keyed in his pin number. "I guess it's stupid to assume everyone in Bluewater Bay knows everyone else, eh?"

"Oh I know him all right." He handed back the card and muttered something under his breath that sounded like "Everyone does."

What? Nate was about to ask for clarification, but Buck had already turned to the next customer. He shrugged and picked up the tray, wending his way through the maze of tables to where Seth was waiting.

Nate set down the tray. After he tossed his jacket over the back of the chair, he unloaded the drinks and plunked the plate with the pastries in the middle of the table. "You like nuts?"

There was that smile again. "You have no idea."

"Me too." He settled into the chair across from Seth. "These are my favorites. Have one." Nate picked up the pastry and took a bite.

Seth poked at the other one with a finger. "Pecans? Not exactly the nuts I had in mind," he muttered.

"So tell me more about the Bluewater Bay Larsons. Are you all related?"

"Unfortunately." Seth took a vicious bite of his pecan twist. "Although not all of them are a waste of space. My aunts are okay. So's my cousin Laura: she's a large animal vet. She's pretty cool. And my grandma, of course."

"Old Mrs. Larson?"

Seth looked down his nose. "'Old' is not a word we use, thank you. We prefer 'seasoned to perfection.'"

Nate chuckled and finished his pastry, licking a smear of caramelized sugar off his finger. "I'll remember that. You must be familiar with that house, then? The one Fennimore built?"

"Ridiculous, isn't it? Clearly the dude liked to show off his bling. It's got a widow's walk, for God's sakes—a fucking tower with a balcony overlooking the Strait of Juan de Fuca."

"But that's what I mean. It's the history." Nate leaned forward, and his knee accidentally bumped Seth's. "You can just *feel* it. The house encapsulates your family, its—its *synergy* with the town. There must be some incredible artifacts in there."

"Well I can tell you about some of those artifacts, although I wouldn't call them incredible. I mean, some of them are impressive, but . . ." He took a sip of his latte, wrinkled his nose, and set it back on the table. "I spent most of this afternoon becoming way too familiar with mummified rodent corpses in the dustier parts of the attic because my grandma is convinced it's infested with squirrels. Plus I live over the garage."

"No kidding? Do you think I could take a tour sometime?"

"I could arrange that." Seth leaned forward, and Nate suddenly felt fingers running along his thigh. "We can start with my bed."

Nate jerked his leg away, heart pounding, mortification sending heat crawling up his throat. "I'm not into that." *Shit, not again.* He'd been so sure Seth understood he wanted to *talk*, not screw.

Seth swallowed audibly. "So you aren't into guys?"

"I mean I don't do sex."

His jaw sagged. "You mean *at all*?"

"Yeah. For the most part."

"'For the most part.' What does that even mean?"

"Just—" Nate sighed. "Sorry. Let's call it a day, okay?" He retrieved his jacket. "Keep the pastries."

He hurried across the room, catching a glimpse of Buck's wry smile as he pushed through the doors. The damp, chilly air outside was a shock against his flushed face. *Why don't I ever learn? Next time, I'll stay home where I belong.*

Seth had never been shot down quite as painfully as tonight. His pride still smarted, even an hour later, walking back to his place. The fog had turned more serious and become rain, which was an excellent reflection of his mood. Piss-poor.

After leaving Stomping Grounds, he'd returned to Ma Cougar's, hoping to find someone to hang out with so he could forget about Nate, pretend it never happened. Not Lucas, because the dude would want to know what'd gone down, but another person. Preferably in front of some of the "theater crowd" so they didn't get the wrong idea—like that he and Nate had left to hook up. He'd prefer it if those people thought he'd left to actually talk genealogy.

In the end, he did find someone, a guy named Evan he could even have gone home with (they'd done it before), but Seth found his sexual appetite had been killed for the night.

Speaking of which, who didn't *do* sex? As in, ever? Or at least "for the most part"?

Lots of people. Nuns and priests for one, like his great-aunt, Sister Regina.

Nate wasn't a fucking priest though. *He just has the sex life of one.*

That explained so much of tonight, didn't it? Like all the confusing signals he'd gotten off Nate after most of his double entendres. Not sure Nate had been getting the message, Seth had made some of his innuendos way over-the-top obvious. He'd hit on straight guys before, sometimes even knowingly, and he was well versed in how they reacted to obvious lines. Straight guys got uncomfortable, even angry, but they didn't pretend that whatever Seth had said was exactly what Seth had meant. Who asked if you liked nuts and actually meant *nuts*?

Nate, apparently.

Turning into the driveway of the Sentinel House, Seth hunched his shoulders, digging his fists deeper into his pockets. He searched the ground for a rock to kick—even a pebble would do—but he kept Grandma's driveway too orderly. Where the hell was a scapegoat when you needed one? He could use one of those mummified mice he'd found in Grandma's attic to drop-kick right about now.

Just then, like an answer to his prayer, another rodent crossed his path. This one was very much alive, the bastard, and larger than anything he'd run across in the house. It couldn't be a rat—he was pretty sure no rats had ears like this one—and the profile was too short and rounded to be a squirrel's. Whatever it was, it looked as if it was carrying something in its jaws as it scurried past and ducked into a hole in the base of the outside wall, right under the damn stairs that lead up to his apartment, no less. Relieved to have something to focus his negativity on, Seth charged through the garage's side door and flipped on the light. *I'll give Grandma a squirrel infestation.*

What he called a garage his mother called "the carriage house," and in this case, her grandiose idea was more correct than his, even though it had been built after the advent of the automobile—barely.

It was a little sturdier than the average garage, and while it held his car and Grandma's, they could have fit at least one more. It also had interior walls, unlike most garages. Seth grabbed a flashlight off the workbench, then began scanning the trim boards, looking for any signs of gnawing or rot.

He might have been carefully maintaining Grandma's house and grounds, but it looked like he'd been neglecting this building some. It appeared fine from a distance—he kept it painted, just like the main house—but as he searched under shelves and behind boxes he found some deterioration. Damn it, he didn't want to replace the drywall in here, it was a fucking garage, for God's sakes. But knowing his family (and even Grandma), they'd want it fixed if they knew it wasn't perfect.

"How did I become the family's superintendent, anyway?" he muttered while shoving aside an old wooden crate with his shoe.

As he neared the southeastern section of the garage, the smell— like rotting meat—tipped him off that he was close to finding his rodent. *This is about to suck.* Swallowing to keep from gagging, Seth kicked aside a half-empty paint can and found a gnawed-out hole in the corner, with lots and lots and lots of twigs falling out of it.

For the first time since he'd started chasing this thing, it occurred to him he might have been happier to ignore it. *Yeah? Who else is going to deal with it?* This was his job, the one he'd shouldered twelve years ago when his parents had ordered him to "pull his own weight" by becoming Grandma's *de facto* handyman.

"Fuck." Now he was as annoyed with this situation as he'd been with Nate earlier. As he stomped back to the workbench for a crowbar, the silver lining presented itself to him: he hadn't thought about being spectacularly shot down for at least ten minutes.

Get over it. You've been rejected before. He shoved the questions about why this one bothered him worse than normal into the back corner of his mind. He had more urgent shit to deal with now.

Back at the suspected nest, he knelt on the floor as he manhandled the panel off the wall with a screech of nails. Just as he caught sight of the full glory of the rodent's nest, a tail disappeared through another hole in the outside wall. Skinny like a rat's, but covered with wiry hair. The kind of tail he could clean out a bottle with.

What the hell was *that?* He'd been hunting pests and larger game in this area his whole life. He would have sworn he'd seen every species of animal that lived around here, but this thing was new.

His puzzlement over that was secondary to his amazement at the collection of shit—and plenty of it was literally shit—in the rodent's nest. Bottle caps, sticks of all shapes and sizes, shredded paper, rusting bits of metal, a piece of broken mirror— Was that a strip of staples for his staple gun?

Gingerly, he used the hook end of the crowbar to pull on a particularly snarled bunch of twigs, and a whole pile of refuse cascaded out, kicking up dust and making him cough, not to mention breathe in a lungful of whatever smelled so badly.

"Fuck this." He hacked as he stood, scanning the rafters for his Have-a-Heart traps. He'd set one tonight and deal with the rest of this shit in the morning.

By the time he was setting the trap up near the creature's midden, it was nearly midnight. *Creature's midden.* Like this was some gothic story, with ghosts in the attic and an unsolved spousal murder.

Okay, so what the hell to bait it with? Some of the rodent's own treasure? Since Seth didn't have a clue what else would attract the thing, he pulled on a pair of work gloves and dug through the pile of crap that had fallen out, trying to find something especially shiny. Most of it was rusty or dirt-encrusted, but he found a particularly long, skinny piece of metal that had a few clean spots on it still. He pulled it out to see if it would work, and as he did, the full shape revealed itself.

Knife. An old hunting knife, if he knew his stuff, and he kind of did. It had a clip-point blade, like a Bowie knife. He rubbed what had to be the handle on the back of his glove, trying to get rid of enough of the dirt to get an idea of what he was dealing with. This thing was either damned old or a reproduction of a Wild West-style knife. Judging by the amount of rust on the blade, he was leaning toward damned old.

Huh. Seth's puzzlement didn't last long once it occurred to him whose knife this probably had been. *Fennimore's.* He groaned. This whole place had been built by his ancestor, and it was full of *objets* that had belonged to him. Once Seth showed this to the family at large— and he had to, even Grandma wouldn't help him hide it, he was certain—they'd be frantically trying to "authenticate" it, and it would stir up the argument he and Grandma were trying to win. Namely, that this house wasn't that important and she should be allowed to move.

Damn it to hell. No longer really caring about the rat, he baited the trap with the piece of mirror he'd seen at first. Then he left everything else lying there—the mess and the paint cans and the crowbar and everything.

The knife he took with him, of course. Carrying it in his still-gloved hand (the thing was gross as hell, antique or not) he was ready to swear it weighed a half ton, and it considerably slowed his progress up his stairs. Once inside, he set it on the spindly table Grandma had insisted he keep by the front door (another ancestral piece of furniture, but not important enough to display in the main house), then he stripped to his skin, left his clothes piled by the front door, and walked straight into the shower for the second time that night.

CHAPTER FIVE

Seth awoke with the distinct sense of having been misjudged.

He couldn't quite remember why righteous anger burned in his chest, but between that and the pounding in his head, he chose to bury his face under the blanket for a few more minutes of sleepy peace.

The pounding wouldn't stop, even when he pinched that acupressure point in the web of his thumb. *I didn't drink* that *much.*

Oooh. Someone was knocking on his front door.

It had to be his mother. No one else would come by this early, and if they did, they wouldn't try to wake him.

I could ignore her. He was nearly to the front door before he'd finished *that* little fantasy, and he didn't even pause before opening up to find—yes. "Good morning, Mom."

Her screaming-orange raincoat made his vision jangle, and his fingers twitched with the urge to shut the door in her face. Except, again, he'd never do that, because—as she said about the pile of dirty clothes in his entryway when she walked in—"Seth Larson, I raised you better than that."

Her lips were pursed in disapproval even as she presented her cheek for a kiss.

Obediently, he pecked it. *Very bad manners to leave dirty clothes lying around in your own home. Check.*

Having grown up with a hypercritical mother had taught Seth to read her mood like a seismograph read tremors, and he knew immediately this was the beginning of a downright miserable visit. Ruffling his hair with his fingers as he shut the door, he wondered if she was the reason for the clinging sense of wounded pride he'd woken up with. He hadn't seen her yesterday, so it had to be something—or someone—else.

Nate Albano.

"Why are you scowling at me?" demanded his mother. "It's not *my* fault your grandmother refused to answer the door at her house. I *had* to come here and wake you."

"Nothing, sorry. Bad dream." He wasn't alert enough to dissect out all the wrongs in that statement. "Just let me throw these in the laundry . . ."

"Pearl's avoiding me," Mom declared once Seth was half hidden in the little utility closet next to his tiny kitchen, stuffing clothes into his washing machine. He rolled his eyes but didn't reply. Of course Grandma was avoiding her. During her last visit, his mother had said his grandmother had a duty to the family to stay in Sentinel House.

"How did you get your clothes so dirty, anyway?"

Seth went for shock value. "I was rooting out a rat in the garage."

Bad move—it led to a diatribe about him living at Grandma's rent-free in exchange for "maintaining the grounds."

He tuned her out until he was done loading the washer.

"—your job to keep the vermin under control," his mother finished as he did. He glanced over at her, sitting poker straight on his settee—another refugee from the main house, but one he liked—crossed ankles tucked in close and hands clasped between her knees. "Did you remember to put in some baking soda?"

"Yes," he muttered as he punched the washer's On button a lot harder than necessary.

"Good. Now let's go find Pearl."

Having his mother following him down the exterior stairs made Seth highly conscious of needing to lay down new grippy tape. In the Pacific Northwest, wood didn't make it through the winter without growing some kind of slime. As he led the way, he kept half his attention behind him in case she slipped.

"You've been living with an old lady too long," his mother said when they'd reached the bottom, cinching the belt around her coat tighter. "I don't need you to help *me* down stairs."

"Mom." Seth sighed. "Grandma won't thank you for implying she's infirm."

"No, I won't." His grandmother's voice floated out from the garage.

Shit. He nearly reached out to reassure his mother, but she was firming her jaw so obstinately that he didn't *want* to touch her. "Don't make it worse," he murmured.

As far as he could tell, she disregarded him entirely.

Before he could consider fleeing, Grandma appeared in the garage doorway. Seth spoke first, in hopes of preempting the looming argument. "Morning, Grandma." He leaned forward to kiss her cheek, and in response she lifted her hands, squeezing his upper arms.

Either that worked or she'd already decided to take the high road with her daughter-in-law, because other than throwing a glare his mother's way, Grandma focused all her attention on him. "What happened in here?"

"I had a raging party with a rat, or something ratlike, at least. I'm going to clean it up before I go to work."

Grandma waved off his words. "It's your first day in your new job, you don't need to do anything now. That mess is in no one's way."

His mother huffed. "He's just going to tend bar, it's not as if he's got a position with real responsibility."

"Well." Seth winced at Grandma's tone. "You can just keep your opinions to yourself, Debra, no one wants to hear them. He's a good boy and works hard." She didn't like anyone denigrating her grandchildren, even if it was their own parent.

"It's okay," he soothed. "Mom didn't mean it the way it sounded, did you?" He turned to her, putting a lot of *Please, Mama, please* in his expression. She'd been susceptible to that when he was little. *Let it work now.*

She sniffed, but gave in. "I just want you to be successful. And I guess this *is* a promotion."

"Nothing is ever good enough for you, is it?" Grandma shook her head, then turned toward the house. His mother followed, and Seth brought up the rear, dreading being stuck with these two when they were feuding. Which had been all the time the last year or so.

Grandma poured them coffee, and they seated themselves in the breakfast nook in silence for a few moments. The air buzzed with impending sparks, like when he'd been a kid and about to pee on an electric fence.

Grandma was the first to whip it out. "Now that Seth has chased the squirrels out of the attic, I can move forward with putting the house on the market."

Jerking slightly—why did she have to drag him into it so early?—Seth slopped a bit of coffee on the table.

His mother *hmph*ed and sipped at her coffee. Probably preparing her next offensive.

Cleaning up his spill wouldn't keep him out of the line of fire, but he tried it anyway. He was standing in front of the running faucet, holding a dishrag in the stream, when Mom raised her voice over the noise of the water. "I hope *you* aren't encouraging Mother's silly fantasy of moving out of Sentinel House."

"Like you said earlier, I'm here to help Grandma with the things she wants done around the house. I do what she tells me to." After shutting off the tap, he turned around to find them both facing him, clenching fingers around their cups in the same way, heads tilted at the identical angle, wearing matching scowls.

Excellent. Damned if he did and damned if he didn't. He forced his lips to turn up into a fake smile, but his cheek muscles failed him within seconds.

Fuck it. He'd done what was asked of him—what both his mother and Grandma claimed they wanted—and he was *tired* of being their pawn, especially since it never did any good anyway. Slouching back to the table, he sopped up the coffee in the brittle silence.

"I think I *will* clean out the garage."

They let him walk out of the kitchen without comment.

Once he saw the mess again, there wasn't that much to clean up after all—less than he'd remembered leaving. As he piled up the twigs and rubbish, sorting out the metal bits automatically, that sense he'd woken up with, of having been wronged, grew stronger than ever.

A short video played over and over in his head while he worked— Nate walking out last night, leaving him sitting in Stomping Grounds to be smirked at by Buck Ellis (now there was a hookup he'd never repeated). Anger built up in his chest like a bad case of heartburn, until he was *soaking* in indignation, mind and body. His arms were full of debris, so he kicked the half-empty paint can hard enough for it to bounce off the wall, then stomped outside to the garbage.

Jesus, did he feel stupid. Like he'd forced his attentions on someone. Oh, God, *was* it his fault? Had he been so into the guy that he'd let his libido convince him innocent comments were really innuendos?

Holding the trash can lid in midair, he tried to recall as much as he could of what he'd said, and what Nate had said, and yeah, he *could* see how there could have been some misunderstandings, but some of that stuff . . . He dropped the lid with a clang. Who the hell left a bar for someplace "more private" with a guy they'd known sixty seconds? People looking for some, at least that was what he'd always thought. Could Nate be from a country where the social customs of hooking up were the complete opposite of what he'd learned?

Unlikely. No accent. Grabbing the broom as he walked back through the garage, he started sweeping.

So . . . the dude really *was* into genealogy?

Intriguing. And dorky, but Seth could kind of understand. He might be sick to death of the way his family revered Fennimore Larson, but he'd always been interested in the family legends. Most of the version he knew had been spun to make his great-great seem much cooler than the guy had been, Seth was sure. The man had been murdered by a former housemaid, but no one ever seemed to mention *why*. He'd always meant to look into it, actually . . .

With Nate?

Yeah, now *that* was unlikely. A laugh burst out of him, and his gloomy mood lifted. This time, when he reminded himself he'd been shot down before, the emotional acid reflux didn't reappear. The guy had said he didn't have sex in general, not that he didn't want to do him specifically.

Grandma came out to the garage as he was tipping the last of the dust he'd swept up into the garbage, to tell him his mother had left then apologize for dragging him into the old argument again, patting his shoulder the whole time.

"Debra just aggravates me to no end," she finished.

"It's all right." And it was; his annoyance wasn't about being involved in the fight over the house, it was in being unable to affect any change. He shrugged, but Grandma continued peering at him, digging her fingers into his arm, so he put his body language into words. "I don't know what to do. About any of this."

Finally Grandma dropped her hand from his biceps and closed her eyes for a few long seconds. Had she been hoping he'd have a solution for her? For a moment, he considered whether he really wanted her to move—he still had no idea what *he'd* do—but then his conscience reasserted itself and reminded him his grandmother's happiness was more important than his own uncertainty. He'd be fine; he'd always landed on his feet before.

"We'll come up with something." This time he reached out to her, giving her a quick one-armed hug.

"Yo, Nate," Morgan called. "Production meeting in ten."

Nate jerked and nearly dropped the sheet of breakaway glass he was trying to mount into a double-hung sash. "Shit, Morgan. Warn a guy."

"Sorry, but I *have* been standing here for the last five minutes while you scowled at that window." She walked over and steadied the glass for him so he could set it in place with glazing tacks. "Your head is just not in the game today, baby."

"Yeah, I know." He hadn't been able to shake his regret from last night's fiasco with Seth. The look on the guy's face when Nate had shut him down—that kind of hurt and shame was just so *wrong*. Nate had heard the expression "his face fell" before, but always thought it was bullshit or poetic excess. But that was what had happened— all the uplift in Seth's face, his eyebrows, the corners of his eyes, his smile—hell, even his *hair*—had drooped. *My fault. I did that.* God, he shouldn't be allowed out.

He drove in enough tacks to hold the glass until he could apply the final trim. "Thanks for the assist."

"No worries. Now, let's go hear the latest raft of bad news."

They walked out of their workshop and across the echoing hangar-like expanse to the warehouse door. Now that the *Wolf's Landing* compound sported two state-of-the-art soundstages, the original warehouse had been repurposed for the art department. Two-thirds of the cavernous building was still open—flexible space used by costumes, props, and anyone else doing work with nontoxic materials. His and Morgan's enclosed workshop took up the remaining third, with a hefty portion of it devoted to storage—a damn good thing, considering how long it took to cure fake glass or build breakable furniture, and how much smashing and crashing occurred in every episode. The show must single-handedly keep several chemical vendors and lumber yards in business.

As they walked through the lot, Morgan waved and smiled at virtually everyone they passed, stopping to hug random people— from actors to craft services minions. Nate kept his interactions to a tight smile and a nod for the most part. After nearly nine months, he knew everybody's name, but had no desire to get closer than an arm's length. Luckily, Morgan attracted all the touchy-feely crap, keeping it away from Nate—yet another reason she was his best friend: she made an excellent deflector shield.

He waited until she'd extracted herself from Suyin, who was carrying a fistful of makeup brushes that scattered pale speckles over Morgan's black T-shirt. "Did you see the latest approved script? Gabriel gets chucked across a corridor—through floor-to-ceiling windows on both sides—and into a cabinet full of specimen jars."

Morgan brushed at her shirt, only succeeding in turning the makeup polka dots to stripes. "Ginsberg is gonna be black and blue for a week."

"Then Gabriel throws Max Fuhrman *back* through two different panes, and he knocks over three lab tables like dominos."

"Think Levi'll do his own stunts this time?" She grinned and waved at a security guard. "He'll need more ice packs than Ginsberg."

"Floor-to-ceiling glass, Morgan. I'm gonna have to build completely new molds to cast the panes for that. A fricking *corridor* of glass."

"Sucks to be you."

"Uh . . . didn't you hear the part about the cabinet of specimen jars? *Full* specimen jars—times all the takes Anna needs to get the coverage she wants."

"Shee-yit." She grimaced. "Okay, I'm definitely on the pain train with you."

"Good. I saved you your usual seat."

"You're all heart, baby."

They arrived at the meeting room in time to see Anna storm off, with Finn Larson on her tail, both of them using outside voices, so the subject of their argument wasn't exactly secret: *Budget* with a capital *B*.

Everyone else in the room was collecting their coffee and notes and filing out. Morgan stopped Emily, Anna's directorial assistant. "Meeting canceled?"

Emily slapped a clipboard against her leg. "You think? They'll be hollering at each other for an hour at least." She shrugged apologetically. "I'll let you know when we reschedule."

"No problem, baby." Morgan hugged her—of course. Which made Emily close her eyes and sigh. Great stress relievers, Morgan's hugs. Maybe Nate needed a few of them himself today.

As they walked back to their workshop, they could hear Anna and Finn blasting each other from Anna's trailer next to the warehouse. Judging by the brief sputters of Finn's voice contrasted to Anna's fucking arias, she was winning on points.

Thank God for that.

Nate held the door for Morgan to precede him. "Ever think how lucky we are to have Anna run interference for us with that joker?"

"All the time."

Nate scowled as they paced across the concrete floor to the workshop. "That asshole is trying to can me in favor of a green screen and a computer."

"Well he's been trying to replace me with a 3-D printer and a vacu-form machine since the first season, so join the party."

"What are the chances we could replace *him*, say with someone who hasn't sold his soul to the devil?"

"He's from Hollywood, baby. Satan owns the place, lock, stock, and BMW."

Nate flipped on the workshop lights. "It's heresy, I know, but sometimes I almost regret that Anna is opposed to all CGI. Have you *seen* the effects notes for the *World Tree* episodes? Hunter wrote it so the damn thing lights up. And levitates."

"I heard that was Kevyan's idea."

"Then the man is evil."

"So I've heard." She grinned wickedly. "But he's keeping us employed, so we should send him cookies. Or custom handcuffs."

Ginsberg popped his head in the door. "Hey, guys. What's up?"

"Speaking of custom handcuffs," Morgan muttered and Nate snorted.

He sauntered in, ice packs strapped to both hips and one wrist. "I heard that. Come on, Morgan, you know I only screwed up the release on the first pair one time. *One time.* Don't you think you could quit busting my chops by now?"

"I say it from a place of the deepest love, baby." She hugged him, ice packs and all.

Ginsberg grinned at Nate over her shoulder. "Morgan's hugs are almost as good as Derrick's."

"I couldn't say."

"I could arrange a hug-off. Just give the word and we're there."

"Morgan's in a class by herself. It wouldn't be fair." Nate nodded at the ice. "Still recovering from last night's shoot, I see. Judging from the vast quantity of broken chairs and tables in the scrap pile, I'm guessing at least three takes on the restaurant scene?"

"Five. Anna didn't like the camera three angles. It was awesome, but the trash cans got extra trashed. Sorry about that." He checked his watch. "Oops. Gotta meet the team to debrief. Later."

He limped out, whistling.

Nate shook his head. "He gets nailed with half the furniture in the room, then tossed through a window into a nest of trash cans—multiple times. Why does he look so happy about it? He have a fetish for ice packs and ibuprofen?"

"I think he's just happy in general. Being stupid in love will do that to you." She sat on the tall stool behind her worktable. "Speaking of which, how'd your evening go after you left with that cute townie?"

Nate's earlier dark mood returned. "You were right."

"Of course I was. I'm always right. About what?"

"He expected sex." Nate pulled one of the pre-cut lengths of quarter-round balsa molding out of the rack. "After I'd known him for all of thirty minutes. How can people do that?"

She shrugged. "Folks are what they are and want what they want."

"Yeah, and this is exactly why I never go out anymore. Everyone assumes that because I'm single, I must be panting to get laid."

"Well most people are."

"That's my point. Sex is the—the default conclusion of any social interaction." He removed the restraining tacks from one stile and ran a bead of glue along the glass. "Assumptions suck."

"As a black woman, you think I don't know about bias, conscious or unintentional? Have you *looked* at Bluewater Bay? We've got more fake werewolves in this town than people of color."

He winced and set down the glue bottle. "Ah shit, Morgan. I'm sorry. I've got nothing to complain about."

"Hold on. I didn't say that. Just because somebody else faces prejudice or intolerance, doesn't mean you have to shut up and take it because theirs is worse, or they've had it longer."

"Thanks for saying so, but—"

She pointed one long finger at him, her fingernail glinting with plum nail polish. "*However*, it doesn't give you a pass on calling them on it, either. Don't take it, but don't be passive."

"But my sexual orientation is my own business. I shouldn't have to explain it to anyone."

"I'm not saying stop people on the street and load them up with ace pamphlets, assuming you even have such a thing. But you *liked* this guy, or you wouldn't have left with him in the first place. Educate, baby. Believe it or not, some people have never heard of asexual, let alone gray asexual."

Nate forgot that sometimes, since his mother was on the ace spectrum too. He'd never had to explain himself, not even the two times he'd felt enough attraction to engage in a relationship—first with Nara and then with Jorge. He was as much a product of experience blindness as the next guy, so he had no right to get pissed if Seth had made a good-faith presumption.

"So." He paid slightly more attention to fitting the trim onto the window than was strictly required, although he glanced at her from under his brow. "Think I should apologize?"

She uncapped a tube of white paint and squirted a blob onto her palette. "If you traumatized some poor guy into thinking he was dogmeat, don't *you*?"

"Maybe." Nate replayed their conversation in his head and winced when he realized how some of his comments might have been misconstrued if Seth hadn't understood the context. "Make that definitely."

"Good on you, baby." She shot him a thumbs-up. "Do what you need to do, but bottom line? Don't be a dick."

Nate nodded. "Don't be a dick. Got it." After work, he'd stop by Ma Cougar's, see if Seth would even speak to him again.

He sat down at his drafting table to work on the plans for the new—God—floor-to-ceiling window molds. He smiled as he lined up the T-square. Future groveling notwithstanding, his heart was lighter than it had been in months.

CHAPTER SIX

Seth was back to his status quo—basic contentedness—by the time he showed up for his first bartending shift. He had his mother to thank for his state of mind. Watching her and the rest of his immediate family failing, over and over, to be satisfied with what they had was a hell of a practical lesson.

Melanie, the bartender who was nominally "training" him, was finishing up at the prep station when he walked behind the bar, and he couldn't help but grin at her as he tied on an apron. "Finally, man, I'm the captain of the ship. No more swabbing the deck." Well more like the second mate, but still. An officer with some say in how things were run.

"Um, hello?" Melanie took one hand off her hip to tap her own chest. "*I'm* the captain."

Seth saluted. "Of course, but you know what I mean."

"You're really excited about this, huh?" She dropped her fake glare and swatted his shoulder playfully.

"Yup, it's gonna be fun." When mixing drinks, he was reminded powerfully of playing with the chemistry set he'd received for his twelfth birthday. His mother had given it to him with dreams of him becoming a research scientist, while Seth had had his heart set on becoming a mad one. Just another indicator that his career path would veer sharply from what Debra Larson had imagined for him.

Career path. He paused while stuffing his backpack—full of extra shirts and deodorant—into a cupboard under the countertop. Truth was, he'd never intended to have a career path. Of course, he'd never been able to imagine life after twenty-five, either. That was when people settled down, and he'd been pretty sure he wasn't the settling-down type.

This wasn't settling down, though. It was change—the antithesis of settling down—and even though Seth hated big change as much as the next guy, he needed the small ones, like new jobs and new mens, to keep him happy.

He began humming "Shiny Happy People" as he looked over the prep station. He'd take his own garnishes from what Melanie had prepared. It wasn't as if he'd never tended bar before—this part was familiar enough. He began lining up the orders that Steve, the bartender going off shift, had left for him.

He'd never admit it aloud, but Seth knew his personality was perfect for a bartender. Benign flirtiness was key, and *that* was as natural to him as criticism was to his mother. She'd once claimed (in a more nostalgic and less judgmental mood) that when born, he'd winked at the nurse who'd slapped his bottom.

In her more characteristic moments, Seth's mother mostly sighed over his lack of ambition. "Your brother's a *lawyer*, you know."

Yeah, he knew, and he also knew his sister-in-law better than his brother at this point in their lives, because his brother was never home when Seth was in Seattle. Considering he'd bunked in their spare room frequently during his seven years of college, that was a lot of time being a lawyer and very little time having a life.

The very first customer he served was someone he knew, Shannon Schumer. She'd graduated from Bluewater Bay High a couple years ahead of him. Seth couldn't remember the name of the woman she was with, but he recognized her as a minor character from *Wolf's Landing*. When he brought them their martinis, he pretended to recognize her, though.

"Hey, how's the set?"

"Great, thanks! I just got written into the next season." Her eyes crinkled joyfully at him over the rim of her martini glass as she took her first sip.

Written into next season. Well, that explained what Shannon was doing—probably an article for the *Bluewater Bay Beacon*.

"Hey, Seth." The smile Shannon gave him was genuine right up until she sipped at her drink and all her facial muscles tensed up. Martinis so weren't her style. The starlet must have ordered.

"Hey, hon." He winked at her before moving on to the next customer, glimpsing her tight-lipped smirk as he turned away.

He was really getting into the swing of things when Nate Albanc walked in. Seth's stomach plummeted like a broken elevator, and his attention wavered from pouring a shot. "Oops," he said jovially to Frank Miller. "Guess you'll get a shot, plus."

Frank grinned, thanked him kindly, and laid down a ten. "I don't need any change."

Seth tried to refocus on work, but he couldn't avoid the stray thought about Nate. Especially since the guy now stood smack in the middle of the bar, near the central set of beer taps. No matter who served him, Seth would have to go there eventually.

Nate had insinuated himself right between what looked like a few sorority girls and a group of local guys who were trying to catch their attention, now doing so with dirty looks at Nate. The sorority girls were giving him the eye from under their lashes. Nate may be old enough to have fathered some of them, but he was still hot as hell.

And oblivious to all of it.

Clearly, the guy really didn't understand sexual attraction. Or he didn't care? Either way, it eased the tightness of Seth's stomach.

All things considered, happy hour was the best possible time for Nate to have arrived, because in spite of deciding not to take their failed assignation personally, the apprehension that built up in Seth's shoulders was uncomfortably familiar. Exactly like it'd used to when he was in high school and one of the jocks had cornered him in the bathroom alone.

As Seth was approaching the barely legal sorority types next to Nate, he slipped up and accidentally met the guy's eyes. Nate gave him a "hello" kind of smile. When Seth glanced down at where the guy's fingers were drumming on the bar, Nate stopped and jerked his arm out of sight.

Giving him a brief smile in return, Seth turned and asked the girls if he could please see some IDs. Hopefully their own identifications. "Sorry, ladies, company policy says I have to if you look under thirty." Or at least, company policy *could* say that, although he wasn't actually aware of it being written down anywhere. He winked at them, as if he believed they were of age and was only following the rules.

The girls pouted, but coughed up valid driver's licenses. Seth's instincts had been telling him they'd want something fancy and fruity, and they'd expect him to help them decide what it should be, and he was right. Considering how long it took (he finally convinced them to try zombies, assuming that if Lucas had hated them, these girls would love them), he didn't blame Nate for starting up the drumming again.

When Seth finally turned to him, he stopped, though, folding his hands together as if he'd only noticed his own recurring fidgeting.

"What can I get you?" The impression he had that Nate was actually nervous about this made it easy to be pleasant.

"Hey." Nate cleared his throat and hesitated a second. Long enough that Seth was almost certain the guy hadn't even come for a drink. *Definitely came looking for me.*

Why the hell would he come here? Did he want to know the Larson family history that much? Whipping his bar rag out from the waistband of his apron, Seth busied himself swabbing down the counter in front of the guy, waiting for him to order.

"How about a Twelve Mile Limit?"

Frozen in the act of placing a beer coaster in front of Nate, Seth's eyes flew up to his face to find some color in the guy's cheeks. "Um . . . is that a prohibition-era drink?" Total stab in the dark, but it sounded like one.

"Yeah, it is." Nate lifted his hand and ran fingers across that beautiful, clefted chin. "You know it? I usually have to—"

"I think I can handle it." Seth put far more confidence into his smile than he felt. *Google-fu don't fail me now.* "Comin' right up." On the assumption that the drink would require him to slice or mutilate some kind of fruit, he headed towards his prep area, pulling his phone out of his pocket and typing *Twelve Mile Limit mixed drink* into the internet search bar as he went.

He couldn't hand this off to another bartender, that threatened his masculinity in ways it was uncomfortable to think about. Besides, nothing would convince Nate that he barely even remembered last night better than a flawless presentation.

Thank God, he found it almost immediately on a list of *11 Unusual Drinks That Will Up Your Cocktail Game.* They had that right—his cocktail game was about to go through the roof.

Oh, grenadine, excellent. They stocked the real stuff, with actual pomegranate juice, and not that colored corn syrup crap, since Seth had insisted Dave buy it as soon as he got the bartender position. In the future, he planned on making his own from fresh fruit, once he'd established himself as a master mixologist. Or mad scientist. *Not to mention made this drink.*

Garnishing the finished Twelve Mile Limit, he tried to keep any triumph (or insecurity) from showing in his expression as he returned to set the martini glass in front of Nate, now seated in a barstool that one of the blond girls had vacated. "Here you go, then."

In spite of it being the busiest time of day, Seth stayed long enough to see what Nate thought of his mixology.

A lot, apparently. He closed his eyes for a moment after his first sip, as if savoring. "Perfect." Then he smiled a smile so dazzling Seth thought he'd been knocked in the head.

So very, very wrong that someone this hot doesn't "do" sex. It was a disservice to all humankind. "Would you like to run a tab?" he asked, ignoring the pointed stares from the people at his end of the bar who'd been patiently waiting. *Only until he answers.*

"Yes. Um." Nate stroked the stem of his martini glass for a second. "I was hoping you could give me a minute, to talk."

Suddenly, Seth very much wished Nate *hadn't* come in during happy hour. Instead of being the best time, it was now the worst. As injured as Seth's feelings had been before, he really wanted to hear what Nate had to say, even if it *was* about the Larson family tree.

"Hey, Seth, man, can I get another beer?" Rob Clarke asked from where he stood next to Nate.

Nodding at the question, he took a pint glass and stepped to the side to fill it. Grimacing apologetically at his semipatient customers he held up the *one minute* finger. As he poured the beer, he leaned closer to Nate and lowered his voice. "I could talk, but can you wait a bit? Happy hour will be over in about twenty minutes, then maybe I'll get a chance?"

"That's fine." Nate nodded, checking his watch. "I have some time to kill."

Through some miracle, just after happy hour ended, Melanie said she could handle things for a bit. "You *need* to take a break," she insisted, glancing at Nate.

So he came around the front of the bar to see what was up with the man who'd apparently come to visit him. As he approached, Bill Purdy got up, heading for the men's room.

That almost seemed like fate. "Hey, I'm using your seat a minute, cool?"

Bill grunted and nodded, and Seth pulled it closer to Nate. It was as much privacy as they'd get. As he settled his butt in the seat, a prickling sense of awareness invaded his chest. Not nerves, he didn't think. More a sense of the unexpected. A heightened interest and curiosity.

Nate turned on his stool, hiking his feet up on the rungs and resting his hands on his knees. Unintentionally, Seth mirrored him, until they sat facing each other, their legs bordering a small physical space between them that seemed private in spite of the noise and press of people in the bar.

"So." Out of habit, Seth lit up one of his flirty—yet platonic—smiles. It was the one he gave Grandma's friends when they came over to play bridge and he acted as their waiter. They ate it up, maybe Nate would be swayed by it as well.

Except, would Nate know platonic-flirty from flirty-with-intent? The dude clearly couldn't pick up on other signals, and Seth really didn't want to make him uncomfortable or give him the wrong idea. Again.

"So." Nate nodded once, then failed to say anything else.

A stab of sympathy urged Seth to make the elephant in the room into a joke. "You've decided you *do* do sex?" he asked overly brightly, plastering on a simple-minded grin.

Nate burst out laughing, and Seth joined in at least partly from relief. *That could have gone just as wrongly as last night.*

"No, no. It's only that . . ." Nate shook his head slightly. "You remember Morgan, of course?"

Oooh, he'd *thought* there might be more there than the guy was admitting to himself. "Yep."

"Well, I told her about, you know—" he lifted his hand and gestured to the space between them "—our miscommunication and, uh . . ." He scratched his ear, as if that would help him find the right words.

Seth certainly couldn't help; he didn't understand at all what the guy was trying to say.

"She pointed out that I probably owed you an explanation," he finished all at once, dropping his hand and his overly upright posture, but meeting Seth's eyes steadily.

"You do? I mean, I don't think you do. You weren't interested, it happens—"

"I misled you. Not intentionally, but she warned me last night that you thought we were going to talk about more than your family, and I didn't listen. I'm sorry if I gave you the wrong idea."

"Nothing to apologize for." Nate hadn't done it purposefully. Still, grinning wryly, Seth conceded the point. "But, yeah. I didn't actually think there'd be that much talking at all."

"Yeah, I get that now." Nate twisted up one side of his mouth before continuing. "I just want you to know—it's not you. It's me. And I know that's about the biggest cliché on the books, but . . ." He took a huge breath, shoulders rising and falling. "Have you heard of ace? Asexual?"

"Yeah. *Ohhh*." Blinking, Seth suddenly understood so much more of last night. And yet less. Nate *had* to be talking about himself, right? "Well, sort of. Basically. Maybe not as well as . . . I think my knowledge is mostly limited to it being the 'A' in LGBTQA. But it means you don't—or, you know, an asexual person doesn't, um, *do* sex." Seth squirmed in his seat, worried he'd somehow gotten something wrong. People tended toward sensitivity about their identities, which he totally understood, but that made it easy to offend or insult.

"Actually, it's sexual *attraction* that we don't do—or do differently." Nate didn't sound offended—he sounded relieved. "We may or may not do sex, depending."

"So does that mean you—"

"I'd rather not talk about it here." Nate jerked his head at the sorority contingent. "If you don't mind."

Out of the corner of his eye, Seth caught Melanie waving at him. "Looks as if my break's about over anyway." He slid off the stool, but then realized he was leaving things at a precarious moment. "But I'd definitely like to talk more. Someplace quieter." *I'm cool with your sexuality*. Or lack of it. That seemed somehow presumptuous to say, so Seth met Nate's eyes briefly, making sure the guy understood he wasn't blowing him off now that he knew sex wasn't ever on the table. Seth didn't want him to feel dismissed, not now that he'd extended the olive branch. *Feels more like the whole olive tree.*

"I'd like that." Nate smiled, a little woodenly, but not as if he were going to bolt at the first opportunity. More like he wasn't super comfortable. "How about— I mean, would you like to come over to my place? For dinner. And talking. If that works for you, that is. Whenever you're free."

For a brief moment, Seth laid his fingertips on Nate's knee to steady himself after the shock of being asked on a date by this man. Until he realized how his touch could be construed, and he pulled his hand away. *Speaking of misconstruing, Nate isn't interested, not like that.* "How about Saturday? I'm working the early shift, my evening's open." *It's not a date.* It was a friend thing. Possibly even an extended apology. He'd really never expected this. They'd had a miscommunication—hey, it happened—but the effort Nate was making was above and beyond.

Could he be *that* into Seth's family history?

Out of nowhere, the image of the knife he'd found last night popped into his head. He hadn't thought about it since he'd set it down on his table. Was it even still there? He couldn't remember seeing it, but he'd never moved it, either. *Has to be there.*

"Saturday's perfect! I'll make—" Nate squinted at him after a few more seconds of Seth staring at him, probably gape-mouthed. "Is something wrong? We don't have to do dinner if you don't want to."

Shaking his head to get his brain in gear, he attempted to explain. "Sorry. No, dinner would be great. You reminded me about something. Turns out I really do want to talk about family history." Nate looked at birth and death records for fun, for God's sake. He could totally give Seth an assist on this.

"Do you?" Interest suffused Nate's expression, just like when they'd first met last night.

"I found something that belonged to Fennimore." Yes, he'd still tell his family, but wouldn't it be best for him and Grandma to have something solidly identified before someone could mythologize it?

"You can tell me all about it this weekend." Nate eased into a smile. "About seven?"

"Can't wait." Movement in his peripheral vision caught his attention. It was Melanie, behind the bar, flailing her arm in his direction like she was going under for a third time and desperately needed a lifeguard. "Okay, I really gotta go, man." This time, when Seth touched Nate, it was intentional. A friendly, "later" kind of nudging of his biceps. Taking a few steps backward, he confirmed once more, just to make sure the message was clear. "See you Saturday."

For the rest of his shift, anytime his mind wasn't occupied with work, Seth's thoughts invariably wandered to Nate. *Very weird.* He'd never had this happen before—when Nate said he just wanted to be friends, he meant he just wanted to be *friends.* No benefits, implied or otherwise.

Lots of guys aren't looking for that. Most of the straight ones he met, for instance—although some straight guys, well, they had some thinking to do on the question of their sexual orientation. Seth didn't generally make it his job to help them in that endeavor. Not unless they were really hot.

Hot like Nate-hot. Sexy, dark, curly hair and chiseled features hot.

Yeah, well, he'd be making a different kind of exception for him.

CHAPTER SEVEN

N ate peered at the eggplant parmigiana bubbling away in the oven. God, he should have thought this through a little more. Maybe Seth hated eggplant. Lots of people did—Nate had himself until his father had taught him this recipe. Or he could despise ceviche. Maybe Nate should have, you know, *asked the fricking questions*.

What if Seth was one of those meat-and-potatoes-only guys? Bluewater Bay hadn't been especially eclectic until the *Wolf's Landing* arrival had expanded the town's culinary expectations. From what Morgan had told him, there hadn't even been a decent Chinese restaurant, something that half the TV crew had nearly quit over— sometimes Szechuan chicken was the only thing that got them through emergency all-nighters.

On the other hand, the town was right on the water. Surely Seth would have a taste for seafood, right? *But maybe not marinated raw seafood, dimwit.*

The last time he'd been this nervous before having dinner with someone was before his first date with Jorge. Of course, besides his father and Morgan, the number of people he'd had dinner with since Jorge walked out—for anything other than business—could be calculated without benefit of any fingers whatsoever.

A muffled *woof* broke him out of his oven-slash-navel-gazing. Tarkus sat at the edge of the kitchen tile—Nate had finally gotten his dog trained to stay out from underfoot during food preparation. Tarkus's ears—oversized and tipped with black tufts—flattened and then perked forward. His favorite toy, a stuffed mallard with both a squeaker and a quacker that had been a present from Morgan, lay at his feet. As soon as he knew he had Nate's attention, he nudged it with his nose, then cocked his head, one eye bright and pleading, the other milky and sightless.

"Hey, buddy." Nate dropped to his haunches next to the dog and buried his hands in Tarkus's ruff. "Sorry, we don't have time for duck-fetching right now. After dinner, okay?" *Your dad is too busy stressing out over—God—his first sort-of-date in three years.*

Right on cue, a knock fell on the door. Tarkus's plumed tail started wagging like mad—the reason Nate had nothing on any horizontal surface lower than four feet off the ground.

He stood, wiping his hands on his jeans—basically transferring Tarkus-fur from his damp palms to his jeans. *So much for dressing to impress.* Although clean jeans and a Henley in a shade other than gray probably wouldn't have gotten him many points anyway. Maybe washing his hands before answering the door would be a good idea. "We're... uh... having company tonight, Tark," he said as he scrubbed up at the kitchen sink. "Not Morgan though, sorry to disappoint. Think you can behave?"

He'd adopted the dog from the rescue league barely a month before he'd moved to Bluewater Bay, and since Morgan was the only person who ever visited, Nate hadn't had much chance to socialize Tarkus in what the dog considered *his* space. He was a big hit at Bluewater Bark, the doggy daycare run by the high school as a community service project, but the only other humans who came near the cabin—the UPS guy, the FedEx driver, and of course the mail carrier—sent Tarkus into a barking frenzy.

Another thing you should have considered. The last thing he needed was for his dog to be as big a dick as Nate had been himself. Or what if Seth was allergic, like Jorge had been?

Another knock sounded. *Right. Answer the door before he thinks you've bailed on him again.*

Nate strode to the door, Tarkus at his heels. "Sit." Tarkus dropped to his butt. "Good boy." He opened the door, and there was Seth—fist raised as if about to knock again. He had that eager, *interested* look that had drawn Nate in the first night, and a smile ambushed Nate's face. "Hey. You made it."

"Yeah, but seriously? I don't imagine you get many other visitors, especially townies. I mean, the log cabin is kinda cool, but nobody I know would risk living next to the cemetery."

"Really? It was a selling point for me."

Seth nodded. "Right. I get it. The whole town history/genealogy thing."

"Exactly."

Seth held up the six-pack of microbrews in his other hand. "My grandma says nobody should ever arrive for a dinner without a hostess gift. She recommends wine, but I don't really go for wine, and you're not technically a hostess, so beer?"

"Works for me." Nate took it. "I haven't seen many of these before."

"I picked out a bunch of the locals. Thought we could try 'em out.' He shifted from foot to foot and shoved his hands in the pockets of his jacket. "So . . ." He cocked his head and grinned. "Can I come in?"

"Oh. Shit. Yeah. Sorry." Nate stepped aside. "I should have warned you. I have a—" Tarkus scrabbled over to Seth and laid down at his feet, turning over to expose his belly "—dog."

"Cool." He dropped to his haunches next to Tarkus, scratching the furry chest as Nate closed the door. "What's his name?"

"Tarkus."

"After Tars Tarkas? In those old Princess of Mars books by Edgar Rice Burroughs?"

A shiver skated down Nate's back. "Sorry. It's from Emerson, Lake, and Palmer, actually. Tark-*u-s*, not Tark-*a-s*. But you read vintage sci-fi?"

"Newer stuff mostly, but everyone's heard of those." He gave the dog one last pat and stood up. Tarkus scrambled to his feet and leaned against Seth's leg, gazing up in adoration. "What kind of dog is he? He looks kinda like a German Shepherd, but those ears . . . and his fur is different."

Nate grinned. "Yeah, his ears are great, aren't they? He's a GSD/Keeshond mix, with maybe something else thrown in. The previous owners didn't know."

Seth sniffed the air. "Smells great in here."

"Yeah, about that. I should have asked. Do you like eggplant?"

"Sure."

"Ceviche?"

"Sounds great."

Nate let out a relieved sigh. "Thank God. I had visions of throwing together mac and cheese at the last minute."

"Nothing wrong with a good mac and cheese either. I'm not picky." Seth wandered into the living room. "Nice. Not as rustic on the inside, but it still fits. You don't see many like this anymore. Most of the ones they put up nowadays are the luxury kind—hardly even qualify as a cabin."

"I need to make the salad, but feel free to take a self-guided tour." He pointed with the measuring spoon. "Mudroom, bedrooms, bathroom, deck, loft. And of course, kitchen and great room. Look around all you want."

"Excellent, I will." Seth meandered around the room, stopping to warm his hands at the fire crackling in the fireplace, peeking briefly into both bedrooms. "What's in the loft?"

"My computer. All my genealogy crap. You know—a nerd retreat."

"Sounds intriguing, do you mind?"

"Be my guest."

Seth *clanged* up the spiral staircase. "Nice." He looked down at Nate over the half wall. "It's just big enough to . . . *fit* around you, you know? I'd love to have a place like this. Grandma's house is the opposite of cozy."

"Yeah, but it's got history. Family history. That's important too."

Set trotted down the stairs again. "Sometimes family history can be a pain in the ass." He paused by the bookshelf under the staircase. "Whoa. This picture—is that you with Nara Sato?"

Nate hesitated mid-tomato dice. "Yeah."

"Wow." Seth's eyebrows rose halfway up his forehead. "I *love* her. She absolutely *shredded* that conservative asshole who sponsored that anti-trans bill."

Nate chuckled. "That one was personal, but she's been known to shred anyone she thinks is a pretentious, insensitive dick."

"I suppose being from Hollywood, you know plenty of famous people, huh?"

"Not really. You kind of have to *be* famous to hang with the famous, and I'm just a special effects guy. I met Nara way before she hit the A-list—we went to the same college. Dated for about three years."

Seth's eyebrows drew together. "So . . . can I ask, *do* asexuals date?"

"Sure. Why not? Besides, ace is a spectrum, not an absolute, and it refers to attraction, not behavior. If you need labels, I'm gray asexual—grace. I feel sexual attraction, but not often—and for me, sex is the *result* of a relationship, not the reason for one." He nodded at Nara's photo. "She was the first."

They'd been really tight—Nate was the only one she'd shared her decision not to have bottom surgery with. Their choice to call it quits after graduation was tough but amicable. They'd stayed friends— she'd introduced him to Jorge after interviewing him for a feature on modern flamenco. She'd been inclined to beat herself up over that when Jorge had bailed, but Nate never blamed *her* for that.

Seth bit his lip. "I can't be a little bit nosy without going *all* the way. It's one of my more endearing flaws."

"Ask whatever you like. If I don't want to answer, I'll say so— although I'll promise you this: whatever I tell you will be the truth."

"Okay then, since you don't mind my asking, how many have there been?"

Nate took a deep breath, suppressing his knee-jerk *none-of-your-damn-business* response. He owed Seth the full story. God knows hiding information had never worked well in his own family. "Two."

"Two besides her?"

"Two including her."

Seth shot Nate a flirty glance from under his lashes. "May I ask how old you are?"

"Thirty-seven."

"Hmmm."

"Weird?"

"Different. So your second . . . um . . . attraction. Did it last a long time?"

Nate smiled wryly. "The attraction doesn't exactly disappear, even if the relationship ends. Nara and I broke up after graduation. Jorge—I was with him for six years."

"If the attraction didn't fade, then what happened?"

"First he wanted to open the relationship so we could have occasional sex with other people."

Seth nodded as he sat on a barstool across from Nate. "Like threesomes?"

"No. I mean he wanted each of us to be free to hook up with others. Of course, me being me, I never took advantage of the opportunity. He did. Three years ago, he left me to marry one of his 'casual hookups.'"

Seth clicked his tongue. "Harsh."

Nate shrugged. "What we had wasn't working for him, I guess. I can't blame him for wanting to be happy. So." He forced a smile. "The eggplant won't be ready for a while, but how about an appetizer?"

Seth opened a beer for each of them and was gratifyingly appreciative of the ceviche. "This is better than anything at Il Trovatore. And that"—Seth put on his fake posh accent again—"is the *height* of Bluewater Bay Italian cuisine, don't you know."

Nate warmed at the praise. "Thanks. It's my dad's recipe. The eggplant parmigiana is his too, handed down from his own father, who'd gotten it from *his* grandmother, who'd actually lived in Albano, the town in Italy named after Dad's family."

"After your family too, right? I mean, you're Nate Albano."

"I am now. But I was Nate Bedrosian until I was twenty-four. Didn't even meet my dad until I was twenty-three. I mean, we've got a pretty good relationship now, after fourteen years of contact." But he'd missed out on knowing his grandparents and at least two uncles and one aunt, who'd died before he'd discovered the truth. And although he had dozens of cousins, they'd all scattered to their own adult lives by then. Their relationships would never be anything other than casual. "It's not the same as being part of the family when you're growing up."

Seth eyed him over his beer. "I'm guessing there's a story there. No pressure, but if you want to share . . ." He clinked the neck of Nate's bottle with his own. "I *am* a professional bartender. We're practically the same as therapists."

Oddly, Nate *did* want to share, something that hadn't even happened with Jorge. "It's not all that impressive. My mom got pregnant after a fling with a colleague. Never told him. Had the kid—me—and raised him on her own. When the kid asked about his dad, she claimed there was no 'father' per se, only donor sperm."

He'd only met his father by chance, and she wouldn't have admitted it then if it hadn't been obvious. *"There's a difference between an 'anonymous sperm donor' and a man you never told about his son, Mom. Talk to me when you figure that out."* That was the last time he'd called her *Mom.* Ever since, once they'd actually begun speaking to one another again, he'd called her *Iris.*

"That's pretty cold."

"Yeah. I've started taking calls from her again, after fourteen years of estrangement, but I can only handle about one a month without having an aneurism."

"I hear you. I can't have more than a two-minute conversation with my Uncle Kirk without wanting to slip a little arsenic into his single malt." Seth scooped up the last of his ceviche. "That was excellent. If the eggplant is up to the same standard, I'll be working it off at the gym for a week."

"How about we take a walk before dinner, then, for a little preemptive exercise? It'll be dark soon, and Tarkus needs a good run at this time of day. That way he'll sleep while we eat and won't give us the puppy-dog eye the whole time."

"Sounds good to me."

They both shrugged into their jackets, then Nate snapped on Tarkus's leash. As soon as the hook clicked on his collar, Tarkus's ears and tail drooped.

Seth laughed. "Why does he look like you're about to take him to the vet?"

"He hates walking on lead. But until we're across the road and into the cemetery, I can't trust him off it. He's already been hit once, and his depth perception is wonky because of his eye. As long as there's nobody around in the cemetery, though, I can let him run free."

"Dude. Isn't that against the rules?"

"I won't tell if you don't."

Seth grinned and shot a thumbs-up. "Your secret is safe with me."

They walked up Nate's gravel driveway, then down the road, Tarkus moping along at their side. Halfway across the field in front the cemetery though, he perked up, prancing along as they neared the gates. He dragged them toward the big oak tree next to the entrance and planted his butt, staring up into its branches.

Nate tugged at the leash. "Tark. Come on."

Tarkus whined and whacked his tail on the ground a couple of times, but his attention stayed fixed overhead.

"What's up with him?"

Nate motioned to Seth and pointed into the tree, where a crescent of red was visible in the fork of two branches. "See that?"

"Yeah."

"It's his Frisbee. One of our first nights here, I made the mistake of playing with him in this field."

"Oh." Seth gave him a cheeky grin. "Bad aim, huh?"

Nate punched him lightly on the shoulder. "No, smart-ass. He did it himself. He's a total Frisbee hound. Half the time, once he catches it, he'll toss it in the air again himself. That's what happened."

"And you didn't retrieve it for him?" Seth propped his fists on his hips and hit Nate with a mock scowl. "What kind of pet parent are you?"

"Have you looked at that tree? No branches low enough to climb, and I didn't feel like bringing a ladder out here and risking my neck for a plastic disk I could replace for a few dollars at the pet store." He nodded at Tarkus. "He, however, has never gotten over it, even though we've gone through at least three Frisbees since then."

"Wuss. *I* think you could have gotten it."

"Yeah? Then you climb up there."

"Think I couldn't?"

Nate grabbed Seth's arm before he could launch himself at the tree trunk. "Hey. That wasn't a dare. I prefer to keep the stunts on the studio lot, where they belong."

"Spoilsport."

But Nate managed to entice both man and dog away from the tree and through the cemetery gates.

Like in a lot of old cemeteries, maintenance of the gravesites varied wildly. Some sections here were manicured closer than a putting green, but in others, the grass grew shaggy around the tombstones. Some areas—either for landscaping value or because the plots hadn't been purchased—were overgrown with low bushes. Whenever Nate and Seth walked past one of these, Tarkus would leap into the midst of the shrubbery, bounding through it like a deer.

Seth laughed as Tarkus flung himself out of the latest patch, shaking himself and scattering twigs in all directions. "Is he always this enthusiastic?"

"Pretty much. I usually spend about an hour brushing all the detritus out of his fur when we get home."

"It must be cool, having a dog. I never did."

"I didn't either, growing up. It wasn't an option in college, and then Jorge was allergic. After he left, though, I decided to go for it." He'd needed something in his life, something warm and alive and affectionate. "Tarkus is actually my third dog."

"Three dogs in three years? That's some seriously bad luck."

"I adopted them from a rescue league down in LA. The first two were older dogs whose owners had intended to put them down because they didn't want to be bothered with the end-of-life care. I figured I could give them that."

Tarkus flung himself into another clump of bushes. "He doesn't seem that old."

"He's not. He's only four, but he got hit by a car—half blinded him and broke both his hind legs. His owners didn't want to foot the bill and were going to—" Nate fought off the throat-closing grief at the thought of a world without Tarkus. "Anyway, the woman in charge of the league called me and I took him. It was tough at first because he needed a lot of care, but I wasn't working much at the time. Since he's younger, at least I'll have him with me for longer."

"That's good. He seems like a great dog."

"And he apparently returns the sentiment." Nate pointed to a headstone in the Larson section. "Check this out. This is one of my favorites. It's pretty recent, but the epitaph is just as peculiar as some of the really old ones." The marker read, *C work at best.* "What do you suppose it means?"

Seth joined him and laughed. "That's my great-aunt. She was a teacher. She didn't have any kids, but Grandma was her executor. She claims that's what Aunt Beryl wanted on her headstone, and I pretend to believe her."

"See, that's what I mean about family. Even when the reality is annoying, it's still . . . I don't know . . . rich." He pointed to the giant marble crypt at the top of a rise. "Like Fennimore's monument. It's the biggest in the whole place, which makes sense given that he's the town founder."

Seth snorted. "It'd be more impressive if the damn thing weren't (a) empty and (b) only thirty years old. My grandfather, uncle, and father put it up because they thought Fennimore's original tombstone wasn't grand enough for such an important asshole."

There. That's what Nate had missed, what Seth took for granted, but was willing to share. History. Legacy. The connection to the past in all its weird, convoluted, *messy* glory. "Tell me about him. Please."

CHAPTER EIGHT

Seth had never knowingly met an asexual person before. He definitely must have met one (much like all those straight people in the nation's Bible Belt who'd crossed paths with a gay person), he just hadn't had a clue.

Now that he did know one, he found himself eager to find out more. Unfortunately, it left Seth even more insecure about exactly what he was bringing to the table here, so to speak. What did he have to offer a guy who wasn't interested in sex?

Apparently what he had to offer was the story of Fennimore Larson, which had been his best guess beforehand. He'd even brought along the knife, but he kept the fact secret until the "right time," having some nebulous idea that it could be both a surprise and a token of appreciation, if that was really where Nate's interest in him lay.

Dude, you have male friends. Lucas and Gabe were his friends. Although he'd kind of wanted to hook up with Lucas in high school, and until about six months ago he and Gabe had gotten it on regularly, so maybe that didn't count? *Whatever. Give it a rest.*

Shaking off his jitters, he stuffed his hands into his jacket pockets, balling them up for warmth. They were going to be in this cold cemetery for a while. Tarkus was clearly not done rooting through the undergrowth and generally racing around like a newly liberated dog. *Okay, the Legend of Fennimore . . .* "Do you want the family-approved version or what I think really happened?"

"How about both?"

Of course he'd want to know everything, not only what Seth believed was the truth. Seth and Nate weren't so different, really. He'd always been insanely curious too, at least once to his detriment.

Nate didn't seem to mind it, though. He hadn't balked when Seth had asked all those questions about his sexuality and exes earlier this evening.

Well, there'd been an obstinate flicker in his eyes for a few moments at one point, but the guy had gotten over it and assuaged Seth's curiosity.

Resting his foot against the plinth of a handy tombstone, he pushed off against it, then let it catch the weight as he fell forward. Over and over, rocking himself. Self-soothing. He probably needed to, in order to tell the sanitized version of the family history. "Fennimore Larson was a very well-to-do businessman, as you probably know."

Nate nodded when he glanced over. Seth nodded back, then returned his attention to his fidgeting. "He was a timber baron—"

"The Timber and Stone Act of 1878, right?"

"Wow, you *really* do your homework don't you?" Seth grinned. "Anyway, so he was in the habit of buying the tracts of land other people had picked up for next to nothing under that act. He of course paid a fair price, unlike all the other timber barons of the time, who took advantage of people who didn't have the money to get out west on their own." It had been common practice to pay someone's way out and then front the $2.50 per acre the tracts cost. Later, as soon as it was legal, the person who'd put up the money got the deed signed over to them, while the bogus settler got a free relocation to America's frontier and a nominal cash payment.

"Mmm." Nate wandered closer to him, his brow creased in concentration, although he was watching Tarkus more than Seth. Definitely listening intently, though.

The guy made a great audience. Flatteringly attentive to Seth's story. "Fennimore built a mill on the West Twin River when he had enough capital, and after *that*, when my great-great-grandfather would make a land deal with a homesteader, he'd offer less cash up front in return for a guaranteed job at the mill. And eventually, that became *no* cash in return for a job and a house near the mill. He'd had the houses built, and owned them, of course, but his employees could live there as long as they worked for him and paid him rent."

"Quite the philanthropist."

Seth snorted. "I don't know about that. Fennimore had his own little kingdom, with his own little castle overlooking it—that's why they called it Sentinel House, by the way—so he could keep an eye on his serfs." But that was part of *his* version of history. He needed to finish the rest of the family-approved legend before he started going off on that. "They—Fennimore and his wife—had a Chinese maid. That's all anyone ever says about her, that she was Chinese. Anyway, she worked for them for years, until one day my great-great-grandmother caught her stealing the family silver or something, and they 'let her go.' Months later, she crept back into the house in the middle of the night, confronted Fennimore in his study, then stabbed him. His wife heard the body hit the floor or him screaming, I don't know, but she came in and caught their former maid 'red-handed,' as they say."

The murder wouldn't come as a surprise to Nate—that part was well documented. He didn't react, didn't say anything, just rubbed his chin, passing his finger over and over that small dimple, and stared at some underbrush shaking in a suspiciously Tarkus-like manner. "So, I take it you don't buy that story? Or not all of it?"

"Do you?" Just then the dog burst out from behind a clump of salal, bounding toward them with a stick in his mouth about twice as long as his body. Panting happily, he dropped it at their feet.

"It does seem awfully convenient they had a Chinese maid to pin it on at a time when Chinese immigrants had almost no rights on the West Coast."

Well, that was kind of embarrassing—he'd hardly considered that angle, mostly thinking about the more personal, familial, details. "That's only the first clue that it isn't right. The biggest for me is why the hell would she come back *months* later and kill *him*? It was Fennimore's wife that dismissed her, and who she had a relationship with." Unless, as he'd pondered more than once, the maid had had a more personal kind of association with Fennimore. If so, that could be why she'd been dismissed.

"Are you sure it was the wife she had the closer relationship with?" Nate asked with a faux-serious expression. Mouth turned down but eyes crinkling. And maybe twinkling. It was too dark to tell out here.

Seth smiled and shrugged his brows as an answer—they really did think alike. Or maybe it was that *anyone* would think of that. "Which is why I think his wife killed him." His pulse picked up noticeably.

He'd never told anyone that and hadn't realized it was that big a deal until the words had come out of his mouth. But, yeah . . . he'd just accused his ancestor of murder.

"So. A cheating bastard offed by his long-suffering wife—who was then willing to let someone else take the rap, getting rid of her rival at the same time?" Nate's tone was dry, but not disbelieving. "Seems at least possible, given the little you've told me. Although if that was the case, Fennimore wasn't the only bad apple to drop off your family tree." He studied Fennimore's monument. "I don't remember seeing the wife's headstone. Did they memorialize her there too?"

"No. She's not even buried in Bluewater Bay. She stayed on in Sentinel House until her oldest son came of age, then remarried and moved to Victoria."

"Who'd she marry?"

Seth shrugged. "Who knows?"

"You're kidding. With the great Cult of Fennimore, I'd expect your family to know all the details."

"Oh, but she wasn't a *real* Larson, don't you know," Seth said in his fake-posh voice. "In fact, I found a picture of her once and someone had written across her face—in *pen*—'Had three children and ran off with another man.'"

"She was a widow with at least one adult child. How does a perfectly legal remarriage constitute 'running off'?"

"That's my family for you."

"Weird."

Seth nodded, not sure what to say now that he'd let out his big suspicion and it had been accepted. He looked down and made eye contact with Tarkus—who'd been flicking his gaze between him and Nate—and the dog immediately zeroed in on him, wagging his whole back end. Picking up the stick, Seth threw it in a great, looping arc. Tarkus raced after it, nearly somersaulting in his eagerness. Either his night vision was better than Seth imagined, or he didn't really care about finding the damned stick, just chasing after it. "He'd love the beach."

"Tark?" Nate's voice held obvious fondness. "Yeah, he does."

"I should take him with me next time I fly kites." He squinted playfully over his shoulder at Nate. "I guess you could go too."

"He'd love it. I'd suffer through it, as long as I don't have to venture onto the water."

Smirking, Seth turned back to the direction Tarkus had disappeared. He could hear crashing and snuffling on the far side of the cemetery, like an excited dog with only one good eye was searching for a stick.

"You hear stories sometimes, you know?" Assuming Nate would realize he had gone back to the original subject, Seth didn't wait for an answer. "A friend of mine—you probably don't know him, Gabe Savage?"

"I recognize the name. Another founding family, right?"

Seth nodded. "Gabe's grandmother has some alternate versions of the great deeds of Fennimore Larson. She heard them from her parents, who were kids when Fennimore was killed."

"What about her legends rings truer than your family's?"

"Other than I know my Uncle Kirk puts a spin on everything? He'd stuff and truss a ham and try to pass it off as turkey on Thanksgiving." He sighed. "The Larsons and the Savages both came here for the timber, but the Savages did it the way it was meant to work. Two brothers each homesteaded a tract, side by side. That same land is Savage Tree Farm—and marijuana producer—today."

Tarkus came loping up again, another stick in his mouth, but it was forked and shorter. This time after he dropped it in front of them, he flopped himself down next to it.

Must be done. Good. Seth hunched his shoulders and turned toward the entrance to the graveyard. "I thought you were going to feed me. I might have to insist on it if you want the *real* story." He'd been joking, but he was cold enough that his voice came out harder than he'd meant it to. He tacked on, "I have something to show you back at your place anyway," to try to erase any nerves he'd jumped on.

"Ah, bribery." Nodding knowingly, Nate reached down to clip the leash back on an unsuspecting Tarkus. The dog stood and jerked his head back, giving his master what Seth would call a glare if he were a human. "Sorry, Tark, but we have to be hospitable to our guest. Otherwise he won't trot out all the skeletons in his family's closet."

Seth laughed and started walking when Nate did. Ambling, really. "Okay . . ." Nate began as they passed out of the graveyard and started across the deserted road. "So, the Savages were loggers."

"Mm-hmm. Are still. Well, Gabe is, he's about all that's left." Unless he and Lucas had kids, which Seth couldn't picture.

"Your family, though, they're timber *owners*."

"My grandfather sold all the timber before I was born, but, yeah, mostly." He shrugged. "Me and a couple of my cousins were loggers for a while. Our rebellious phase. Their mothers liked it as much as my parents did."

Nate stopped in his tracks to gape at him. "You're a logger?"

Yeah, that always threw people off. In gay bars, it tended to turn guys *on*. Nice to know it worked in platonic relationships too. "I wouldn't say I'm a logger, just that I could be, and I've occasionally worked as one. Lately only if Gabe needed another sawyer on his farm."

"A sawyer." Studying the ground, Nate began walking again, slowly. Seth fell into step beside him and waited for him to ask. "Meaning what? You cut the trees down?"

"Exactly that." He didn't like to brag, but it was considered the most macho of all jobs on a falling crew. His cousins had always grumbled about that, but the truth was that Seth wasn't burly enough for some of the other positions, plus he had a knack for getting a tree to land right, so that it didn't bring down others or violate riparian zones. The fines for destroying the environment were high enough to trump the fact he was gay for every crew foreman he'd ever met.

"Not a skill set I'd normally associate with a bartender." Nate sounded vaguely impressed, which led to Seth's vague embarrassment. He couldn't swear his cheeks hadn't flushed a little, and he didn't have a clue why he was squirming inside. Confused and uncertain, he didn't say anything else, and neither did Nate, not until they'd climbed his porch steps and Nate was opening up the house.

"You're full of surprises." Nate's tone was amused, and for the briefest second, as Seth walked through the doorway, he thought he felt the touch of Nate's hand on the small of his back.

Regardless of whether the touch happened, Seth found himself as flustered as a teenager on his first date for the next ten minutes.

FOR A GOOD TIME, CALL...

He fumbled the salad as he was setting it on the table, and nearly tripped himself with his own chair when he pulled it out to sit down.

Maybe he *was* a teenager on his first date—he'd never actually dated as a teenager. Or really as an adult. Not like this. Two guys spending time together in each other's company with no intention of capping off the evening with mutual orgasms.

Yeah, he really was rusty when it came to this friendship thing. *Bad Seth. Focus.* Nate was talking, for God's sakes.

"—do you like it?"

"Uh," Seth sipped his beer, then decided to come clean. Setting the bottle down, he offered Nate an apologetic smile. "Sorry, I zoned out for a minute there."

Nate had just taken a bite of the food he'd dished up for himself, so other than waving one hand in the air, he didn't respond. While Seth waited for him to finish, he finally forked up his own eggplant parmigiana.

His experience with eggplant was limited to the few times his mother had made it when he was a kid, so he was pleasantly surprised when it was not only delicious, but firm and not at all mushy. "This is great," he blurted, still chewing.

Nate's table manners were better than his own, as he demonstrated by wiping his mouth with his napkin before saying, "Thanks. That's exactly what I was asking."

After they'd taken the edge off their hunger, Nate started telling him a little bit about work—stories of the actors behind scenes, and prop and set anecdotes. Ways to make it look as if someone were getting the shit kicked out of them without actually harming them. Much.

"Sounds like a hella fun job. So is that what you're doing for the *Frankenstein* production? Wreaking havoc without actually doing it?"

Nate's grin took on a hint of slyness, and Seth recognized that little gleam in his eye. Not from having seen it in Nate's before, but because he knew how that twinkle felt—it was joy in messing with people. Not harming or humiliating them, but spicing up life a little. Yeah, they *really* had a lot in common.

"Oh yeah," Nate said.

"What are you doing?"

"No way." Nate waggled a finger at him. "You've got to come see it if you want to know."

Looked as if Nate expected them to spend a lot of friend time together. Which reminded him. "Hey, I have something to show you." Reaching around the back of the chair, he found his coat pocket and the fished out the knife he'd found the other night. "We can look at it while we eat." He was only halfway through dinner, and he sure as hell wanted to finish what Nate had cooked.

But maybe this wasn't a great idea after all, because it looked dirty as hell. Rustier and more disgusting. He'd dug it out of a rodent's den for God's sakes, what was he doing pulling it out at the table?

Nate whistled softly, and when Seth looked, there was a different light in the guy's eyes. Interest.

"I found it in Grandma's garage. It had to have been Fennimore's." Carefully, he set the knife down between them, then stood, wiping his palms on his thighs. "That thing's filthy. I'm going to go wash my hands again." Should he have put it on a napkin?

"Mmm." Totally absorbed in inspecting the knife, Nate was leaning forward and peering intently at it. He didn't seem to feel it violated the sanctity of his dinner table or anything.

When Seth got back, Nate was still squinting at it. Chewing, so he must have continued to eat, but totally focused on what Seth had brought him. Seth understood—there was something about the thing. He'd barely looked at it since he'd found it, not until right before he'd left tonight. It was much more intricately worked than he'd realized at first. It had a pommel, or whatever that knob at the end was called, which was decorated with designs chased into the metal.

"Are those someone's initials?" Nate's voice was hushed, as if they were in a library.

Seth nodded. "That's what it looked like to me. I can't really make them out, though." It also had a mother-of-pearl handle, which he didn't know how he'd missed. Fennimore had liked to show off his wealth. A knife like this would be right up his alley.

"So, why are you showing me it again?" Now Nate was peering at *him* intently, head tilted just so. Completely absorbed. It gave Seth a little bit of a thrill, capturing the guy's attention so completely.

Swallowing his bite quickly, he responded with his planned answer. "I thought you might have an idea how to research it. Find something out about it." *Stupid*—it sounded like an excuse, now. An excuse to spend more time with him.

Nate's expression wasn't scornful though, or patronizing. Nate's plate was clean, and he pushed it aside and used his napkin to pick up the knife and set it down right in front of him. "It'd help if we could make out these initials."

"You don't think they're Fennimore's?" He hadn't really considered that, other than rejecting the fleeting thought.

Pointing at the handle, Nate shook his head. "There's so much dirt encrusted in the monogram that it's hard to tell, especially with that chip in the mother-of-pearl. Makes it look more like a *T* than an *F*."

Well, yeah, he'd seen that himself, but he'd assumed it was just distorted. "Huh." Seth scooped his last bite of food onto his fork. It was the one he'd been saving, laden with sauce and toasty cheese and a solid cube of the eggplant. Always save the best for last—his personal motto, but a lot of the world worked on the same principle. It was why orgasms came at the end of sex.

Stop bringing everything back to sex. This is just platonic. If nothing else came from tonight, he'd figured out one thing: he didn't know how to do "strictly friends" with a guy. That was plain old sad at this point in his life.

"I take it that means you like my cooking."

Nate's voice surprised him out of his thoughts, and he opened his eyes, which made him realize he'd closed them to savor the flavor of the food fully. He couldn't help but laugh at himself a little. "I *love* your cooking. Please don't tell me if you're one of those people who can only do one dish well. I want to pretend everything you make is this good."

Smiling, Nate picked up his plate and started toward the sink. "Let's say I have more than one signature dish."

Good, he'd take that to mean the guy cooked everything well.

"So, the knife . . ." While Nate was rinsing his plate, Seth brought his own over, waiting for Nate's train of thought to come out of his mouth. "I've got a few resources, so I'm sure we could figure out a few things."

Excellent.

"I might need your help though."

"Happy to give it." Seth crossed his arms over his middle and leaned his hip against the counter. "What do you need?"

They spent nearly an hour in front of Nate's computer, looking through old *Bluewater Bay Beacon* issues that had been uploaded to the internet. They didn't figure a lot out, except that the Chinese maid had had a name—Hsiang Ah. In the coverage of her trial and hanging, her Chinese name was only mentioned briefly, and she was referred to mostly as "Adeline."

"Do you suppose she chose Adeline herself, or would Mrs. Fennimore have foisted it on her?" Nate mused.

Seth snorted. "Knowing my ancestors, *they* picked the name." He glanced over in time to catch Nate stifling a yawn.

Time to go. "Seems like figuring out her name is enough for the night, huh?" He was strangely proud of them for finding it, actually. "I was serious about taking Tarkus to the beach," he blurted out of nowhere, then resolutely didn't wince. Damn it, but he really did want to hang out with Nate again.

"Cool." While navigating his mouse to click on something, Nate nodded. "I was serious about going to see *Frankenstein*. Opening night, if you can swing it." He glanced sidelong at Seth, a smile quirking his lips. "That way you won't be able to pump anybody for spoilers and ruin the shock and awe."

As he prepared to go, they made nebulous plans to meet up again, and Seth didn't force the guy to commit to a date. He was really starting to get the hang of this friends-only thing. He liked it better than he thought he would.

But, on Seth's way out the door, Nate confused the hell out of him.

"Hey," he said softly, grabbing Seth's arm in passing. "Thanks. For the company, for the stories, for giving me another chance. I had a good time."

Then he leaned forward and kissed him on the cheek.

"Sure," Seth said before stumbling out the door in a daze.

CHAPTER NINE

"I kissed him." Nate's words were muffled and hollow—not surprising, since he was wearing a full-face respirator while he and Morgan finished pouring the breakaway glass goop into the mold for the first of those giant windows.

Morgan peered at Nate from behind her own respirator. "You know I can't understand you when you're masked up. I could swear you just said 'I kissed him.'"

"I did. Right here." He tapped the faceplate with one gloved hand. "Last Saturday."

"I am going to *murder* you, Nate Albano. You should have told me first thing Monday morning, not sprung it on me out of the blue on Thursday afternoon."

"I know." He offered her an apologetic smile. "Sorry?"

"I ought to whack you upside the head for that, but in this rig, I can't." She flipped him off instead. "We're cleaning up here and then we are taking a freaking break so you can tell me the whole story—in detail, at which point I might *still* whack you upside the head."

When they stepped out of the workshop and stripped off their protective gear, Morgan pointed him toward the warehouse door. "Outside."

Nate nodded and trudged toward the door. Maybe if he attempted to explain his feelings to Morgan, he'd stand half a chance of understanding them himself.

"Nate." Her voice lost its drill-sergeant edge.

"Yeah?"

"Come here, baby." She enfolded him in one of her world-class hugs, and his eyes prickled with the threat of tears. *Shit.*

He disengaged, turning his head away so she wouldn't see him lose it. "Canteen? I could do with some coffee."

Morgan seemed to know exactly what he needed, because she fell into step beside him, quiet, not even bothering to do more than wave to her many fans on the way across the lot.

They collected their coffee and retreated to a two-top in the far corner, away from a gaggle of noisy grips.

Morgan sipped her coffee, her dark eyes soft and kind. "All right, baby. You're clearly freaking the fuck out. You want to tell me about it, or wallow some more?"

Nate wrapped his hands around the base of his cup. "Wallowing hasn't gotten me very far. I'm more confused now than I was when he left Saturday night."

She raised her eyebrows. "By 'he,' I assume we're talking about Cute Bartender?" Nate nodded. "And when you say 'left'—where exactly was he that he needed to leave?"

"My place. I invited him over for dinner to, you know, make up for being a dick."

"When I told you to make it right, I was imagining something more along the lines of an apology—not a cozy evening at Chez Albano."

Nate scowled into his coffee. "It seemed like a good idea at the time."

"I'm not saying it wasn't, but it's not like you. It's like pulling teeth to get you to go out for a drink with the crew, and as far as I know, you've never had anyone up to your place except me."

"I know."

"So why the change in game plan?"

The knot lodged in Nate's stomach since Saturday night coiled tighter. "I . . . I *like* him."

"You like lots of people, even if you act like a sociopath, but— *Ooh*. You *like* like him." Her smile bloomed. "That's great."

"No. It's not. Do you know how many times I've felt even a hint of sexual attraction for anyone? Twice. Maybe three times, if you count the crush I had on my seventh-grade science teacher. It's not like I have a lot of basis for comparison here."

"Why do you *need* to compare it?"

"How do I know it's a real thing, that it's not, I don't know, desperation?" He'd tried to convince himself he hadn't been devastatingly lonely after Jorge left. The dogs had helped, but since neither Ratchet nor Sophie had lived for more than a few months after he'd adopted them, he'd had to deal with their losses too. He'd never stopped to consider whether he'd chosen to take on animals at their end-of-life because *he* didn't want to commit, to get too attached.

Of course, with Tarkus, that ship had sailed after the first week. The first ten minutes, for that matter.

"I mean, Nara's confidence and . . . and excellence at everything she did was part of the turn-on. And Jorge—well, he *shone* when he was onstage. I defy anybody to resist that kind of brilliance."

"And the science teacher?" she drawled, cocking an eyebrow.

"He was just . . . cool. Enthusiastic, you know? We could suggest anything to him, any experiment, any tangential idea, and he'd say, 'Let's try it and see what happens.' He'd lead us down the rabbit hole with no qualms, and we still managed to complete the curriculum before students in the other teacher's class. We used to fight over who'd get to push his wheelchair—not that he needed our help. He had the upper body strength of Atlas."

"And this is relevant why?"

"Seth is a *bartender*, for Chrissake. He doesn't have anything in common with the others."

She tapped her fingers on the table, lips pursed. "Did anyone ever tell you you're an achievement snob?"

"Is that even a thing?"

"Yeah. We call them groupies."

He gave her the stink-eye over the rim of his cup. "I am *not* a groupie. Lord knows we see enough of that kind of behavior around here to tell the difference."

"If you say so, but bartender or not, there must be something there, or you wouldn't be this freaked. Normally, you've got a pulse beat of forty-two. Forty-three in a real crisis."

"Very funny."

"Come on, Nate, you've known him for less than a week and spent a total of, what, four hours with him? Do you really expect a relationship to go from zero to sixty that fast?"

"But that's the point. Maybe that's exactly how it works for other people." He leaned forward. "My statistical frame of reference is minuscule, so I'm half-afraid to let it go any further, and half-afraid to hesitate in case the feeling dissipates."

"Don't borrow trouble, baby. You don't even know if he'd be into it anyway."

"God, don't I know it. I mean, he's part of this *town*, for God's sake, not just a guy who'll only be here until the fans get sick of *Wolf's Landing* or until Finn Larson convinces the other producers that CGI is cheaper than practical effects."

She reached across the table and flicked his forehead with her finger. "Don't sell yourself short either, you dope. You're a catch. You're smart, gorgeous, funny—when you aren't being a curmudgeonly bastard. Don't rush to commit, but don't give up before you try either. Let him get to know you." She straightened, excitement making her eyes sparkle. "I've got it. Invite him here."

"Here?" Nate looked around. "To the canteen?"

"Don't be dense. To the lot. Give him a tour."

"I don't think people who actually live in Bluewater Bay are interested in that. It's for tourists."

"Not the public tour. The *private* one. Our space. What *we* do. I'm sure you could get permission from Anna."

"You mean *you* can get permission from Anna. You could probably get special dispensation from the pope if you tried."

"Don't exaggerate." She clapped her hands. "It's settled. In fact, let's make it tomorrow. I don't want you to have a chance to chicken out."

"Is that a challenge?"

"You know it, baby. Go big or go home."

"Go big. Right. I can do that." So why did he feel so fucking small?

As Seth stood, alternately looking at the half a pomegranate he held in his left hand and the citrus reamer in his right, he realized there was a lot he didn't know about the fruit. The juice wasn't going to be difficult to get out, he was pretty sure, since it was currently dribbling over the edge of the peel and down between his fingers. One dark-red rivulet was starting down his wrist.

"Okay," he muttered, setting the pomegranate back on the cutting board. He had the basics down for making grenadine, with a couple of different recipes printed out even, but obviously getting from finding a pomegranate in the supermarket to "combine the juice with the sugar in a saucepan" was going to be a little different than he'd thought.

Maybe he should have done more research before bolting out of his place with a half-assed plan this morning. But he'd needed to leave to stop thinking about Nate Albano.

He's not interested. And it wasn't even personal—he wouldn't be interested if Seth were a woman, either. Not unless he had romantic feelings for him first.

What did it take to elicit romantic feelings in a guy like that? Seth owned it—he really wanted to know, but he could also accept that he wasn't likely to be the right person.

Except Nate had kissed him, and even though he'd been kissed good-bye on the cheek by men before, Seth couldn't stop, well, *mooning* about it. That kiss was 100% of the reason he'd decided he needed to make grenadine. To avoid thinking about how dry Nate's lips were, yet how soft. How they'd felt grazing across his cheek. And about that slight hint of moisture on his skin as Nate had pulled away.

Footsteps behind him told him he wasn't alone anymore. "What are you doing again?" Dave, Ma Cougar's head bartender, asked, accompanied by the clatter of a rack of beer glasses being set down.

"Making grenadine." Sighing, Seth barely stopped himself from running his purple-stained fingers through his hair. That was all he needed—his hair was light enough to show the streaks, and he'd be pomegranate juice marked like hell.

"We have grenadine." Now Dave was looming over his shoulder. He moved on before Seth could turn, though. "It even has real pomegranate juice in it."

Well, yeah, because Seth had insisted they needed the better one

"Don't you want us to be known as master mixologists?"

"I don't care." Seth could practically hear Dave's shrug in his tone. Just like he'd said earlier, he was happy for Seth to tinker if he wanted.

as long as he didn't poison anyone and didn't expect to get paid for his hours "messing around."

"You be careful what you agree to, man, or I may just invent some world-famous cocktail and get your job."

Dave snorted. "Be my guest," he said, voice echoing in from the pass-through to the kitchen. The dude truly didn't care—he was one of those retirees who'd returned to work to keep from getting bored. He'd gotten the position as head bartender when there was a lack of qualified people to promote, and he made no secret of the fact that he was doing them a favor by taking the job.

So really, Seth was gunning for his position already, and they both knew it.

"Is it too early for a beer?" someone new asked.

"Uh..." Seth glanced up to find Shannon Schumer parking herself on a barstool. "How'd you get in?" They didn't open until eleven. And technically, he wasn't on shift until three thirty.

"I know a guy." Shannon hiked her thumb back over her shoulder, smirking. Of course she did—she was dating the dining room manager, Alan.

"That's the problem with living in the same tiny town you grew up in," Seth said half to himself.

Shannon assumed he was talking all to her, of course. "Repeating your past over and over?" At his quizzical look, she said, "I dated Alan in high school. Right after I broke up with Jim."

"Ahhh." She and Jim Schumer had just gotten divorced. "Well, in that case, maybe a beer *is* in order. But really, why not be classy and have a mimosa? It's what the septuagenarian set has when they come in for lunch." Since, of course, they came in for lunch at eleven on the nose, complaining about having to eat later than normal.

She squinted at him suspiciously, like he was trying to sell her a bill of goods. Or short her on alcohol content. "Can I get a double mimosa?"

"Why not?" After all, he'd already broken with tradition by serving the senior citizens a community mimosa in a punch bowl. Old Herman Thompson had gleefully dubbed it a *miboasa*. *"Because it's a veritable boat of champagne!"*

Seth had been forced into it, though—they went through so many wine glasses when they came in that the dishwasher wasn't able to keep up.

Once he'd made Shannon a large mimosa in a pint glass and set it down in front of her, she fixed him with an intent look. "So what's new with you?"

Immediately an image of Nate surfaced in Seth's mind, but he shoved it back into his subconscious. "Nothing much." He forced ease and friendliness into his voice. "You?" That was what she was really looking for—someone to listen. A little bartender therapy. He was here anyway, even if he wasn't on shift. Might as well let her get whatever was eating her off her chest while he continued to figure out his grenadine.

She sighed, and then let him have it with both barrels. Seth surreptitiously eased his phone out of his apron pocket and surfed the internet on it behind the counter while playing shrink for her. Listening to how sick she was of writing stories about *Wolf's Landing*, the cast of *Wolf's Landing*, developments during the current *Wolf's Landing* season. "For variety, I sometimes interview Hunter Easton. You know"—she flicked her fingers in the air and added unnecessarily—"the creator of Wolf's Landing."

Seth made about his fifteenth sympathetic noise in the past ten minutes, and began peeling the pomegranate at his prep station according to the directions he'd found, doing it just like they did in the pictures, minus the preliminary cuts, since he'd already halved the thing.

"I really, really need a story that has nothing to do with that—" she shifted her eyes side to side, then leaned toward him and hissed "—*fucking* show."

He held up his purple-stained palm to stop her. "There's no call for that kind of language, missy."

She smirked and took a gulp of her drink. "Anyway, you got anything for me?"

"Huh?" Scooping up the seeds, or *arils* as the websites insisted on calling them, he put them in a bowl to take them to the blender. Shannon could probably talk over the noise.

He was right. "You're a bartender," she half yelled over the whirring of the blades. "People tell you stuff all the time. What's the gossip?"

He pushed the Off button. "I'm sorry, ma'am, but that would violate the bartender code of confidentiality."

"How come I was 'missy' before but now I'm 'ma'am'?" she whined.

He really had no answer for that. As he turned to look for a strainer to get rid of the seed chunks, he saw a man coming toward the bar, intent in his step. *Damn it.* "I need to get out of here."

"What? The place just officially opened, people are coming in." Shannon pushed her glass closer to him. "And I need another."

"I'm not working right now. It's not my shift."

She sputtered a laugh. "Um, I think you are. I don't see anyone else back there, and you've already served me. Twice, hopefully."

Dave appeared right then, flicking a look at Seth and then asking the new customer how he could help. Trying to keep a low profile, Seth poured his pomegranate pulp into the strainer and let it drain while he made Shannon another drink, quickly. He could finish his grenadine in back.

"Hey, he came to visit you the last time I was here." Shannon was looking toward the door as he set down her double mimosa.

"Careful," he warned, pulling her bill out of his apron pocket to present to her. "You're starting to sound like a bar fly."

"No, I'm serious." She waved her index finger in front of his face and then pointed toward a guy who'd almost reached the bar.

Nate. "Oh hey." Seth winced inwardly at how welcoming he sounded. But Nate had surprised him. He couldn't help that he'd done nothing but think about that kiss since Saturday— *Stop it.*

"Hey yourself," Nate said a little awkwardly. Cute-awkward, the way someone who wasn't used to trivial social interaction would say it. Still rocking the cute-ward, Nate angled slightly toward Shannon. "Hey there, you play Justine in Frankenstein, right?"

"So you've met Shannon?" Seth still felt obliged to tell her, "He's part of the *Wolf's Landing* crew, you know."

She squeezed her eyes shut and groaned, which Nate totally caught, so when she plastered a smile on her face and held out her hand to shake, he hesitated a second before taking it.

"Sorry." She grimaced. "I wouldn't expect you to know, but I'm a reporter for the *Bluewater Bay Beacon*, and I was just telling Seth, um . . ." She rolled wild eyes his way, looking for help.

Barely keeping himself from laughing, Seth saved her. "It's okay, he won't be offended." He didn't think. That was his gut feeling, but in truth he didn't know the guy that well. *I only know how his eggplant tastes and how it feels when he kisses my cheek.* Jerking himself out of that line of thought, he turned back to Nate. "She was just telling me how tired she is of writing pieces about the show."

"I shouldn't complain." Shannon slumped over her glass. "I mean, the only reason I'm a *paid* reporter is because of *Wolf's Landing*. We were too small before to have actual staff."

By then, Nate had relaxed, and it looked as if he was trying to not smile too broadly. "Believe me, there are things about the show I'm not too fond of—the producer for instance. But it's got its good points. Speaking of—" he shoved his hands in the pockets of his jeans and turned fully back to Seth "—would you like a private tour of the lot?" He winced, his cheeks turning pink above his stubble. "God, I did it again, didn't I? I don't mean *that* kind of private—but something other than the public stuff with the tram and the gift shop and the selfies in the interrogation room set. I could show you where Morgan and I work. How we build the effects for the show."

"Oh." Seth blinked, surprised into single syllables. But it made sense, they were friend-guys, and guy friends hung out, right? "Yeah, that'd be cool." The idea took hold of him as he answered, so that by the time he was done, he was grinning. "Fascinating," he added, to prove he was multisyllabic when the occasion called for it.

"Great! How's tomorrow morning?" Nate had already been smiling, but now it was downright dazzling. At least, it made Seth feel like a deer in the headlights. Seth only half listened as Nate explained he had to get back to the set right away since he'd just nipped out really quick to buy a part at the hardware store . . . something like that. Seth's mind seized on the fact that Nate was essentially playing hooky to come talk to him. *Do guys do that for just friends?*

Well, he didn't know, did he? This was his first purely platonic experience, wasn't it?

He kissed my cheek.

Yeah, and Lucas kissed me hello the other night.

Nate was stepping back from the bar, leaving, and Seth lifted his hand in a wave. "Bye." God he *was* a teenager, wasn't he?

"I'll call you with the details." Nate nodded and turned, making his way toward the door.

Seth only watched him halfway there before he felt Shannon's stare boring into the side of his head.

"We're just friends," he blurted.

"Uh-huh." She snorted, then took another swig of her mimosa.

Yeah, he wouldn't have believed that, either. He couldn't fix it now, though, so he went back to work, or not-work, rather.

"He's *very* nice to look at," Shannon said approvingly as Seth cleaned up his juice-making mess, preparing to go into the kitchen to mix up the grenadine that had been going to save him from thinking incessantly about Nate. *Didn't work.*

"Seriously." He paused, sighing and meeting her eyes for a second. "He only wants to be friends."

"Could have fooled me," she muttered, as she dug through her purse. "Here, will this cover it? I don't need any change." She handed him twenty-five dollars. "Thanks, Seth, and if it makes any difference, he couldn't do a lot better in his choice of friends."

Blinking, he stood there stupidly as she left and her words sunk in. Did he deserve them? He wasn't sure he did. Nate had made the friends-only thing very clear, even answering Seth's prying questions about his past relationships, and in return Seth had still been reading sexual intent into every action the guy made. Analyzing every action to see if there was something deeper.

Now, that seemed kind of rude. Misleading, even. Would Nate have asked him to the set if he realized Seth was mooning about that stupid kiss on the cheek? God, he was repeating the night they met. Not listening to what Nate was actually saying, but hoping for more.

He didn't want to be that kind of friend. He wanted to be real friends, whatever that might mean. *Okay*, he resolved, *no more reading into everything. I'll take him at his word.*

Which meant he really needed to make grenadine, now, to keep himself from repeating the pattern.

CHAPTER TEN

For about half an hour, Nate was certain Seth wasn't going to show. On the other hand, he'd headed over to the gift shop forty-five minutes before the time they'd arranged to meet, so in case *Seth* showed up early, he wouldn't feel like Nate was standing him up.

He seriously needed to get a grip. For Chrissake, he was on the downhill slide to forty, not a fricking teenager. *Yeah, but today's average teenager probably has about ten times as much dating experience as I do.*

Then Seth was there, climbing out of a white Honda sedan, and when he caught sight of Nate, his face lit with the smile that made Nate's knees wobble. Just for a second, but still—an unmistakable wobble. *Yep. Grip definitely needed.*

He took a deep breath and walked over to meet him, doing his best to at least impersonate an adult. "Hey. Glad you could make it."

"Yeah." Seth glanced at the chattering crowd clustered around one of the tour trams. "I've never visited the set before. Do we have to buy a ticket and get on that bus-let?"

"Nah. You're getting the special tour. Maybe not as exciting, if you're a big *Wolf's Landing* fan— Wait, *are* you a fan?" God, maybe he'd planned this whole thing wrong.

Seth chuckled, shoving his hands in the back pockets of his jeans. "No. No worries there."

"So you won't be disappointed if you don't see the stars?"

"Nope. I've served most of 'em lunch enough times that the mystery is over. I'd rather find out what *you* do."

"Okay, then. Right this way." They walked through the gates into the compound proper, Nate lifting a hand to the security guard.

Seth paused once they were inside the fence. "Whoa. This place is a lot bigger than I thought. I didn't think there was enough room in this part of town for buildings that big, let alone this many of them."

"Does it bother you, Hollywood taking over your town?"

"I may live here, but trust me, I don't take ownership. The rest of my family, now, that's another story."

"They haven't gone Hollywood, eh?"

Seth snorted. "Not likely."

"You know, back in the early days of silent film, when the industry was just getting started, the original residents of Hollywood felt the same way. They used to put up signs in businesses and boarding houses that said 'No Movies.'"

"What, just to let people know they didn't have, like, a multiplex inside?"

Catching Seth's teasing smirk, Nate chuckled. "'Movies' was what they called folks who worked in film. Old Hollywood was not excited about all the riffraff, although there were plenty who took advantage of it too. The ones who weren't barring the doors were throwing up shacks on their lawns and renting them out to would-be actors—who mostly spent their days in corrals at the studios, hoping to get tapped for extra work."

Seth grinned at him. "So you study Hollywood history too, along with Bluewater Bay and Larson genealogy?"

Heat rushed up Nate's throat. God, he probably looked parboiled. "I'm just . . . fascinated by history, by connections. My mom raised me, and she didn't have any extended family. I guess I was always looking for a place to fit in. One of my online genealogy friends is the Hollywood expert. He's a little enthusiastic, so I've picked up some tidbits over the years."

Seth took a half step closer and nudged Nate's arm with his elbow. "It's cool."

Nate put his hand on Seth's back to steer him between the two new soundstages toward the warehouse. *Warm, even through his jacket.* Nate was tempted to sustain the touch, but when Seth shot him a startled glance, he dropped his arm to his side.

"Do you miss Hollywood? I mean this has to be a little different."

"A little. But I didn't get involved in the industry until I was an adult, and it was . . . unexpected."

"Unexpected? Jeez, I thought a career in film and TV had to be practically engineered from birth."

"From birth I was expected to work in live theater. My mother is a director—Shakespeare, and if you want to talk about snobbery, try convincing a Shakespearean scholar of the value of a TV show about werewolves."

"So why didn't you do that?"

"I almost did. Graduated with a degree in technical theater. Had a job offer from a rep company in Chicago."

"Chicago isn't exactly next door to Hollywood. How'd you end up out west?"

"I met my father."

Seth winced. "Oh. Right."

"He was an agent for years. My tech theater skills translated well enough to film and TV work, and Dad had the connections to get me in the door. I worked SFX on several of Levi's films and—" he opened the warehouse door and gestured for Seth to go inside "—the rest is history."

Seth peered up at the distant ceiling with its banks of fluorescent lights. "Now this place I recognize, although it's had a major facelift since it was the boneyard for Bay Building and Salvage." He nodded at the workshop wall, two-thirds of the way across the building. "It used to be one big empty space. Well, except for the metal shelves full of second-hand toilets and reclaimed bricks. The racks of costumes are an improvement."

"Back in the early days, this was the original soundstage, so it was still open. Once the show took off, though, and they built the two new ones, they turned this place over to the art and tech departments"

"I remember that, I think. Didn't they used to rent out space in that creepy industrial park out by Holly's Haus of Imports?"

"Yeah. Transportation was a real pain in the ass, apparently. Better to have everything on the lot." He led the way into the workshop and closed the door. "Morgan and I do most of our fabrication in here" Nate pointed to the giant fans high overhead that vented to the outside. "It's closed off from the rest of the building with double-thick walls and has serious ventilation, because the materials we work with are kind of toxic. The prosthetics team uses it too, and the costume department when they need to chemically distress costume pieces for a character like Max Fuhrman, who always looks as if he just crawled out of a blender."

Seth goggled at the fans. "Jesus. Those things are the size of the propellers on the *Titanic*."

"Yeah. And they're not even enough. We use the big portable fans too, when we're working with the really nasty stuff."

"It's not . . . I mean, sure, it's dangerous, but it's not like *dangerous*, is it?"

Nate grinned, Seth's obvious concern warming him. "That's what protective gear is for. Sometimes we look like we're suited up for a space walk. Come on. I want to show you the storage area."

"I want to show you the storage area"? God, could he be any more awkward? That either sounded like another inadvertent double entendre or the lead-in to the most boring segment of an IRS tax archive tour. Yeah, what guy could resist *that* kind of temptation?

Seth, however, didn't lose the look of bright-eyed interest he'd worn since he arrived. His evident curiosity was irresistible, and Nate had to force himself not to edge closer.

Morgan walked in from their tiny office, carrying a sheaf of the oversized paper they used for storyboarding stunts and effects. "Hey, Mr. Bartender. Welcome to our crazy world."

"Seth, this is Morgan Fitzgerald. Morgan, Seth Larson."

Her eyebrows shot up. "Larson?"

"Not *that* Larson." Nate grinned at Seth. "The *Bluewater Bay* Larsons."

"Well then, that's all right, and since you're not useless—here." She handed the drawings to Seth and grabbed his elbow, steering him over to the corkboard that ran the length of one wall. "Nate, get the pushpins. We don't have much time."

He grabbed a box of pins off the supply shelf. "Time for what?"

"Time to set the stage." She took the first rendering from Seth and waggled her fingers until Nate handed her a couple of pins.

Seth peered at the first picture as he handed her the second one. "Did you draw these? They're really good."

She beamed at him. "Thank you, sugar."

Nate frowned at the sketch of the set with the glass corridor he'd been complaining about for two days. It had somehow acquired a row of exterior windows that hadn't been present before. "Did the script change?"

"No. But I want to see if we can get Ginsberg to at least *pretend* that a stunt scares him."

"Good luck with that," Nate muttered.

Seth fumbled the next drawing before handing it to Morgan. "So ... Ginsberg? He's one of the guys that runs the Burnt Toast B&B, right?"

Morgan nodded. "Part owner. He's also the stunt double for Carter Samuels, one of the show leads." She gestured to the storyboard. "So what do you think?"

Seth peered at the pictures. "Holy shit. Is he on *fire* when he falls off that ledge?"

Her grin grew wider. "Yes, indeed he is."

He walked back to the beginning of the series and tracked the sequence. "So he crashes through three of those big panes of glass ... then falls through the hole in the floor ... and smashes that desk ... and the wolves drag him *up* the stairs." He turned to her, wide-eyed. "Four flights? And *then* comes the fire and the fall?"

She tilted her head, considering. "Hmmm. I might have overdone it just a smidge." Morgan turned to Nate. "But Gins was super disappointed when a guest performer got to do that big fall a couple of seasons back."

"He may have been relieved," Nate said. "Didn't he have a broken wrist at the time?"

She waved her hand in dismissal. "It was definitely disappointment. Trust me and play along."

Just then, Ginsberg bopped into the room with his usual jaunty stride—his own, not the walk he used when he was eerily copying Carter's movement patterns. "Hey, guys. You wanted to see me?"

"Hey, baby." Morgan enveloped Ginsberg in a hug, which he returned with interest.

Seth sidled over until he was standing right beside Nate. *Play along?* he mouthed.

Nate brushed his fingers across the back of Seth's hand and shot him what he hoped was a reassuring smile while they waited for Morgan to disengage. "Don't worry," he murmured. "He won't be mad at *you*."

Seth flashed a quick grin, accompanied by a shrug. "Why should I be worried? I'm not the one setting the dude on fire."

Nate moved forward to slap Ginsberg on the shoulder. *Time to improvise.* "So, Gins. We're working up our build lists for the FX for the season finale, and we've got a . . . ah . . . continuity question for you." He caught Morgan's approving nod out of the corner of his eye as he pointed to the storyboard. "Do you remember whether that desk you smashed in season two was the two-pedestal faux-oak model or the green metal institutional type?"

Ginsberg laced his fingers together behind his back and strolled over to the storyboard, studying each panel for a good fifteen seconds before moving on to the next. Nate forced himself to avoid Morgan's gaze for fear he wouldn't be able to keep a straight face.

He made the mistake of glancing at Seth, though, and his breath caught. Seth's lips were slightly parted, his eyebrows quirked above eyes that fairly sparkled. *Anticipation.* That was what it was. *He digs this. I bet if we'd filled him in, he'd have been on board one hundred percent.* If Nate hadn't already felt drawn to Seth, that look would have sealed the deal.

Ginsberg reached the last rendering. "Nice try, guys."

Morgan didn't so much as blink. "What do you mean?"

He snorted. "Nate never touches anyone but you, Morgan, so *that* was weird enough, but a continuity question? *Seriously?* Since when do you guys not have every detail documented in your notes? Even if I hadn't already seen the script, I might have bought it if it weren't for that." He sauntered toward the door. "But this sequence looks like way more fun. I bet we could get Hunter to sign off on the change. Later."

He strolled out of the room, humming the *Wolf's Landing* title theme.

"Well, shee-yit." Morgan propped her fists on her hips. "That didn't go the way we'd planned."

Seth choked on a laugh. "So that whole thing really was just you two messing with him? That's *excellent!*"

"Unfortunately, the whole thing backfired." Nate yanked a pushpin out of the cork and lobbed it across the room to the worktable. "Damn it, now we may actually have to build this stuff."

"That guy is either totally brilliant or completely whack." Seth shook his head. "I mean, getting tossed out a four-story window on fire didn't tip him off, but the question about the desk did? And he *prefers* the dive of flaming death?"

"That's Ginsberg for you." Morgan tilted her head, studying the storyboard. "Good thing I decided to leave out the plunge into the giant vat of ice water."

"I'm surprised you restrained yourself," Nate said.

"Well, I couldn't figure out why police headquarters would have a giant vat of ice water hanging around. Oh well." She started to remove the drawings. "It was worth a try."

"So." Seth turned to Nate, smile wider than ever. "What's next? I believe I was promised a *storage* tour."

Nate laughed and gestured to the exit with a bow. "Right this way, sir. Who needs actors and stuntmen when you could hang out with the real stars of *Wolf's Landing*—the breakable sets and props."

As usual, when Nate picked up Tarkus from Bluewater Bark, he had to practically pry the dog away from Conrad Paulson, one of the three regular kids who'd fallen for Tarkus like a ton of Styrofoam bricks.

"Can't he stay a little longer, Nate?" Conrad pleaded. "I'm off in twenty minutes. I could walk him home for you."

"Be serious. It's almost five miles—double that by the time you got back—and you've got school tomorrow."

"I know, but we were working on a new trick, and he's almost got it. Come on, Tark. Show him. Army crawl!" Tarkus dropped to his belly and crept forward a few inches, then rolled to his side and whined softly. "See?"

Nate snapped his fingers and Tarkus scrambled to his feet, panting. "Hate to tell you, Conrad, but he's known how to do that since I got him."

"Really? But he acted like he didn't know the command."

"Hmmm." Holding Tarkus's gaze, Nate held out his hand, palm down, then clenched his fist. Tarkus immediately dropped, this time crawling all the way to Nate's feet before he flopped over, pawing the air feebly in addition to the whine. "He's really good at faking it." Nate hunkered down and scratched Tarkus's belly until the dog half closed his eyes in bliss, one rear paw twitching. "I think he could have given Rin Tin Tin a run for his money."

"Who?"

"Never mind. See you tomorrow."

He snapped on Tarkus's leash, led him out to the parking lot, and opened the door of the Jeep so the dog could hop in and settle down on his blanket in the backseat. He glanced back at the daycare window. Maybe he should take Conrad up on his offer—not to walk so far, but to let Tarkus stay for a little longer. Bluewater Bark had extended hours. Maybe Nate should take advantage of them. Go over to Ma Cougar's for a drink. Just to unwind—didn't have anything to do with the fact that Seth would be working the bar.

In a pig's fricking eye.

For some reason, Nate couldn't believe that this feeling, this compulsion to be close to Seth, could be real. He had the impulse to keep testing it, poking at it like a sore tooth, to see if repeated exposure would make it fade to the same sexual indifference he felt for everybody else.

Nah. That was just pathetic. Besides, he'd promised Seth he'd research the knife. If he found anything interesting, *then* he could stop by the bar. Maybe tomorrow. Or the next day—no point in seeming too eager. It might give Seth the wrong idea. *And inviting him to dinner, then kissing him on the cheek didn't? Get your head in the game, Albano.*

Now if he could just figure out what the alleged game actually was . . .

"Am I out of my mind, Tark?" Tarkus just panted quietly, jaws open in his doggy smile. "Yeah, that's what I thought."

When they got home, he fixed Tarkus's supper, threw together a salad for himself, and wolfed it down before unpacking the cleaning supplies he'd borrowed from Morgan's kit. When Seth had entrusted the antique knife to him, Nate had wrapped it in an old T-shirt to protect it until he could read up on the best way to clean mother-of-pearl. Exposing the knife now, his breath caught at the idea that this was a tool someone long dead had used—that Seth's *ancestor* had used. According to Seth's tale of Fennimore's sensational murder, the man had been stabbed, possibly with a knife just like this one, but the murder weapon was never found, even though they'd hanged that poor Chinese girl for the crime.

For something so old, the knife wasn't in as rough a shape as it could have been. Yeah, there were scratches on it—some that looked like tiny teeth marks, which fit with where Seth had discovered it. Mostly, though, it just seemed to suffer from an excess of dirt. *I can handle that.*

Using a brush with soft nylon bristles, he whisked as much of the loose surface dirt away as possible. Then, he used a swab soaked in soapy water to remove the next layer. After he'd rinsed with clear water, he blotted it dry and played a flashlight over the surface. The initials etched into the handle were still inlaid with dirt, but they were a little easier to make out. What they'd thought was an *F* or possibly a *T* was actually an *E*.

He squinted at the other two initials—a *C*? No, a *G*. He swabbed the initials again, removing more crusted dirt, because that last letter didn't look anything like an *L*.

M. EGM, nothing remotely like FLL—for Fennimore Leroy Larson.

Wait a minute. EGM? The sheriff—Fennimore's poker buddy, the guy who'd handled the inquest and arrested Adeline, the Larsons' maid—his name had been Edgar Gaines Monteith. A chill raised the hairs on Nate's neck. *God, was it possible?* Could Seth have discovered the murder weapon after all this time?

And if the murder weapon had belonged to the man who'd been in charge of the whole investigation—

"Holy shit."

Nate raced up the stairs and woke his computer. He'd already spent so much time trolling through the Bluewater Bay historical records that he knew where to look, so he pulled up the newspaper archives and went to work.

CHAPTER ELEVEN

Inspired by the drink he'd made his first day for Nate, the Twelve Mile Limit, Seth had been experimenting. Prohibition-era drinks were very popular right now. They had a sense of class that more modern cocktails couldn't compete with. Still, some updates were in order. And he had one option all ready, as he found out when he went back to check on some of his concoctions in the restaurant's kitchen.

During a quiet moment, he sprang it on Melanie, dragging her to the wraparound. "It's called a Mary Pickford, after the silent film actress—"

"I *know* what a Mary Pickford is." Melanie's eye roll was all in her tone of voice.

"—I used a secret ingredient though. Try it." He nudged the glass closer to her. "G'ahead."

Her expression was wary, but she at least picked it up, hesitantly sniffing it first. She eyed him over the rim. "I'll give you my verdict after you help that group that just came in."

Turning, Seth found Lucas's father standing near the central taps. "Oh, hey there, Mr. Wilder." He was with some old logging buddies, all of them retired, gnarled, and lined. "What can I do for you gentlemen?" This wasn't their typical hangout, but Carl Wilder came in with his family a lot. Judging from the way he was beaming around at his crew, he'd dragged them here himself.

"Told you we'd get good service here. I know the bartender."

"Everyone knows him. That's Old Lady Larson's grandson," Dick Codger said, pointing a crooked finger toward Seth, wavering it around a couple inches in front of his nose. *He* had some nerve, calling Grandma "old."

"We know the bartender at Tiny's, too. Went to high school with 'im," grumbled Roger Stoddard.

Ignoring them, Carl spread his hands in the air expansively. "Order whatever you want, boys, it's all on me." Amid the mutterings of acceptance that followed his pronouncement, he leaned forward, telling Seth confidentially—in a carrying voice—"It's been a good harvest season for Savage and Wilder." He winked, using the whole left side of his face.

Seth smiled at him and tried to ignore how bloodshot his eyes were. "You boys walk here?" He at least needed to be sure of that.

"Don't you worry, son, none of us are driving. That's what we got wives for."

"Dontcha got any Bud Light?" Dick interrupted, squinting at the fancy microbrew tap handles.

It took Seth a while to get the fractious group of aging townies settled—they finally perked up when he suggested a pitcher of Local Logger Lager; that name guaranteed it'd be a hit around here—so of course he had a backlog of drinks from the dining room to make when he was done. It was almost an hour before he spoke to Melanie again.

"Your drink was good," she said from behind him, reaching past his arm for some clean pint glasses from the dishwasher. "So good, in fact, that I'd let you offer it to customers as an unadvertised special."

Seth barely stopped himself from whirling around and spraying soda water everywhere. *She liked it?* But he played it cool, glancing over his shoulder after he'd topped off the highball glass and raising his eyebrows. "You would, huh?"

Her smirk told him she knew how happy that made him, but really, he didn't mind her knowing. Anyone would think that was cool, wouldn't they?

"Just tell me again you made your mixer in the restaurant's kitchen."

"Definitely." He even still had his food handler's license.

His first victim showed up shortly after he got the go-ahead from Mel. It only took him a few seconds to talk Shannon into trying it. "So, you're experimenting on me? I don't know . . ." She squinted at him, settling her purse on the empty stool next to her. "I get it on the house, right?"

"You weren't this picky about that martini you ordered last week," he teased as he started mixing the drink.

"That's the same kind of glass." She pointed at it accusingly. But then she smiled, waving her hand dismissively. "Whatever, I'll try it. Can't be worse than vermouth."

"I've been making these mixers—they're called shrubs."

"A shrubbery?" she asked, mimicking the accent and intonation of one of the knights from the Monty Python movie. Then she wrinkled her nose at him. "Wait, you can make your own, like, ingredients? For use in the bar?"

"A shrubbery." He parroted her impersonation before answering. "As long as I do it in the licensed kitchen, I can. Shrubs're also called 'drinking vinegars' because they're made by mixing sugar and fruit— or some other flavoring—with vinegar and letting them steep together for a while. Days, or weeks." Honestly, he'd started using this particular one a little earlier than advised, but it had tasted right. She'd like it, he was certain—her flavor profile seemed very sweet and sour to him. "Anyway, this drink—" he paused to concentrate on measuring the rum "—it calls for maraschino cherry liqueur." As he poured it into the shaker, he glanced up to see the "yuck" squinch everyone made when maraschino cherries were mentioned. "There's none in here."

"You used this 'shrub' instead?" She lifted her chin to be heard over the sound of the ice clattering around.

Straining the drink into the glass, he nodded. "Yeah, I use this shrub I made—it's cherry-based, so I figure it's the same basic thing, plus Dave laughed his ass off when I asked him to buy some maraschino liqueur."

"Smart man." She picked up her drink and sipped, then her eyes went so wide he could see the whites of them. "This is *good*. So good I'll even pay you for it."

Warmth flooded his rib cage, as if he'd just saved a cute, wriggling puppy from the pound. But he had to go help other customers, so he couldn't make her tell him again how great his drink was.

When he made it back to check in on Shannon, someone new was inhabiting the stool formerly claimed by her purse. As the woman turned her head, he recognized Guy Parker's wife.

"Hey, Elle. What can I get for you?"

"Exactly what she's having." Elle hooked a thumb at Shannon's drink. "Those are awesome. Are you in charge of all the specials?"

"Nah." He shrugged, hoping his extreme pleasure at people's reactions wasn't too obvious, but blood was rushing to his cheeks. Busying himself with her order made it easier to hide.

"I should get the food columnist at the paper to do a piece on you." Shannon's voice was slightly rounded, not quite slurring, but not hitting her consonants briskly. He checked, but she hadn't even finished her drink. Maybe she was tired. She was in *Frankenstein* wasn't she? They'd probably just finished rehearsal.

But more importantly— "The *Beacon* has a food columnist?" He set Elle's Mary Pickford in front of her.

Shannon made a face. "Not really. Ty—you know, over at Flat Earth—is trying to convince the editor to let him do one, though. Thought I'd help him out."

It looked like Ty was really branching out. Seth could help with that too, he supposed. Besides, if he ever wanted to leave Bluewater Bay, he'd have a local feature story to put on his résumé.

"Okay, sure. I'll have to check with management first, though." Glancing around, he realized he didn't have anyone waiting to order. "So, how about you? Any interesting stories you're working on lately?"

She nearly snorted Mary Pickford through her nose, but before she could swallow and answer, something over Seth's shoulder caught her eye. From her seat she could see the entrance to the restaurant while he had his back to it.

"Oh, hey, there's that guy helping with Frankenstein," mused Elle, chin in her hand and focusing the same way Shannon was. "He's *really* good-looking."

A tiny thrill ran up Seth's spine, but he didn't turn immediately. He knew though—it *had* to be Nate, right?

"Nate," Shannon confirmed, glancing at Elle and smiling in a way that made him uncomfortable. Not like they had any designs on Nate's person, more like they wanted Seth to have designs on his person.

Biting his tongue to keep from blurting out *We're just friends*, he turned to see the man himself. Heading his way, with messed-up hair and a wild, excited look in his eye. As if he'd been out on Sandy Bluff during a winter storm, reveling in the lightning dancing too close to him and the wind beating him around.

So sexy. And moving so fast he was in front of Seth within seconds, lurching to a stop and planting his hands on the counter.

"It wasn't a *T* or an *F*, it's an *E*!"

Head whirling from the intensity of Nate's stare and the force of his entry, Seth tried to make sense of what he'd said. Why the hell would he barrel in like this, as if he had some grand pronouncement, looking into Seth's eyes the whole time, then come up with something so out of nowhere? What the hell could he even be talking about— *Ohhh!*

"The knife?"

"The knife," Nate said a split second after him. "The monogram on the hilt is EGM, which happen to be the initials of the sheriff at the time. The same sheriff who arrested Adeline."

"What knife?" Shannon butted in. "Who's Adeline and why was she arrested?"

"Wait, *what?*" Seth shook his head, ignoring her clear interest and still facing Nate. "It's really not Fennimore's?"

He shrugged, smiling lopsidedly. "Does he seem like a guy who'd have someone else's monogram on his knife?"

"Then how did it get in Grandma's garage?"

"Hold it, back up. You found some *knife* in your grandmother's garage?" Shannon's tone had become so strident, Seth couldn't ignore her anymore.

"Yeah." Still, he kept his focus on Nate. "A very old one, which I thought was my great-great-grandfather's."

"Except . . ." Nate's lopsided smile grew, as did the glimmer of excitement in his eye. "It's not, and you know what that means? As we say in show biz—' he waggled his eyebrows "—*the plot thickens.*"

"Oh, I so get it," Seth breathed, speaking mostly to himself. He one hundred percent understood the thrill of history and genealogy right this second. No boring recitation of family legend by his uncle Kirk had ever made his heart trip along like this. "How do we find out more ab—"

"That!" Shannon crowed, startling Seth so much he almost stumbled, even though he'd been standing still. She hung half-over the bar, her pointy finger stabbing the air with each of her words. "*That's* the kind of article I want to write. I *need* to. For my sanity."

Clearly. "Hang on." He threw up his hand, palm out and white bar rag incidentally wrapped around his thumb. Like he was surrendering or something. "I don't— I mean, would they care? Your readers?" His heart was really thumping away now.

"Town history like this? I'm sure they would. I mean, Fennimore was *murdered.*"

He hadn't even mentioned the knife to Grandma yet. And his uncle Kirk would *freak out.*

Oh, that sounded appealing.

"Well . . ." Glancing over at Nate, he once again got caught by that mischievous gleam in the guy's eyes, and felt an answering buzz kindling in his own. "We have to do some more research, right?"

Nate nodded, his lips compressed as if he was trying to contain his grin. "Yep. And I could use your help with that."

"Okay." His pulse drummed in his ears so loud he couldn't hear himself speak. They definitely heard him, though, because Shannon whooped and, at the corner of his eye, her fist pumped the air. But he wasn't looking at her; most of him was focused on Nate and that glowing exhilaration. For a second, he thought the excitement would physically spark between them, arcing over the bar. "I wonder how this'll go over with the family?"

He barely cared at the moment, not now while he and Nate stood there in silence, as if they could figure out the answer through prolonged eye contact.

"Bartender," someone called.

Oh, yeah. *Damn it.* He was at work.

With Seth sitting so close to him, peering over his shoulder at the computer monitor, Nate was having trouble concentrating. Seth wasn't having the same issue, apparently. His whole attention was focused on the timeline Nate had thrown together last night, his knee bouncing as if he couldn't contain his enthusiasm, lips parted a little, eyes shining.

Focus, Albano. This is about the story, *about something that matters to him, not about your stupid ambivalence.*

Nate cleared his throat and used the mouse pointer to indicate each step in Adeline's doomed journey.

"We got this far last night. Even though there's no birth certificate, the ledger from the doctor's office shows the bill for attending the birth." Nate hesitated, unsure if he'd drawn the right conclusion. Sure, Seth didn't seem at all sentimental about Fennimore—or have many illusions about him—but the guy was still his ancestor. "We're both on the same page regarding the likelihood of Adeline's baby being Fennimore's, right?"

"Yup." Seth's tone was a bit irritated. "I *told* you that already."

"Just checking. Now take a look at some of these lost-and-found ads."

Seth squinted at the monitor. "Are you shitting me? They include missing wives and servants in the same list as lost dogs and watches?"

"Let's just say white male privilege—especially straight, Christian, white male privilege—isn't exactly a new thing." Nate pulled up the next document. "Take a look at our friend EGM. Over the course of the five months leading up to the murder, he advertised for lost stuff thirteen times. A coat. A watch. A horse."

"A horse? How could he lose his horse? The guy was way too careless with his shit."

"But in all those ads—and thirteen seems pretty excessive—you know what was interesting? He never advertised for the lost knife."

Seth tilted his head, looking over at Nate. "Something's not lost if—"

"You know where it is," they said simultaneously.

"Asshole," Seth muttered, then blinked rapidly. "Not you. That guy."

"Wait. There's more."

"What are you, an infomercial host?" Seth lifted one eyebrow and lowered the other, the picture of fake skepticism. "If you're hawking cubic zirconia, I'm not buying."

Nate forced a chuckle, but his hand on the mouse was a little clammy anyway. Seth might *say* he wasn't invested in keeping his ancestors' reputations intact, but when push came to shove, they were still his family. "While I was digging through the records, I found the notice of your great-great-grandmother's second marriage. Guess who the groom was."

Seth's eyes widened. "No way—*Monteith*?" Nate nodded, waiting for anger and denial, but instead, Seth cackled evilly, rubbing his hands together. "This is *fantastic*. Uncle Kirk is gonna rupture a blood vessel. What else have you got?"

Heaving a relieved sigh, Nate turned back to the monitor. "Well, the anti-Chinese sentiment began to appear in the newspaper ads almost immediately after Fennimore's death. See?" He brought up the screenshots of the yellowed ads of local businesses touting their goods and services. "Before the murder, they're this weird combination of outrageous and self-deprecating—like they're trying to boast about how great their stuff is, but don't want to draw down the wrath of God for hubris or something." He pointed to the ads from the week after the murder. "Here, she hadn't even been convicted yet, but it's already starting." Each ad had a tiny line at the bottom: *No Orientals.* "They go on like that for about two months. Then they peter out."

Seth snorted. "What, Bluewater Bay suddenly grew a social conscience?"

"Hardly. Look—after the exclusion ads start to disappear, we also see these." Nate pointed to a whole line of ads for servants. "In the months before the murder, there were virtually none. Combine the sudden need for servants with the disappearance of the exclusion language—"

"The Chinese had all left town?" Seth reared back in his chair. "Unbelievable. The bastards fucking drove them out."

"That's what I think, and Bluewater Bay wouldn't be the first or only community to do it."

"If they—"

Quack. Tarkus nudged Seth's knee, his duck in his mouth. He *quack*ed it again, then laid it at Seth's feet.

"Hey, boy. Whatcha got there?"

"I think he's offering it to you. You should be honored. He guards that thing like it's a Holy Grail made out of bacon."

Seth picked it up and gave it an experimental squeeze, activating the squeaker this time. He stood, waggling it in front of Tarkus, who crouched down, tail swishing madly.

"Oh yeah. Somebody wants to play. Somebody wants his squeaky duck, yes he does." Seth feinted to the right, then left, Tarkus matching his moves and *ruff*ing in excitement. "Uh-oh. I think it—yes, it's going to flyyy." He launched the duck over the half wall to the living room below. Tarkus lunged after it. "Oh my God. No—"

But Tarkus just put his paws on the top of the wall and peered down, whining a little. He cast Seth a reproachful look and headed down the stairs.

Seth collapsed in his chair. "Holy shit, Nate. I'm sorry. I thought he was gonna jump."

"Hey, don't worry about it." Nate rubbed a circle on Seth's back. "He's got some impulse-control issues, and his depth perception isn't great, but he's got this place figured out."

"That's a relief. Now where were we?"

"Well, we know that the entire Chinese population decamped after the whole sorry episode. We can see some specific evidence of how they were treated here. The newspaper accounts of the arrest and trial mention Adeline's mother, Mei, being hysterical and having to be removed from the room. They barred her from the jail too. She wasn't allowed to see her daughter before the execution."

"Which means Adeline couldn't see the baby either."

"No." Nate's throat tightened, thinking about that poor girl abandoned, falsely accused, isolated from even a last sight of her child. "Probably not." He swallowed. "But look here. The day of the execution, Mei was taken away by two women that the reporter obviously loathed almost as much as he did Adeline. Harriet Bunson and Mamie Rose Keeler."

"Who are they?"

"He wrote about them a few other times—apparently they were suffragists, and a major pain in the ass for the fine, upstanding men of the town, your illustrious and not-very-lamented ancestor included."

"Figures." Seth snorted, crossing his arms, and his obvious indignation warmed Nate's heart. "Well, good for them."

"Yeah. And check this out. They wrote this totally insulting letter to the town leaders that got published in the paper—"

"Wait. If it was insulting, why did the editor run it? He was one of Fennimore's poker buddies too."

Nate grinned. "Because he wanted to gloat. The women wrote it as they were leaving town."

"Okaaay. That's kind of patronizing, but I'm assuming it's significant?"

"They moved to San Francisco—and took Adeline's baby and Mei with them."

Seth grabbed Nate's arm. "Really? We found them?" He looked at his hand and immediately released his hold.

No. Put it back. Being touched—Nate missed it like crazy. "But you're right. We've got a firm lead, because Harriet and Mamie Rose weren't exactly shrinking violets. In fact, they were totally badass. I've found mentions of them—letters to the editors, articles about protests—in newspapers from San Francisco to Santa Barbara to Hollywood. If Mei and the baby were still with them when they hit Hollywood, we have a chance of locating them. My friend—"

"The Hollywood expert?"

"Yup. He's got that town nailed. Now if—"

A whine from the top of the stairs interrupted them. Tarkus limped toward them, favoring his left hind leg.

"Jesus, Nate. He's hurt." Seth jumped up and rushed over to Tarkus, running his hands over the dog's flank. "Is that my fault? Did he—"

"Hey, hey, hey." Nate followed him and rested a hand on his shoulder. "Relax. He's faking."

"Faking?" Seth looked up. "Seriously? He *does* that?"

"Yup. He had to alter his gait when he was in casts after he was hurt, and he had so much practice that it's like a self-taught trick. He pulls it out whenever he wants to make me feel guilty for ignoring him."

"Yeah?" He grinned. "Maybe it's time we took a break, then. But I'm sure no poor, injured puppy would want to play Frisbee on the beach."

Tarkus immediately bounced to his feet, and Seth laughed, his shoulder vibrating under Nate's hand. *This feels good. Warm. Comfortable.* Seth hadn't complained about the length of time they'd spent on research. He played with Nate's dog. He didn't seem to mind that sex wasn't really on the table. He was a good guy.

God help me, I really like him. Now what am I supposed to do about that?

efore taking Tarkus and Nate to his favorite beach, Seth stopped by his place to get his Death Star kite. The day was partly clear, and judging by the way the clouds were booking across the sky, the winds aloft were strong. Nothing looked more unominous on such a nice day than a planet-killing battle station swooping around in the blue. Nate would appreciate it.

As he turned into the driveway, his whole world twisted sideways with the car for one disorienting second. Déjà vu and vertigo all rolled up into the sudden realization that he never brought guys home with him except for sex.

It was stupid, but he couldn't quite overcome the feeling that Nate would somehow know that and interpret Seth inviting him up as a come-on.

"Um." He turned the key in the ignition, shutting off the engine, brain whirling. He reached back to pat the muzzle currently snuffling in his ear. Tark had shoved his head between them as soon as the car stopped, his blue Frisbee clamped in his jaws—he hadn't let go of the thing since they'd left Nate's place. "I'll just run up and grab my kite, okay? It'll only take a second. You guys can stay here."

Nate shrugged. "Sure. Take your time."

Well, that hadn't been a big deal, had it? Except for him.

So he left Nate in the car as he bounded up the stairs to his place. It took him long seconds of emptying his front closet onto the floor before he found the kite, still in its original packaging, but he was back out the door in less than three minutes, he'd guess.

Unfortunately, a danger he hadn't anticipated had reared its head—Grandma was standing next to the passenger side of the car.

smiling and chatting with Nate, who'd clearly gotten out to talk to her. Tarkus refused to be ignored, of course, hanging his head through the open window, watching attentively—although he still hadn't dropped the Frisbee.

Damn it.

"Hello, dear," she called when Seth reached the bottom of the stairs and was walking toward them. He had to pass by her before getting back in the driver's seat, so he did what had recently become normal for them—kissed her on the cheek.

"Hey, Grandma." Then he snuck a look at Nate, relieved that he was smiling naturally and seemed relaxed. "Um, you two have met, I take it?"

Nate murmured something affirmative.

Grandma beamed. "I love to get to know your friends."

Yeah, he bet she did. Thank God *she* didn't know he usually only brought guys here for sex.

"I was just telling Pearl what we're doing—"

An alarm wailed in Seth's head—he was waiting for a good time to reveal the existence of the knife, but what if she already knew? If Nate had said something first . . . Well, it'd be fixable, just, he didn't like upsetting her. Okay, yeah, and he felt guilty for not saying anything yet.

"—and she asked me if we're going to *your* beach."

Seth laughed, partly in relief. The gleam of mischief in Nate's eye reassured him. "Yeah, it's called Larson Beach Wayside. Another family heirloom. When Grandpa—" Seth nodded his head in Grandma's direction, to indicate he meant her husband "—sold all the timber land, he set that parcel aside and donated it to the county for parkland." He squinted at his grandmother in a faux-annoyed way.

She lifted her chin and pursed her lips, but it didn't hide her smirk. "With the amount of time you spend there, one would think your grandfather had donated it to you."

A snort slipped out. "It's too bad he didn't."

Amusement bled from her expression, and she looked past Seth, over his shoulder at the main house. "Yes, it is too bad."

Stupid thing to say. It had to have reminded her of the millstone Grandpa had left around *her* neck. "We've gotta get going, Grandma."

He leaned forward to kiss her cheek again. "Don't worry, I'm working on something about the house," he whispered in her ear. Not that he couldn't tell her now, but he'd rather do it later. Right now he wanted to go to his beach and hang out. Absorb what they'd found out and really think over what he wanted Shannon to say.

Not to mention fill Nate in on the parts of the situation the dude knew nothing about. Seth hadn't even brought up getting Sentinel House ready to sell. Damn it, he'd have to explain it. *Today*, he promised himself.

Nate lifted a brow, as if he realized Seth wasn't being completely up front about something, but he said good-bye to Grandma and got back into the car when Seth did.

"Um, thanks." Using the excuse of watching the road as he drove, Seth avoided Nate's gaze. "For not telling her about the knife. I haven't had a chance to, yet, but I will before Shannon prints anything."

"No problem." Nate's tone was perfectly normal.

"Listen, there's stuff I need to tell you," Seth began, but then he didn't say anything else for a minute, half concentrating on getting them through the first couple of intersections.

"If you aren't comfortable—"

"I am. I mean . . ." He twisted his grip around the steering wheel for no reason other than stress. "Okay, the thing is, Grandma wants to sell the house."

After too many seconds of silence, he glanced over to see a frown on Nate's face. The same one he wore when he was thinking. The guy didn't often speak before thinking, and Seth appreciated that more than he would have expected.

"Shannon's story won't kill any deal, will it?" So sweet, that he looked concerned. "She's running it by you before it goes to press, right?"

"Yeah, and I'll have some veto power." They'd discussed only a few of those details last night, and planned to get together for coffee tomorrow to iron things out. "Also, she needs to know what we found today." He sighed, wondering if he really was the slacker most of his family claimed he was. "I should have told Grandma already, and I should have emailed Shannon—I mean, I should be doing those things right now, but I'm doing this, instead." He struggled not to add the obvious, but the words wouldn't stay inside. "With you."

"Hey, I get it," Nate said after a few moments of silence. "People underestimate the effect history has on them, especially personal history. You probably need some time to process it." When Seth glanced over, he smiled slightly.

"Thanks. Um, there's more."

"Wait until we're at the beach," Nate said just loud enough for Seth to hear over the sound of tires on pavement. "We can talk about it there."

For a split second, Seth closed his eyes, but only that long. He was driving after all.

They pulled into the small, roadside lot for "his" beach, driving past the sign, half-hidden behind overgrown salal, but still legible. *Larson Beach Wayside*.

Nate didn't say anything more about the name, though, and Seth consciously let go of his discomfort and worry as he climbed out of the driver's side. "I totally need this right now."

Tarkus interrupted whatever Nate was about to say in response, scrambling through the front seats across the guy's lap to shoot out of his open door. They both laughed, and then Nate went after the dog, wrestling the Frisbee away from him and tossing it toward the water. Tarkus took off after it while Seth got his kite out, opening the package for the first time and putting the plastic in the garbage can at the access point between the lot and the beach. Sometimes when he came out here, he spent the first hour picking up trash that other people had left or that had washed ashore, so he'd be damned if he'd contribute to it.

It was perfect weather, at least for the Pacific Northwest. Too windy for shirtsleeves, but perfect for a kite. Nate took a walk, following the shoreline to the east end of the little crescent of sand.

Meanwhile Tarkus actually dropped the Frisbee to lunge at the Death Star, then barked like crazy at it as Seth ran west, trying to get the kite to catch the breeze. It didn't take much before it lifted off. "Good boy. Ravage the Dark Side." While Seth couldn't help praising Tark's instincts, he wanted to keep the thing intact until he'd flown it at least once. It looked as ridiculous as he'd hoped it would with the sun-washed fluffy clouds and bits of blue as a backdrop.

After he'd played out most of the string and the kite was at altitude—close enough to make out some detail, but far enough away that it just might really be a space station orbiting the planet—Nate wandered up, a couple of smooth stones in his hands and telltale grains of sand around the pockets of his coat.

"Damn, young Skywalker." Nate squinted up into the sky. "Think they have TIE fighter kites too? Because that would be epic."

When he turned his grin on Seth, blood rushed to Seth's head. The guy was so amazingly attractive, to the point that just looking at him made Seth as high as his kite. He couldn't tear his gaze away, not with the way the muted teal of Nate's jacket made his eyes pop, and the intensity of his smile. Seth was trapped by him; worse, he was *drawn* toward him, being pulled forward as if Nate had him on a string and was reeling him in.

Fortunately, before Seth did anything dumb like press his lips against Nate's, Tarkus dropped the Frisbee at their feet and barked, ending the moment of enchantment.

Seth got his head back in the game, searching the sand for a rock big enough to anchor the kite with. "Definitely better than my Strawberry Shortcake one. That's best for stormy days."

Nate laughed, then threw another of what would be many Frisbee tosses for Tarkus. Although Nate had said the blue Frisbee was a poor second to the treed red one in the dog's eyes, it didn't seem to matter: he looked as happy as Seth felt.

Seth was working up to explaining the rest of the situation with his family when Nate asked him about work. Specifically, about the "unadvertised special" Mary Pickford Seth had made for him when he'd dropped by the night before to talk about the knife. So now, Seth ended up explaining his drinking vinegars—after the prerequisite amount of time repeating "a shrubbery" in silly British accents—and his other plans for the bar. "It's awesome, more than I expected. I feel like a mad scientist. Dude!" He whipped his head around to catch Nate's eye. "You think they'd let me wear a lab coat?"

Nate laughed as much as he'd hoped, and Seth's insides squirmed in Tark-ish delight.

"Shannon said she'd see if the 'food columnist' wants to do a story on my shrubs." As soon as he'd said it, he wished he hadn't, although he couldn't put his finger on why, exactly. Because he'd been bragging? Maybe?

Nate's eyes lit up. "That could really be a boost to your career."

Oh *there* was why—he'd given Nate an opening to lay some expectations on him. *Except this is Nate.* Nate, the guy who seemed to like him the way he was. *You're overreacting.* Shrugging it off, he killed the subject as well as he could. "I think it's more likely to be a boost to *Ty's* career, since he's the columnist."

It wasn't until the sky was just starting to turn yellowish from the setting sun, and Seth was thinking about reeling in the Death Star, that they ended up talking about the knife.

"It does seem like an old-fashioned mystery, doesn't it?" Seth mused.

"The story of the Chinese maid who came back and murdered Fennimore is a little too pat for that time period."

Experimentally, Seth tugged the kite string, and it bobbed in the sky, wavering and swooping for a few seconds. "What if I've seen too many British crime dramas lately?" He'd taken to watching them when he got home from work at 1 a.m., because they were interesting but not so absorbing he couldn't fall asleep.

Nate kicked at a rock in the sand. "Well, I haven't, and for my money, this Edgar Gaines Monteith is a much more plausible suspect than Adeline, especially since he later absconded with Fennimore's widow. Hell, maybe your great-great-grandmother was in on it."

As Tarkus came trotting up, he bent to scratch behind the dog's ears. Tark sat panting, finally giving the Frisbee—and Nate's arm—a rest, letting his master shower him with affection.

"It makes sense. Even if we assume that Adeline's baby was Fennimore's, what would she gain by killing him? Seems like she'd be more interested in getting his help, or recognition for the child. But with the anti-Chinese prejudice at the time, she'd be pathetically easy to frame for the crime, especially if you happened to be the law officer on deck."

"That's exactly what I've been thinking." Which reminded him of another thing . . . "The Larson family tree could have a whole, unknown, illegitimate branch. Is it stupid that I hope the baby was a girl?" He swallowed, because this part was what had made him want to come to the beach rather than talk to Grandma or Shannon. "Larson men have a history of bulldozing others to serve their own best interest. Like this thing with selling the house. My uncle is opposed to it because he thinks it makes him look bad, and he's convinced my father to oppose it, also. They don't think her feelings are important."

Nate's brow crinkled up. "Is it that she wants the approval of her sons? Will she sell if she doesn't have it?"

Seth took a deep breath, bracing himself. He *hated* this. "Grandma's husband—my grandfather—put the house and most of their assets into a trust before he died. He had terminal cancer and he wanted her to be 'taken care of' once he was gone. He named his sons, my father and uncle, as the trustees. None of his daughters, just his sons." As far as Seth knew, none of his three aunts had ever even been asked their opinion about the estate.

Nate's eyebrows flew up, and he whistled soundlessly. "Throwbacks to pre-Nineteenth Amendment days, eh? Do you think they're treating her like that because she's not a 'real' Larson?"

Seth shrugged, busying himself with rolling up the kite so he could fit it back into the tube. "Call me cynical, but I'm pretty sure that kind of chauvinism is a trait passed on from father to son, and it probably all began with Fennimore."

"Hey." Nate's palm landed on his back, and Seth froze. He hadn't realized how cold he'd become out here, or maybe it was that Nate's body heat was so potent. "Every family has its baggage. I told you about my mother. Strange as it seems to us, they do these things because they want to protect us somehow." Before dropping his hand, he rubbed Seth's lower back a couple of times, the way people did when they wanted to offer comfort.

"Yeah, I guess." He turned to face Nate. "That's why Grandpa set things up the way he did, but it's not working the way it should. Kirk wants to hang on to this legend he's spun, and he doesn't care enough about his own mother to see that's not the best thing for her. I don't understand how he could be raised by her but turn out like this."

Nate cocked his head. "Are you worried that the Larson family Y chromosome has a douche bag gene? Because if that's the case, don't be. Attitudes are learned, not inherited, and even if they were, I'm pretty sure you escaped the taint."

For a moment, he thought Nate was going to hug him. He held himself as still as possible, hoping it would happen. Instead, Nate caressed him again, squeezing Seth's upper arm with his fingers.

They were still standing there, gazing into each other's eyes, when Tarkus barked. Glancing over his shoulder, Seth found the dog halfway back to the car, looking at them like they were dumb humans who didn't know when it was time to leave.

"Guess we've been summoned," Nate said, but he didn't move. "Come back to my place for a while? No pressure. We don't have to talk about this anymore."

"There's one more thing you should know." Seth swallowed. "I've kind of promised Grandma I'd figure out some way to help her convince Kirk and Dad to let her sell, and Shannon's story is my first attempt."

Nate's mouth quivered, as if he was fighting a smile. "And I suppose I'm helping you with your dastardly plan to undermine them? You're using me for my investigative skills, aren't you?"

Seth laughed outright, and then punched Nate's upper arm. "Yeah, that's it. I only want you for your Google-fu."

Nate was grinning now, but Seth suddenly realized what he'd said. *I promised I wouldn't do that anymore.* "Wait, um, you know." He cleared his throat. "When I say 'want you,' I meant, just, you know, friendship . . . yeah." *Bad save.*

Rolling his eyes, Nate scooped up Tarkus's abandoned Frisbee, then pulled Seth around so they were facing the parking lot, and nudged him until he started moving. "Don't be a dork."

That didn't seem possible. "I'll do my best."

As soon as Nate opened the cabin door, Tarkus rushed in, slurped up half the contents of his water dish, and then flopped down on the rug in front of the fireplace.

Seth laughed—and the way his eyes crinkled at the corners, his cheeks pink from the sun and wind, made Nate's breath catch in his throat. *He's happy. He can be happy with me.* That didn't mean Nate made him happy, per se. *But he made me happy. I had a really good day, and it wouldn't have been nearly as good if he hadn't been in it.*

"I take it that Tarkus is one of those guys who just rolls over and goes to sleep as soon as he gets his way," Seth said with a mischievous smile.

"You . . . uh . . . you met many of those?"

Seth shrugged. "Oh you know. My share, I suppose."

They stood by the door as awkwardness settled over them like a midnight fog. Seth shuffled his feet, glancing sidelong at Nate and then at the door. *Does he want to leave or does he want to stay?*

Do something. Say something. But what? "The knife. You want it back, right?" He escaped to the living room, where he'd laid the knife, still wrapped in the T-shirt, on the mantel. He handed it off to Seth.

"Thanks." He tucked it in the pocket of his jacket. "It'll help to give it back to Grandma when I confess about the newspaper article."

"I cleaned it. Well, you know that. You saw it. But . . . yeah." Nate rubbed the back of his neck. "So. You probably have to get back home or work or meet a friend or something."

"Actually, I've got the night off, and Grandma is visiting her friend Eleanor." For some reason, Seth's cheeks turned even pinker. "And I'm with a friend already, right?"

"Then . . . stay for dinner and a movie?"

Seth's smile was blinding. "Sure. I think I was promised mac and cheese at one point."

Nate grinned, the tension in his neck easing. "Not exactly a promise, if I recall, but I can do that. You like bacon in it?"

"Who doesn't? Um, hey, can I use your computer to send Shannon an email with what we found out?"

"Sure. There's no password, so just jiggle the mouse to wake it up."

"Thanks." Seth trotted up the stairs, but stopped halfway up. "You are way too trusting. What if I was an evil spammer? You'd be totally screwed."

"I'm not worried. But if your evil spamming plans involve collecting millions of dollars from deposed Nigerian princes, I want my share."

Seth snorted a laugh and *clonk*ed the rest of the way to the loft. From the staccato tapping of keys that followed, he had a lot to say—and was a decent typist too. Yet another un-bartender-like skill.

While Seth was upstairs, Nate put water on to boil for pasta and grated cheddar, parmesan, and gorgonzola. He minced bacon and tossed it in a skillet—he'd add cream too. Screw heart-healthy, at least for tonight.

After coming back downstairs, Seth looked over Nate's shoulder. "Can I use one of the stove burners, or will I get in your way?"

"Go for it. What are you making?"

"Simple syrup. I thought I'd handle beverages since you've got dinner covered."

"Cool. Saucepans are under the counter there, and sugar's in the canister next to the fridge."

Seth hummed around the kitchen, occasionally brushing against Nate's arm or back as he prepared his cocktail ingredients. Nate didn't think it was on purpose—the kitchen wasn't that big—but he took comfort from it anyway. *This is nice.* Even though they were working on different tasks—Nate had his back to Seth most of the time as he put the mac and cheese together—it was still . . . companionable.

"Here." Seth handed him a highball glass filled with ice and a colorless, slightly cloudy liquid. "Try this."

Nate eyed the mint garnish. "What is it?"

"I haven't decided yet."

"You mean you're going to put more stuff in it?"

"No, you dork. I mean I don't know what I'm going to call it yet. I'm trying out a new idea."

"You made up a new drink just now?"

"It wasn't easy. Your liquor cabinet is really weird. I mean, Aperol? What the heck is that?"

"It's an Italian aperitif. A present from my father. You'll note it's unopened."

"Yeah, along with the orange-flavored vodka and coconut-flavored rum. Anyway, I had to get creative since I didn't have any of my own secret concoctions." Seth flapped his hands at Nate. "Go on. Don't be a baby. Try it."

Nate took a cautious sip, and the flavors of mint and anise bloomed on his tongue. "That's—" He took a bigger sip. "That's *great*. I'm impressed."

Seth shrugged. "Well, I *am* a bartender."

"Still—" Nate sipped again. "Really, *really* good. Better than anything I had in Hollywood."

"Thank you." Seth's ears had gone pink at the tips.

"Ever think of starting a drink blog? If you keep inventing stuff this tasty—" He savored another mouthful. "I bet you'd get a ton of followers. You'd probably be able to monetize it too."

"There are already a shitload of cocktail blogs."

"But do any of them have anything as good, as unique as this? I think you should consider it." Nate offered an encouraging grin. "Think of it as an internet tip jar. And who knows? It could turn into more."

Seth's brow crinkled up briefly, but then smoothed out again. "Nah. I don't want to spend all my time trying to duplicate someone else's success. Whatever. Let's eat, because I may not have been promised mac and cheese explicitly, but the movie was a firm guarantee."

While they ate, Nate mentally reviewed his rather eclectic list of favorite films. They could always watch one he'd worked on, but Levi's indie stuff was a little dark, and the Chad Eastwick flicks weren't even something Levi wanted to think about. Besides, Nate wasn't in the mood for dark or explosive tonight.

As they cleaned up, putting dishes in the dishwasher and leftovers in the refrigerator, he got it—the movie that fit his mood for the day. "Have you ever seen *Big Eden*?"

"Don't think so. Is it sci-fi?"

Nate huffed out a laugh. "Hardly. Although some people might argue that it's fantasy. It's a really sweet gay love story where the people in a small town aren't all bigoted, homophobic assholes."

"Nate." Seth singsonged his name, giving it about six syllables. "Are you a closet romantic?"

Heat rushed up Nate's throat. "I—"

"Hey." Seth gripped Nate's shoulders and met his gaze. "I'm just giving you shit. There's nothing wrong with a little romance. I mean,

I can't say I've had a lot of experience with it myself, but I don't have anything *against* it."

Good to know. "It's, you know, a relationship story."

"And for you, the relationship is the reason, not the result. I get it. Sounds awesome."

"I like the actor who plays Henry, the lead. He was a friend of my mother's—they'd done a couple of shows together, so I knew him when I was a kid. He's a quirky-looking guy, really interesting performer. I love how Pike, the other lead, hides what he's doing, how he's taking care of Henry." Actually, Nate suspected Pike might be grace, like him, but that could be wishful thinking—him looking for some kind of cinematic affirmation of his own personality. "Besides, there's a dog in it, and I think Tarkus has a crush on her."

"Excellent. I'm always up for new things. Let's go for it." Seth poured them each one of his magic concoctions and wandered over to the sofa while Nate grabbed the remote.

As soon as Nate sat down, Tarkus got up and trotted over, staring balefully at Seth and heaving a huge doggy sigh.

"What did I do?"

"You're in his spot. That's why there's a blanket on that cushion, and why your butt is now probably covered in dog fur." He spread his hands out in surrender. "Yes, I'm one of those annoying people who allows their pets to sit on the furniture." Because frankly, he liked the closeness and the company.

"Guess I'd better move, then. The chair or . . .?" Seth glanced pointedly at the middle cushion, eyebrows raised. When Nate nodded, he scooted over.

Nate pulled the movie up on Netflix, and as soon as the first post-title shot appeared, Seth tapped Nate's knee excitedly.

"Hey, I recognize that guy. He played a serial killer on *Criminal Minds.*"

Nate smiled at him, at the enthusiasm that was such an integral part of Seth. "He played a killer—or at least a potential killer—in *Minority Report* too, which is really weird, because he's the sweetest guy. This movie is a lot more like I remember him."

Nate leaned back as the scene played out, and it seemed like the most natural thing in the world to throw his arm across Seth's shoulders.

After one startled glance, Seth smiled and snuggled in to Nate's side, Tarkus's head on his knee.

Nate couldn't remember ever enjoying a movie more.

CHAPTER THIRTEEN

The morning after their beach day, Seth began getting caught up on chores he'd been slacking on to hang around with Nate. While he was spreading oat straw over the garden, putting it to bed for the winter, he found most of a hide and one hind leg of the rat-creature that had started all of this. "This" being the current situation he found himself in—apprehensive about the next issue of the *Bluewater Bay Beacon*, and preoccupied with a guy who was supposed to only be a friend.

He'd never bothered figuring out exactly what kind of animal it was, which proved how consumed he'd been with other thoughts. After he put the tools away in the garden shed and took the stairs two at a time to his place, it only took a few minutes on the internet to identify the rodent as a woodrat. Related to a packrat, but not actually a rat at all. It was supposed to be pretty rare around here, so it made sense that he'd never seen one before.

Sitting at the computer after all that physical activity made his muscles cramp, so he stood, stretching his arms high over his head and then out to the sides, when something caught his eye. Across the room, but visually right at the tip of his fingers, was the knife. He'd brought it home from Nate's last night, intending to give it to his grandmother. Not that he really thought it would make up for not having told her in the first damn place, but it was all he had to offer.

Damn it. It was time to stop stalling and go find Grandma before it was too late to yank the story.

Shannon was probably already of the opinion that it was too late.

The thought of what would happen if Grandma *did* insist on killing the article almost stopped him. He'd be trapped between two angry women, was what would happen. He avoided putting himself in that position, especially since the last time he'd found himself there—when he was chaperoning a gay-bar-hopping trip for a group of thirtysomething bachelorettes (minus the bride for reasons Seth had never understood) and had felt it necessary to cut some of them off. After that disaster, he'd promised to never intentionally incur the wrath of more than one woman at a time.

That particular fiasco had been Lucas's fault, and *there* was someone he'd made a promise to. The first time Seth had run into him after the incident, he'd sworn revenge to Lucas's face. He still owed the guy for that. That had been six months ago, he really needed to get on it.

Later. For now, he grabbed the knife, wrapped in a clean shop rag, and made his way to the main house. He found Grandma sitting at the kitchen table in her lavender "track suit"—her version of the housecoats some women her age wore when they were at their leisure.

She was reading the paper—not the *Bluewater Bay Beacon*, the *Seattle Times*. As he came to stand next to her, the only noise was the rustle of pages turning and the faint beat of his pulse in his ears. After a few moments, when she looked up questioningly, he unfolded the bundle and offered it to her.

She recoiled. "What's that old thing, and why did you bring it into my house?"

"This was in the garage." Not quite an answer, but by now she'd have figured out what it was. It was cleaner than when he'd first found it—Nate had done a hell of a job on it—and the shape was obvious. When she turned her gaze on him, he met it steadily, ready to own up to his wrongs. It had been years since he'd done anything like this—waited to be disciplined. Actually, he doubted he ever had. His memories were all about hiding from punishment, not meeting it head-on.

Grandma refocused on the knife, leaning closer to where it rested in his palms.

"I found it that night I found the rat's nest," he offered after a minute of her silence.

"That was almost two weeks ago." She tilted her head, studying him. "You look like you're expecting me to take you out behind the woodshed for a whuppin.'"

When she pushed out the chair next to her, he sat, continuing his confession. She needed to know the full extent of what he'd done. "A, um, friend of mine helped me investigate it a little. We found some interesting things about the knife when he started researching it."

"Why would you need to *investigate* it if you found it here?"

Of course, she assumed what he had. What anyone would—that it belonged to an ancestor of theirs. In answer, he laid it on the table between them.

She squinted at him, then it, unwrapping the knife further. An audible breath escaped her as she touched it gingerly, running her fingertip over the engraved initials. "This didn't belong to any Larson. Whatever it is you know, you'd best tell me."

She'd already heard about Adeline being found over the body—*every* Larson had—but she wasn't aware of the other details that had led him and Nate (and Shannon) to a very different conclusion about who had murdered Fennimore. Grimacing, he filled her in. On how Edgar Gaines Monteith was the sheriff and apparently a poker buddy of Fennimore's, and how much anti-Chinese sentiment existed at the time. "And, on top of all that, Fennimore's widow marries Monteith?" Grandma just stared at him, so he finished up with, "We can't prove anything, but it's an awful lot of coincidences."

Gape-mouthed, she didn't say anything for long seconds. "Oh my," she finally whispered. "Kirk won't be happy about this at all. It'll sully the Larson name . . ."

That was his cue to *really* own up. "Shannon Carr—she used to be Shannon Schumer, remember?" At Grandma's nod he went on. "She's writing a story about it for the paper. A local color sort of piece, because she's sick of writing about *Wolf's Landing*."

Oh God, Grandma had gone pale. Seth put a hand under her elbow, as if he could keep her from toppling over, even though they were sitting down. "Maybe, um." He licked his lip quickly. "Maybe I can call Shannon and we can ask her not to run the story?"

"No," Grandma said before he'd finished speaking. Her voice became stronger as she went on. "No. It's no good hiding the truth. In fact, it might be time to force some truth on your uncle." Taking a deep breath, she glanced at him out of the corner of her eye. "It could help us too. That's the only way I'm getting out of this house. If he thinks it's a liability rather than an asset."

Well, yeah. That's what he'd been hoping, but it was secondary to the other stuff, now. "Grandma, there's more."

"More?" She reared back in her seat.

"Adeline, the maid? She'd had a baby a couple of months before the murder, and we kind of think . . ." Wait, why exactly did they think that Fennimore had to be the father? Maybe Adeline *had* been fired because she was pregnant, but that didn't mean it was his baby.

Before he could voice any of that, Grandma had gone white as a sheet and stood up. "Follow me." Her voice was barely louder than the scuff of her slippers on the hardwood.

She took him up to the second floor, all the way at the other end of the house, to what had been Grandpa's den. It had also purportedly been Fennimore's, as had the desk dominating the room. Seth had never really thought about it before, but as he walked through the doorway, he realized in a prickling rush that this was the room where his great-great-grandfather had been stabbed to death.

Grandma didn't seem affected by that. Walking around to the back of the desk, she bent over and wrestled the bottom drawer open. When she straightened up again, she was holding a familiar-looking archival storage box. It was where they kept all the most important historical documents. Like the original deed to this land, and the certificate from a long-ago mayor designating Fennimore as an official Honored Citizen.

A chill ran up Seth's spine, and his hair—already standing on end—tried to levitate off his scalp. "Grandma?"

She shook her head, lips compressed while she set down the box and dug through it, using a lot less care with the yellowed documents than he'd come to expect. Near the bottom of the stack she stopped, squinting at something for long seconds before ripping it from under the other papers and holding it out toward Seth.

Her hands trembled, making the paper crinkle ever so slightly as he stared at it. Grandma shook it deliberately when he didn't take it right away.

Damn it. He had a feeling Grandma knew whether Fennimore had been the father.

And he was right. It was a document that read *Birth Return* at the top. What looked like a very old, very official one, most of the fields filled in by hand in that elegant penmanship everyone had used a century ago.

The baby on the record was named *Finnimore Larson*.

"It's not spelled the same way," he said stupidly. "And this is from King County." The doctor—whose name was the only illegible thing on the record—listed the city of birth as Seattle. Fennimore had been born on the East Coast, much, much earlier than the date on this document: *February 13, 1903*. The same year Fennimore had been murdered. Only a couple of months before then.

So, not Fennimore's birth certificate for certain, then. As if he didn't know whose it was. Some things jumped out at him immediately— the baby was labeled as *yellow* in the *Color* field, and the line following *Father's Name* was blank. So was the *Legitimate or Illegitimate* field. Squinting, he focused enough to find the information he needed.

And yes, there—the mother's name was Hsiang Ah.

Paper crinkled, and he immediately let go of the birth record, which he'd inadvertently clenched. He watched as it fluttered down onto the desk. "That was her name—Adeline's—her Chinese name. It was in the *Beacon*. It's *got* to be his baby too." He doubted she'd name the kid after Fennimore for any *other* reason. Had she done it to force him to acknowledge it?

"I hope so." Grandma gripped the edge of the desk, her knuckles going white. "Because if it's not *that* baby's birth record, there might have been more than one of Fennimore's bastards running around."

Grandma said "bastard." Realizing this was a bigger shock for his grandmother than him, Seth hurried around to her. The antique chair squealed as he pulled it out, then gave another high-pitched protest as he sat her in it.

Peering up at him, her eyes seemed huge, very dark against the paleness of her face. "We've never known exactly whose it was, but your grandfather found a secret compartment before he had the desk refinished, and that was in it. This always seemed like the most likely possibility. An illegitimate child."

"But . . ." He shook his head. "How would he even have gotten it?"

She snorted an unamused laugh. "I think we have plenty of examples to show us that Fennimore wasn't above throwing his money around to get what he wanted." She gasped before adding what had apparently just occurred to her. "Or Adeline brought it to him that night . . . that could be how she became their patsy. Oh, I've always *said* that man was a jackass." She smacked the desk with the palm of her hand, frowning angrily now. "This would be just like him, to hide the evidence of his own child. And to force himself on that poor girl! Then they *hung* her." Grandma's eyes were accusatory, as if he'd had something to do with it.

"We don't know that he forced himself on her." God, he hoped not. He might have to change his name if they ever found out that was true. He was already considering losing his breakfast at the thought.

"No, we don't, I suppose." She didn't sound convinced, and her anger almost visibly bled out of her all at once, as she slumped in her seat. "Seth, it's not right for me to tell you this, but . . . the Larson men have a history of philandering."

Seth gulped, the sound loud in the room. Did she— Was she saying that—

"Not your father," she said quickly. "But *his* father." A single tear fell from Grandma's eye, and as she wiped at her cheek, everything about her went back to the grandmother he was familiar with. She sat up straight and firmed her chin, continuing in a much stronger voice, one tinged with anger. "And his father, and so on. Generations. The whole damn town talked about it."

"I'm sorry," he offered, as if he could speak for the past Larson men by proxy. God, poor Grandma. There didn't seem to be a lot more to say, so they simply looked at each other, probably wearing identical frowns. Hers certainly reminded him of looking into the mirror.

Slowly, Grandma's color returned, and her spine got even straighter. She put the birth certificate back in the box, laying it right on top, before covering it. Then she stood and dusted off her hands on her lavender jogging pants. "Well."

"Yeah."

"I'm not going to hide this. I won't be a party to it. You tell Shannon to run that story." With that, she marched out of the room, nose in the air.

The next couple of days, Seth went everywhere and did everything he should—worked at Ma Cougar's and did his chores around Sentinel House—and the entire time, he felt as if he were holding his breath. Waiting. Whether it was for Shannon's piece or to see Nate again, he wasn't sure.

In any case, his schedule conflicted with Nate's, so he had to settle for a phone call.

He hadn't wanted to tell Nate any of his new, nauseating discoveries, but he'd ended up spilling it all once he heard Nate's voice, though. Not only the news of the birth record and the Larson predilection for infidelity, but the possibility that Adeline had been coerced into sleeping with Fennimore.

"Shit," Nate muttered.

"Why didn't I think of that before?" Seth's voice sounded quavery in his own ears. Another similarity between him and Grandma.

"Are you okay?"

"Not really. This is downright sordid. I almost wish I'd never found that fucking knife."

"Hey." Nate's tone was gentle. "Discovering unexpected or unpleasant things about your family is a shock. Believe me, I get that. But you're not Fennimore. Your reaction makes that clear, don't you think?"

"I suppose."

"No supposing about it—you want justice for Adeline, right? Or at least vindication. If you'd known about the possible rape beforehand, would you have wanted to suppress the truth? Left her on record as Fennimore's murderer?"

Seth nearly choked. "Oh my God, *no*."

"Like I said, babe. You didn't inherit the douche bag gene. You're a good guy." Nate must have covered his phone with his hand then, because his voice was muffled for a moment. "Sorry. I've got to get back to the set. You gonna be all right?"

Babe? "Sure, eventually." Was Nate one of those guys who called all his friends pet names? Seth wouldn't have guessed that. "I mean, I don't feel like I can't go on or anything. I'll be fine."

"Okay, then. I'll talk to you soon."

He did feel better after confessing to Nate, even though nothing was solved. Maybe he'd just needed to confide the whole mess in someone he trusted.

Plus, he called me "babe."

CHAPTER FOURTEEN

*N*ate wasn't alone in the bed.

"Nara?" He reached for her, and she flipped her long ebony hair, and it was short, the skin no longer ivory but brown. *Jorge.* But Jorge couldn't be there. He'd walked out of Nate's life and left him alone. But here he was again, his back broad, his hips narrow, but no scar on his back where the doctors had fused his vertebrae. *Before the accident,* when he'd still loved Nate. Jorge rolled onto his back, and Nate's breath stalled. He'd always been so beautiful, although more so when he was in motion, attacking a performance with the passion Nate had always found irresistible. *God, I haven't touched skin in so long.*

But when Nate reached out and placed a trembling hand on Jorge's stomach, the skin under his fingers was paler than Jorge's, paler than his own. Lightly tanned, underlaid with a rosy flush and furred with soft blond hair.

What?

Nate snatched his hand away when a warning bell sounded, and Seth—*Seth?*—said, "You can't have everything your own way. What about *my* needs?"

The bell got louder, more insistent, and Nate woke up to his cell phone nearly vibrating off his nightstand, his father's picture illuminated on the screen. He grabbed it.

"H'lo?"

"Sounds like I woke you. Sorry, son."

Even after fourteen years, Nate couldn't help the warmth that spread through his chest when his father called him "son." He suspected his dad had the same feeling, because in any conversation, he was bound to drop the S-word at least twice, which didn't bother Nate a bit.

"No worries, Dad. I need to— Holy crap, look at the time. I'll be late for work if I don't get moving."

"Sorry, I'll call later."

"No, it's okay. We can talk while I get ready." Nate kicked the tangled sheets away from his legs and swung around to sit at the edge of the bed. Tarkus, curled on the oversized doggy bed in the corner, immediately perked his ears, although he didn't get up—by this time, he knew the morning routine as well as Nate did. "Putting you on speaker." He shivered his way to the dresser. Christ, it was getting *cold* in the mornings. "How's retirement? You still hustling your unsuspecting friends on the golf course?"

"Do you realize how excruciatingly tedious golf can be when it's the only thing you're allowed to do? I'm on a self-imposed hiatus until I can stand to look at the damn clubs again."

Nate dragged a pair of sweatpants on over his boxer briefs and fought his way into an old Henley so he wouldn't freeze his butt off while he fed Tarkus. "Dad, remember what the doctor said. Exercise, but not too much of it."

"That quack," he grumbled. "He won't even let me walk the course. I have to ride in a damn cart."

"That's because you had a heart attack." He trotted into the living room, where it was even colder. No point firing up the wood stove or the fireplace though—not when he had to leave in under thirty minutes. He opened the door to let Tarkus bound outside, checking automatically to make sure the gate was latched. "Follow orders, okay? I'd like to have you around for a while longer."

"Yeah, yeah. Boredom's likely to kill me before another attack."

He filled the coffee maker reservoir with water. "Hey, you're not going to believe this, but I'm doing some work with the local community theater company."

"You took a job in live theater? I thought you said you'd never—"

"Not a job. Just a consult. Helping out a friend with some SFX for his *Frankenstein* production."

"A friend?" His father's voice rose on the word. "A *special* friend?"

"For God's sake, Dad, I'm not thirteen." No, they hadn't even known each other then, thanks to his mother's secrets and lies. "It's Levi Pritchard. I owe him this job, so it's the least I could do."

"Oh." His sigh was audible even over the noise of the coffee grinder. "When's the production?"

"Final dress is tonight. They open tomorrow, then run for three weekends."

"Wish I could come up and catch the show. I'd like to see your work."

Nate laughed. "As much as I'd like to see you, we're not talking red-carpet material here. Just a community theater group, but they get some attention from the Seattle papers because of Levi's status, so it's all good."

"I can't help but think that if you've resorted to stage work, you must be getting tired of the hinterlands. Ready to come back to Hollywood? There are a lot of interesting projects coming up, and Levi's not the only one with clout. My contacts haven't completely dried up. I'm sure there's someone . . ."

Nate finished his father's comment in his head. *Someone you didn't completely fuck up your professional relationship with.* Not likely. And when the bottom line was at risk, Hollywood brass didn't give out second chances.

"Nice try, Dad, but the job is going great, and the show has legs like you wouldn't believe. Besides, I like the town. It's got its own pretty crazy history, you know? Maybe not as out there as Hollywood, but—"

"But you're finding plenty to keep you interested."

"Yeah." He thought of Seth, brow furrowed, as he studied the evidence of Adeline's fate on Nate's computer; or later, as he ran down the beach, whooping like a loon, while Tarkus raced away from him with the Frisbee in his jaws. "Yeah, I am."

"Nate? Are you— That is, I haven't heard that tone in your voice since before Jorge got hurt. Have you . . . have you *met* someone?"

"Why would you jump to that conclusion?"

His father sighed. "Can't blame me for hoping, son. I don't like to think about you being alone."

Nate paused after setting Tarkus's food bowl on the floor. Was he ready to admit that he *might* have met someone? He wasn't entirely sure himself. But his dad sounded so down. The least Nate could do—

Tarkus yipped at the door, startling Nate out of his funk. He jogged to the door and let the dog in. "Sorry." Tarkus pranced across the room and dove into his breakfast.

"Sorry about what?"

"Nothing. Just talking to Tark." Nate licked his lips. "The thing is . . . I might be seeing someone. Sort of. I think."

"Well there's a definitive statement for you," his father said dryly.

"I'm not sure *he* thinks we're seeing each other. I mean, I come with some unusual baggage." Besides, Nate had kind of told him they *weren't* seeing each other—and never would be—the first time they'd met.

"Everyone has baggage, son." A three-"son" conversation. Shit. Nate must be sounding especially pathetic today. "We just need to find someone whose load balances ours."

"Deep, Dad, very deep." Nate headed to the bathroom. "Listen, I've gotta jump in the shower or I really will be late. Talk to you again soon?"

"You bet. Love you, son."

"Love you too, Dad."

While Nate was in the shower, he remembered how down Seth had sounded after he'd talked to his grandmother. The *Beacon* came out today—when Shannon's story hit, would it make Seth feel better or worse? *Better, surely.* He'd been pretty disgusted about the Fennimore whitewashing job and Adeline's victimization. Having popular opinion behind him was bound to bolster his confidence.

Wish I knew what the article actually says. He'd grab a copy at Stomping Grounds, along with a couple of bagels because he had no time to eat, not if he was going to get Tarkus to Bluewater Bark and make it to the studio by the eight-o'clock production meeting.

As it turned out, he didn't even get his bagels. After handing Tarkus over to his enthusiastic fan club—who had to chat Nate up for fifteen minutes he didn't have—he barely pulled in to the staff lot in time.

He sprinted from his car to Soundstage Two and slid into a chair next to Morgan just as Anna finished her regular glare at Finn.

Morgan cut a glance at him. "Nice save, Mr. I'm-Never-Late-for-a-Meeting," she murmured. "Hot breakfast date?" Just then, Nate's stomach growled loud enough to attract the attention of half the room. Morgan grinned. "Guess that would be a no."

"Settle, people." Anna lifted an eyebrow. "And somebody get Nate a doughnut so I can hear myself talk."

"I've got him, Anna." Morgan handed him a Stomping Grounds bag.

Nate tried not to rattle the paper as he pulled out the pastry—a pecan twist, the same kind he'd shared with Seth that first night when his comments had been so wildly misconstrued. Maybe someday Nate would be ready to put the pecans on the plate again, so to speak. *Too soon.* But the idea that it might be possible was strangely pleasant, and carried him all the way through a nightmare of a meeting.

As he and Morgan headed to their workshop afterward, for once Nate wasn't the one fuming the loudest. "Can you *believe* that asshat Larson? How does he think we can cut the budget by using *real* bottles from the canteen instead of the breakaway ones? Yeah, he'll cut the prop budget, but our workers' comp rates—not to mention the hospital bills for the stunt performers—will go through the roof."

"I don't think he was serious. He's been in the business long enough to have that much sense. I think he was just grasping at straws because Anna shut down all his other suggestions."

"Well he shouldn't have said it, then," she said. "It's irresponsible and demoralizing for the crew and the cast. We're people, damn it, not dollar signs. He needs to remember that."

She flung the warehouse door open—so hard it clanged against the wall—then charged inside.

"Hey." Nate trotted to catch up with her. "What's the matter? It can't only be Finn—this isn't any different than his usual bullshit, and usually you're the one telling *me* to cool off."

She strode into the workshop and picked up the newspaper off her drafting table. "I'm pissed off at this whole town right now. Have you *seen* this?" She waved the paper at him.

"Not yet, and I won't if you don't stop playing keep-away with it. Show me."

"Look." She unfolded the paper and slapped it on the table. "Institutionalized racism—hell, worse than that. Legally *enforced* racism and scapegoating. Right here."

Nate glanced at the headline. Shannon's story. *Their* story. "This is great."

"*Great*? This is outrageous. It's appalling. It's—"

"Hey, hey, hey. Yeah, it's all of those things. The great thing is that it's in the open now, right? Adeline can be vindicated."

She folded her arms. "Fat lot of good that does her. Or any of the Chinese citizens—*citizens*!—who got run out of town back in the day."

"I know. But since we can't change the past, we can at least work for justice in the present. I don't know if restitution is possible—"

"It ought to be," she growled.

"Does it make you feel any better that Seth and I are trying to trace Adeline's mother and baby?"

Her scowl lifted. "You don't say. You and *Seth*, huh?"

Nate fought the urge to duck his head and shuffle his feet like he'd been caught doing something shameful. "He's got a vested interest, you know. It was his ancestor she was convicted of killing. He's the one who found the knife that started my search, so you kind of have him to thank for bringing this to light."

"Hmmm. Maybe."

"No maybe about it. But your attitude is exactly what we were hoping for when we handed the story to Shannon. Public outrage. No more sweeping the dirt under the rug of history. Admit the wrongdoing and . . . and . . ." *What about the other suspicion?* Nate hadn't wanted to say anything to Seth, to make him feel any worse than he did, but even if Fennimore hadn't physically overpowered Adeline, the power imbalance between them made a consensual relationship highly unlikely.

"Yeah. And what?"

"I . . . uh . . . guess we figure that out next. I wonder if Seth has seen this yet?" Nate pulled out his phone and keyed in a text message. Something upbeat—to keep his mind off the other thing.

Early results are in re: Beacon story. Success! Pro-Adeline sentiment with tempers running high against F.

He stared at his phone, expecting Seth to respond. Nothing.

And still nothing, all day long, no matter how many times he checked his phone. Morgan finally yanked it out of his hand and tossed it in a drawer.

"You'll get that back at the end of the day."

"Yes, Miss Gulch."

She chuckled. "And your little dog too. Now get to work."

The day the story was published, Seth went into work early to start a new project: limoncello. His nerves over telling Nate the bare details of his family history had been nothing compared to his anxiety now.

"Hey," Dave called from the doorway into the kitchen after Seth had been puttering in there about an hour. "Shannon's here, wants to talk to you."

Excellent. He supposed he had to go say hi to her and probably be there while she celebrated the publication of a non-*Wolf's Landing* story.

He found her at her usual spot—seated at the last stool of the wraparound, facing the main entrance. Dave had already served her up a double mimosa. They had her to thank for the inclusion of that on the menu, now. It was very popular.

"Isn't it great?" she gushed as soon as he was within hearing distance. "My editor is thrilled."

"He is?"

"Eh." She shrugged. "Well, he's not bitching, so that qualifies. Did you read it?"

"Skimmed it, and it looked pretty much the same as your first draft." He'd read that before finding out the rest of the family dirt, and thank God. Reading it a second time was beyond him. "Are you getting any feedback yet?"

"Not really. It only came out today, so I didn't expect much anytime soon." Her face changed, from beaming in delight to confused eyebrows as she refocused her gaze over his left shoulder. *Know what that means.* Someone was coming their way. *Please let it be Nate.* It wouldn't be, though. By the indisputable rule of Murphy's Law, it'd be someone in his family.

"Oh, hey it's your—"

"Seth." *Uh-oh.* His mother's voice. Was Kirk here too? Closing his eyes, he took a second to compose himself.

"Young man, your mother's talking to you." Well, that answered *that* question.

Pivoting, he faced them, separated only by the counter. Smiling perfunctorily, he hid the way his hands fisted in a bar towel from his apron. "Mom, Uncle Kirk. Do we really have to do this now? I *am* at work." They didn't need to know he wasn't actually on shift for three more hours.

The confrontation itself was inevitable, and for once he planned on telling them how he really felt. Normally he took a page out of his father's book and went along to get along. Oh, speaking of . . . "Dad." The guy was standing behind Mom, face unreadable as usual, but not glowering angrily at him the way the other two were. He nodded once.

Kirk got right to business. "Yes, we must do this *now*."

"We went by the house and you weren't there." His mother doubled-down on her glare. "Your uncle took valuable time away from his own schedule and you owe it to—"

"As did your father," Kirk interjected.

"Yes." Mom waved a hand in the direction of her husband, but didn't actually look at him. "He left his office too."

For his part, his dad glanced uncomfortably around at the customers near them. His family had clearly attracted attention. It was lunch hour, so the bar itself wasn't crowded, but the dining areas were.

"Now, do you have a break coming up?" Pointedly, Kirk looked at his wristwatch, then crossed his arms over his chest.

Unbelievable. "I can give you fifteen minutes."

Kirk's eyes narrowed, and his fingers clenched. Look at that, they had similar physical reactions to each other.

"Let's find someplace private," Seth's father finally chimed in.

He couldn't take them to an unused table or the break room. He hesitated a moment, until, much like Shannon had a few minutes ago, his mother's eyes focused over his shoulder, widening in recognition. They'd know who wrote the piece. Would they give Shannon a hard time too?

Well, he couldn't let them do that.

He jerked open the counter at the pass-through and marched off toward the kitchen without really knowing where he was leading them. He considered pretending he smoked, so he could force his family outside in the rain and possibly irritate them by exhaling in their faces, but that seemed petty. Plus, Grandma would tan his hide if she thought he'd taken up cigarettes.

Nettling them really wasn't worth ruining his health, anyway. They ended up in the tiny alcove that hid the entrance to the storage room from the bar area, crowded too close for comfort, but there wasn't a lot of choice. Jockeying them around, he arranged it so that he was the one most visible from the bar, where Shannon was leaning back on her stool, openly watching.

Uncle Kirk and his mother stood front and center, with his father still hanging back, slightly behind his wife, and looking politely indifferent, now that they weren't in public. Why had they even brought him?

Kirk stepped a half foot toward him, establishing his dominance in the coming discussion.

Unthinkingly, Seth widened his own stance and firmed his jaw. His defensiveness would be obvious, but no way could he back off. This was too important. Not only because Grandma wanted to move, but because the whole damn mythology of their family was built on lies. Sickening ones.

"So, what can I do for you?" he asked.

"You know perfectly well what you can do for us," Mom snapped.

"Um, no, actually. I know you're here because of the article in the newspaper—"

"You were *quoted*. You gave them—her—" Mom pointed at the wall separating them from the bar where Shannon sat. "You gave her this story, and you never said a word about it to us. That's completely unacceptable behavior. You had a duty to tell us first."

"Grandma agreed to the article." After the fact, but still.

Kirk scowled. "It wasn't her decision to make. Father left us in charge of Mother to keep her from doing foolish things—"

"You know what I think of that." They'd discussed this before, and at least once, nearly in this same spot. It was the other time Seth had stood up to them, so both his father and uncle knew Seth thought they were severely misinterpreting their own father's wishes. And more, doing it out of selfishness.

Well, Uncle Kirk was. His father's motivations remained a mystery.

"Regardless of how you feel about it, you just remember that we let you stay in that place rent-free, for the past twelve years."

God, this *again*? "Yes, and you remember that for that entire time, you've expected me to maintain the property, all of it. I've had to learn everything from electrical work to plumbing to house painting—"

Kirk scoffed at that, as if house painting wasn't a skilled job. What Seth wouldn't give to make him get up on a ladder and see how easy it *wasn't*. "My point is, and has been, I met all those expectations and I've saved the family thousands. I'm sure it makes up for any rent you could have charged me for a studio apartment over a garage."

Once again, his father spoke up. "That's really not the purpose of this discussion. This is about the knife you found, which you didn't inform any of us about." For a moment, Seth thought he might say more, but he subsided into silence.

Silence that his mother filled. "And all that business you made up about your great-great-grandfather. That's just *shameful*."

"*None* of it is made up." That was the real shame. "All of it is clearly documented, exactly the way it's explained in the article. A friend of mine, Nate, is an experienced genealogy researcher. He found most of that stuff on the internet in less than a day—only a couple of hours."

"Who cares what this Nate guy says he found on the internet?" Kirk smirked unpleasantly.

"I saw the records," Seth said through his teeth.

"They're just records!" His mother threw her hand up into the air. "They're impossible to interpret."

It had seemed pretty black and white to him. Literally. Well, more black on yellowed paper.

Kirk threw a quelling look at Seth's mother, then tried more of his brand of patronizing logic. "How can he know anything? He's just some man who's got no connection to us. He's certainly not family, so how could he possibly understand the deeper motivations behind what Fennimore did?"

There were so many things he could say, but Seth cut to the chase. "Grandma showed me the birth record."

Kirk and his father knew immediately what he was referring to: he could see the understanding all over their faces. His father paled, and Kirk went so red it approached purple.

"What are you talking about?" Mom asked, hands on her hips and scowling. "What birth certificate? You aren't suggesting that maid's baby was actually related to us, are you?"

"That's exactly what I'm suggesting. Grandma thinks he might even have forced himself on her."

Seth's father jerked slightly, and for a split second shock widened his eyes.

"That's ridiculous," Uncle Kirk nearly shouted. His voice rebounded on them in this tiny space, and he lowered it to a hiss. "He can't have forced himself on someone he never had a relationship with. This is unproductive. We will discuss it further, later." Kirk performed an angry pirouette and took the first step of what would clearly be a bombastic exit, then lurched to a stop. "We don't want *that* business getting out. I expressly forbid you from telling *any* reporters. Or anyone else." His narrowed eyes met Seth's over his shoulder for a second before he marched off, with Seth's mother closely mimicking his movements. Although her confusion was still clear. As they passed Shannon, the look Kirk gave her was the visual equivalent of spitting at her feet.

Presumably by "that," Kirk had meant the birth certificate. Seth sighed, then realized his father was still standing in front of him, eyebrows raised.

"Son?"

When was the last time Dad had called him *that*? "Yeah?"

"You really opened a can of worms, here."

Unbelievable. "Thanks for the heads-up, Dad."

"Listen . . ." He adjusted his tie, then patted down the front of his suit in exactly the pompous way Kirk would. Seth braced himself for whatever bullshit his father was about to spew. "We should meet for coffee soon. I have some, um, unrelated business to discuss with you."

Then he left too.

Well what the hell did that even *mean*?

CHAPTER FIFTEEN

Nate still hadn't heard a peep from Seth by the time he got to the Playhouse for final dress. Levi had invited the residents from Bluewater Bay Senior Estates to the rehearsal, and the house was half-full. He ducked backstage to check in with Jack and Levi. He wanted to congratulate Shannon on the story too, but he didn't want to distract her before the show.

Levi was huddled next to the fly rail with Jack and Darla, but grinned when Nate walked up.

"Hey. Ready to see how your effects play to our test audience?"

"Some of them don't look too steady on their pins. Are you sure we're not inviting tachycardia with some of the effects, not to mention seizures from the strobes?"

"We issued a content warning with the invitation, so everyone here is prepared for thrills, chills, and action-packed adventure."

Nate chuckled. 'That line sounds like an ad for a vintage horror film."

"Where do you think I got it? It's on at least three of the posters in the lobby." Levi gripped Nate's shoulder. "Seriously though—your effects give the show exactly the boost I wanted. I can't thank you enough."

"If you want to repay me, don't tell my mother I'm doing theater work again. I'll never hear the end of it."

Levi laughed and slapped Nate's back. "No worries there. I doubt Iris Bedrosian knows me from the third spear-carrier on the right. Sit with us during the show?"

"Sure."

Nate left Levi to confer with his staff, and after checking to make sure Jack didn't need him for anything, Nate wandered back into the lobby while he waited for curtain time.

If he wanted to be honest with himself (although why start now?), he'd missed live theater. The pace, the vibe, the immediacy—so different from TV. Still its own brand of crazy, of course, but one with completely different stakes.

If an effect didn't go off perfectly on performance night, there was no safety net—no chance for a dozen retakes to get it right. He still shuddered at the memory of a long-ago performance of *The Philanthropist*, when the gunshot effect in the shocking opening scene had failed. The poor actor had sat with a gun in his mouth—and nothing happening—for nearly a minute, which felt like fucking forever under lights with several hundred people staring at you.

But watching an effect go off perfectly, and hearing the audience *oooh* or *ahhh* or shriek in response? It was an adrenaline rush like no other.

Maybe he could talk to Levi about getting involved in future productions from the beginning. If he kept his involvement low-key—and under his mother's radar—he could feed that still-active theater jones without compromising his own principles.

Nate entered the auditorium and joined Levi and Darla in the back row. Levi had a legal pad on his knee, and he clicked his pen, in-out, in-out, until Nate gave him a pointed look.

"Sorry." He tucked the pen in the pocket of his shirt.

"Nervous?"

"Always. Not for me. For the cast and crew. There's nothing I can do to help them now."

"Don't worry." Nate nodded at Darla, then jerked his head at the stage where the actors were no doubt taking their places. "Your team is great. The audience'll love it."

Levi shook his head as the lights dimmed. "If they don't either laugh everyone off the stage or suffer simultaneous heart failure."

But he needn't have worried. The audience gasped and jumped and screamed at all the right places. While the performance didn't go off without a few snafus—one costume malfunction and a couple of missed sound cues—it was a solid show. As soon as the house lights came up after the final curtain, Levi excused himself and dashed backstage.

Nate moved over one seat to sit next to Darla. "I think we need to fix the light levels in the laboratory scene, for the Creature-disappears-off-the-table effect. As it stands, I could see the table flip."

Darla tapped her lips with a pencil. "What if we stagger the lightning effects? Victor is already heading downstage. If he moves farther stage left to draw the audience's attention, and we hit them with a double lightning bolt, Jack can time the flip between the flashes, when everyone's eyes will still be adjusting."

"Perfect. Then the crew will have time to unstrap Tv so he can hit his mark in the corner before Victor lights the desk lamp."

Nate surreptitiously checked his phone again as the audience was filing out. Still nothing from Seth. *He's not obligated to talk to you. He's probably busy. Or at work.*

Darla spoke into the headset for a moment, then turned to Nate. "Levi's giving notes after the cast gets out of costume. He wants to know if you can hang around for it."

"Sure." Not like he had anything else to do, with Seth maintaining radio silence and Tarkus being spoiled rotten by Morgan for the evening—she was taking him to Bluewater Bark in the morning too.

The cast began straggling out from backstage. Shannon, since her character had gotten offed (for the second time) shortly after intermission, was one of the first. Nate ambled down the aisle and sat next to her in the front row.

"Hey. Great performance. You expired beautifully. Twice."

She grinned. "Thanks."

"I wanted to tell you—the story was awesome. You should have seen the reaction from my friend at work. She was ready to march to the mayor's office and demand everything from a public apology to an official Adeline Appreciation Day."

"Oh." Shannon's brow puckered, and she bit her lip.

"What's wrong? That's exactly the reaction we were hoping for."

"I know, but—" She glanced behind her, at the other actors chatting amongst themselves. "I think it kind of backfired on Seth. His mom and uncle showed up at the restaurant and—" she lowered her voice "—there was a *scene.*"

Alarm chased a lightning path down Nate's spine. "Is he okay? Did they do anything to him?" God, was *this* why Seth hadn't responded to his texts? If Nate had been a party to Seth being ostracized from his family ... He had more than enough experience to know how much that sucked.

"I don't know. He looked kind of agitated, but I had to leave before we could talk much about it, for you know—" she gestured to the stage "—this."

Nate checked his watch. It was late, but he'd still have time to get to Ma Cougar's before they closed and make sure Seth was okay, as long as notes didn't take too long.

But when notes went on and on and *on*—and then Jack needed to consult on the table-flip mechanism—closing time disappeared into the rearview. *How could I have forgotten the miserable time suck of tech/dress rehearsals?*

As soon as he was released though, he raced to his car. Seth said he was usually at the bar, closing up, until at least one, and it was barely past that now. Was it too late to stop by? It wasn't as though he didn't know where Seth lived, and Seth had seemed like a total night owl in their evenings together—not that there had been many of them.

"Screw it." He shoved the Jeep into gear and tore off at decidedly illegal speeds for Sentinel House.

Seth was exhausted but wired when he finally left work that night. Well, morning, actually. He'd worked what was becoming his regular closing shift, which meant not getting out of Ma Cougar's until at least one.

Thank God he had the next two days off. Maybe he could decide how to answer Nate's text sometime in the next forty-eight hours.

Risking water damage to his phone, he pulled it out of his pocket just before turning into the driveway of Sentinel House to read it again. Nate had it right—tempers were running high because of the *Beacon* story—but Seth was having a hard time calling it a success. He stared at the glowing screen long enough that the words were nearly obscured by drops of drizzle.

"Excellent," he muttered to himself, then wiped the phone off on the leg of his jeans and put it away before climbing the stairs to his place.

Once he was dry and in pajama pants, he threw himself onto his bed, snatching the remote out of the air when his body landed on the mattress and launched it high. *Heh.* He could unwind with an episode of his current British crime drama and maybe forget the scene at work with his family, and all of Shannon's worried questions after. He'd told her next to nothing, mostly because he was just so fucking tired. Exhausted by his mother and uncle and their ongoing battle to make the whole world see things their twisted way.

God, and Kirk had said they'd discuss it more later. If only his fucking father would grow a pair and speak up. Assuming whatever the guy had to say would be supportive of Seth and Grandma's position, and not Kirk and Debra's. The jury was still out on that, and nothing that had happened this afternoon had given Seth any more of a clue.

Except he was almost certain his dad had been appalled by the idea that Fennimore had raped his maid. He had to realize that the master-servant relationship wasn't okay even if Adeline *had* agreed to it.

Or maybe Seth wanted a reasonable parent so much he was hallucinating.

Give yourself a break. Thinking these things wouldn't help him relax. He'd worry about future arguments with his family and how to answer that text in the morning.

Five minutes past the opening credits of *Foyle's War*, he heard someone on his stairs. Not Grandma—her light had been off when he'd come home, plus the creaks and groans that warned him he was about to have a visitor were too loud. Whoever it was, their footsteps were too heavy to be his grandmother's.

Good lord, was this what his uncle had meant by "discuss this later"?

Not wanting to answer the door in nothing but pajama pants, he'd managed to pull a sweatshirt on by the time whoever it was knocked, hesitantly. *Definitely not Kirk.*

Nate? The guy knew where he lived, after all . . . but wasn't he at that final rehearsal Shannon had been going on about? She'd given him the impression it might run all night.

Only way to find out was to answer the knock. He swung the door wide, and there stood the man himself, dripping a little in the rain and looking apprehensive, shoulders hunched and hands in his pockets.

"Hi. I know it's late, but, well, are you okay? After our conversation the other day, and then not hearing from you . . . and when Shannon said your family gave you shit today, I was worried."

Any irritation he'd felt over Nate's text melted away. If it had ever even been there. "C'mon in, you're getting wetter by the second."

Nate walked through the door, but stayed right there next to him while Seth shut it. Before he could let go of the knob, Nate's fingers were gripping his wrist. "Tell me." His lips—his very sculpted lips—were only inches from Seth's. So close and so beautiful that Seth almost couldn't pay attention to Nate's next words. "Was it bad?"

"Well . . ." He blinked, trying to remember. *Oh, nice.* That was the first time he'd managed to forget all day. "Yeah. I mean, they came to the bar and we had it out, sort of."

Nate nodded, his mouth firming, then he dropped his hand from Seth's arm.

Damn it.

"We knew there'd be blowback, but you shouldn't have had to deal with it alone." Nate took a couple of steps into the room and then turned. "I'm really sorry."

Seth had no response, even though Nate stood there like he expected one. So he shrugged and led the way to the settee in the middle of his living area. "You want something to drink?" He had beer, but that was really about it. Maybe some milk . . . but it could be pretty old. He mostly ate up at the house with Grandma.

The cushions sighed as Nate sat down next to him, stretching one arm along the back of the couch and still peering at Seth with that concerned look in his eyes. "I'm fine. No need to be the good host for jokers who show up unannounced in the middle of the night. But will you tell me what happened?"

"Pretty much what you'd expect. Total denial. Noisy denial." Forced to shrug again, Seth started to remember that Nate's text *had* seemed pretty uncaring today. Except . . . "Did you think they *wouldn't* get their knickers in a twist?"

"I have to admit, I wasn't thinking about them at all—I was only thinking about you and how much you wanted to make things right. If anything, I guess I assumed they'd appreciate your concern and sense of justice—because they damn well ought to." A smile flitted across Nate's face before being replaced again by that concerned expression. That look went a long way toward convincing Seth that the guy really had had no idea. "Why didn't you warn me?"

God, this shrugging thing was getting old. He needed some new moves. "I thought you'd know. I've told you how they impose their will on me and Grandma all the time, and taking *me* for granted is an honored family tradition." He'd never say it aloud, but even his grandmother did, on rare occasions.

"Yeah, well, in my family, denial takes an icy, passive-aggressive form—avoidance and noncommunication, that's our playbook." Nate let his head flop back to lie on the top of the settee, facing the ceiling. "I should have realized the story would be incendiary for you personally, not just for the Cult of Fennimore in general. If I'd have just *thought* about it, we could have asked Shannon to soft-pedal the piece. Publish just enough to help your grandmother, but not enough to—"

"Shut up. No." For a second he covered those perfect lips of Nate's with his fingers, but then yanked his hand away when his skin started to tingle. "I mean, I wanted it out there. Something has to change around here, and that's as good a push as any. And after what Grandma told me . . ."

"Did that come up too? Shit," Nate whispered, still staring at the ceiling. He didn't seem to have noticed Seth's fingers on his mouth at all. "I'm guessing they weren't exactly excited to find out you knew about the birth record."

"Well," he stalled. "It's like you said, tempers were running high."

Nate winced and jerked his head up to look at Seth. "Uh-oh. I take it from your tone of voice that you weren't thrilled with that text."

"It's no big deal." And it wasn't. He'd been under stress and overly sensitive. The way people reacted had been a good thing, viewed objectively. Ish. "A bunch of customers mentioned it to me at work today. Coworkers too. Everything from, like, horrified interest to outrage about the maid. It had the desired effect." On most of the public.

"But not with your family."

"That was inevitable." He waved it off. "I knew it was coming, so I was prepared." As much as possible. "Honestly, though, I'm kinda done thinking about it. Tell me how your day was. How'd *Frankenstein* turn out?"

A grin transformed Nate's face, and that mischief sparked in his eye. "Terrifying. Jumpstarted a few pacemakers in our septuagenarian test audience."

"So, that's a good thing?" Seth teased. "What was it you did for them again?"

"Nice try, but you're getting nothing out of me." Nate waggled a finger at him. "No spoilers, or it'll ruin the effect when you see it."

"Am I going to see it?" Speaking of pacemakers, his heartbeat faltered.

"We talked about it the other day. Guess I shouldn't have assumed your acceptance." Nate cocked his head. "But you *are* coming to the opening with me tomorrow, right?"

"Are you asking me or telling me?"

"Which approach will get you there?"

"Either. I'm easy." Especially if Nate was involved.

Uncle Kirk's "later" discussion happened the next afternoon before the *Frankenstein* opening. Yet again, Dad would be no help—Mom and Kirk hadn't even brought him this time. Mom dragged Seth out of his place up to the house, where Kirk insisted they "meet" in the formal sitting room. Seth sat next to Grandma on the damask couch as a show of solidarity, but it ended up working to his uncle's advantage—instead of a united front, they were more like a couple of naughty children.

Kirk paced back and forth in front of them, his hands clasped behind his back, lecturing. He reinforced the impression that they were misbehaving kids by chalking up the article to them "acting out,"

refusing to see the validity of their points, and actually chuckling—
chuckling!—at the suggestion that he let Grandma move.

"Don't say any more," Grandma murmured to him when Kirk was
at the far end of the oriental rug, about to turn around and come back
past them. "Let him have his damned say and let's get this over with."

It was infuriating. Seth did his best to look bored. Grandma
successfully ignored her son, but at the expense of being so angry by
the time he was done that Seth was sure she could chew up nails and
spit out bullet casings. Once Kirk had left, she was nearly incoherent
with anger for a good five minutes.

Once she'd calmed enough, they discussed whether they could
stomach giving Shannon the birth certificate. "We don't know if that
baby had descendants," she insisted. "We don't know what making
this public might do to *that* family. I'd rather not screw up someone
else's as well."

"You can't blame yourself for how Uncle Kirk turned out." Seth's
money was on Grandpa messing him up.

Apparently, Grandma agreed. "When he was a boy, he'd do
whatever he wanted knowing his father would always take his
side." She scooted to the edge of the cushion and pushed herself up
from the couch, wobbling a little. Seth gripped her elbow to steady
her, and she smiled at him for a second. It didn't last, though. She
was back to sighing and shaking her head before he dropped his hand.
"It's high time someone put my self-righteous son in his place, but
talking to him is like beating my head against a pompous brick wall. I
swear, that boy . . . he makes me want to *do* things."

She left the room before Seth could ask her what things, but
he thought he understood anyway. Crazy things, that was what she
meant. Again, it was time to up their game.

CHAPTER SIXTEEN

The night of the *Frankenstein* opening, Nate had planned to meet Seth for dinner beforehand, but the *Wolf's Landing* crew had gotten a last-minute shooting schedule change, and he'd had to scramble to prep the set pieces for the new scenes. He practically ran from his car to the sidewalk in front of the Playhouse with minutes to spare before curtain time.

Seth was standing at the foot of the stairs leading to the big double doors, hands in the pockets of his jacket. His eyebrows were drawn together and his gaze was fixed on the ground at his feet. He didn't notice Nate huffing down the street, until Nate touched his elbow.

He looked up, blinking as if he was having trouble placing Nate. "Oh hey. You're here."

"I'm so, so sorry. I'd never—"

"Hey, no worries. I haven't been waiting that long anyway." Seth sighed, glancing up at the marquee, although his gaze seemed unfocused.

"You okay? You seem a little preoccupied."

Seth appeared to give himself a shake, like Tarkus emerging from the bushes, and that killer smile lit his face. "Nah. I'm good. Looking forward to the shock and awe."

Nate grinned. "Outstanding. Shall we?"

They walked into the lobby as the lights flashed, joining the last stragglers making their way into the auditorium. Levi had made sure they had great seats, smack in the center of the house, and apparently they weren't the only ones—Ginsberg was in the row behind them, snuggled into Derrick's side, the big man's arm draped across his shoulders, and Carter grinned at them from the seat next to their empty ones—the only free seats in the aisle.

"Way to make an entrance, guys."

"Yeah, sorry. I had to make sure the sixteen windows Gins has to fly through tomorrow were ready to go."

Ginsberg groaned. "Derrick, get out the ice packs, honey. I'll need some TLC tomorrow."

Derrick chuckled. "You don't fool me. You love it."

Nate put his hand on the small of Seth's back. "Everybody, this is Seth. Seth—Carter, Derrick, and you already know Ginsberg."

Ginsberg lifted a hand in greeting. "Hey, Seth."

Derrick, on the other hand, mock-scowled. "I hear your grandma is planning to give us some competition."

"Damn it, is that rumor already making the rounds?" Seth grimaced apologetically as they sat. "I was going to talk to you guys about it once we know what's happening with the place, but the way things are going, you might never have to worry—"

"Don't listen to him." Ginsberg poked Derrick in the ribs. "Giving customers a choice is a good thing. It'll encourage us to step up our game."

"Yay, capitalism." Seth met Nate's gaze. "I think?"

Nate chuckled. "Absolutely."

The seat on the other side of Carter was occupied by a twentysomething girl, and judging by the way her gaze was glued to his profile, she wouldn't be seeing much of the action onstage.

"Isn't Levi joining you?" Nate asked.

Carter snorted. "Not likely. I want to enjoy the show, thanks."

"But you and Levi are famous for watching things together. I've heard stories—"

"Movies at our house, yeah. Or shows he's not involved in. But something he's directed? No way. He telegraphs."

Seth blinked. "He what?"

Carter smiled. "He'd never do it as an actor, but when he directs, he knows everything—and I mean *everything*—that happens onstage. So he anticipates what's coming next. If you watch him, you know when to brace for incoming, because he tenses up, leans back in his seat like this." Carter pushed himself back, gripping the seat rests, his head half-turned away, jaw clenched. "Spoils the surprise for the rest of the audience. Plus, he huffs."

"Huffs?"

"Whenever something happens that he doesn't like—an actor dropping a line, a missed lighting cue—" he grinned at Nate "—an effect that doesn't go off as planned. He makes this disgusted huffing sound. Trust me. You don't want to sit next to him at a performance. Nobody does."

The house lights started to dim, and Seth leaned close to Nate and whispered out of the side of his mouth. "Exactly how many surprises do we have to brace for?"

Nate nudged Seth's shoulder with his own. "Shock and awe. You'll see."

As the house went dark and the curtain rose, Seth patted Nate's hand. "But you'll save me, won't you, Obi-Wan?"

Prompted by a flutter in his belly, Nate laced their fingers together. "Absolutely."

Seth glanced at him sidelong, but didn't pull away.

Can't get more perfect than this.

The first act effects went off without a hitch, and the audience response was exactly what Nate had intended—although this time, he filtered the success through Seth's reactions. When the Creature disappeared from the table, Seth jerked against his arm, and when it appeared suddenly in the corner of the lab, Seth clasped his other hand around Nate's, gripping it tight.

Did I think it couldn't get more perfect? I was wrong.

When Shannon's character, Justine, was wrongfully hanged at the end of the first act, Seth flinched and then released Nate's hand, going very still as he stared intently at the stage. *Shit. It's like Adeline's story. I should have thought about that. Warned him.*

When the house lights came up, Nate turned and grasped Seth's arm. "I'm sorry. I should have realized this might be a trigger for you. I—"

"No. It's okay. I mean, it's *not* okay, obviously, for Adeline, but I'm fine. I hadn't really thought about the details of her, you know, situation, but that kind of brought it home."

"Want to go grab a drink in the lobby? I doubt they'll have anything as tasty as that drink you invented the other night, but we might be able to score a beer or some wine."

"Definitely could use a drink." As they stood and made their way to the lobby, Seth shoved his hands in his pockets and glanced back at the stage. "You know, I thought I knew this story. But jeez. I'm gonna have nightmares for a week."

Nate rubbed the back of his neck. "Yeah, about that . . ."

"You're telling me the second act isn't gonna help me sleep better?"

"I seriously doubt it."

"Better make that drink a double."

During intermission, they chatted with Carter, Ginsberg, and Derrick while they sipped beer from tiny plastic cups—although Seth might have downed his first one in two gulps (not that Nate was watching the way his Adam's apple nudged the edge of his golden stubble). *Talk about shock and awe.*

Ah, hell—I'm rolling with it. So when they took their seats for the second act, Nate threaded their fingers together and rested their clasped hands on his knee. A smile spread over Seth's face as the curtain rose, and he gave Nate's hand a squeeze before turning to the stage.

As the climax of the play grew nearer—and with it, one of the more startling effects—Nate found himself watching Seth almost as much as the actors. But then he got involved too—Levi had done a great job staging this show, and the actors were turning in stellar performances, amateurs or not.

When Victor destroyed the Creature's prospective mate (and Shannon's Justine died a second time), Seth shivered. So naturally Nate had to put an arm around him. For comfort purposes only, of course. *Whose comfort would that be, exactly?*

With Seth warm against him, despite the armrest cutting into his side, Nate forced himself to focus on the stage. Elle, as Elizabeth, paced across the bedroom—the very scene Nate had first witnessed when he'd answered Levi's distress call.

She pushed aside the heavy velvet drapes, and Darla's moonlight special bathed her in an eerie glow. A muffled thump sounded, and she whirled, her hand flying to her mouth. She crept toward the door, but halfway there, she noticed a tiny mound of dust on the floor.

She frowned—the dust hadn't been there when she'd passed by on her way to the window.

A trickle of dust drifted down to settle on the mound, and she followed the line of it—past her waist, her shoulders, the top of her head, all the way to the ceiling.

Bam!

A giant fist crashed through the ceiling, and the audience—Seth included—jumped, half of them shrieking along with Elizabeth as the Creature dropped through the hole to land in a crouch in front of her.

He rose slowly as she backed away, until he towered over her—Jack had gotten the set proportions exactly right, forcing the perspective of the walls so the Creature looked even larger and Elizabeth more fragile.

Elizabeth began to scream, the Creature blocking her body from the audience's view. Her scream rose to a crescendo—and then cut off.

A beat. Two. Three. Then the Creature dropped his arms to his sides, and Elizabeth crumpled to the floor, her blue eyes wide and sightless in death.

Blackout.

Following the latest family meeting disaster, Seth had spent most of the day talking himself out of arson.

Tonight was about Nate and this play, though. Seth didn't feel like dragging his pretentious, overbearing, sordid relatives into the spotlight again. Fortunately once the play started, he forgot all about them.

When the monster had come through the ceiling, Seth had jumped and screeched along with half the audience. The moment resonated with him, with the need that he had to do something over the top. The show was over, they'd applauded, and he was following Nate out of their row of seats when it hit him.

Nate could drop Frankenstein through Grandma's ceiling.

Well, not Frankenstein, but maybe . . . Fennimore? *The ghost of Fennimore Larson.*

Oh, that had a nice ring to it.

"Seth?" Nate was looking at him quizzically. They were standing still in the middle of the exiting crowd, people swarming past them like rocks in a river. "Anything wrong?"

"I just— I thought of something." The idea burned so brightly he could feel it in his grin. "So." He hooked his arm through Nate's and started them forward again, sauntering along. "You like doing that stunt stuff, huh?"

"Please. This is stage magic, not 'stunt stuff.'"

So cute, the way he got a tiny bit indignant. "Okay," Seth said agreeably.

"What did you think of Ty's big entrance in Elle's death scene?"

Also cute, the way he wanted Seth's opinion. "It was a stunner, that's for sure, but you know what? You telegraph too. I mean, fantastic effect, but the way you tensed up right before? I knew *something* was coming."

Nate raised an eyebrow. "Oh really?" He nudged Seth's ribs with his elbow. "You still jumped a foot."

"Hell yeah. Like I said, great trick. So great in fact, that I might have a proposition for you." He'd meant to go on, but hearing himself, he suddenly wondered if Nate would think he was trying to put sex back on the table. Then he shook his head at himself internally. *You need to get over this.*

"Yeah? I'm listening." That spark was already kindling in Nate's eyes and he didn't even know where Seth was going. Or did he?

They reached a door that led from the auditorium to a hallway behind the stage, and Seth reluctantly let go of Nate's arm. "How'd you like to haunt a house?"

Nate's grin was spectacular. Like Seth had presented him with a beautifully wrapped gift. And he saw where Seth was going immediately. "A house like, say, Sentinel House?"

"Yep." Seth shoved his hands in his pockets and rocked back on his heels, then forward onto his toes, sure his grin was matching Nate's in wattage. "That's exactly what I mean."

Nate's brow wrinkled, probably because his brilliant mind was already spewing forth brilliant ideas. "I can see how it would be fun, but how exactly will it work?"

"Oh, *there's* a brilliant idea. *Have a plan.*" He snapped his fingers, and it apparently conjured up the first few details of one. "Well, I guess if we want word to get out that the house is haunted, we need someone to haunt. A victim. I have just the guy . . ." Haunting Sentinel House was an even better idea than Seth had first imagined. Not only would it show Kirk the extent of his and Grandma's resolve, it was going to enable him to get even with Lucas.

"Won't haunting the house—you'll pardon the expression— scare off potential buyers? We don't want to make it harder for your grandmother to sell."

"Pshaw!" He executed an exaggerated *forget about it* wave. "We're only haunting it as a stunt, temporarily. We can stop once the message gets pounded through my uncle's thick skull."

"And that message is?"

"That if he's going to refuse to listen to reason? We'll resort to being *un*reasonable."

The grin melted off Nate's face. "Don't get me wrong, I'm totally onboard in theory, but we've already had one plan backfire on us. The last thing you need is another family shit-storm. Are you sure this'll give you the desired results?"

Okay, that deserved honest thought. "I *think* so. We'll have to run it by Grandma, of course, but if I'm right, this is exactly the kind of thing she wants to do. And really, I'm not sure the first plan backfired so much as didn't produce *all* of the desired effects."

Nate's question was obvious in his expression, he didn't need to voice it.

"This would be like . . . showing him the strength of our resolve. Making a spectacle of the house—making it an object of gossip—is what he wants to avoid. So, we do exactly that. Shannon's article? That was the civilized protest march, next step is a more radical form of civil disobedience."

As he explained it, Nate's brow smoothed out, then he began nodding along, and by the time he had finished, Nate was exactly how Seth liked him best—lit up with excitement. Dancing eyes and spectacular grin.

"I've got a few ideas already, although I might need Morgan's help for a couple of them. The game is definitely on."

Excellent. Now all he had to do was talk Grandma into it. Although he was sure that wouldn't be difficult.

A haunted house. How cool was that? Nate used to stage one in his mother's garage from the time he was eight until he'd left for college. Now that he had more advanced skills though—and a sidekick like Morgan—he could take the effects to the next level, all for Seth's benefit. It had to be subtle though. Nothing too gruesome or outrageous. Something that could skate so close to the edge of possibility that they could push their victim squarely into the *I'm a believer* camp.

As Nate was mentally cataloging options, Levi caught sight of him and barreled over, movie-star grin lighting his face. He pumped Nate's hand. "I can't thank you enough."

"I didn't do all that much. You did it—you and your cast and crew. I hope you get the audiences you deserve, because, hell's bells, man. You all hit it out of the fricking park. Well done."

"The effects had a lot to do with it. If you—"

"Leonato."

Nate froze. Nobody called him by his birth name. Nobody except . . .

He turned around and there she was, in the Chanel-covered flesh: three-time Tony winner, umpteen-time winner of any other directing prize you could name, the woman who'd convinced Nate he'd been conceived from a vial of anonymous frozen sperm. Her hair had gone completely silver since he'd last seen her in person fourteen years ago, but—typical of Iris—the style, reminiscent of a classic Audrey Hepburn pixie cut, was impeccable.

"Iris. What are you doing here?"

Her mouth tightened a fraction, and in the harsh fluorescent light of the hallway, every line on her face was cast into unflattering shadow. "When have I ever missed one of your opening nights?"

Nate was weirdly comforted by Seth's presence at his side. "You—"

She turned a gracious smile on Levi. "Since Leonato hasn't done the honors, allow me to introduce myself." She held out one fine-boned hand. "Iris Bedrosian." Levi took it with an odd half bow, as if he were greeting royalty. *Yeah, my mother has that effect on people.* And really, in theater terms, she *was* royalty.

As she chatted with Levi, congratulating him on the show, tucking her hand in his arm to stroll down the hall to meet the cast, Seth leaned close, pressing against Nate's side. "So. Your mom, huh?"

"Unfortunately. I can't believe she'd show up unannounced."

Seth gave him some side-eye. "Okay, seriously? If she'd announced herself, would you have been here to greet her?"

Fair point. But still . . . "Tonight should be about the cast, about Levi—not a showcase for Iris Bedrosian, slumming it in Bluewater Bay."

"I think you're being kinda unfair. She's not doing any overt spotlight stealing."

Nate frowned, drawing away from Seth. "I told you what she did. What it meant to me and my father."

Pulling him into a little nook, Seth lowered his voice. "Yeah, but she came all the way here, to Bluewater Bay, just because you staged a few tricks for a community theater troupe. My mother won't even pay for her own drinks when she shows up at Ma Cougar's to harass me. I have to deal with the lecture *and* pick up her tab."

"But—"

"Your mom is *proud* of you. Look, you've refused to see her for years, and I can't imagine she wanted your reunion to be *here*." Seth glanced her way. "She came because she wants to be in your life so much she's willing to risk public humiliation."

Nate huffed out a breath. "Your mother probably didn't tell you your father was essentially a turkey baster though."

"No, although she might have wished he was sometimes." Seth stroked Nate's arm. *Nice.* "Look, your mom was what, twenty-four, twenty-five, when she got pregnant?"

"Twenty-two, actually."

"Maybe you could cut her a little slack, then. I mean, I can't claim every decision I made at that age was brilliant. Jesus, I can't manage brilliance *now*. Besides, how do you think she found out about the show?"

"It's not a secret."

"It's not a secret in *Bluewater Bay*, but she was where? New York?"

"Minneapolis at the moment, I think. The Guthrie."

"Somehow, I doubt the Bluewater Bay Community Players are big news in the Twin Cities, know what I'm saying?"

"I guess."

Seth poked him gently in the ribs. "So who did *you* tell about this gig?"

"Nobody. Just my ... my father." Christ, could his parents actually be in contact with one another? True, he'd never asked his father how he felt about the whole thing—not after weathering that first furious confrontation when the truth had finally come out.

"So maybe *other* interested parties have decided to forgive and forget, yeah?"

Nate shrugged as he watched his mother obviously charming the collective pants off Levi and the rest of the cast. When he was a kid, he'd been the recipient of that charm too—he'd never questioned her devotion to him, had trusted her implicitly until that trust was shattered by the fundamental lie of his paternity. He didn't know if their relationship could ever get back to that point again—it was like one of the breakaway windows he manufactured by the hundreds: once shattered, it was destroyed for good.

But maybe he could build a different kind of connection. *God knows, I'm the master of unconventional relationships.*

Seth nudged him again. "Come on. She's taken the first step. Give it a shot. If it doesn't work, you can always go back to the way things were before. At least you can try."

"Yeah. You're right." He took Seth's hand. "But you're with me, right?"

"Abso-fucking-lutely." Seth insinuated his fingers between Nate's.

They arrived at the growing clot of actors and crew that surrounded Levi and Iris in time to see her cock her head, surveying Levi from head to toe, and say, "You would make an excellent Bottom."

Nate sucked in a breath. "Mom!"

Levi laughed. "It's okay, Nate. She means *Nick* Bottom, one of the mechanicals in *Midsummer Night's Dream*."

"Exactly." She patted Levi's arm. "I've been toying with the notion of setting it in gangland Chicago, with Hippolyta as a gun moll and Hermia and Helena as chorus girls. From what I've seen, your company should be able to carry it off."

"You want to direct?" Levi's voice broke on the last word. "Here?"

"Why not? You have a lovely little jewel box of a theater. The seats could perhaps use an upgrade—"

"That's next on the priority list," Guy Parker blurted, his arm firmly around Elle's waist. "We'll spare no expense."

Iris inclined her head. "Excellent."

Levi ran a hand through his hair. "I . . . uh don't really act in the shows anymore. Not a lot of time, with the *Wolf's Landing* shooting schedule."

"We'll arrange to do it during the show's hiatus, then. I'm determined, Mr. Pritchard. Your comedic talents have been sadly underrated." She nodded at Shannon. "Miss Carr, please call me regarding that interview. I'm leaving town tomorrow at noon, but perhaps we can meet before my flight."

Shannon nodded enthusiastically, waving a business card. "Yes. First thing. I mean, as early as you want. Wherever. I mean *thank you!*'

"I look forward to it." Iris turned and met Nate's gaze. "May I speak to you privately for a moment?"

Seth gave Nate a prod in the small of his back. "Go ahead. I'll be right over here, watching for you to send up the bat signal if you need me." He dodged past Guy to give Shannon a hug.

Nate didn't blame him for retreating to a safe distance. When Iris Bedrosian demanded privacy, Nate didn't know anyone in the US, UK, or the entire Pacific Rim who could deny her. The woman had directed Anthony Hopkins, for God's sake, *and* Christopher Walken—although not at the same time. *There's a nightmare for you.*

He turned to Iris, and as they strolled down the hall, she took his arm. With the echo of Seth's words to support him, Nate managed not to yank himself away.

"I'm pleased you're venturing into legitimate theater again."

"It's *Frankenstein*. At a community theater."

"It's a classic text. Shelley's commentary on the nature of the soul, on our responsibility for our own creations and our relationship to the infinite—"

"Okay. Fine. But tell me the truth. This . . . this sucking up to everyone." He gestured to the cast, who were still milling around in the hallway, casting starry-eyed glances at Iris—which was pretty ironic considering their director was a fricking TV icon. "Is it a ploy to earn my forgiveness?"

"Don't be coy, Leonato." She patted her hair. "Of course it is."

"Iris—"

"You called me Mom earlier." She looked up at him, and once again he was struck by the fact that she'd aged. *Of course she's aged, idiot. It's been fourteen years since you've deigned to meet her face-to-face.* "Could you— Do you think you might do that again?"

He swallowed. "Why . . . Mom? Why didn't you tell me? About my father? Why didn't you tell *him*? Didn't you feel anything for him at all?"

"I did." She shifted her gaze to a point beyond his shoulder. "I didn't expect it, you know. By most people's standards, I suppose the attraction would be considered tepid, but it was more than I had ever felt before. You of all people should understand that." She glanced down the hall where Seth was laughing at something with Ty, who was still in his Creature makeup. "But it wasn't enough to justify the changes I would have had to make in my life to accommodate him."

"You had to make changes to accommodate me."

"Yes, but that wasn't a hardship, my dear. That was my privilege and my joy."

Heat prickled at the corners of his eyes. "Still, we had the right to know. Both of us."

"In hindsight, perhaps my choices weren't ideal for all parties. But as much as I wanted you, I wanted to live my life on my terms as well. You've always wanted the same for yourself. Do you think I deserved less?"

When she put it that way, he sounded like a self-righteous prick. But . . . "I wanted a father."

"And I wanted a child *and* a career. What if your father hadn't wanted the same? Or had, but at a cost that I wasn't willing to pay? Nothing I knew of Robert at that time hinted that he was willing to compromise his own career for mine or for you. Ultimately, I had to choose what I wanted. I'm sorry I hurt you. I never meant to.

I never meant to hurt Robert either, but I had to prioritize, Nate, and he came last."

She's never called me Nate before. "Did he tell you about this show?"

"Yes. He also told me that you might have formed a meaningful connection with someone." She nodded at Seth. "Is that him?"

When Nate followed her gaze, Seth looked over and smiled at him—that same brilliant flash of *interest* that had captured Nate's attention that first night. Something kindled in his chest—not a bonfire, not even a blaze, just the quiet warming glow of an ember.

"Yes. Yes it is."

CHAPTER SEVENTEEN

Grandma had been on board with the haunting plan before Seth and Nate had finished explaining it the next day. Nate had had the idea of asking Shannon if she'd like to do a story on it, and even she was on board.

Convincing Lucas took more work. Seth had been counting on the guy's ego, but he'd misjudged it.

Which was why, when Seth was working a closing shift by himself, Lucas's butt was in a barstool being manipulated into acting as the patsy. Not his butt, his whole person. "So, will you come give Grandma your opinion on the house?" Or, rather, come be a haunting victim. "She's nervous about putting it on the market, and I think it would help if she had someone outside of the family telling her it's sellable."

"Why me again?" Lucas squinted at him.

Gah. "Because." Placing a dirty pint glass in the dishwasher first, Seth held up his hand, extending his fingers as he ticked off his points once more. "First, we aren't ready for everyone to know about selling the house, but I've already told you. Second, you recently sold a house in Los Angeles. Third, you're a professional artist, therefore Grandma assumes that you will be able to offer a valuable opinion."

Lucas's head bobbed side to side as he apparently thought it over. "Okay," he finally said, then swallowed the last of his beer. "When were you thinking?"

"Sunday afternoon." He probably needed to take extra steps to be certain the dude showed. "How about I text you that morning?"

"Yeah." Lucas nodded. "I'll probably need the reminder."

Seth gathered up the dirty wineglasses littering the bar, and when he turned back, Gabe was standing behind Lucas's stool. "Hey." Seth grinned at him. "Haven't seen you in forever."

"Hey, man." Gabe extended his hand across the bar, so Seth clasped it a second. That was nice. He had to admit, he'd been worried Gabe was backing off from the friendship.

"Want a beer?"

"Nah." Gabe looked at his boyfriend as he explained. "We gotta get moving. Momma wants us to come for dinner."

Shortly after they left, Evan Miller came into the pub. The guy sat himself down at a secluded stool that Seth had to pass by frequently. Whenever Seth was close, Evan would engage in some light chitchat. Some about the weather, and some about Shannon Schumer's divorce. She and Evan had been in the same graduating class.

"She's changing her name back to Carr," Seth told him. It was probably the most meaningful thing he said in the three hours the dude sat there, nursing his way through two beers. To be honest, he didn't much want to talk to Evan.

At eleven thirty Seth gave last call, which caused a mini-rush. The few drinkers left besides Evan were sitting at tables, in intimate little groups. Preparing to say good-bye or to leave together, depending on their circumstances.

Seth was pretty sure Evan was here in the hope that *they'd* leave together.

"Hey, man, what time do you get off?" Evan called from his end of the bar. The smirk he flashed after the question wasn't at all subtle.

Get off. Yeah, I get the joke. Seth treated the question at face value, the way Nate had his innuendos early on. "I won't be done until about one."

Apparently taking that as an invitation, Evan hung around.

I'm not interested. How did he tell him, though, if that was even why Evan was here? Seth wasn't sure of proper protocol. Sure, he'd told guys he wasn't in the mood—he'd told Evan that the same night he'd met Nate—but this was different. Because it wasn't that he wasn't interested in sex, it was that he wasn't interested in sex with Evan. Ever again.

There was only one person he was interested in doing anything with.

Best to be direct. After all the other patrons had paid and left, he brought Evan his bill, setting it on the bar right under his nose. "Time to settle up and go. I need to close."

"Didn't think you meant me too." Evan ducked his head, giving Seth a very practiced—and familiar—look from under his lashes. Seth had never found it particularly sexy (dude had smallish eyes and average lashes) but he'd responded to it in the past as a signal that sex was on offer.

How sad was it that, when Seth had taken him up on the offer, he'd done it because he'd had nothing (or no one) better to do? Staring at Evan—who was growing increasingly agitated—it was so obvious: Seth didn't really *like* him. He barely knew him. They weren't friends. The only things they had in common were growing up in Bluewater Bay and being into sex with guys.

"Hey." Throwing his chin up to flip his bangs off his forehead, Evan regarded him narrowly. "You want it or not, dude?"

"No," Seth blurted, then didn't act on his urge to lessen his bluntness. He gripped the rag he'd been wiping down the bar with in between his fists, pulling it taut and twisting it. Evan's gaze fell to Seth's hands and his forehead wrinkled up. What was he reading into Seth's fidgeting? Nerves? Didn't matter.

"What's with you, man? You used to be a good time."

That surprised a short bark of laughter out of him. "I think I'm done with the good-time guy thing." He paused to take a deep breath. "Sorry, Evan, but I think that, um, aspect of our relationship is over."

"What relationship?" He sneered, then threw back the last swallow of his beer like it was a shot. "Whatever, you aren't worth chasing after." He tossed a ten on the counter and turned to go, stalking out.

Well. Easier than he'd expected.

Thoughts of Evan didn't linger long after the man himself left. Because Nate took front and center in Seth's mind.

He had no clue how to deal with a guy he was so attracted to who didn't want him in return. At least not sexually. Nate *did* seem to be into their friendship, which was great. Seth had consciously chosen not to read into Nate's frequent affectionate gestures. Not even when he'd put his arm around Seth as they watched *Frankenstein*, or the way Nate had held his hand. He'd just let it happen, leaned into it. Because while the guy might not want sex, he did want contact—a physical connection—or he wouldn't have done those things.

Seth was dying for much more intimate touches from Nate, though. It would figure, wouldn't it, that when he found a guy he wanted a real relationship with, he couldn't have it?

Not that he was in love with Nate, just . . . He didn't know. Could it simply be his own curiosity getting the best of him? Like kombucha—Seth couldn't claim to love the flavor, but he was compelled to keep tasting it. Maybe to figure out why it was so evocative, or because it had some nutrient his body craved, he couldn't say. He only knew he wanted to put it in his mouth, over and over again.

Which was the same thing he wanted to do with Nate. One of the things he wanted to do with Nate. Over and over again.

Could that ever even happen? He knew Nate had had relationships, sexual ones, but he didn't understand how that worked for someone like Nate, not really. Romantic feelings, he'd said. That was what it took to get him interested.

Seth didn't know about Nate, but *he* had plenty of romantic feelings.

An hour later he was at home, lying on his bed in nothing but pajama pants and looking up *gray asexual* on his laptop.

It had to be Nate's imagination that the *click* of the hammer mechanism for the broken mirror effect sounded so loud. But even though the workshop wasn't any emptier than usual—Morgan sat at her table, squinting in concentration as she put the finishing touches on a plaster bust destined to be the remorseful ghost of Fennimore Larson—the sound seemed to echo in Nate's brain.

Maybe it was because the rest of the warehouse was deserted. *Yeah, that has to be it.* On regular work days, the place was never this silent—noise bled into the workshop despite closed doors and reinforced walls. *Or maybe it's all in your head. Just deal, Albano.*

He screwed the housing in place on the back of the mirror frame. "I really appreciate you giving up your day off to help me with this."

"Are you kidding?" Morgan grinned at him as she squirted another blob of red paint onto her palette. "This is *historic*. Nate Albano, interested enough in a guy to build him a big scary Valentine's present—in *October*? No way could I resist playing Cupid's assistant."

He scowled and turned away to remove the clamps from the other two mirror frames. "It's not like that. I'm just helping out. We're friends."

"Uh-huh." Her tone was dryer than the pile of sawdust at Nate's feet. "Mighty elaborate favor for someone who's 'just' a friend."

He hung the clamps on their hook with more force than necessary. "Mmmphmm."

"Don't get me wrong, baby—you always go the distance for your job. But how many people would you go to this much trouble for outside of it? I can count them on one hand." She held up said hand and waggled her fingers. "Your dad." She curled her index finger into her palm. "Levi." There went the middle finger, thank God. "Tarkus." Ring finger. "Me." She grinned and tucked her thumb away then pointed her little finger with its Wonder Woman–themed manicure at him. "And now Seth."

"So?" Christ, could he sound any more defensive?

"I'm just sayin', Nate. Looks like your ice has finally cracked. In fact, if I didn't know you better . . ." She shot him a sly smile before turning back to Fennimore. "I'd say you're almost giddy."

He lifted a frame onto his workbench. "I'm not." But for the third time in his life, he wanted to be. Did that mean he was sending out mixed messages? *Yeah, you think?* The daily phone calls and texts, the dates, *the touching*. Yet he'd never actually admitted—to Seth or to himself—the feelings that had been growing in him, twining around his battered heart, maybe even nudging his comatose desire into sleepy awakening.

Maybe he should say something. In his mind, he heard his father's voice, the testy tone he trotted out whenever Nate waffled over a decision: *Time to make soufflé or get out of the kitchen.* But what if Seth wasn't interested in Nate's soufflé? What if Seth thought Nate's soufflé was too damn much trouble for not enough substance in return?

"Morgan?"

"Hmmm?"

"Do you think I'm a selfish asshole?"

Her eyebrows shot up. She set down her paintbrush and hustled over to give him a hug—which he gratefully returned. But didn't that prove his point? He always let her initiate the hugs, never offered any of his own.

"Not selfish, baby. You're always there when anyone needs you, but you don't volunteer anything that'll take you out of your safe little *Wolf's Landing* box. I'm sorry I missed the *Frankenstein* opening, because from what I hear, all *kinds* of drama was on display, and I don't mean on the stage."

He froze in her embrace. Was this about the scene with his mom? "What do you mean?"

"Oh come on. *Holding hands* with Seth at the play? Actually snuggling with him? Mooning over him with googly eyes—"

He reared back to glare at her. "I have *never* had googly eyes."

"That's not what Ginsberg said," she singsonged.

"Ginsberg—" he ground out between clenched teeth "—is a giant gossip who needs to stick to flying through windows and falling off of buildings." *Time to deflect.* He disengaged and strolled over to her worktable. "Whose face did you steal for this anyway?"

"P.T. Barnum's. He looks kind of like Fennimore, and it seemed appropriate, given that you're trying to sucker someone into heart failure."

Nate studied the bust: its eyes bulged, its fleshy jowls sagged in horror, and the hair ringing the bald pate stood nearly on end. "In every picture I've ever seen of Barnum, he looks more smug and less like the second victim in a B-grade horror movie."

She shrugged. "So I took some liberties with the mold. Sue me."

"Man, you *really* don't like Fennimore."

"You think?" She jabbed her paintbrush at his neck, adding another lurid splash of red. "Bastard deserves to be shot. It's almost too bad he's already dead."

Nate squeezed the back of his neck, suddenly wondering exactly what kind of backlash he and Seth had unleashed. Yeah, it made sense not to perpetuate the myth, especially at the expense of Adeline and her baby. But . . . "You don't— I mean, you're not mad at *Seth*, are you?"

"Seriously, Nate? Sins of the fathers?" This time, she flipped the paintbrush, poking his chest with the handle to punctuate her words. "I. Do. Not. Project. Blame where it's due, baby, and no place else."

Whew. "Good. I didn't think so, but . . . good." *Let's hope the rest of the town feels the same way.*

She tossed her brush on the palette and nodded at the three mirror frames. "Now let's mount the glass in those puppies so we can get out of here. I'll gild and age the frames in my studio at home." By the time she was done, nobody but a true expert would be able to tell them from the real Victorian article. "You're building the false wall, I assume."

"Seth said he'd take care of it." Nate had offered to help, but Seth had been insistent—yet oddly chill about it, as if building an entirely superfluous wall with a hidden peephole was something he did every day. Nate tried not to stress about it, beyond reiterating his offer to help, and restrained himself from nagging Seth for a progress report. "I've got a baby Fresnel on loan from the Playhouse, complete with its own dimmer, so I can rig the lighting effect for Floating-head Fennimore."

Morgan helped him secure the glass in each frame, and Nate double-checked that the frame with the trip hammer got the glass that had been treated with a protective film that would keep the broken pieces in place: they wanted to crack the mirror on cue, not scatter the polymer shards all over Pearl's vintage carpet runner.

When they were done, Nate schlepped the mirrors out to Morgan's truck. "I'll wait for Floating-head Fennimore's paint to dry, then take him home. Let me know when the mirrors are ready and I'll come by your place to pick them up."

She grinned. "Not on your life. I'll bring them over to Sentinel House on Saturday. I want to see everything in place. Will that be a problem?"

"No." He drew out the word, raising an eyebrow in time with it. "But are you more interested in the SFX, or in how I act with Seth?"

"Baby, that's the most unbelievable effect of all, and I can't freaking *wait* to see it!"

CHAPTER EIGHTEEN

The excitement that built up in Seth's chest before seeing Nate was familiar, but today it was even stronger. He'd probably go so far as to call it nervous apprehension.

What he'd learned about gray asexuality hadn't helped that much. The various interpretations were all over the place, so he had to go with Nate's own words and the observations he'd made. Nate was capable of being attracted to people he felt a strong attachment to. Seth thought it was possible that Nate was developing those feelings for him.

But how would he know? Would Nate make a move? *Yeah, you just sit tight until he kisses you.*

Or Seth's own feelings overpowered him and he kissed Nate.

Sighing, he turned back to inspecting his wall. It was another reason for his anxiety—he'd learned nearly everything he knew about carpentry either by doing, or by being told how to do by the guys at the hardware store.

Well, and a lot of shows on the home and garden channel.

Whatever. The wall was done, it looked good enough. Nate wouldn't expect much from two days of work, would he? Plus, of course, there was Seth's longstanding rule of never worrying about other people's expectations.

Even a person he was romantically interested in. Who might be romantically interested in him?

"Are they here yet?" Grandma's voice grew louder as she came into the entry hall. A waft of deliciously scented air followed her all the way from the kitchen.

"Not yet. Are you baking something?" Pie, hopefully, although this smelled a bit more savory. "Cheese sticks?" *Yum.*

"Dog biscuits," she said, adjusting her apron. It was different than the one she'd had on earlier. And had she *ironed* it? "I just love that Tarkus. You know, I've always wanted a dog, but your grandfather, well . . ." She shook her head.

Yeah, I know. He was a dick. Even after living with her all these years, he'd had no idea she'd had it so hard with Grandpa until all of the family's dirty laundry had been aired. The old guy had died when Seth was twelve, so his few memories were fuzzy. None of them seemed to be the warm variety of fuzzy, though.

The fact that she didn't even control her own money should have been a clue.

Seth was about to go hug her, but finally he heard noises on the front porch. Footsteps and the faint click of canine claws. Seth opened the door before Nate could knock, and Grandma called, "Welcome!"

As soon as he saw Nate, his nerves started jangling. "Hey, Grandma made Tarkus treats, but not us." *Nice opener.*

"Hush, you." Grandma slapped him on the shoulder. "Let them in." She took over, thank God, starting the tour of the house, chattering at Nate, petting the dog. Sneaking biscuits out of her pocket for Tarkus.

Grandma and Tarkus didn't make it past the kitchen, which was only the third room they visited. Fortunately, by the time his grandmother had stopped pretending she had any interest in the humans, Seth's more steady personality traits had reasserted themselves. He managed to show Nate the basics of the first and second floors. He could probably skip the third floor servants' quarters, but there was one cool thing he'd like to show him upstairs.

"Come up to the widow's walk." Seth pulled down the folding attic stairs from above a false ceiling panel.

Nate followed Seth up, the treads creaking under their feet. "Good thing Tarkus is worshipping at your grandmother's feet. I'd never trust him up on the roof, but I wouldn't want to leave him at large in the house either."

"You think he'd get in trouble? He's fine at your place."

"Yeah, but my place isn't a virtual porthole into the past."

"You worry too much. We have more heirlooms than we know what to do with." Seth led Nate around boxes and furniture— antiques judged unfit for display—to one of two identical dormers. The windows set in them were actually small doors.

"Damn." Nate ran his hands over the frame, studying the way the hinges were hidden in the trim boards. It was charming, the way he needed to touch things to really see them. "The workmanship. It's incredible. You never see that care and attention to detail anymore," he said once he'd satisfied his curiosity and was clambering out next to Seth. "Selling it will be like losing a family member. A shame, really."

Seth's alarm must have been all over his face, because Nate threw up a hand and said, half-laughing, "Hey, it's not my place to judge. If your grandmother is ready to move on, that's her right. But I sincerely hope whoever buys it doesn't decide to 'modernize' the soul out of it. I'd hate to think the links to the past would be lost because some joker with more money than sense decides the master bath needs a giant whirlpool tub. Or worse, some cretin who'll gut the place of all the original fixtures because he can sell 'em for a mint on eBay."

Actually, he could see Nate's point. It was kind of a shame, but not so much of one that Seth wanted to step up and keep the place, if he even could have afforded to. "Well, if the B&B people buy it, they want all the furniture for 'atmosphere.'"

Nate flashed him a grin, then, like they were both responding to some unknown signal, they turned toward the Strait of Juan de Fuca. It wasn't a picturesque view today, instead it was a melding of clouds and ocean. Somewhere offshore, fog bled down into the sea, or maybe the water was evaporating into the sky. A horizon line was barely discernible. It could have been twenty yards out or two thousand, it was impossible to tell.

"On a clear day, you can see Canada." Seth wondered how many people had stood here and said exactly that. "I kind of like it like this, though. It's more ..."

"Authentic," Nate finished for him. It was the perfect description. They were allowed to see the Sound out of costume because they were locals. It would answer the door in sweatpants for them.

In spite of the looming mist, it was dry enough that Seth could sit on the ledge where the roof met the walkway. The butt of his jeans might get damp, but he didn't care.

It had been years since he'd come up here, and he'd forgotten how small it was. The whole thing was barely long enough for pacing, about twelve feet, built between the only two windows set into the roof.

Showing Nate the house had given him a weird sense of nostalgia. Wistful nostalgia, reminding him of when he'd been a little kid and his world had seemed so familiar and right. Before he'd figured out he'd never fit into the Larson Man mold. Before he'd figured out he wasn't straight.

"I was insanely curious as a kid," he mused.

"I'd argue that you still are, but where did that come from?" Nate's voice was as quiet and reflective as his had been. Again, perfect. A sign he understood Seth's mood and validated it.

"It's how I figured out I was gay," he said, surprising himself with the admission. "By being curious. I wasn't only curious, though, I was careless. Impulsive. You remember me telling you about that chemistry set I had, and how I'd mix things together to see what happened without thinking about the consequences? My whole life was that when I was younger: acting without thinking about the end result. There was this guy . . ." Was he really going to tell this story? He never did, not without strong incentive. He turned to see Nate looking at him, waiting. "It's really humiliating." Again, he said it before he thought, but it seemed okay. Safe.

"You don't have to tell me, you know. Not if it makes you uncomfortable. But if you want to share, I'd be honored, and I promise I won't laugh."

"I might feel better if you did. Everyone else I've ever told it to was horrified." Understandably. He doubted there were many survivors of such complete public shaming. He couldn't hide from it, though—the story had become legend in his high school. The whole town, actually . . .

"Bluewater Bay High is so small that in order to have enough players for most sports, everyone eligible had to want to play, so sometimes there just wasn't a team for a particular sport. When I was a freshman, the juniors and seniors had a basketball team."

People often smiled at this point, because they thought they knew where this was going, but Nate didn't. He just regarded Seth steadily, his eyes somehow radiating *trust me*.

Seth did. "There was this one guy, Theo. He's not around anymore, he left town as soon as he graduated. Anyway, he was really, really good-looking." So much so that he might almost have eclipsed Nate in a side-by-side comparison. "But, like, not in a traditional way, you know? Pushed all my buttons, though." The guy had been almost the opposite of Nate, actually, with a nearly too round face that still managed to be stunning. Theo's dimples had had the power to wipe all thought from Seth's head.

Nate murmured some kind of acknowledgment.

"Theo went to a different grade school, and he was a few years older than me, so when I started high school, I'd never seen him before." Bringing his feet up onto the ledge in front of his butt, he wrapped his arms around his shins and rested his chin on his knees, gazing out at the strait. He trusted Nate, but that didn't mean he needed to watch his expressions while he told this story. "He was the one."

"The one what?"

"Like, I kind of knew I was different, but after I saw him, it became impossible to *not* know I was into guys."

"Oh, that 'one.'"

"I kept trying to figure out *why*. Why was I gay? I thought he held some kind of answer. I used to follow him around. Between classes, down to the coffee shop after school. Into the locker room."

For a brief second, Nate's fingers caressed his arm, and that was enough to make him continue.

"So, one Friday night, the basketball team was playing a home game, and I went to watch him. Theo. But of course seeing him *play* wasn't enough. After the game, I followed him and the rest of the team into the locker room—I don't know what I thought I was doing, but by the time I walked in, they were naked, or close enough. *Theo* was naked. And I was . . . mesmerized. Compelled to watch him." It sounded so perverted, now, but he refused to whitewash what had happened. He knew he wasn't the only fourteen-year-old guy out there whose hormones had overcome his reason, and he wasn't going to deny it had happened. "I got hard. Like, so fast—crap, I nearly came in my jeans, and I'd grabbed myself to keep from, you know—" he nearly did it now to demonstrate, but managed to stop himself "—and that's when one of the guys was throwing his jock into his gym bag and he overshot it, so he had to go pick it up. I didn't see him coming in time. He got a little too close, and there I was with my hand on my dick." He swallowed compulsively. "I wasn't *doing* anything, but you know high school.

"I didn't even *try* telling them I wasn't gay. It didn't matter. I never tried to stop the rumors or anything. Shit, if I'd been straight and just holding on to my dick to keep from peeing, they still would have told everyone I was gay." He'd barely known that himself. Lucas had fought tooth and nail every rumor that *he* might be gay in high school, but Seth had just accepted his social stigmata and suffered.

Nate's hand closed on his arm. "Did they hurt you?" Nate's voice was low and almost fierce, his gaze intense. He touched him again, palm sliding down Seth's back, and Seth realized he'd been expecting it. It was becoming habit between them. "Because if they did—"

"There's nothing you can do now." Nice to know he'd like to, although Seth wasn't sure he deserved the sentiment. "I can't blame anyone but myself." He always said that, as if he were okay with having been publicly outed in a seriously humiliating way.

Suddenly, Nate's arms were wrapped around him, holding him close. "Look, I can't say that lurking in the corner of the locker room to spy on your crush isn't a little creepy, but you were a kid, and if those assholes injured you, then that's on them—and on the school authorities if they let it happen."

"You know . . ." He took a moment to breathe before going on, enjoying the feeling of having told someone who just accepted it. No judgment, not that he could detect. "I was so— My hormones were so *starved* then, and I'd just figured it out, my sexuality. I didn't know it would, like, take me over. It was like my higher brain function had shorted out. I was all instinct and desire and—" he shrugged "—I really couldn't stop myself. Tell you what, though, I wish I'd found a better hiding spot."

Nate didn't laugh, but neither did he.

"Christ, Seth. Bluewater Bay might have its good points now, but back then, when it was so narrow and suffocating and as far as you knew it would never get any better? Why did you stay? If they treated you so badly, why didn't you get the hell out of Dodge?"

There it was, the thing he'd been struggling with since running into Evan. As he answered, though, the real reasons began to coalesce.

Drifting into his mind and out his mouth, bleeding together like the fog and water. "If I'd left . . . I'd never have come back. Not because of my memories, but because of how other people remembered me. I'd have worried what people were saying about me every time that story got passed around, and eventually, I'd have been too scared to face people. As long as I'm here, I can prove it, you know? Prove that one stupid mistake doesn't define you. What I did doesn't make me, I don't know . . . It doesn't *make* me anything." Tension he'd probably been storing since the other night ebbed out of his shoulder muscles. So much that he almost felt shaky. Like he'd just put down something five times his weight.

Nate's arms tightened around him. "I just . . . I hate to think about you being alone. You didn't deserve that."

"I had my cousin Laura and some other people." Yeah, he'd been bullied fiercely all four years, some of it physical. "Girls would escort me into the ladies' room so I didn't get jumped in the guys'. It could have been worse. Matthew Shepard was *beaten* to death, for God's sake. I barely ended up with any bruises. I survived." He let his hand rest on Nate's knee, not gripping it like a lot of him wanted to. "I did better than survive. I'm . . . good." He could even smile about it, right now, gazing into Nate's dark-rimmed gray eyes. Until he realized he was leaning toward him, and he'd parted his lips, expecting Nate to kiss him. His body was telling him it was inevitable, that Nate *wanted* to.

Am I imagining this? Nate's breathing had picked up and his lips were parted too, and Seth was torn between retreating and closing the gap between them.

Before finding the answer, Nate ended the moment, suddenly pulling back. "Morgan's going to be here any minute."

"Oh." Swallowing, Seth stood. Yeah, he'd probably imagined that. *Stupid hormones all over again.* "Excellent. We should probably go downstairs, then. Need to get this haunting show on the road."

Nate stood after Seth squeezed past him, heading back to the door they'd come out of. He didn't look back the whole way through the attic or down the stairs, even though he was tempted to.

Nate had come *this close* to kissing Seth. *Near-disaster much, you idiot?* Aside from the piss-poor timing—with Seth's grandmother downstairs and Morgan expected any second—it would have been a total dickhead move. While he was still wrestling with his own tangled feelings, he had no right to make any kind of tacit relationship promise to Seth. That wouldn't be fair. *Don't lie. You're afraid to put it to the test.*

Afraid was an understatement—he was freaking terrified.

So instead, he did what he did best and avoided the issue entirely to concentrate on the task at hand, stopping on the "haunted" landing to run his hand over the smooth surface of the false wall that hid the door to the servants' stairs.

It was a perfect location for their plan—the landing was extra deep, so reducing the area by two feet didn't make the turn of the stairs feel cramped. He couldn't see a single seam, the corner joins were invisible, and the paint matched the rest of the stairwell perfectly. Furthermore, no hint of construction debris remained anywhere that he could detect. "This is outstanding work. If I didn't know better, I'd say this had always been here."

Seth shrugged. "No big. I've been maintaining this house for more than a decade."

"Really?" Nate glanced around. The house had the usual Victorian gloom, but none of the genteel decay that a lot of old gingerbreads developed over the years. "I had no idea you had this kind of talent. You've done a terrific job."

The tips of Seth's ears turned pink. "If you say so."

Why does he try to sidestep compliments about his work? No wonder he's content to wait tables or bartend. Probably nobody ever encouraged him for his real abilities. Well, Nate could handle that. "You know, with this level of skill, you could land a gig with a high-end remodeling firm without breaking a sweat."

Seth's eyebrows bunched over his nose. "Why would I want to do that?"

"But you could get paid for it. Really well. Historically accurate Victorian restoration is big business, and not everyone has the experience to do it right. I bet you could name your price."

"No." Seth edged away, shoving his hands in his pockets. "I'm happy with the job I have, Nate. You don't need to worry about me."

"But—"

The front door opened, and Morgan called from downstairs, "Hey, guys. Where do you want these mirrors?"

"Stay there. We have to take them around back." Nate made a mental note to revisit the idea of encouraging Seth to branch out, develop some of his obvious skills and interests, once they had some time alone. Maybe tonight they could have dinner at his place again. They wouldn't have another opportunity for a while, since Seth had evening shifts for the next few days and Nate had to be on deck for a series of night shoots.

The two of them trotted down the stairs, Tarkus accompanying them in a clatter of toenails. *Time for a trim, before he starts catching those things in the underbrush.* Guilt washed through him—not a lot, but enough. He'd been spending so much time with Seth lately that he hadn't been paying close enough attention to Tarkus. Not that Tarkus seemed lonely—how could he be, with his teenaged fan club at Bluewater Bark, Morgan (at whose feet he was currently lolling in adoration), and now Pearl, with her homemade dog treats.

Morgan handed the big mirror in her arms to Seth. "Here. Be useful so I can hug my baby."

"You guys are sure affectionate with each other," he said as he tried to keep the ornate frame from jabbing him in the throat.

"She's not talking about me," Nate said dryly.

Sure enough, as soon as Seth had a firm hold of the mirror, Morgan squatted next to Tarkus and hugged him around the neck. "You're neglecting my god-dog. Look at the state of his fur—he needs a good brushing."

"Well, don't do it now, or Seth's grandma will need the industrial-strength vacuum from the shop. Are the other mirrors in your truck?"

"Nope. Right there." She pointed to the frames leaning against the wall. "Your breakaway, and one with two-way glass. You really gonna break three mirrors in this scam of yours?"

"Just one, I think. But we need an understudy, just in case." Nate picked up another mirror.

"Gotcha." She stood, then frowned at her hands. "Look at this—if I wipe my hands on my jeans, I'll scatter fur from hell to breakfast."

Seth changed his grip on the mirror. "I wouldn't worry about it. He's been running around here all morning, following Grandma and getting under Nate's feet. I think the fur coating for everything in the house is pretty much a given."

"Not cool, not if your grandma needs to keep things pretty for her buyers." She hoisted the remaining mirror. "What about this? Once we stow the props, I'll take Tarkus back to Nate's place and you can remove the evidence of canine occupancy."

Seth let the way down the hallway, through the butler's pantry to the door to the servants' staircase. "Sounds good to me. I've got a vacuum that can do the job—the cobwebs we collect around here make Tarkus fur look like nothing but pixie dust."

Nate followed the two of them up the stairs, trying not to trip over Tarkus, who didn't want to be left behind. Normally he didn't like leaving Tarkus alone in the yard for long—let alone in the house. He was a little too resourceful, way too curious, and hadn't an ounce of self-preservation sense. But they were almost done, and Tark had surely worn himself out enough for a nap with all the traipsing around after them.

"Hey, guys," Nate said. "Do the two of you want to have dinner at my place? I haven't managed to get to the grocery store lately, but we can stop on the way. Pick up whatever you'd like."

Morgan shot him a grin over her shoulder. "Sorry, baby. I've got a lady-date with some of the gals from the costume department. I'll leave Tarkus in the yard. He can hang out in his pup-tent until you get home."

Seth set the mirror down in the narrow space behind the false wall. "Tarkus has a tent, huh?"

"Morgan's being poetic. It's not a tent. It's more an igloo made of fiberglass."

Morgan set her own burden on the other side of the stairway. "This is the two-way piece. See this mark on the back? Make sure you don't mix them up."

Nate set his mirror next to Seth's. "I know how to set a stage, Morgan. I've been doing this longer than you have."

"Never hurts to verify, baby. Now I've got to run. Is Tarkus's leash downstairs?"

"On the table by the door. Thanks."

"Yeah, Morgan," Seth said. "Thanks for doing all this. I really appreciate it."

"My pleasure." Despite the narrow confines, Morgan hugged Seth, and then Nate. "Come on, puppy-boy. Auntie Morgan will get you a nice soup bone on the way home."

She vanished down the stairs with Tarkus at her heels, and suddenly the space seemed *smaller* than it had with them in it.

"So." Nate stuffed his hands in his pockets and tried to keep his elbows from bumping into the walls—or Seth. "You want to come over for dinner once we're set?"

Seth smiled, and Nate couldn't catch his breath, as if the air had been sucked out of the space. *Talk about your haunted-house effects.*

"Awesome. What else have we got to do besides de-furring?"

"Just haul Floating-head Fennimore up here, and maybe test the door on the third floor."

"Okay. I've got a vacuum that'll suck the—" Seth smirked. "I mean, I'm on vacuum duty. Do your stage magic woo-woo, and I'll meet you downstairs after. Deal?"

"Sounds good to me."

"Great. Then . . . *break*."

Seth raced down the stairs.

An hour later, they had everything in place and had de-Tarkified the house.

Nate repositioned one of Pearl's Queen Anne chairs on the runner in the entry hall and dusted his hands off on his jeans. "Done. That didn't take long."

Seth coiled the vacuum hose and stowed it in a cupboard under the stairs. "Nope. We didn't need to send Tarkus away after all."

"Are you kidding? If we hadn't, we'd've had to start all over again before we even finished. He has an endless supply of fur, although it's not as bad now as it was in the spring." Nate peered up the stairs at the landing. The stage was set—now all they needed was a patsy. "How are you planning to convince Lucas to be your unsuspecting victim?"

Seth waved one hand airily. "Don't you worry, I've got that covered."

"Yeah? Good deal." Nate checked his watch. "You up for an early-ish dinner? We can pick up a chicken to throw on the grill. I've got a recipe for a great lemon-rosemary marinade—"

"Dude. You realize you just won and lost Bluewater Bay redneck points within two sentences? Grilling?" He flashed two thumbs-up. "But lemon-rosemary marinade?" He blew a raspberry.

Nate grinned. "Shut up or I won't let you have any."

"Oh no. I know you better than you think—you'd never violate the sacred bro hospitality tradition. Not when I'm bringing the beer."

"Beer? Not shrubbery?"

"*Shrubs*, not *shrubbery*." Seth flapped his hands, shooing Nate out the door. "And I make a lot more than just those. Of course, I only share my secret cocktails with guys who don't threaten to deprive me of lemon-rosemary–marinated grilled chicken. Come on. I'll drive."

"You sure? You'll have to bring me back here to pick up my Jeep later."

"It's five miles, not five hundred, and it's not like your car'll get jacked on the streets of Bluewater Bay."

Nate laughed. "True. You're on, then."

They mock-bickered in the grocery store—Seth threatening to toss barbecue sauce in the grocery cart on top of the bag of lemons—and all the way to the cabin. Nate was still chuckling when they pulled in the driveway, gravel scrunching under their tires.

"I'm telling you," Seth said, "real lumberjacks don't grow beards."

"And you're a real lumberjack?"

"Meh. More like a meta-lumberjack. That's why *I* can have a beard."

"'Meta'? Seriously? What did you study in college?"

"The question is, what *didn't* I study? I was sort of a free-range student. I think I took every 101 class in the catalog. Lots of breadth. Not much depth." He climbed out of the Jeep and slammed the door. "Hey, looks like you got a package. Expecting presents?"

"Just some genealogy books." Nate hauled the grocery bag out of the rear of the Jeep. "I hope the UPS guy got here before Morgan dropped off Tarkus."

"Why? He can't get to the front porch from the backyard. It's fenced, right?"

"Yeah, but you'll find out at the haunting how vicious Tark can sound when something gets to him—I used a recording of the UPS truck as one of the sound cues to set him off tomorrow during the haunting."

"That terrifying, huh?"

"The hound of the Baskervilles has nothing on him, and I don't want the UPS guy to refuse to deliver to me. Internet shopping is—"

"There you go. Losing redneck points again." Seth scooped up the package and waggled it in Nate's face. "We do *not* talk about internet shopping."

"No?" Nate opened the door and flicked on the lights. "You've never ordered anything online?"

"I didn't say that—but we don't call it 'internet shopping.' We refer to it as 'porn acquisition,'" Seth said in his fake-posh voice.

Nate laughed as he unloaded the groceries. "I stand corrected."

"I'm telling you, it's all in how you spin it. At least, according to my Marketing 101 class." Seth wandered through the living room and looked out onto the deck. "If you— Uh . . . Nate?"

"Hmmm?" Nate was rummaging through his crisper drawer searching for the arugula, although that would probably put his man-points in jeopardy too.

"The gate in back is open."

"What? It can't be. I never open it, not with Tarkus . . ." Nate rushed across the room, leaving the refrigerator door hanging open. "He should have been at the door already. He's always there to greet me. He knows the Jeep." He yanked open the door and ran onto the deck, the wind whipping through his hair and slicing through his shirt.

Shit shit shit. The gate was hanging open. What idiot built a fence with a gate opening outward instead of inward? If Tarkus had been determined enough to get out, he could have worked it open, but usually he didn't bother, far more content to hang out in the yard.

Ah hell. The UPS truck.

Nate's hands shook as he dug his cell phone out of his pocket. "Maybe Morgan hasn't dropped him off yet. It hasn't been that long since she left, and she always takes him the long way around. Claims he likes riding in her car better than the Jeep." He was babbling, he knew it, but *damn.* He fumbled the phone, dropping it in the damp grass.

Seth scooped it up and handed it back, placing a warm, steadying hand on Nate's cheek. "Hey. Chill. We'll figure it out, 'kay?"

"One of the reasons I rented this place was that there wasn't a lot of traffic, but there's some. He only has one eye, his depth perception is funky. And the woods. What if there's a bear? He's too friendly. He might not realize—"

"Bears are never seen this close to town." Seth sounded confident, but was that a flash of uncertainty in his expression? He shifted his grip from Nate's shoulder to the back of his neck, squeezing, grounding Nate a little bit. "He's a smart dog, right?"

Nate clenched his eyes shut and nodded. "Yeah. But he—"

"Nate. We'll *find* him. Trust me."

He took a shuddering breath and opened his eyes, meeting Seth's concerned gaze. "I do. Absolutely."

"Well then. Let's go get our boy."

CHAPTER NINETEEN

Nate lurched through the gate and charged up the driveway, gravel crunching and skidding under his trainers. He glanced wildly around, then took off in the direction of the highway as Seth caught up to him. In the twilight, in the murk between the double lines of towering firs, it was hard to make out anything but shadows.

Then the headlights of an approaching car illuminated a huddled mass on the verge, and Nate's heart tried to leap into his throat. *No Please no.* He stumbled to a halt, afraid to go any farther, afraid to know the truth.

"Hey." Seth was there, beside him, lacing their fingers together, and his felt so warm in comparison to Nate's cold ones. "Do you want me to scope it out for you?"

Nate nodded, unable to speak. Seth squeezed his hand once, then strode down the road until he reached the lump. Nate closed his eyes. *If I keep my eyes shut, that's one second more, ten, a whole minute, that I can still believe Tarkus is all right.*

Seth's footsteps approached, muffled by the rank weeds that lined the road. Was he walking slow? Fast? Which was better? Why did it feel like a year since Nate had seen that dreadful unmoving lump, yet no longer than a blink of an eye?

He jerked when Seth gripped his shoulders. "Nate. It's not him. It's not. It's just a pile of burlap sacking."

"Not him?" Nate's voice wobbled. "Oh God. Not him?"

"It's not. I promise."

Nate sucked in a breath and tried not to break down. *There's still a chance. He could still be okay. But where is he? How can I find him?* "I don't— I can't—" Why were his teeth chattering? It wasn't that cold.

Then Seth's arms were around him, holding him close, sharing warmth until Nate's shuddering lessened. "Better now?"

He wasn't, not even close. He wanted to stay here in the circle of Seth's arms, but that wouldn't help Tarkus, so he nodded and moved away reluctantly. "Sure. Let's go." He headed toward the highway, but Seth grabbed his hand and pulled him to a stop.

"Where are you going?"

"That's the path the UPS truck would take—up the drive, turn right, and take the service road up to the highway."

"But why would Tarkus follow it? By the time he got out, would the truck even be here anymore?"

"I don't *know*. I wasn't here. I shouldn't have—"

"Chill, Nate, okay? Now, I've only known Tark for a little while, but he doesn't seem like a dog who holds a grudge. I mean, the UPS guy isn't always on his mind, right? He doesn't hang out by the door waiting for the chance to take a chunk out of him."

Nate blinked at him, not understanding. "No. Of course not. But when he hears it, he goes ballistic. If he had the chance to chase that truck—"

"What if he didn't chase it? He's a dog, a smart one, but by the time he got out, he'd be over the UPS truck. He'd use his freedom more wisely." Seth took his shoulders again and gave him a little shake. "Come on. I've got a hunch." He grabbed Nate's hand and pulled him the other direction.

"Where are we going?"

Seth gave him an encouraging smile. "Following the love, not the hate." Seth said something else, something about trees and a gate, but Nate was so far from okay that his hearing kept skipping out on him.

Unresisting, he let Seth lead him down the road toward the cemetery, although he couldn't help looking back over his shoulder at the headlights zooming by on the highway. If Tarkus was up there—

Seth started to laugh, and Nate whirled, yanking his hand away. Christ, did he think this was a joke?

"It's okay." He captured Nate's hand again and nodded toward the cemetery gates. "He's right there, he's fine."

Barely visible in the gathering darkness, Tarkus sat at the foot of the oak tree, staring up into the branches. A sob caught in Nate's throat, and he broke into a run, Seth pounding along beside him, until he could drop down next to his dog and hug him around the neck.

"Tark. God, Tark, I thought I'd lost you."

Tarkus just panted, with a soft whine thrown in every now and then, although he wasn't paying any attention to Nate at all. Nate kept his face buried in Tarkus's ruff, despite getting fur up his nose, unwilling to let go. Dimly, Nate registered odd scrabbling sounds, a soft curse, more scrabbling, a thump.

Suddenly Tarkus leaped to his feet, tail wagging like mad, yipping excitedly, and dumping Nate onto his ass. Nate looked up to see Seth hand Tarkus that damned red Frisbee.

"See? This, he remembers. Love wins out over hate."

Nate blinked, glancing from Seth to the tree. "You climbed the tree? You *climbed* the *tree*?"

Seth raised an eyebrow, squinching his face. "Sure. Seemed like the best way to keep Tark from making a break for it again."

"But the Frisbee was stuck *miles* up there!"

"It was like ten feet. No big. I am a professional, after all."

"Yeah, but—" Nate's acrophobia kicked in big time when he imagined being up that high without even a ladder. "I can't believe you *climbed the tree*. You found my dog and you *climbed the tree*."

Seth's expression turned mystified. "Seriously, why is the tree such a big deal?"

"Because . . . because I'm afraid of heights."

"Wait, you are? Seriously?"

"As a freaking heart attack. Why do you think I left that damn Frisbee up there in the first place?"

Seth grinned. "You know, if you're that easily impressed, I've got some other mad redneck skills I can wow you with." He took off his belt and looped it around Tarkus's collar for a makeshift leash. "What do you say we get this guy home?"

Nate shambled along, still zoned out from multiple shocks, although Seth's stride was as jaunty as usual. Tarkus pranced between them, the red Frisbee locked in his jaws, as if he hadn't a care in his little doggy brain—which he probably didn't. The relief that had washed through Nate when he realized Tarkus was safe was being replaced by a stronger feeling—one that he hadn't felt in years.

Seth—he'd talked Nate down off the ledge; he'd protected Nate from the potentially devastating sight of his dog dead by the roadside; he'd been sharp enough, intuitive enough, to find Tarkus; and he'd *climbed a fucking tree.*

Once they made it back inside, Nate made sure Tarkus had water and food, although he might as well not have bothered: as Seth released his belt from its impromptu leash duty, Tarkus paid no attention to anything but the Frisbee.

Seth scrunched his nose as he peered at his fingers. "Yuck. My hands are filthy." He dropped his belt on the floor and held up his hands like a doctor waiting to glove up. "You got any industrial-strength hand soap?"

"Sure. Under the counter. Also hand sanitizer, olive oil. The usual suspects. Help yourself." Nate squeezed Seth's shoulder. "But don't go anywhere, okay? I'll be right back."

Stalking into the mudroom, he grabbed a roll of wire off the shelf above the soapstone sink, then headed outside to secure the damn gate. Nobody ever needed to use the thing again as far as he was concerned. Five loops around the latch could be overkill, but he wasn't about to go through this again. Next time, he might not be so lucky.

Lucky.

He stood in the yard, heedless of the wind kicking up and penetrating his shirt like an ice beam. *I'm lucky. Here. Now.* The cabin lights glowed soft and golden in the windows and French doors along the deck, gilding Seth's hair as he scrubbed his hands and turned his head to say something to Tarkus, who'd curled up on his bed with the Frisbee between his paws. Seth walked into the living room and knelt by Tarkus's bed, offering him something from his pocket—probably one of Pearl's homemade dog treats. *So lucky I found him. He fits this place. He fits us. He fits me.*

Something warm expanded in Nate's chest—and *hello*: his dick stirred in his pants as well. *I want him. I do.* But would Seth want him back? Only one way to find out.

He circled the deck, entering the mudroom to stow the wire and wash his hands at the sink. Peering at his reflection in the window, he made a valiant—although not entirely successful—attempt to tame his hair with his damp hands.

He scrubbed his palms along the outside of his jeans. *Now or never.* Taking a deep breath, he walked out of the mudroom in time to see Seth about to thread his belt through his belt loops.

"Leave it off."

Seth's chin shot up, his eyes widening. "That . . . seems a little unfair. Why am I the only one with his pants sagging down his ass?"

Nate held Seth's gaze as he unbuckled his own belt and drew it off. He tossed it on the counter. "Better?"

Seth blinked rapidly. "Uh . . . Nate? What exactly are you doing?"

Nate closed the distance between them, then grasped Seth's waist gently and pulled him close. "Making soufflé."

"Aren't . . . aren't soufflés those big poofy things that rise until they practically escape their pants—uh, pans?"

"Mm-hmm." Nate nuzzled Seth's neck, the spot just below his ear.

"Um, so . . ." Seth inhaled the word. "Is something *rising* now?"

Nate pressed his pelvis forward so the heated bulge at the front of Seth's jeans aligned with his own. "What do you think?" he murmured, his lips grazing Seth's skin.

"Am I . . . uh . . . Oh my God Nate, *really*?"

Pulling back, Nate smoothed Seth's hair off his forehead. "Is that okay? I don't want to push you into something you don't want, but I'm feeling so . . . so *close* to you right now. Like you're here." He grasped Seth's hand and pressed it over his heart. "Inside."

Seth's eyes were huge, blue irises almost swallowed by his pupils. "Do you want to get . . . closer?"

"Yes." Nate pressed a kiss to his throat.

"How—how close exactly?"

"This is good. For a start."

"Hold on a minute, will you?" He pushed Nate back. "Look, I'm *totally* into this, being with you, but I need more, I don't know, *information* from you. Like—like I think this means you have, you know . . . feelings for me."

Nate couldn't help his grin. "Sorry. Wasn't I being clear? Yes—I am *so* there."

"Thank God." Seth's shoulders drooped and he swayed a little before Nate steadied him. "Because I have feelings for you, lots of them, and, um . . ." Seth bit his lip. "I've never been with a guy I've really cared about. This is—will be my first time. If we, you know— Wait . . ." He blinked, forehead puckering in confusion. "What's happening exactly?"

Then he blushed. *Adorable.* "We're exploring." Nate stroked Seth's cheekbone, following that lovely wash of pink along the edge of his beard. "Finding ways to make each other happy—and in case you haven't noticed, it makes me insanely happy to touch you. You've got all these fascinating textures and colors and—" Nate sucked at the spot below Seth's ear. "Tastes. Like an interactive game."

"I'll give you interactive," he muttered.

"Excellent. Let's start with this." Nate dove in for a kiss, moaning when Seth opened for him. But he didn't take it deeper, not yet. Soft. Sweet. Thorough, but not sloppy. *God, I've missed kissing. I've wanted to kiss him for days now.*

But then Seth pulled back from the kiss—*damn it!*—although he seemed as breathless as Nate and kept his fists bunched in Nate's shirt. "I'm trying to *talk* to you. I thought that's what people with feelings for each other did before kissing." He focused on Nate's chin rather than his eyes. "I mean, I don't know *what's okay* between us. You pretty much know I'm up for anything, especially with you, but I don't want to—I'm *terrified* of hitting one of your limits. I mean, what if what makes me happy freaks you out?"

A fair question. "Then I'll tell you, but I'd never hold an honest mistake against you." Nate ran his thumbs along Seth's jaw as he tried to find the best way to put his desires into words, something that had never been easy for him. "If it makes you feel any better, though, I was totally into sex with Nara and Jorge. I didn't initiate it all that often, but when they wanted it, I was there. Invested. In the moment. Because making them happy *did it* for me."

"So the fact that you're coming on to me now . . ."

Nate quirked an eyebrow. "Welcome to the exception that proves the rule."

"What if . . ." He swallowed, and his blush deepened. "What if I asked you to strip?"

With excitement prickling his skin like static, Nate made a valiant—and probably unsuccessful—attempt at nonchalance. "Like this?" He let go of Seth—reluctantly—and peeled off his Henley.

Seth sucked in a breath as Nate balled up the shirt and tossed it onto the sofa. He popped the top button on his jeans, but Seth grabbed his wrist, then let go as if the contact had burned him.

Seth rubbed his palms along the outside seams of his own jeans, staring intently into Nate's eyes. "You mean it. You really want this" It's not—I don't know—a pity fuck or misplaced gratitude?"

"First, you're not pitiful. And second, if it was nothing but gratitude, I'd buy you a drink, not do everything but beg you to touch me. Because in case you haven't noticed, I've been doing most of the touching so far."

"Oh really?" Seth's eyes kindled—finally!—and he slid both hands up Nate's belly and over his pecs. "What do you call this?"

"About fucking time."

CHAPTER TWENTY

There was only one way Seth could show quite how much it mattered that Nate wanted him, so he initiated full-body contact, wrapping his arms around Nate's solid shoulders and pressing their bodies together, his chest molding to Nate's. *Skin.* God, he loved touching this guy. And being touched by him.

Nate engulfed him, towering over him and bracing his thighs outside Seth's. Arms so tight around him ribs creaked, although he wasn't sure whose. It was better than he'd imagined, and he'd imagined plenty the last few nights. But he hadn't known that every time he'd pull a breath in through his nose that the scent of Nate would feed his excitement, or how Nate would taste as they kissed.

It consumed him until they stumbled. Nate was pulling him back, somewhere, and Seth lost his balance, nearly bringing Nate with him. "What?"

"Bedroom."

"We're really doing this?" Damn it, why had he asked? If Nate was going to decide this was a mistake, Seth wanted him to do that afterward. *Please don't let this be extreme gratitude.* The pathetic thing was that he'd take it even if he knew that was the reason. He'd take whatever he could get from Nate. He'd even consider himself lucky to have been kissed if Nate called this off right now.

But Nate didn't. "Yeah, we're doing this."

He stopped outside the bathroom door, gripping Seth's shoulders when Seth tried to keep nudging him toward the bedroom. "Hang on a sec," Nate half panted. "Gotta get some lotion."

"Oh." Seth blinked as some of the cold water of reality splashed on him. Of course Nate probably didn't have lube, and he could forget condoms. *He* didn't have anything with him—he'd never thought this would happen. "Yeah, that'd be good." Really good, because he'd love to suck Nate off, sometime, but right now he wanted nothing more than Nate's naked body on top of his, weighing him down while they found a rhythm together. "Hurry."

He didn't need to say it, because Nate had already been in the bathroom and was slipping back out the door as Seth spoke, a pale-yellow bottle in his hand. All Seth saw was the word *unscented* before he was working them toward the bedroom again. He needed this so badly. *My first time.* So weird, but it was. The first time he wanted to be with someone because it was *them*, together, not because he wanted to get off.

Getting off was secondary. What he really wanted was for Nate to have a good experience. For him to be so totally consumed by it that Seth could tell by looking at him that Nate wasn't bored or just doing it for Seth. *It can't just be gratitude.* Romantic feelings, that was what Nate had said.

The way Nate kept touching him, kissing him over and over, until he could barely get his shirt over his head, convinced him Nate did want this as much as he did. That Nate was totally absorbed.

Seth shoved that thought away as he pushed against Nate's shoulders, making him stop. Not out of uncertainty, but because he wanted to watch as he revealed Nate's dick for the first time. He rested his head on Nate's collar bone and looked down between them as he popped open the jeans and shoved the briefs out of the way.

"Jesus." God, he'd wanted to see this forever. Since the night they met. Not Nate's dick, but his own hand on it, stroking him. Not to mention hearing the way Nate groaned, or feeling how his Adam's apple bobbed against Seth's forehead as he swallowed. "Need that lotion."

He looked around, finally spying it on the floor, but before he could reach for it, Nate had pushed him backward onto the bed. The mattress bounced under him and Seth nearly laughed out of happiness. Nate's expression was so intent, though, that it killed any amusement.

Reaching down, Nate unfastened Seth's jeans and worked them under his hips, shoving them down his legs in one continuous motion.

Then—*oh, fuck*—Nate dropped to his knees next to the bed and, more carefully, peeled down the waistband of Seth's briefs. "OhmyGod." He couldn't look. Just the brush of Nate's breath on his cock threatened to make him come. "Hold on, hold on," he whispered.

Nate didn't, though. Still touching him as if he were delicate, he pulled Seth's briefs down to where his jeans were wrapped around his calves, then untied his shoes.

"You don't have to—"

"Chill," Nate ordered, taking Seth's shoes off, then his clothes.

Seth bit his lip. He was a sucker for a guy who exerted control. "'Kay."

Spreading his hands wide, like he needed to touch as much skin as possible, Nate caressed Seth's legs, skimming his hands up from the ankles, passing behind his knees, and along his thighs until he was gripping Seth's hips. Again, breath touched Seth's dick, but this time he jackknifed into a sitting position and grabbed Nate's shoulders. "Don't. Come up here, please?"

As Nate stood, Seth grabbed the bottle, then took advantage of being at eye level with Nate's cock, stroking it in his hand, spreading the lotion around. It was his turn to be the undresser—disrober?— and he aimed to drive Nate nuts while he completed the job. Difficult with one hand, but not impossible, since at some point Nate had toed off his own shoes.

Scooting back on the bed as Nate crawled over him, Seth made sure they were positioned for maximum physical contact. He pulled Nate down on him, then began caressing him everywhere, rubbing and writhing and generally encouraging Nate to find his groove. Anything would do it for him—he could come from having his palm massaged, if it was this man doing it.

He could, but he'd rather have it like this, with his legs tangled around Nate's and his hands kneading Nate's ass and his tongue in Nate's mouth while Nate thrust against him.

Seth barely made it, hanging on to his orgasm by his fingernails, until Nate was groaning in his ear and spilling on Seth's groin, then he let go of the tiny bit of control he'd had, moaning loudly enough that he'd probably be embarrassed later, then sucking on Nate's tongue as aftershocks pinged around inside him.

So much better. He'd never come like that. It wasn't about the strength of the orgasm, it was about the way his heart had swollen up and exploded at the same time. In a good way. Exploded like a piñata, showering happiness and bliss all over Seth's body and mind. "Fucking fantastic," he murmured.

"Mmm." Nate seemed to agree. His head was resting against Seth's neck, and for a second there was a hint of moisture and the brush of Nate's lips against his skin, under his jaw.

As reluctant as he was to leave the warm nest of blankets—and warmer expanse of Seth's back—Nate slipped out of bed at his usual time the next morning. Although he didn't have to report to work until two, since he was scheduled for night shoots for the next three days, they had a haunted house to stage.

Seth murmured in his sleep and nestled deeper into the pillows, but didn't wake. From his bed in the corner—that damn red Frisbee tucked between his paws—Tarkus tracked Nate to the bathroom.

I could have lost him. If not for Seth, he could be gone. But if not for Tarkus, Nate might never have had the courage to take the final leap into intimacy with Seth. With Nara and Jorge, although the attraction had been there, he'd waited for them to make the first move. This time, he hadn't been willing to wait, to trust to chance.

In the days before Nara, when Nate imagined he might be able to go along with sex with no real connection, if only to belong, he'd tried it once or twice. It hadn't turned out well—wasn't worth the hassle and recriminations and the burden of expectations for so little return. Turned out, if he didn't put out—one way or another—his erstwhile partner withheld touch as a punishment.

Which made no sense—if you wanted intimacy, why refuse to be intimate, even if it didn't go as far as a come-shot? Orgasms lasted maybe fifteen to thirty seconds, if you were lucky. Cuddling and kissing could go on for hours. Making a life—*sharing* a life—sleeping with someone to *sleep* with them, the closeness in the night, the companionship, knowing you weren't alone, meant more to him than where he stuck his dick—or if he stuck it anywhere at all.

He'd seen how other men his age—*and younger, because let's face it, you're not a kid anymore*—seemed to charge into sex with little thought for the *after*. Yeah, maybe they had enough regard for consequences to take appropriate safe-sex precautions, but they didn't think a lot about the *emotional* precautions. Where did you find a condom for *that*?

After last night, Nate doubted there was an emo-condom in the universe hefty enough to protect him from his feelings for Seth.

And what about *Seth's* feelings? He'd allowed Nate to mesh their lives in a way Nate hadn't let himself want since Jorge. What could Nate give him in return? What if Seth wasn't ready for Nate's peculiar brand of devotion?

Confidence. Yeah, Nate could give him that. The self-assurance to face his family, pursue a real career path that wasn't hedged by their expectations. The freedom to follow his dreams. *I just have to figure out how.*

He took a quick shower, but when he heard Seth murmuring to Tarkus, he didn't bother to shave. He cracked open the bathroom door to see Seth crouched by Tarkus's bed in nothing but his boxer briefs. The curve of his spine as he rubbed the dog's belly—God, sculptors would barter their first- *and* second-born to capture something that perfect.

Wrapping a towel around his waist, Nate padded over and trailed his fingers along Seth's bare shoulder. "Good morning. We don't have a lot of time before your friend arrives. Want to grab a quick shower while I make breakfast?"

Seth gave Tarkus a final pat and stood. "Good morning to you too." He kissed Nate's cheek. "Probably be a good idea, huh? I mean Lucas can take his chances, but I try never to smell like sex when I meet my grandmother."

"About that—"

"We don't have to figure this all out now, Nate. I'm good with just knowing you might like that kind of . . . closeness with me again." He lowered his gaze, his fingers twirling in Nate's chest hair.

With one knuckle, Nate raised Seth's chin until they could look each other in the eyes. "No. That's not what I meant. Our connection—" Nate wrapped his arms around Seth's waist and pulled him close, skin to skin. "*This* connection is important to me. When I said it was the exception—well, I may not initiate sex very often, but if it means we stay close—"

"I'm not going to force myself on you. It's not the same if I know you don't really want it."

"That's not— Please believe me, I—I *desire* you. It's just that my brand of desire may not take the form you're used to." *Way to sell him on the product, Albano.* "What I mean is this isn't a one-way connection, you know? If you want something—something more than I'm giving you—please, just tell me. Being with you, touching you, is no hardship. Far from it."

Seth bit his lip and dug his fingertips into Nate's back. "It's no hardship if you *don't*—" His cell phone went off. "Sorry. That's probably Lucas. I should get it to make sure he actually shows up." Seth answered the call and walked into the bathroom, shutting the door as he greeted his friend.

Damn it. That discussion hadn't gone the way Nate planned at all. *Story of my life.* How did you frame the conversation when the other person's frames were completely different? How could he make Seth understand how huge a deal this was for him? One way or another, he needed to figure that out before Seth decided Nate was too high maintenance to be worth the effort.

By the time he dressed, fed Tarkus, brewed the coffee, and had an omelet ready to slide out of the pan, he still hadn't figured out the answer to that little conundrum.

Seth strolled out of the bedroom, running his fingers through his damp hair. "I really need to start keeping my hair product in my car. How am I supposed to keep my 'do in place?"

Well, that was something. Seth apparently hadn't rejected the notion of showering here again—which presupposed spending the night. "I'll pick some up. What brand?"

"Don't, I'm kidding." Seth flicked his fingers in dismissal, and Nate's heart sank. "I'll bring some over next time." *Next time—heart bounces back.*

"That's . . . great." He divided the omelet between two plates and set one in front of Seth. "A little piperade to start your day."

"Mmm. Another Italian specialty?"

"Actually, it's Basque, but I learned it from my dad."

Seth sat down on a barstool and inhaled the steam rising from the eggs. "Mmm. Smells most excellent."

"Thanks." Nate nodded at the coffee by Seth's plate. "Coffee's up too. A little milk, right?"

Seth tilted his head, his hand poised halfway to the cup. "You remember how I take my coffee?"

"Sure. I saw how you doctored it when we stopped for coffee at the studio canteen after the tour."

"That's so sweet." He took a sip and closed his eyes. "Perfect. My mother *still* doesn't remember, and she's had about a thousand times more chances.' He dug into the omelet. "Oh my God. This is incredible. If you keep feeding me like this, you'll never get rid of me."

That's a fantastic plan. If I keep taking care of him—food, coffee, moral support—maybe the relationship will take care of itself.

"What did Lucas want?"

Seth shrugged. "He's bringing Gabe with him."

"Gabe?"

"Savage. His boyfriend. He won't be as easy to fool as Lucas."

"A skeptical sort, is he?"

"It's not that." Seth took another bite of eggs. "Jesus, this is good." He chased it with a gulp of coffee. "But Gabe knows me better. I have *tells*."

"You play poker with him or something?"

"No." Seth stopped cutting up his omelet and met Nate's eyes. "We, um, we used to fuck."

Nate froze with his own fork poised over his plate. "You—you were in a relationship with him?"

Seth rolled his eyes. "God, no. We were friends with benefits, and he ended the benefits as soon as Lucas was back in town. It's okay. I saw it coming, plus—in his case—just friendship is fine with me."

"Ah." Nate stabbed his omelet with extra force, wishing it were Gabe's hand—or maybe his dick.

"Hey. Look at me."

Nate responded to Seth's cajoling tone—how could he not?—and looked up. "Hmmm?"

"It was nothing serious, okay? Gabe was always waiting for Lucas, and I knew it. We just hooked up when it was convenient. And once the convenience stopped, so did the sex. It's a different thing altogether."

"You deserve to be more than a *convenience*."

"Sometimes convenience is all you need." Seth shook his head. "It worked for me too."

"Oh." Did *this* suit Seth too? Would he walk away when it didn't suit anymore, the way Jorge had done?

"It's not what I want now, though." He grinned. "For one thing, I never got piperade out of that deal."

Nate forced himself to laugh. "Well, there's that, I suppose." He finished the last of his eggs. "So. You remember your cues?"

"Yup. When we're on the landing, I have to say 'rodents.' Then upstairs, I have to trigger the sensor for the door."

"And make sure they don't come back downstairs again until I have time to reset the mirror."

"Mmm, I like a man who establishes control."

"I can, when the occasion warrants."

"Sounds like fun." Seth shot him a flirty look from under his lashes. "You'll have to give me a list of warranted occasions."

Oookaay. Nate's skin suddenly felt a couple of sizes too small in several key locations. "I'll—I'll definitely think about it. But, for now, we'd better get going."

Because whether or not their plan succeeded in getting the other Larsons to back off and let Pearl sell her house, Nate would take savage satisfaction from scaring the bejesus out of Gabe Savage.

Seth was pretty sure Grandma would notice he hadn't come home last night. She'd known he was with Nate, and she'd definitely have checked for his car before going to bed and when she got up. He wasn't normally an early riser, so if it wasn't there in the morning . . .

And yes, she'd have paid attention because she wanted to know what was going on between him and Nate. The looks she'd given him yesterday before going off to have lunch with Eleanor had made that clear.

This morning at Nate's had been a little awkward, and Seth imagined it wouldn't get any better once they showed up at Sentinel House and Grandma started asking barely veiled questions.

Nosy old woman.

Correction, nosy woman seasoned to perfection.

"You good over there?" he asked Nate, sitting in the passenger's seat of his car. Once the words were out, Seth nearly squeezed his eyes shut in embarrassment. He couldn't do that, though, because he was driving.

"Fine." One of Nate's eyebrows twitched quizzically, but he went expressionless. "Why wouldn't I be?"

"Just checking." *Shut up. You're making this worse.* "Do you want the heater on?"

Excellent. He clearly wasn't done with the oversolicitous questions.

"Really, I'm fine." Warmth enveloped Seth's hand on the gearshift. Nate, touching him. Reassuring him.

That made things both a little better and a little worse. This right here? This situation would have benefited from his having had a boyfriend in the past. Then he'd have a clue how to behave the morning after. He knew all there was to know about how to act around a casual hookup over breakfast but next to nothing— Scratch that. He knew *nothing* about how to make sure the guy knew he was interested in waking up next to him for the foreseeable future. Should he just say it outright? *I want to be your boyfriend.*

Partner. That was the PC word. "I want to be your partner," he whispered, then ripped his hand off the steering wheel and slapped it over his mouth. The car veered toward the shoulder, which meant he had to grab the wheel, so he lost physical contact with Nate. Tarkus yipped his displeasure at being thrown around in the backseat too.

Damn it.

When they parked in Seth's driveway, Nate didn't get out right away. "Are you okay?" he asked instead, capturing Seth's hand again, but this time pulling it over onto his thigh. "You seem a little on edge." A wave of something that wasn't all warmth began to radiate up Seth's arm, comforting him enough that he could laugh. Well, chuckle, in an embarrassed way, but still.

Time to lay it on the line. "I'm just freaked out about . . . Tell me again you really want to be with me. Like this, and—" He jerked his head back the way they'd come, trying to indicate the bed they'd slept in together. "And like that. I don't *do* this, Nate, or I haven't done it. Had romantic relationships. I'm afraid I'm going to fuck it up somehow." When he realized he'd dug his fingernails into Nate's jeans, he loosened his grip.

Nate looked at him forever, eyes especially deep and serious. "You don't need to stress about it. I'm not exactly a flighty guy, so you don't need to worry that I'll suddenly take off in a fit of pique. We'll figure out the relationship as we go along, okay? So just . . . be yourself, I guess. That's worked pretty spectacularly so far." As Nate spoke, the knot of anxiety began to unravel in Seth's chest.

"I can do that," he said on a relieved breath. Then, well aware the chances Grandma was watching were fifty-fifty, he leaned over the console and tilted his head, pressing his lips against Nate's perfect ones for a few seconds. Long enough to spark up a little heat inside him, in his heart and his gut. "I like this," he whispered. Again with the being stupid, but he had all these feelings inside him that wanted out, and he couldn't seem to bottle them up. *The guy I am doesn't want to hold back.*

"Mmm." Nate kissed him back before they finally got out of the car. When Seth glanced up, he saw the café curtain on one of the breakfast nook windows twitch.

Well, Grandma would have figured it out anyway. And honestly, he was glad she knew. She'd be happy for him.

"All right." Seth rubbed his hands together in anticipation. "Let's go haunt the shit out of this place."

CHAPTER TWENTY-ONE

"You won't have any trouble selling this house," Lucas announced ten seconds after he walked in the door. "It's perfect, Mrs. Larson."

"Aren't you sweet." Grandma beamed at him, then allowed Lucas to give her a gentle hug hello. That was a little weird, because they barely knew each other. Apparently Lucas was a more affectionate guy than Seth had realized. That or he had a soft spot for Grandma.

As Lucas began nattering on to her, complimenting her on the house and how historically accurate it was, Seth raised an eyebrow at Gabe.

The guy smirked. "It *is* pretty damned impressive. Didn't know you were so good with detail work."

Without missing a beat, Lucas—in the middle of telling Grandma that Gothic Revival was his preferred nineteenth-century architectural style—punched Gabe in the upper arm, hard enough that Gabe massaged it while sulking. "Not what I meant," he muttered.

Right then, Tarkus came trotting in, plumy tail swishing close to a narrow table bristling with antique vases and figurines.

"Oh, good boy." Grandma beamed at him, completely blind to all dangers he might present. "There's my puppy." Bending over—was that her spine creaking?—she clasped the dog's head between her hands a moment, then scratched him thoroughly behind the ears. "Meet our visitors, Tarkus. This is Lucas and Gabe. They're a couple."

Panting happily, Tarkus paid no attention to them, instead he stared hopefully at Grandma.

"Didn't know you had a dog." Gabe frowned. In spite of what Grandma had said, the dog clearly wasn't a puppy, and he and Gabe used to spend enough time together that the guy could reasonably expect to know if Seth had had a pet of any kind.

"He's Grandma's," Seth said quickly.

Tarkus helped out by completely ignoring him in favor of sniffing at Grandma's pockets, where she stowed her homemade dog treats.

"This place is really well-kept. It looks so *period*, you know?" Lucas was craning his neck, examining the crown molding in the entry hall. "Is that chandelier original?" Now Lucas was goggling up at the fixture.

Calling it a *chandelier* was kind of a stretch in Seth's mind. It was more of a multibranched pendant lamp with a few crystals hanging off of it.

Okay, fine, it was a chandelier.

"Seth does all the restoration work." Now his grandmother was beaming at him. Would she scratch behind his ears too? "He's been responsible for the upkeep on Sentinel House for the past twelve years. Oh, dear, that reminds me." Her smile melted into a grimace. "I forgot, there's something I wanted you to look at—that doorway to the servants' stairs on the second-floor landing is doing that thing."

That was his first cue. "Last time didn't fix it?" Befuddlement with a hint of apprehension, that was what he was aiming for.

Grandma shot him a quelling look—had he overacted?—before placing her hand on her chest, in a perfect embodiment of worry. "I'm afraid not." She turned to Lucas and Gabe and then nearly blew it. "Can I offer you two some coffee?"

What was she *doing*?

"Or would you like to follow along? It might help if you saw the problems we need to fix as well as the good points, hmmm?"

Oh, nicely played, Grandma. She might have missed her calling. Seth would let her take the lead from now on in this charade, since she was clearly a better actor than him.

Lucas and Gabe followed along, with a few more gentle nudges from his grandmother. "Don't worry if you hear any weird noises. It's just the rodents in the attic," Seth announced as they began climbing the steps, Tarkus scampering along behind them. "I'm pretty sure," he added, as if speaking to himself.

Then came Grandma's next bit of brilliance, at the mirror hanging on the wall of the landing halfway up the first flight. Just after she'd passed it and Lucas was about to, it cracked, loudly enough that they all halted at the noise. Tarkus did his part by staring at the wall and whining, no doubt detecting Nate's presence.

"Oh no," Grandma quavered. "Not that damned mirror *again.*"

Her distress was so real that Seth actually reached to comfort her, placing his hand under her elbow, before he remembered this was according to plan. Nate was doing a hell of a job behind that false wall. "Grandma, don't worry. I'm sure it'll, you know, resolve itself the same way it did last time."

He must have played it right, because she didn't give him any dirty looks. Instead she sighed and waved him on. As he turned to head upstairs again, he spied a glimmer of confusion in Lucas's face.

Excellent.

When they reached the top of the flight, the door was ajar. Nate had made it automatic, since he couldn't run out from behind the wall, around to the kitchen and then up the servants' stairs in the three seconds it took them to climb a dozen or so steps.

Or maybe it was remote controlled? Either way, it meant he was sexy and talented.

Seth shut it, making sure the latch clicked audibly. "Seems fine, Grandma." The second he turned, it sprung open again—and Tarkus growled right on cue, hackles raised, because Nate had embedded the distant sound of the UPS truck in the mechanism somehow.

He repeated that maneuver a few times, with Grandma getting increasingly agitated. The only moment of danger was when Gabe said, "Want me to take a look at it?"

"Absolutely not." Grandma said before Seth could do more than blink stupidly. "You're our guest. We'll just leave this here, and Seth can figure it out later."

"Yes, Grandma," he said obediently, earning an eye roll from her as soon as the other two turned their backs.

Okay, yeah, that had been out of character.

As they traipsed back downstairs in a line, like a group of climbers after summiting the mountain, the real fun began.

"Oh my God," Lucas gasped as he caught sight of the mirror on the landing. He stopped so suddenly he teetered, and Gabe reached out for him. "The crack is— Oh my God what *is* that?"

Craning his neck, Seth could just make out Fennimore's face floating in the mirror—the miraculously unblemished mirror—like a scary clown meme. It was sternly eyeing Lucas as he stood frozen in front of it. Well, frozen except for the tremor in the hand he'd slapped against his chest.

In the pulsing silence after Lucas's screech, Grandma waited a beat or two for Tarkus's whine before pushing forward to peer into the mirror. "Oh, that's, well, we think that's Fennimore."

"Fennimore *Larson*?" Gabe reared back, nearly losing his balance too, but he recovered fast. The image flickered out a split second before Gabe shoved in front of Lucas—to protect Lucas or to see what had freaked him out? Squinting suspiciously, Gabe poked his finger toward the mirror, not quite touching the glass. "Didn't that have a crack in it?"

"Yeah, sometimes it does that," Seth said helpfully. "I think it's a heat thing, like cool air makes the crack widen and, uh . . ." He shrugged, doing his best impression of a straight guy who believed he knew everything.

The look he got from Gabe wasn't particularly trusting. "Babe, what did you see?" he asked his boyfriend.

Lucas's gulp was audible, and his face was as white as the proverbial ghost (although in Seth's opinion, the "ghost" that had appeared in the mirror was downright florid). "Fennimore? Maybe? Who's Fennimore?"

God, did the guy not read the papers? Not that Seth did much himself. "He's my great-great-grandfather. You know, the guy that built this house. He was, um . . . he was murdered here."

Dun-dun-duuun, wouldn't have been out of place after that little announcement.

"You think you saw a face in the mirror?" Gabe asked reasonably.

"I don't—I don't know?"

Honestly, Seth almost felt sorry for Lucas for a second, there. *Remember the bachelorette party.* Okay, yeah, no mercy. The guy had this coming.

"Oh dear." Grandma patted him. "I saw him too, but I'm sure it's my imagination. If he were *really* haunting the house, I probably would have noticed before."

"So, you think *I* saw him because of your imagination?"

"No, honey, I think that was in *your* imagination." Grandma patted him some more, then flapped her hands to try to move the guys along. "Now, who wants that coffee I offered? It'll get cold if we stand here jawing about phantoms in the mirror all day."

Yup, they needed to get moving: there was more haunting to be done. As soon as Lucas turned and started—hesitantly—down again, Seth let himself smile. When Gabe glanced over his shoulder, he barely killed his amusement in time.

Gabe waited for him, letting Grandma and Lucas go on ahead. "Hey, man. I was going through some stuff the other day, and I found one of your old Hickory shirts. Forgot to throw it in the truck though."

"Only one? I'm surprised I didn't leave more there." When he'd logged with Gabe, the implicit understanding was that once they were done for the day in the woods, they'd spend the rest of the night in Gabe's bed. Or other convenient surfaces in his place. "Don't worry about it. I don't need it back."

Gabe shrugged. "Won't fit me, and I don't think Lucas's gonna wanna be wearing it around much."

Yeah, he and Lucas might be friends, but Lucas still didn't like remembering when Seth and Gabe were that and then some. Which reminded him, right here where they were standing, Nate would be able to hear every word, and judging by this morning, Nate didn't like knowing about that any more than Lucas.

"By the way," Gabe continued before Seth could urge him along. "Ran into Evan Miller, and whatever you said to that dude? He's telling everyone you aren't *up* for a 'good time' anymore."

"Excellent," Seth groaned. "The impotence offensive. If I'd known his ego was so fragile, I would have made up an excuse the other night. Jesus, I thought I was being *nice* telling him I'm not . . . Whatever." He shook his head and let Gabe fill in the blank however he wanted. Gabe *and* Nate. *Really don't need to discuss this right here.* He took a step, watching Gabe to make sure he was following.

Gabe didn't move his feet, but he did let his gaze flicker to the dining room archway. *Great.* He didn't want Lucas to hear this any more than Seth wanted Nate to. "Evan's trashing you to everyone. Like, if you ever want to get laid—"

"I really couldn't care less."

Something in his tone—probably the annoyance—made Gabe's eyes go wide. "Well, now, that's a different tune than you used to sing."

"Sorry." Not that he was sure what for, exactly. "Things're . . . different, now."

"You seeing someone? Like, seriously?"

Shrugging, he attempted to force himself not to blush. Being blond sucked sometimes.

Gabe had mad skills—he could smile smugly and whistle at the same time. "Never thought you'd tie yourself down to one guy."

If he was seeing someone, that didn't mean he wasn't seeing other guys. *But you won't, because that would hurt Nate.* That, and he didn't *want* anyone else. "You did," he finally retorted. *Excellent comeback.*

"Yup." The dude finally started down the last few steps, still smugly smiling, but at least now it was about *his* boyfriend instead of Seth's . . . relationship.

When they got to the dining room, Grandma was at the buffet, next to the coffee service she'd laid out. "Seth, dear, set out the cups so I can pour." As she lifted the thermal carafe, her hand shook noticeably. "Did you see— Never mind. My imagination again." She squinted into the far corner of the room an extra second before shaking her head and attending to the coffee.

Tarkus played his part as well as Grandma played hers. Seth was pretty sure he could only hear the recording start up because he was listening for it. It was in the corner Grandma had drawn attention to, around the ten-seat table, but Tarkus made out the sound of the UPS truck just fine—nothing wrong with his ears, after all, just the rest of him—and he started freaking like a hound of hell had dressed up as the mailman. When Seth lunged to grab his collar, he truly believed he needed to in order to keep Tark from rooting out the speaker. Of course Tarkus wasn't acting, he believed the malevolent man in brown was encroaching on his territory, and he growled and barked and salivated and showed his canines just like it was delivery day.

"Oh, I hate it when he does that," Grandma said in a low voice, although loud enough to be heard. When he glanced at her, she was clutching her chest. "Just when I've convinced myself there's nothing there."

"There *is* nothing there," Lucas insisted, then ruined it by adding, "Right?" He stared intently at the corner, then started toward it.

Seth improvised, grabbing the guy's wrist as he passed to halt him. "No, don't. Sometimes people get, um, shocked."

"What?" Lucas's eyes bulged out of their sockets.

"Shocked by what?" Gabe asked.

"Like, electrically shocked. We don't really understand." Seth bit his lip, faking reluctance to say more, since he really had nothing else to add. "Wiring in old homes like this, it's sometimes, um—"

"I hoped . . ." Grandma's voice held the perfect amount of tremor. "I—I have to sell this house. I was hoping, when you two boys came by, *it* wouldn't—" she gulped in a parody of Lucas on the stairs earlier "—disturb things."

"*What* wouldn't?" Lucas actually stamped his foot.

"Well . . ." Should he say it or let the guy get himself there? "We don't really know." Better to let Lucas come to the obvious conclusion. At least, he hoped it was obvious.

Exhaling shakily, Lucas blinked a few times, then asked, "Um, I think I've seen enough. Can we end the tour now?"

Nate was so proud of his coconspirators. Pearl—God, she'd been brilliant. If Levi ever decided to stage *Arsenic and Old Lace* at the Playhouse, Pearl would be a shoo-in as Aunt Abby, the sweet, no-nonsense septuagenarian poisoner.

Seth had remembered his cues, timed them exactly right. Even Tarkus—who was only responding to the recordings of the approaching UPS truck in his usual way—hadn't blown his lines. All the effects had gone off without a hitch.

Then Nate just had laid on the dining room UPS recording a little longer than was strictly necessary because . . . Gabe fricking Savage. *Don't pad your part out of pique, Albano, or you'll ruin the whole thing.*

It wasn't bad enough that the guy hadn't reacted to the haunting effects with anything other than *meh*—and Nate had really wanted to turn his crank at least a little. But his casual, borderline contemptuous remarks about Seth's reputation and past? They'd flipped a switch Nate hadn't even realized he had.

Nate's sexual attraction wasn't quick to ignite, but once lit, it burned slow and steady, even if it wasn't as hot as he'd heard other people brag about. Last night, with Seth, it had flared for only the third time in his life. Seth was *his* now—and that meant Nate was all in, and he intended to prove it by showing Seth he was focused. Devoted. Protective.

Seth might not have had a lot of experience—or any, if Gabe was to be believed—with long-term relationships, but at least it sounded as if Seth had turned down a chance for a hookup. This Evan Miller character—who the hell was he anyway? Even if he and Seth had a history, he had no right to talk shit about Seth that way. Nobody did. The dickhead needed to back off—and it didn't sound like Gabe had made the least push to encourage that. *Asshole.*

Maybe Gabe and Lucas needed a demonstration that Seth was both off the market and not without a champion. *A grand gesture— that's the ticket.* Or at least as grand as Nate could manage at short notice.

So he hustled down the back stairs, crept through the kitchen and outside. He couldn't risk screwing up their plot with an ill-timed unscheduled cameo, so he lurked out of sight, waiting for Gabe Savage to say one. More. Thing.

Grandma pretended to be reluctant to let Lucas and Gabe leave, but she didn't force them to see anymore. "Maybe next time," she said as they walked out onto the wraparound porch with their guests.

Seth had a feeling there wouldn't be a next time. Even after Lucas found out the place wasn't haunted.

As Lucas and Gabe said their good-byes, Shannon drove up and parked on the street in front of the house. They'd expected to still be inside when she arrived, but she could probably improvise, right?

She acted all the time. Everyone came down the steps to stand on the lawn and wait for her.

Her smile as she got out of the car didn't seem strained, neither did her wave. "Hey, Seth. Hey, guys." As she reached them, she greeted Grandma. "Hello there, Mrs. Larson."

Shannon hugged Grandma—what was it about his grandmother that made his friends want to paw at her? Seth couldn't be sure, but he thought Shannon whispered something in her ear.

"I've been working on that story you and Seth proposed," she said as she disentangled herself. "The special-interest piece about the history of Sentinel House? I think I can get my editor to go for it if we come up with a unique angle. So, is there anything especially unusual about it?"

Shannon got the same sort of glare from Grandma that he had when he'd overplayed his part. Still, Grandma managed to smooth any too-obvious moments over. "Well, dear, it's on the national historic register, of course, and in a few minor, specialized guidebooks. One's about Victorian architecture of the Olympic Peninsula."

"Oh." Shannon wrinkled up her nose. "That reminds me. I'm sure it's just a joke or someone overreacting, but when I was researching the house, I saw it on a website that lists haunted houses. On a couple of them, actually. One even called it the most haunted house on Puget Sound."

"Oh no." Grandma fanned herself with a tissue. Where the hell had she gotten that, from between her bosoms? If you asked him, she was working the frail old lady bit too hard.

"Oh my God," Lucas called, pointing back at the house. "That—that thing in the dining room, it was—I saw it! On the mirror in the staircase! Ghost of Fentenmeier!"

"Fennimore," Gabe corrected.

"Fennimore!" Lucas repeated, gesticulating wildly.

Shannon leaped right on that. "You saw something? Would you let me interview you about it for the paper?"

Unexpectedly, Lucas clammed up, pressing his lips together like a thirteen-year-old who'd zipped them shut and thrown away the imaginary key. His gaze pinged from Shannon to Seth to Grandma and back again, over and over.

Uh-oh. Now Seth saw it: the flaw in their plan. Lucas was concerned Grandma couldn't sell a house that was haunted. They all stood there, him and Shannon and Grandma teetering on the edge of owning up, not sure if Lucas would still agree to look like a fool in the local paper and swear he saw a ghost if he knew he'd been set up.

Then, of all people, Gabe came to the rescue. "Haunted, huh? Congratulations, Mrs. Larson." He gave her that easy grin that he'd been flashing around since he was old enough to carry a chainsaw. "I hear the right people will pay big bucks for a haunted house. Why, if you were to sell it to someone who wanted to turn it into a bed and breakfast, that could be the clincher right there."

A bed and breakfast? Lucas must have said something.

"Sure, it might narrow your market a bit, but you could gain big from a feature like that. Better to get it out in the open than to try and hide the evidence, I say."

For the first time, Grandma seemed at a loss for words. "Oh . . . why you might be right, Gabe."

"Hey." Another visitor—everyone turned as Nate came sauntering over from around the corner. "You weren't at your place so I thought I'd check the house." Seth tried to read his expression, see if he'd caught the conversation with Gabe, but Nate looked normal.

Automatically, Seth went toward him, so that he and Nate ended up standing just a little apart from the others. Kind of like Gabe and Lucas were. Like a couple.

More revealing though was when Nate put his hand on Seth's back, leaving it there as he faced the group. That probably answered the question of whether he'd overheard him and Gabe, but more importantly: *he's staking his claim on me.*

Once again Seth found himself trying to fight off the heat in his face. Really, though, he couldn't have been happier about it if Nate had peed a circle around him.

Actually, this more subtle approach probably made him happier than that would have.

Speaking of circles, Tarkus was trying to dance one around Nate, now, although he was as ungraceful as ever.

"That dog," Grandma said. "I swear, he'd go home with you if I let him." Beaming, she came up to Nate and gave him a hug—something

Nate obviously wasn't prepared for but returned anyway. Seth thought the guy looked as pleased as he'd felt when Nate had staked his claim on *him*.

"Boys." Grandma turned toward them. "Have you met Nate Albano? He's a friend of Seth's."

What the hell. Seth basked in Nate's possessiveness as introductions came and went, and then Gabe and Lucas finally got a move on. Shannon followed Lucas to the pickup to finish interviewing him.

Gabe hung back long enough to give Seth a bro-hug—he must have wanted to get in on the action also—during which Nate actually moved closer rather than backed off. Once done, Gabe flicked a glance at him and then asked them both, "How long do you reckon you'll keep this place *haunted*?"

Grimacing, Seth told him the truth. "Shannon's editor would only agree to print a false story on Halloween if we played it off as a gimmick in the next edition." For a week, everyone who read the paper would think the place was legit haunted. But people would forgive a lot in the spirit of holidays.

Plus, to some people, the name Larson still carried weight in this town. That or the editor wanted to hug Grandma as much as Seth's friends did.

"Well, don't worry about Lucas. I'll break it to him once you've accomplished whatever it is you're aiming at here." He gave the house an appraising look over Seth's head. "Trying to sell the place, huh? Doesn't your uncle have some say in that?"

Seth snorted, and apparently that was answer enough for Gabe.

CHAPTER TWENTY-TWO

The stretch of beach was about as desolate as you could get, which was one of the reasons it was a regular spot for *Wolf's Landing* location shoots—at night anyway. During the day, it was something of a tourist attraction for show fans, since it was the same spot where Levi had broken character to declare his love for Carter the first time.

That must be why the two of them were gazing into each other's eyes as if they were alone on the shore and not surrounded by crew setting up lights and checking camera angles, Levi touching Carter's hand or arm or face as if he required the connection. Carter was soaking it up like oxygen, and the look on his face ... *God.*

Nate was so there with Seth—and there were *signs* that Seth might be thinking long-term too. He patted his pocket, where he'd tucked the note from Seth, inviting him to go crabbing. *A handwritten invitation.* How freaking charming was that?

"Yo, Nate." Morgan waved a hand in front of his face. "You in there?"

Nate blinked. "Yeah. Sorry."

"You've been a thousand miles away all night. Time to get your head in the game, don't you think, since you're about to set Ginsberg and C.J. on fire?"

Nate squinted at the clouds scudding across the sky, at the actors' clothes flapping in the stiff breeze. "Not unless this wind dies down. Too risky."

"Tell that to the asshole." Morgan nodded at Finn, who was gesturing wildly at a glowering Anna.

"What the hell is his problem now?"

"Budget. What do you think?"

Finn's voice carried to them easily. "Do you know what this shoot is costing? Not only our crew but the firefighter paramedics too. Can we just get on with it? There's nothing flammable on the frigging beach for half a mile."

"If you don't count the actors," Nate muttered. "No way can we do this stunt tonight unless the weather report is right for a change and things calm down at midnight."

"Absolutely not." Anna's tone brooked no argument. "Give it up, Finn. We're not going to stage a dangerous stunt in unsafe conditions just to make the bean-counters happy. Now get out of my way so I can at least film *something* tonight."

Finn stomped away from Anna, his dramatic exit somewhat impaired by the way his loafers took on sand. Before he completely escaped the nimbus of the floodlights, though, his expression changed from angry to satisfied.

Morgan raised her eyebrows. "Nothing good has *ever* followed Finn looking that smug. Come on." She held her finger over her lips and nodded to where Finn had stopped beyond the makeup trailer, his cell phone to his ear. She gestured for Nate to follow her.

You're going to hell, he mouthed. But apparently he'd be joining her there, because he let her lead the way to a spot shielded by the trailer.

"That's right," Finn said gleefully. "Weather conditions again. This makes how many times? Yeah, if this doesn't convince the other producers to switch to CGI— I'll email the cost overruns to you tonight."

As Finn's footsteps crunched away, Nate shared a troubled glance with Morgan. "If he finally convinces them to go with the green screen SFX—"

"He won't. Anna won't allow it. *Hunter* won't allow it, and Hunter is God—or at least Oz, the great and powerful, remember."

"Yeah, but—"

"Nate! Morgan! We're switching to the boat fight. Could you set up, please?"

"Sure, Anna." Nate trudged down the beach to one of several rowboats that was about to meet its doom. While he still had a job, he might as well do it right.

Four hours later, though, the wind still hadn't abated, and they'd gone through all six of the break-away boats. On the last take, Ginsberg had face-planted in the sand just as a sneaker wave had overrun the set, soaking his wig. Suyin had torn the makeup trailer apart but couldn't find the backup wig, so Anna had called a dinner break while a PA made an emergency trip to the production lot.

Nate was in no mood to dine with everyone at the craft services tent, so he, Morgan, and a handful of other crew had driven a few miles up the highway to a roadhouse that had barely adequate burgers.

"We probably should have stuck with craft services." Morgan tossed her napkin on the table. "At least their salads aren't brown around the edges."

"Sorry. I needed some space."

She patted his arm. "I know, baby. But I'm telling you, you don't have anything to worry about."

"Morgan, we *all* have something to worry about. Even if Finn doesn't win this battle, this show can't last forever. At some point it'll be over."

She shrugged. "So? That's the nature of this business. We didn't get into it because we wanted to sit at the same desk for forty years in exchange for a gold watch and a retirement party."

"I know, but . . ." Damn it, he'd started putting down roots—or at least entangling himself with a guy who had roots so deep they went back over a century. "I gotta pee before we head back."

"Take your time."

Nate was so exhausted that for a moment, standing at the urinal, staring at the wall, he didn't register what he was seeing. Bathroom graffiti was a given at dives like this—crude dick pictures, unimaginative insults, misogynistic bull-crap. The words and numbers scrawled in front of him were typical: *For a good time, call:* followed by a phone number.

A phone number he recognized. *Seth's phone number. Not Seth's handwriting.*

Nate's brain snapped back on line with a vengeance as anger curled in his chest like a rabid tiger. This was on par with the way Seth had been outed in high school—an involuntary advertisement, a total invasion of privacy. Nobody had the right to do that. *Not to Seth.* Not to anyone.

He zipped up, washed his hands, and stalked out of the john. "Morgan. I need your Sharpie."

"What makes you think I have a Sharpie?"

"You always have a Sharpie. You always have three. I need the black one."

She cocked an eyebrow at him, but pulled a black Sharpie out of her go-bag. "Remind me to stop being so damn predictable."

"Dependable, not predictable." He all but snatched the thing out of her hand. "Thanks." He stormed back to the john, shouldering one of the grips out of the way at the door. "Sorry. Won't be a minute."

Once inside, he locked the door. Uncapping the Sharpie, he changed all the threes in the phone number to eights. For good measure, he changed the one to a seven. *There.* Even if that was a real number, no way would it be local enough to get anyone in trouble. Later he could come back with some industrial-strength cleaner and remove the whole thing. He froze with his hand on the doorknob. *How many other johns from here to Sequim have the same graffiti, the same implicit claim that Seth is nothing but a good-time, no-strings guy?*

"He's not that," Nate muttered as he flung open the door and scared the grip into fumbling his coffee cup. "He's more. So much more." *And he's mine.*

Finally—at about two in the morning—they'd managed the fire effect. It went off without a hitch, thank God, and they were able to strike the set by three thirty. By the time Nate got home, he was dead on his feet, so he should have fallen into bed and passed out.

But for some reason—maybe the coffee he'd sucked down on location just to keep his hands from freezing—as soon as he walked in the door, he got an unwanted second wind, so he stomped upstairs to his computer. When he woke up the monitor, the first thing he saw was an email from Bailey, his online genealogy friend with the hard-on for Hollywood history. He opened the message. *Three attachments? Seriously?* Christ, Bailey got more wound up in his research than Nate did, which was saying something.

Nate opened the first attachment, containing a series of articles about the two suffragists and their actions in the Los Angeles area.

Harriet and Mamie Rose apparently had found their calling, working with the young women who'd flocked to Hollywood for a chance to be stars in the fledgling film industry, but instead ended up penniless, starving and/or victims of the male-dominated studios. They frequently mentioned their housekeeper, Mei, and why she'd been raising her grandson. Nate was relieved to note that the boy, although he'd been named after his father before Adeline's ill-fated visit, was now going by Morey Larson.

The next attachment was all about Morey. Apparently, he'd gotten in on the ground floor of the film industry too. At first he'd just been a driver for Famous Players-Lasky, but apparently had been so adept at keeping volatile stars out of trouble that he'd risen in the studio management hierarchy. The list of "incidents" he'd helped cover up—with connections in the corrupt police force and DA's office—was truly hair-raising. He'd married a Swedish silent film starlet, had three kids—a son, named after him, and two daughters— and died of a heart attack at fifty-eight.

His son had stayed in Hollywood too, although he'd been a director, not a "fixer" like his father. He'd gravitated to television and married an heiress, for God's sake, but not until later in life. They'd had only one child, a son, whose name was—

"Holy shit."

Finn Larson.

CHAPTER TWENTY-THREE

Seth's grand scheme to get them the heck out of Dodge on Halloween—the day the haunting story came out—didn't go exactly as planned. To crab this time of year, he had to take them past the Tatoosh-Bonilla line. Seth got them out in the open ocean and looked over to see the excitement on Nate's face, only to discover the guy'd gone green.

Under questioning, Nate confessed to being afraid of large bodies of water. Seth tried to take them back to shore, but Nate wouldn't let him. "I've gotten this far, the least you can do is catch me crab."

So Seth did. Because if Nate wanted it, he wanted to provide.

Plus, knowing the guy had gone crabbing with him just because it made Seth happy was a huge turn-on.

Watching a sexy man eating crab . . . that was almost more erotic than Seth could handle. They'd begun dinner with Nate's spectacular cioppino, which was the only reason Seth had gotten any food in his stomach. After that, his own crab lay in front of him, half-forgotten, because he couldn't stop looking at the guy next to him. The dab of butter on Nate's chin highlighted his cleft, and he kept closing his eyes as he ate, savoring the taste. To add to Seth's enjoyment, Nate proved, over and over, that he could suck the meat right out of a crab leg.

By the time they'd finished, Seth was half-hard simply from good food, good company, and good tongue technique. A mind-movie began on his internal screen—straddling Nate in his chair and riding him.

Instead he jerked himself out of his seat, then, since he was standing anyway, took their plates to the sink and scraped them, his heart attempting to lunge out of his rib cage the entire time.

So far, they'd only been together that once, due to conflicting schedules, and Seth had been following Nate's lead, then.

If Nate started something, Seth was at least assured that Nate wasn't—*say it*—making love with him only because *he* wanted it. Nate wanted it too. And the way Nate looked at him and how he touched Seth's naked skin was almost reverent.

He wants me. Not sex, but sex with me.

It was of paramount importance to Seth that he was making love with Nate.

Earlier today, just being with Nate had been enough for him. It gave him what he'd ached for most when they hadn't been together—closeness. Intimacy. Being able to touch Nate whenever he wanted, even if it was just a hand on his arm or a kiss dropped on his cheek, had been enough at first.

Tonight he wanted more, though, a lot more. He wanted to see Nate respond to him. Be affected by his touch. He just didn't know exactly how to begin.

He was afraid. Of making a move. He hadn't figured out what was okay and what wasn't between them, hadn't found the boundaries.

He'd never find them if he didn't take a chance.

Done rinsing the plates, he set them carefully in the sink, then considered taking out the trash—they'd need to tonight so the place didn't start to smell. *Not now, stop stalling.* Turning, he braced his hands on the counter behind him, ready to make his move.

Nate stopped him, though. Or rather, this view of Nate—his black wavy hair streaked with just a little gray and still tousled from their day on the water. Those long, strong fingers idly fiddling with the salt shaker while his beautiful lips quirked up with the glimmer of a smile.

He was so . . . *amazing.* Perfect in some ways and perfectly flawed in others.

This is probably what love feels like. Being in love.

I'm in love with Nate Albano.

Does he love me? Heart now trying desperately to jump up his throat, Seth went back to the table, standing next to Nate. When Nate looked up, he straddled one of his thighs and leaned down closer to him, moving in for a kiss. A real one, not the small, affectionate kind. Taking the initiative for the first time.

If Nate rebuffed him, it might kill him.

Nate kissed him back, though, tilting his head up and stroking Seth's beard with his free hand. He opened right up when Seth nudged his lips, asking to be let in.

Success. When Seth ended it, pulling away to gaze into Nate's gray eyes, he was lightheaded. Too dizzy to go further right now—too dizzy to *stand*—he ass-planted in the seat next to him.

Nate didn't seem to notice his dorkiness. He turned sideways toward him and trapped one of Seth's legs between his own, then reached out, cupping his hand over Seth's knee and squeezing it, fingers resting on Seth's jeans. "You wanna move this into the bedroom?"

"In a minute." Seth took his hand, playing with the thumb, caressing it. "Did you have fun today?"

Nate quirked an eyebrow. "You know I did."

Because he'd already asked, a couple of times. "Except for the, you know, terror of the high seas."

Leaning closer to him, Nate said, "Today was amazing. Thank you for taking me," then kissed him briefly, pulling back just far enough to look into his eyes. As if he understood Seth needed to drive things tonight.

"They don't call me the good-time guy for nothing." Seth could feel his face heating up, but he didn't drop Nate's gaze. "Thank *you*," he murmured, then lifted Nate's hand and swirled his tongue around Nate's thumb before sucking it into his mouth. From under his lashes, he watched Nate's pupils dilate and his eyelids lower.

That was a hell of a beautiful response to his touch. It made him want to do a lot more of it.

Releasing Nate's thumb with a last slurp, Seth stood and held out his hand in front of him. His erection was right in Nate's line of vision now, and Nate gave it a flattering amount of his attention.

"Where are you taking me?" he asked Seth's groin.

Seth took the liberty of speaking for his dick. "Bedroom."

Nate stood and let Seth lead him away from the table and into the bedroom. Not like their first time, in a stumbling mass of tangled bodies and hormones. More sedately, until Seth reached the edge of

Nate's bed, where he turned to slide his arms around Nate's shoulders and kiss him, pulling him down onto the mattress with him. There was nothing sedate about *that*.

After their first time together, Seth had worried that the piñata effect was a one-time thing. That, once burst open, his heart was spent. Now, he was happy to find that it was a self-healing organ, already swelling with happiness. He'd never felt that before, that sex involved much more of him than his physical body. It was as if he'd discovered a sixth sensory organ. Or an extra penis. *Heart penis.*

Yeah, no.

"What are you laughing about?" Nate whispered, kissing Seth's smile. Pressing on his shoulders, he propped himself over him when Seth lay back.

"Just—" He kissed Nate's insistent mouth before finishing. "I was thinking dorky things. About myself. About how you make me feel."

"How's that?" The words were as much of a caress as Nate's lips and fingers, brushing gently across Seth's skin and making him shiver.

"How do I feel? About you?" Working his hands under Nate's T-shirt, he peeled it up his back, tracing the bumps of his spine. Before he answered, he pulled the shirt over Nate's head, skimming it along his arms and watching the skin pebble up at his touch. "Does it matter?" he teased.

"Yes." Nate's brows bunched, as if he actually thought Seth might be serious.

Seth smoothed them out with his fingertips, soothing the inner Nate with words. "I know it does."

"So how do I make you feel?" Nate wasn't playing any more, he needed an answer.

Gah. Just say it. "Cared for." *Definitely blushing.* He could barely keep his gaze connected with Nate's. "And caring." As a declaration it was kind of weak. His self-protective instincts skittered away from saying it outright—the L-word—though he knew one thing he *had* to tell him now. Seth placed his palms on either side of Nate's face and held him still. "I've never felt like this about anyone else. Ever."

"Good," Nate breathed. "That's a—a good thing." Nate kissed him for real, then, no playing around anymore. Then he began the serious business of working Seth's shirt over his head. After, Seth executed a sneaky leg lock and rolled them both, still wrapped around each other, so that he was on top.

He pulled away until their lips were barely separated. His rubbed against Nate's as he spoke. "There's something I want to do."

He felt rather than saw the muscles in Nate's jaw tense up. "Yeah?"

"Yeah." Holding his breath, he waited a second for Nate's response. "Okay." Nate swallowed.

As Seth worked his way down Nate's naked chest and abdomen, muscles all over him got more tense rather than less, even with Seth using his gentlest touches. "Relax," he whispered, then dipped his tongue in Nate's belly button.

Nate squirmed. Okay, yeah, not the most calming caress. Seth switched his focus, tracing the lines of Nate's ribs with his lips, speaking as he did. "It's nothing weird. Not kinky. I just want to . . . taste you."

Why he chickened out at the last second he wasn't positive but it probably had to do with the term *blowjob* seeming so out of place when talking about them, together. Nate would understand wouldn't he?

Seth tangled his fingers in the thickest line of Nate's hair, the one that arrowed down from his navel. Following it until he could dig his fingertips under Nate's waistband, he pulled open the top button of Nate's jeans. That *pop* was such a satisfying sound. Also satisfying was the way Nate rolled his hips as Seth unwrapped him slowly. *Now* he was relaxed.

Time to wind up his sexual tension.

When he pulled Nate's pants off, he followed them all the way down, rubbing a cheek against Nate's erection while exploring his legs. They were as furry as the rest of him, of course, and strong. He took off Nate's boxer briefs in the same teasing way, only coming back up to his dick when he had him completely naked.

Nate's skin reached its full glory on his cock. A delicious shade of purple red. "Fine wine."

"What?" Nate gusted a brief laugh.

"The color of your dick." Seth kissed it. "It's burgundy."

When he pulled it into his mouth, Nate gasped. Like everything else with Nate, this was completely different. That extra sense guided him, and for the first time in his life, sucking cock was emotional as well as physical. Underneath all the normal sensations—the taste of Nate's skin and the smell of his body and the stroke of Nate's fingers on his face—was another layer Seth had never known was there. A part of Nate that was more energy than mass, and responded to Seth's touch, and even shared the sensations with him. When he moved his tongue a certain way or took him especially deep, he could feel it as a ghost touch on his own dick, and it made him crazy. He wanted it to be good for Nate, because he wanted *everything* to be good for him, but also because that made it better for himself, which made him want to make it better for Nate and so on, until Seth was writhing, nearly ready to come against the sheets, heart deafening in his ears.

Just as Nate was about to explode—Seth could sense it, right there, reaching for him—he sat, curling his body over Seth's, and touched him everywhere he could reach, all at once, as if he couldn't stand coming on his own and he was trying to increase that biofeedback loop. Nate's groan vibrated in Seth's throat, and when he came, Seth only had to touch his own dick before he was too, a beat behind Nate's orgasm and surfing its waves.

When he hauled himself up Nate's body and snuggled up to Nate's chest, they were both breathing hard. Nate worked his hand under Seth's chin, into his beard, and tilted it so he could kiss him. So deep it felt almost like sucking him off again. He rolled so they were side by side, gentling his kisses slowly. Seth wasn't sure when they stopped exactly, just that eventually they were lying there, his forehead against Nate's chin and Nate's arm weighing him down. Keeping him there.

Good. Seth wasn't planning on letting go of him, either.

When Nate awoke the next morning, Seth was cuddled against his side, his head on Nate's chest. Seth hadn't put any product on after his post-crabbing shower last night, and now his hair was soft and a little flyaway against Nate's neck and chin. Nate found it incredibly endearing—as if Seth had lowered all his shields, trusting Nate to see him without artifice.

Last night had been . . . unexpected—a word Nate was starting to associate entirely with Seth. It could be his epithet—the unexpected

Seth Larson. Or his superhero power: Seth the Unexpected, surprising even the most jaded of opponents. Nate had no desire to be an opponent though—after last night, *partner* echoed in his heart as a deep contentment settled into his bones.

Seth murmured in his sleep and snuggled closer, and Nate tightened his arm around him. *Wonder what he'll decide to do, now that he'll have the chance to follow his dreams?* What were his dreams, exactly? It wasn't like he'd ever had the opportunity to do anything about them, not with his family using him as unpaid labor for the last decade or more. With his eclectic skillset, he could do anything he wanted.

Nate cataloged possible careers for Seth in his mind. Would he be interested in a job on *Wolf's Landing*? Excitement tingled in Nate's belly. *That would be perfect.* If Seth got into one of the tech departments—set construction, for instance, which he could totally do, if his work on Sentinel House was any example—then he'd be qualified for other jobs in Hollywood once the show wound down and they had to leave Bluewater Bay.

He dropped a kiss on the top of Seth's head, which made him nestle closer and fling an arm across Nate's stomach.

Nice. But I really need to pee. He slipped out of bed, chuckling when Seth made grabbing motions against the sheets. "I'll be right back."

"You better," Seth mumbled into the pillow.

Always.

Humming as he pulled on his briefs, Nate strolled to the bathroom to take care of business. As he washed up, he eyed the shower. Would Seth be up for a little shower massage, so to speak? Nate had never gone that route before, but it might be fun to try it with Seth. *I want to try everything with him.*

His earlier contentment amped up, fizzing in his veins like one of Seth's magical cocktails. Not just contentment. Anticipation. Hope. *Joy.* Seth had awoken new desires in him that he'd never had before, and Nate intended to cherish every one of them.

In return, he'd do whatever it took to make sure Seth was free to pursue his ambitions, to achieve his full potential without the burden of his family's obligations. Nate winced when he remembered the bomb he still hadn't dropped—that Seth's family included another member who'd be about as welcome as an outbreak of Ebola.

Finn Larson. Christ. Despite Nate's assurances to Seth that douchebaggery wasn't an inherited trait, Finn seemed to be a solid argument in favor of nature vs. nurture. He was also a money-focused guy with an eye to the main chance. Hard to tell what he'd do once *he* found out the truth. Would he try to challenge the Larson trust—and if he did, would it be a good thing or a bad thing? Maybe Seth would know. So as much as Nate hated to break the peace of their morning, it was time to come clean. *Then* maybe they'd try out the shower.

When he got out of the bathroom, Seth was sitting up, blinking sleepily. He stretched, a lovely arch of his spine. "Morning."

"Hey." Nate strolled over and sat on the edge of the bed, capturing Seth's hand and kissing his palm. "Do you have to work today?"

"Nope. Day off. How about you?"

"Night shoot, so the day is free." He toyed with Seth's fingers. "So there's something we need to talk about."

Seth eyed him warily. "That's kind of a loaded statement. Is this a good talk or a bad talk?"

My question exactly. "I'm not entirely sure." Nate swung his legs onto the bed and draped his arm across Seth's shoulders. For an instant, Seth stayed tense before tucking himself against Nate's side. "So the other night, we were on the beach for a night shoot, and Finn Larson showed up."

"He's like a bad penny, isn't he? Whatever that means."

"I actually know that. Back in the—" Nate shook his head and kissed Seth's temple. "Never mind, but I totally get your point. Just to get away from him, Morgan and I bailed on craft services and drove to the Roadhouse for our dinner break."

"I don't blame you. I'd probably go there and risk food poisoning or a beer bottle in the head if the alternative was dinner with Finn Larson."

Nate shifted uncomfortably, then rested his chin on the top of Seth's head. No way would Seth take the Big Finn Reveal well. Did Nate really want to bring the guy into the room with them—hell, into bed with them? Maybe he should pick a better time—

"Go on." Seth poked him in the ribs, making him flinch. "Oho. Ticklish, eh?"

"Yes." Nate grabbed Seth's hand before he could land another jab, and the little chuckle that escaped as he nestled close again pinged all Nate's protective circuits. Hard. But how could he protect Seth from something rooted so far in the past? *I can't.* On the other hand, that same night he'd done one thing that had had an immediate effect—one thing he could be proud of. "Funny thing, though. While we were at the Roadhouse, I went into the restroom."

"Wow, you were all kinds of daredevil, weren't you?"

"What can I say? I guess Ginsberg's rubbing off on me. Well, I mean not, you know, *that* kind of rubbing off—"

Seth laughed, sending vibrations through Nate's chest. "Relax, Nate. I'm so over your accidental awkward innuendos."

"Thank God for that. Anyway, I found your phone number on the wall over the urinal."

"Huh?" Seth pulled back far enough to meet Nate's gaze. "Really?"

"Yeah. Along with the old 'For a good time, call' chestnut."

This time, Seth pulled away, tensing under Nate's arm. "It was probably— Listen, this guy, Evan? He came into the bar last week and he was looking for some . . . you know. Some."

Nate squeezed Seth's shoulder. "I know about that. I heard you talking to Gabe at the haunting."

"Thought so," Seth muttered, then took a deep breath. "I tried to tell him—Evan—I *told* him I wasn't into anything with him anymore, like, ever, and he didn't take it well. I mean, you heard what Gabe said—"

"Yeah." Scowling, Nate tightened his grip. "And Gabe should have stepped up and told Evan to shove it right then." That earned him an eye roll, and when he tried to pull Seth against him, he met resistance. "I don't think this was related though—looked like it had been there a while." He dropped his scowl, attempting a smile if that would get Seth to lean into him again. "I had your crabbing invitation in my pocket, so I could tell it wasn't your handwriting—"

"Hold on a second." Jerking away, Seth scrambled to the other side of the bed and turned to stare at Nate. "You *compared* the writing? Wait, you seriously had to *make sure* I wasn't trolling for sex in the

Roadhouse bathroom? What the *fuck*, man?" Throwing off the sheet, Seth stood, then immediately bent to grab his briefs off the floor.

"No! I mean you and Gabe talked about your old rep, and just last night you said they didn't call you the good time guy for nothing." Okay, forget the eye roll—that look was a total glare of death. "But this—well, it was obvious it wasn't you who'd done it, but that's not the point."

Yanking his underwear on, Seth planted his hands on his waist, face like a thundercloud. "Well, then, Nate . . ." his voice was ominously polite, "what exactly *is* the point?"

The hell if he knew. How had he fallen down this rabbit hole anyway? He'd been trying to avoid the Finn Larson shit pile and instead put his foot in an even bigger one. "I just wanted you to know that I fixed it. I borrowed Morgan's Sharpie and changed the number, so nobody will bother you anymore."

Seth threw his arms in the air, exasperation clear in his expression. "Jesus, Nate, nobody actually *calls* those numbers."

"But they could, and *that's* the point." He kneeled on the mattress, wishing he had more on than a pair of briefs. "It's personal information, Seth. *Your* personal information. It should be your decision when and how and *who* to share it with—not have it broadcast to any asshole taking a piss at the Roadhouse. This violated *your* privacy, *your* choices—like when you were outed in high school."

Seth's jaw dropped, and he sucked in a sharp breath. "I cannot *believe* you just said that." He turned and walked out of the bedroom, the sunlight on his bare skin doing nothing to soften the line of his spine or the tension in his shoulders.

Ah shit. Nate practically fell off the bed in his haste to follow, snatching a pair of sweatpants off the hook on the back of the door and trying not to break his neck as he struggled to step into them and walk at the same time. "Seth. Wait. That didn't come out right. I was trying to protect you, that's all."

Seth already had his jeans on and didn't even look at him, just continued scrabbling for something under the couch as Tarkus sniffed his hair. "Are you really sure it was me you were protecting? Because from my perspective, it looks more like you were trying to protect yourself from my past."

"That's not it at all. Your past is irrelevant." He wrapped his arms across his stomach, gooseflesh rising on his arms from more than the chilly air. "Why is it a bad thing for me to want to look out for you?"

Seth stood up, his socks balled in his fist. "I'm thirty, Nate. I can look out for myself."

Nate blinked. "You're thirty? I assumed— That is, you seem younger."

"Is that why you've gone all paternalistic on me?" He dropped down on the sofa and yanked one of his socks on. "You think I'm a child?"

"Of course I don't."

"Then why treat me like one?" Seth yanked on the other sock.

"That wasn't my intention. I'm sorry if it seemed that way." Nate skirted the sofa, and although he desperately wanted to sit next to Seth, to touch him, ground them both, he remained standing. "If it had been Morgan's number on that wall, I'd have done exactly the same thing."

The tension drained out of Seth's shoulders, and he hunched forward, hands dangling between his knees. "Shit. I guess I might have too . . . I kind of overreacted, huh?" He patted the cushion next to him, and Nate accepted the invitation before Tarkus could zip in ahead of him. "How did we end up talking about this, anyway?"

Nate rested his hand on Seth's back and breathed a relieved sigh when he didn't pull away. *Dodged a bullet there.* Although Seth was still a little tense under his touch. "Finn Larson."

"Right." Seth snorted. "That dude can stir up shit when he's not even around. What was he doing at your shoot anyway? Is that a normal thing?"

"More normal than we like. But this time, he had an agenda. He's got it into his head that CGI would be more cost-effective than practical effects."

"Would it be?"

Nate shrugged. "Filming all those action scenes against a green screen? I kind of doubt it, but I'm not a CGI jockey. If he has his way, though, I'll be out of a job."

Seth turned to him, eyes wide. "But it might not happen, right? How much of a possibility is this?"

"Oh it'll happen someday. One way or another, we both know my job in Bluewater Bay is short-term. It could happen tomorrow, if Finn prevails, or if the fans hop on a new bandwagon, or if Hunter Easton decides he'd rather write about zombie motorcycle gangs than werewolf cops."

Seth grabbed Nate's hand. "But . . . that means—"

"It means we should be prepared for possible futures, that's all." *Aaand the kid goes for broke.* He kissed Seth's forehead. "So here's the thing. I'm in this relationship for the long haul, you do get that?"

Seth nodded. "And I told *you* that I care for you, a lot. I even . . . I'm *serious* about you." He gestured between the two of them. "About this."

"Thank God. We're on the same page, then." He pressed a kiss on Seth's lips this time. "So I was thinking. Now that we're on the verge of getting your family off your back, I could check with the head of the set department, maybe get you a job on *Wolf's Landing.*"

"But . . ." Seth's brow puckered, and he retrieved his shirt from the floor. "Why? I've already got a job."

"I know, but without your family obligations tying you down, you've got other opportunities. You've got the skills for an entry-level set carpenter, and I know you'd move up fast once they got to know you." He grinned and flicked a lock of Seth's hair. "You'd be primed for department head once we get to Hollywood."

"You're making a lot of assumptions, Nate." Seth's voice carried a warning edge as he pulled on his shirt, causing Nate's belly to tighten with worry. "Why would you think I'd want to work on that stupid show? Or in Hollywood?"

"Oh." Nate laughed nervously. "Right. You're not a fan. The entertainment industry is the world I know, where I've got connections and could do you the most good, but that's not your only option. Would you rather go back to school? You could turn your bartender amateur psychotherapy into a *real* counseling degree."

Seth's scowl had melted into a cool, almost contemptuous smirk and Nate's palms started to sweat.

God, I'm screwing this up. He chuckled, a pitiful thing laced with nerves. "But if you don't like psychology, something else. I mean, you don't want to be a bartender all your life, right?"

Seth lifted his chin—Christ, were those tears glittering in his eyes? "And what if I did?"

"But—" Nate swallowed, trying to switch his train of thought onto a different track. "Look, all I want is for you to be happy. Whatever shape your happiness takes is fine with me—as long as I'm part of the picture."

"What would make me happy—" Seth scooted away until his back was pressed against the sofa arm "—is knowing you think I'm good enough for you."

Nate reared back. "What? You're good enough. You're *better* than good enough."

"As long as I'm not a bartender." He didn't phrase it as a question.

"I didn't say that. But you've got so much potential. Why would you want to—"

"To waste my life? Is that what you were about to say?"

"I—"

"Because if it was, you can save your fucking breath. I've heard it all before. Everyone, from my first-grade teacher on, yammering on about my fucking *potential*." He crossed his arms, closing him off from any possibility of touch. "You know why I stuck it out as the Sentinel House handyman all these years? Not to impress anyone or fulfill somebody else's expectations, but because I *like* it, and because I wanted to help the one person who's never told me I'm not good enough for them—Grandma."

"But . . . but that's the point. Your grandmother will be out of the house, and you'll both be commitment-free. You can do whatever you want. You can do so much better—"

"Aren't you even *listening*? I *wanted* to help Grandma and I *like* being a bartender." Seth stood up and crossed to the French doors where his shoes lay jumbled in a pile with Nate's. Tarkus followed, nudging Seth's hand until he relented and scratched his ears. "Letting other people plan my life never did shit for me, and I decided a while ago that I'd only be meeting my own expectations, no one else's."

"I can understand that."

"Do you?" Seth gaze was intense. "I'm not so sure. Because you're giving me a whole new set of standards to meet—your own. Why would I want to exchange one set of expectations for another?"

"That's not— I didn't mean it like that. Why can't I want what's best for you?"

"You know what? *I* get to decide what's best for me, and I like the way I am. If that makes me beneath the great Nate Bedrosian/Albano, heir to a goddamned Hollywood dynasty, so be it." He wiped his hands on his jeans, brushing off Tarkus fur, his lips pressed in a thin line. "It's a huge disappointment for me too, finding out you're a fucking snob and I can never make the grade."

Nate's jaw dropped, and the air whooshed out of his lungs. "I don't— I've *never* thought of myself that way. And I definitely don't think of you as *less.*"

"No?" Seth lifted his chin. "Then why didn't you introduce me to your mother that night at the play?"

"It—it didn't occur to me."

"Of course it didn't," Seth muttered, then opened the door to let Tarkus outside.

"Come on, Seth, cut me a break here. I hadn't seen her face-to-face in fourteen years. Don't you think I might have been a little gobsmacked?"

"How hard would it have been? I was standing right there."

"Hell, *I* didn't want to be standing right there."

"Oh, so you were doing me *another* favor?" He kicked Nate's shoes aside to free his own. "Protecting me from your mother—or were you really protecting yourself? Keeping your underachieving 'friend' on the down-low?"

"Is that how you see yourself? As my dirty little secret?" Nate thrust himself off the sofa and stood, hands fisted at his sides. "Christ, Seth, I haven't exactly tried to hide you."

"No. Just *change* me, with all your suggestions about monetized blogs and Victorian renovations and, Jesus, *psychology*? Seriously, Nate?" He shoved his feet into his shoes. "You know what? I'm done." Seth stalked toward the front door, the untied laces of his sneakers clacking on the wood floor with each step. He grabbed his jacket from the back of a barstool as he passed.

Fear and anger and despair tangled in Nate's brain, darkening his vision at the edges. "That's it? You're walking out on me too?" *Just like Jorge.*

Seth froze with his hand on the doorknob. "What do you mean, 'too'?"

"It's pretty obvious, isn't it?" Steeling himself so he wouldn't break down, Nate's tone was a little more contemptuous than he wanted. *Leaving? Please don't leave.* "Good-time guys aren't into commitment. They always bail before shit gets real."

The way Seth's face paled and shut down—*God, that was the wrong thing to say. Why did I say that?*

"Yeah," Seth said, voice wooden. "I guess I *am* meeting your expectations." Then he turned and *walked the fuck out.*

"Seth?" Nate shook off his paralysis and rushed across the room to stand in the open door, the cold wind against his chest reminding him he was still half-naked—not that it mattered. Nothing mattered except Seth, slamming his car into gear and peeling out of the driveway.

Nate's knees buckled, and he sat down in the open doorway with a thump. *Alone again.* God knew he ought to be used to it by now. Why the hell had he imagined this time would be any different?

CHAPTER TWENTY-FOUR

Seth made it home on autopilot, not really aware of driving or even climbing his own stairs. How long he stood there after letting himself in the door, he didn't know, but eventually he came to frozen in his entryway, staring at his tiny apartment.

Wondering how it was that discovering he was Nate's guilty pleasure made him feel dirtier than years of casually sleeping around ever had. He'd worried so much about proving that he was committed to Nate that he'd forgotten a guy like him might not be good enough to commit *to*, not without meeting some expectations first.

Met one of his expectations though, didn't I? He threw his keys onto the spindly table in the entry, hard enough that it marred the surface. It didn't make him feel any fucking better—the scratch he'd put in the wood seemed uncomfortably familiar too. His heart had wounds like that all over, and then some.

Should have listened better. He should have realized that when Nate made comments about starting a blog or carpentry work, what it really meant was that the guy had a yardstick for acceptable partners and was measuring Seth against it. If he'd listened, he'd have realized someone who'd learned to be happy with what he had wouldn't be good enough for a guy like that. He didn't approach life seriously enough, and didn't have the kind of motivation that counted.

"Ugh." Yanking down the zipper of his jacket, he let it fall off of his arms and onto the floor, then flung himself onto the settee like a wounded teenager. It screeched a foot or two across the floor when he landed.

And fuck, the *outing*. He'd told Nate about high school because he *trusted* him, emotionally, not so Nate could use it to prove some point in the middle of an argument. Jesus, wasn't it enough that he'd had to tell him about "fixing" that fucking graffiti?

What had the guy even been trying to say?

Squeezing his eyes shut tightly, Seth tried to remember. Something about protecting him. Nate had even told him like it was some kind of favor he'd done—as if it wasn't an issue at all. As if Seth's whole *past* wasn't an issue.

Maybe because for him, it's not.

"Fuck." He let his head flop back on the couch, staring at the ceiling for answers. Is *it only my issue?*

That couldn't be right, otherwise why had Nate needed to mention the graffiti at all? Did he think Seth *wanted* to know there was shit like that out there? No, Nate had done it because he wanted to prove something.

Again with the proving shit. Proving he'd protect Seth to the best of his abilities.

Okay, that can't be right either, because it doesn't sound that bad.

Kind of paternalistic, but . . . sweet. *If he's sweet, why does this hurt so much?*

He tried to hunt down the causes for his pain again. He caught a flash of it, of the hurt, but it was like he was chasing a ghost down a long, interminable hallway. Hard to make out and impossible to catch. So instead he turned to the other new feature in his emotional self: the spot in his heart that belonged to Nate.

It was bruised, yes, but not destroyed. There was still life in it. Fuck, letting it die was going to be painful. Because what he'd said was true—he couldn't be happy unless Nate believed he was good enough as he was. He needed someone who could look at him and *not* find him lacking.

He'd believed he had. Damn, he'd really fooled himself, hadn't he?

His eyes prickled painfully. Taking the teenager theme further, he covered them with his hands, digging the heels into his sockets hard, trying to make everything go black. Stop the ache from spreading. But again, he was fooling himself, because the throbbing hollowness had started in his chest and migrated out from there. All he was accomplishing was to keep it from spilling out of him.

Trapping it inside might kill him, though. *Fuck this.*

Shoving himself upright—which the settee protested by creaking angrily—he stood and started undressing. If he was going to cry, he was going to go do it in the shower like a real man. An adult one.

"Hellooo," Morgan called as she walked in the door. "I knocked, but you—" She stopped, probably wondering what the hell Nate was doing sitting on the floor next to Tarkus's bed. "Nate? Did you forget you were supposed to help me load tonight's pieces into my truck?"

He blinked at the westering sunlight splashed across the living room floor and struggled to his feet. "Shit. What time is it?"

"Nearly five. Our call isn't until ten, but I thought we could get this out of the way in case you had dinner plans with Cute Bartender." She grinned and fluttered her eyelashes.

"I don't."

Morgan's smile faded as she scrutinized his face. God knew what he looked like. He certainly felt like eighty miles of rough road. "Baby, what's wrong?" She opened her arms as if to hug him, but he stepped back, warding off her touch, palms out.

"Stop. Please."

"Jesus, what happened? Is Seth okay?"

Nate choked on a laugh. "How would I know? He walked out." His breath got lost somewhere south of his heart. "He . . . walked. Out." He whirled and slammed his fist into the sofa cushions, causing Tarkus to cower in his bed, ears flattened. Christ, now he was terrorizing his dog too. His shoulders began to shake with the effort to hold himself together. "He fucking walked *out*, Morgan."

Her keys clattered to the floor, then she was there, gripping his shoulders with her strong, capable hands. She gave him a little shake. "Step back from the ledge, baby, come on. Seth is *not* Jorge. He's not seeing someone on the side."

"I know he's not like Jorge, but what if he's like me? I walked out too—on my mother. For fourteen years. This is probably karma—I'll be paying for it for another twelve lifetimes." Or twelve relationships.

She gave him a shake. "Maybe instead of having yourself a big-ass pity party, you should ask yourself *why* he walked."

"I don't have to ask. He told me. Apparently he'd rather be exploited by his family for the rest of his life, stuck in a subsistence job in Backwater Bay than accept any help from me."

She pressed her lips together and raised an eyebrow. "If *that's* how you tried to sell him on you and your relationship, no *wonder* he kicked your ass to the curb."

"Christ, Morgan, I didn't say *that*. Exactly. But that's what he heard anyway."

"Maybe you weren't listening with both ears either." She led him away from the sofa, arm around his waist. "Not everyone wants a career with a capital *C*, you know. Bartending isn't exactly minimum-wage servitude, and just because *you* think it would be a nightmare, doesn't mean it's not a legit path for Seth. Don't project, baby. People are different." She gave his shoulder one last pat. "Which is a good thing. Can you imagine if *everyone* on the planet had Ginsberg's jones for action? You wouldn't be able to go shopping without worrying whether the cashier would leap over the counter and take you out in a hail of M&Ms and Snickers bars."

Nate scrubbed his hands over his face. "I'm not really in the mood for this right now."

"Too bad. You need to get your shit together because these effects tonight are no joke and you need to be *present*. Do you love him?"

He glared at her. "You think I'd be this wrecked if I didn't?"

"Did you *tell* him so? Or did you move right on into 'Get it done' mode and start making plans?"

"I—" Had he? In so many words? "Maybe not. But he had to know, didn't he? He knows I'd never— Not with someone I didn't feel strongly for."

"'Feel strongly' isn't the same as 'love.' Words matter, baby."

Nate winced. "I think some of my words were a little toxic. But he gave some back too." *"Heir to a Hollywood dynasty"? Really?*

"Shee-yit. If anybody ever needed emotional hearing aids, it's the two of you." She smacked him on one shoulder. "Go see him. *Talk* to him. And what's more important, *listen* to him. But don't melt down.

You're scaring my god-dog, and though I love you like a brother, I won't stand for that." She bent down to scratch Tarkus's belly. "And this time, baby? Don't just get it done. Get it *right*."

CHAPTER TWENTY-FIVE

After showering, Seth spent a couple of hours in bed trying—unsuccessfully—not to think. Lying there, he kept reliving his last few moments at Nate's this morning, as he'd walked out.

Seth had been able to see the pain flickering in Nate's eyes from across the room. He'd read it as easily as he'd always been able to see mischief or excitement in them. When Nate had made that comment as Seth left, about good-time guys never sticking around . . . *Maybe he didn't really mean it.* Maybe Seth had hurt him so much he'd lashed out.

By the time Seth had reached the door, *he'd* definitely said things he regretted now.

Shoving himself up, he bothered to put on some clothes before pacing a circuit around his apartment, turning the argument over and over in his mind, like he could dismantle it if he could just figure out its structure. The more he dwelled on it, the more convinced he became that the good-time guy issue *was* all him, and he'd overreacted. He'd freaked out because he'd been desperate not to have his first real argument with his first real—and only, he'd hoped—partner.

Jesus, I really overreacted. Did I fuck everything up?

The only way to find out is to talk to him. He'd have to reach out. Apprehension tightened his chest, then spread to his gut. Oh, wait, that might be hunger. Glancing at his alarm clock, he realized it was already evening, and he hadn't eaten anything since last night.

There was no food here, in his apartment. If he was careful, he could nip in and out of Grandma's fridge without seeing her. Then he'd work up the courage to call Nate.

Approaching the house in stealth mode, he peeked in the window before determining the coast was clear.

He'd forgotten to factor in the infernal Law of Murphy, which had been plaguing him lately, so as he let himself into the kitchen, he found his mother entering it from the dining room.

"Well it's about time," she announced, planting her fists on her hips.

Seth lurched to a halt as the door swung shut behind him. *No escape.* "What are you doing here?" Not more of her crap, not *now*.

She gaped at him a second, then recovered enough to snap, "Waiting for you, what do you think? I left you three messages to come up to the house in the last hour."

"I didn't get them." Truth was he hadn't been paying attention to anything that wasn't Nate.

Her nostrils flared, then she pivoted on one foot with the efficiency of an angry drill sergeant. "Come along." She led the way out of the room. At least, she would have led the way if Seth had been following, but he didn't see why he'd do that. He doubted she was here alone, and he wasn't dumb enough to walk into that ambush, whatever it was about.

The article. Absorbed in the uncertainty of his relationship with Nate, he'd forgotten all about it.

Eh. Who cares?

Exactly who cared became clear as, after piling ham and cheese and veggies in his arms, he nudged the fridge shut with his foot to reveal his parents, Uncle Kirk, and Grandma standing on the other side of it.

Mom and Kirk were glaring at him, Dad was looking everywhere *but* him, and Grandma had her stare fixed on the breakfast nook. The brilliant red of her cheeks clashed with the white of the rest of her face.

"Where have you *been*?" demanded Kirk. Most of his anger bounced off Seth's shield of depression. He shrugged and set his armload of sandwich fixings on the island.

"Answer me," thundered his uncle.

"Don't you speak to Seth that way," snapped Grandma, eyeing him angrily enough to set him on fire with her laser vision. "You have *no right*."

Kirk rounded on her, towering over her. "After what he's done to ruin our reputation in this town?"

"He didn't do it alone." Debra turned her ire on Grandma also.

"I have every right," Kirk continued, leaning toward Grandma. "After I've let him live here, he owes me an explanation for that article—"

"I owe you *nothing*." Seth put himself between them, shielding Grandma, inches from Kirk's face. "I've worked for everything I have. None of it was simply handed to me."

Uncle Kirk retreated, a calculating set to his mouth. Probably surprised at Seth's calm, but he'd have prepared for this. He'd have a half dozen offensives cued up to fling at Seth. Not to mention whatever he'd already said or planned to say to Grandma.

This is just about control, now, isn't it?

Well, fuck that.

"Grandma." Seth kept his attention unwaveringly on Kirk as he spoke. "I think you should pack a few things. It might be best if you and I went to a hotel." It would be ironic if they ended up at the Burnt Toast, wouldn't it? "For the foreseeable future."

Pulsing veins popped out on Kirk's forehead, which was all the warning Seth got before his uncle lost all cool and was yelling in his face. "You aren't leaving here!"

"There's no need for you to leave," Dad said at the same time. Somehow, in spite of the volume of Kirk's voice, Dad's was the one that dominated the room. "Not until you're ready."

What did that mean? As Seth whipped his head around to look at his father, he could feel Grandma doing the same behind him.

Kirk whirled on him too. "What are you talking about?"

"I'm talking about Mother selling the house. Or rather, *us* selling the house and dissolving the trust."

So, Dad *was* on their side? Thank God. Seth relaxed his stance, stepping away so he was close to Grandma but no longer crowding her. Next to her, though, so he could protect her again if needed.

Okay, he could see how wanting to protect the people you loved could make you do things.

"If Mom wants to move so badly, I think standing in her way is only going to cause us more problems." Dad dipped his chin toward

Grandma. "I can't imagine how she's planning to escalate the situation if haunting the place was the next logical step."

Not the most encouraging way to put it, but still supportive . . . wasn't it?

Scowling, Kirk took a step toward his brother. "Even if we sold the house—*which we aren't doing*—the money would go directly into the trust account. But giving in to these—these *antics* is exactly the wrong thing to do. She'll use the same tactics the next time she wants something unreasonable, and God knows what she'll ask for."

"A pony?" Dad offered.

Kirk choked, face growing redder and mouth flapping.

Whatever. Before Kirk could recover, Seth took advantage of the moment to appeal to their logic. "Do you even understand why it is Grandma *wants* to move?"

Dad shrugged, and for a brief moment, Kirk's face went slack with surprise, then he tossed his head like a cow shaking off flies. "She wants to take it easy. She doesn't want the upkeep of this place, which is why we need you—"

"No. As you've pointed out, I do all of that for her, that's not the problem. There's one thing I can't do for her, though. I can't be her friend Eleanor. I can't be her whole social life." And God knew her sons weren't trying to fill in that gap.

"That's ridiculous! All she needs is this family." Once again, Kirk was advancing on Grandma. "Your socializing years ended when Father died."

What a dick.

Grandma snapped, going up on tiptoes and shouting in his face. "My damned husband may have given you control over my life, but he certainly didn't intend for you to make me miserable." She rounded on Seth's father. "*Either* of you!" Her voice cracked then, and Seth gathered her into his arms. Holding her safe, he glared over her head at those fucking assholes who'd upset her, daring them to try anything else.

She wasn't exactly wracked by sobs, but the silence in the kitchen—in the whole house—was so thick it seemed like she was crying into a megaphone.

Dad stepped toward them, and instinctively, Seth turned away, protecting her with the bulk of his body.

Halting, his father held up his hands in a gesture of surrender. "Mom . . ." Was that quaver in his voice real? "I'm sorry about this. All of it." As he slowly approached again, Seth let him, although still wary. Not letting his father do more than pat Grandma's shaking back.

"Kirk." Dad kept this attention on Grandma as he spoke to his brother. "I'm not going to stand by and let you bully Mom—or my son—anymore." His gaze flickered up to meet Seth's for a moment. "I've let you do it far too long already."

"What are *you* going to do?" The nastiness in his mother's voice was tactile, and the sneer she aimed at her husband made her look like a stranger. Someone he'd never known. "Kirk has to consent—"

"Shut up, Debra." Shoulders slumping, Dad cut her off as quietly yet effectively as he had Kirk earlier. He turned to face his wife, positioning himself so he was clearly on Seth and Grandma's side. "You don't know what the hell you're talking about. Neither of us can make any unilateral decisions, not unless the other allows it. That's what I've been doing, letting Kirk make the decisions—what *you've* wanted me to do—but I'm done."

Seth's mother gaped. She sputtered. She whipped out an accusatory index finger. "*Philip*. I never— This is inexcusable, how could you—in front of your son!"

"He's your son too."

Apparently that was so offensive to her she lost the power of speech. Instead she screeched, nostrils at full sail, and stamped her foot. With a last glare she marched out of the kitchen, her footsteps echoing through the house, then growing louder again. Seth just caught a glimpse of her orange coat as she stomped through the entryway. The front door bouncing off the wall as she flung it open made Grandma wince, and they all jumped when it crashed shut behind her.

"Well." Dad cleared his throat. "Mom, as long as you're staying tonight, can I sleep in my old bedroom?"

Grandma sputtered with either laughter or some sort of hyena-esque crying. When she pulled out of Seth's arms, he caught a glimpse of her smiling face, although her eyes were as reddened as his had been earlier.

Reaching for her younger son, she patted his face, then held it between her palms. "Of course. You can have your old room back."

Dad swallowed. "I'm sorry for letting Kirk ruin your life and for everything I did that contributed. Can y-you forgive me?"

"You always were a mama's boy." Kirk seemed to have recovered enough to start slinging insults.

Dad had some of his own, though. "Better than being Daddy's little shit."

Whatever scintillating comeback Kirk was going to serve up was cut short by the sound of the doorbell.

Seth hadn't been in his apartment when Nate had knocked. Judging from the extra cars in the driveway—all of them much higher end than Seth's Civic—Sentinel House wasn't empty, but despite Morgan's warnings about rushing to "get it done" over getting it right, Nate didn't want to wait any longer. If Seth wasn't inside, maybe Pearl would know where he was.

The door cracked open and Pearl peered up at him. *She's been crying.* Outrage flared in Nate's chest. What sick bastard would have made her cry? Unless . . . was she upset because *Seth* was upset? Could this be Nate's fault?

Why not? Everything else seems to be.

"Hey, Pearl. I'm sorry to disturb you, but I was . . . ah . . . looking for Seth. Do you—" The door opened farther to reveal Seth standing behind his grandmother. "Oh. Hi." He glanced between Pearl's tearstained cheeks and Seth's stony expression. "This is a bad time, isn't it?"

"You think?" Seth opened the door the rest of the way to reveal two men looming in the vestibule.

From their resemblance to each other—and the fact they shared the same nose as Seth and his grandmother . . . *The Brothers Larson, I presume.* The one in front was scowling at Seth, and the one in back was scowling at the one in front. Given that Seth was scowling at Nate, he felt like the caboose in a fury train.

"I was hoping we could talk. That you'd still want to talk."

"Nate, this is really—"

"Nate?" the one in front boomed. "Is this the *Nate* who spread all those lies about our ancestor?"

"Uncle Kirk," Seth said through clenched teeth. "As I've said before, they aren't lies. We have evidence."

"Evidence? Or 'alternative facts'? Regardless, it's irrelevant. Our duty, both legally and morally, is to protect our heritage."

"Jesus." Seth rounded on his uncle as if Nate weren't even there "Don't you mean your status? Your precious reputation as a leading citizen?"

"It's the same thing."

"No, it's not. You're not interested in making Grandma happy. You don't even care about this house, not really. You just want control so you can keep up appearances for the least amount of money." Seth put his arm around Pearl's shoulders. "Otherwise you'd be glad to dissolve the trust. Then you wouldn't be responsible for Grandma anymore."

"The trust is for the protection of her *assets*," Kirk bellowed, getting right up in Seth's face. "It's for *Mother's* benefit."

"Seriously?" Derision fairly dripped from Seth's voice. "Show me the benefits to her, because I don't see any, and I'm pretty sure she doesn't either. Seems like the only one benefiting from the trust is you."

Okay, clearly Nate had walked in on another battle in the Larson family civil war, and it didn't look like this one was going anywhere either. Seth and Pearl needed some kind of wedge, something that threatened not only the family reputation, but its foundation.

Get it right.

Nate took a step forward to stand next to Pearl—he hadn't worked up enough courage to stand next to Seth yet. "You know, if you're trying to negotiate a solution to a family conundrum, don't you think all members of the family should be represented?"

Kirk barely glanced at Nate. "My niece and other nephew don't concern themselves with this town any longer, and my sister-in-law is in total agreement with me. Our sisters and their children understand this isn't their affair."

"I wasn't talking about them," Nate said. "I was referring to your second cousin."

That caught everyone's attention. "Is this more of your genealogy garbage?" Kirk growled. "Because we don't care about some poser in Kalamazoo who might be named Larson. It's not an uncommon name. Our family is totally accounted for and it's—"

"Missing an entire branch. There's another direct male descendent in Fennimore's line, and he's right here in Bluewater Bay."

All the Larsons' jaws dropped at that news. "What? Where?" Kirk spluttered. "Who?"

"The great-grandson of Fennimore Larson by the woman who was framed for his murder." Nate paused for effect—not that he needed it, but sue him: he had theater in his blood. "*Finn* Larson, executive producer of *Wolf's Landing.*"

"What the fuck?" Seth's outcry didn't match his uncle's for volume, but it cut right through the other noise and into Nate's heart. *Shit. He doesn't sound happy.*

"Language," Pearl murmured.

Nate glanced at Seth, but although his mouth was working, no words were forthcoming, so Nate plowed on.

"Depending on the specific terms of the trust, if it refers to 'heirs and assigns,' Finn might be one of the de facto beneficiaries. You know—" Nate pretended to look around the entry with an appraiser's jaundiced eye "—I bet he'd love to film some scenes from *Wolf's Landing* here. There's a plotline coming up next season with a wealthy reclusive werewolf who'd live in exactly this kind of house."

Kirk's face resembled an eggplant by this time, although Nate couldn't get a read on Seth's dad, and as for Seth? *Not promising.* Pearl was the only person who seemed marginally entertained, and even she looked a little strained around the eyes.

"Of course," Nate continued, "there might be some damage if we have to stage any fight scenes here, but our crew is really good at replicating historic artifacts. You'll never know the difference."

Kirk drew himself up, inhaling until he was puffed up like a Macy's Thanksgiving Day parade balloon. "You will *not* reveal this . . . this nonsense. To anyone."

"You know, *sir*, this 'nonsense' isn't yours to control. I don't know what the legal ramifications might be, given the generations separating Finn and Fennimore, not to mention the shocking treatment of Finn's great-great-grandmother, but Finn has a right to know that he's a part of this family. What he—and you—do with that information may redefine the way the name 'Larson' is viewed in this town forever. Don't you think it would be a good idea to make those negotiations amicable?"

"You— He—" Kirk whirled on Seth. "This is all *your* fault. You and that . . . that *genealogist*. If you'd just left well enough alone—" He glared at his brother, buttoning his overcoat with quick, jerky movements. "Very well. Sell the damned house. But I warn you, Philip, I refuse to dissolve the trust, and I'll do everything in my power to protect it."

Seth's dad—Philip—nodded. "Suit yourself, Kirk. I guess Finn and I will see you in court." Then he grinned and tossed off a two-fingered salute.

As Kirk marched past them and out the door, Nate dared a glance at Seth, offering a tentative smile.

Seth didn't return it. "Can I talk to you for a minute? Outside?"

"Um . . . sure." Nate followed Seth outside, his belly in the vicinity of his toes, in time to see Kirk's Mercedes peel onto the street, narrowly missing a passing Volkswagen. Seth led the way around the porch until they were out of sight of both the front door and the driveway.

Seth stopped, but didn't turn around, and Nate's stomach dove farther—maybe all the way to the center of the Earth. "Why didn't you tell me?" Seth's voice was low and tense.

"You mean about Finn? I started to tell you this morning, but somehow we got derailed." *There was an understatement.*

"How long have you known about this?"

"Since . . . since before the crabbing trip. The same night I found your number—" *Better not go there again.* "I was . . . ah . . . looking for the right time."

Seth spun and faced him. "You've known for days and you think *this* was the right time? Jesus, Nate."

"But . . . but it worked, right? Your uncle gave in, so your grandmother will get to sell the house."

"Gah!" Seth clutched his hair. "Yes, it worked. Thank you, even, but *that's not the point.*"

"It's not? But the results—"

"Fuck the results. You didn't give me a *choice*. You bulldozed your way into the conversation, then *you* decided it would work, so you just blurted it out. Finn Larson? *Jesus.*"

"You said that."

"I know. But *Jesus.*"

Nate tried to scare up enough saliva in his dry mouth to swallow. *No success there.* "I only wanted to help. I mean, you didn't seem to be making much headway otherwise."

"We *were*, actually. But you barged in and what, had to be the hero? Because you always know what's best for me? For us? For everyone?"

All the air left Nate's lungs, as if he'd been gut-punched for real. Seth was putting him on the outside—not part of *us*, therefore firmly in the *them* camp. "I'm screwing this up royally, but you walked out, Seth. You *walked out.* I had to at least make a push to—"

"Stop." Seth dashed his hand under his eyes. "I just can't, okay? What you said before and now this . . . I need time to—to think. I can't fuck this up again."

Time. Okay, that wasn't an absolute *get the fuck away from me and never come back.* He'd take it. "How . . . how much time?"

Seth planted his hands on his hips and looked away. "You're telling me you really want to try and work this out? Us?"

"Of course I do."

He swallowed. "Then I'll let you know." Seth glared at him out of eyes brimming with tears, then turned and took two steps away before he stopped again, not looking at Nate. "And for God's sake, if you can possibly control yourself, *please* let us handle talking to Finn Larson. *Jesus.*"

He walked out of sight around the corner of the house. Even after Nate heard the front door close, he couldn't make himself move. *Maybe "time" means ten minutes.*

But after ten minutes, twenty, thirty, of shivering on the porch without any sign of movement from inside, he finally gave up and trudged back to the Jeep. He really hoped that Seth's time would be measured in hours rather than days, weeks, or—God forbid—years

How can I get it right if I can't even get it the fuck done?

ack inside, Seth found Grandma and his father in the den at the rear of the house. He and Grandma sat here in winter sometimes, because the fireplace made it so cozy. Bonus, it was where Grandma's tiny stock of liquor was stored.

He poured them each a shot of whiskey. *Make it a double. Even for Grandma.*

"I'm a professional," Seth told her when she tried to refuse the glass. "Bartender's prescription." Bitterness flared up his throat for a split second, but he firmly shoved Nate out of his mind again, standing next to the empty hearth and sipping his drink in the very-much-less-tense silence.

Until Grandma said to Dad, "That Nate, he's a nice boy. Seth's seeing him, did you know?"

Dad glanced up, for the first time showing interest in something other than his knees. "That so?" His brow wrinkled up. "How come he didn't stay?"

Deep breath. Carefully he set his highball on the mantle. It was that or chug it. "We're . . . taking a break."

"Oh no," Grandma murmured. "Tonight's really been a shit-storm, hasn't it?" She downed the rest of her drink in one gulp.

"*Mom!*"

"Language," Seth snapped. She kind of deserved that after earlier.

Snorting at them, she held out a hand toward Seth. "Help me up, please. I'm a tipsy old woman." He cupped her elbow and let her use him for leverage. Spine bowing more than usual, she stood unsteadily in front of her son's chair.

"Philip, I'll get you some fresh sheets for—"

"I can do it." Seth crossed his arms over his chest to show he meant business. "You go to bed."

She didn't argue, which told him just how much tonight had worn on her.

"I don't have any clothes," Dad said conversationally after Grandma left. "I can go by the house in the morning for a suit, but I've never really taken to sleeping in the nude."

"I'll get you something. Sweats and a T-shirt?" They were the same size, and about the same build, although his father had put on more weight around his middle than Seth remembered him having. They really hadn't seen much of each other, had they? "Dad, thanks for—"

"Seth, I'm very proud of you," he interrupted, but didn't let Seth react. "And I know where Mom keeps the linens. Just get me something to sleep in."

"Hang on." He didn't need to go all the way out to the garage. His own clothes dryer had a dead door switch, so he'd been using the one in the house. His last load should still be in it—he'd thrown it in and turned it on before going over to Nate's the day before yesterday.

Man, that seemed like forever ago. Too much had happened between then and now, with the blow up this morning, then what his family had piled on, and then Nate again.

Groaning, Seth bumped his forehead against the dryer, which he'd just crouched down in front of. He couldn't remember walking into the room, he'd been so absorbed in revisiting the disaster of today. In wondering if he could work things out with a guy who thought life was something to be constantly "fixed."

Whatever. He yanked open the door and found that yes, exactly what his dad needed was waiting for him.

Back in the little sitting room, Dad's head was lolling on the back of the armchair and his eyes were closed, although he blinked heavily and rubbed at them after Seth walked in.

"Are you going to bed? It's, um—" Seth glanced at the clock on the mantel. "It's eight thirty." Although he'd love to be tired enough to sleep. Forget everything.

"Is it? Huh." Yawning, Dad scratched his abdomen under the dress shirt he still wore. His smile was so relaxed Seth could almost forget they'd just had one of the worst collective family fights ever. "I've got my laptop and some work in the car to keep me busy, but I think I could sleep."

"I can't," he responded unthinkingly. "I'm fine on my own," he added.

But Dad shook his head and pushed himself up out of the chair. "How about I pour us each another drink? I told you at the bar that I wanted to talk, and now seems as good a time as any." He licked his lip in a gesture Seth hadn't seen in years. That was what he did when he was considering important things. Weighty decisions.

"'Kay." It would be better than going over and over everything Nate had said today—the shit they'd *both* said. So he sat in what had been Grandma's chair and accepted his refreshed glass when Dad handed it to him.

His father sat down with a satisfied groan and sipped at his drink.

Slouching, Seth did the same, relaxed for the first time in hours. The alcohol had finally started to work through his system.

"I've asked your mother for a divorce." Once again, Dad's tone was completely conversational. *I'm proud of you, I've asked for a divorce, the forecast is calling for rain.*

Seriously? "Oh." The most surprising thing about the news was that it surprised him at all. Although ninety percent of his surprise was that Dad had taken the initiative. He had a strong urge to pat his father on the back. "Wait, when? Tonight?"

"No. Six months ago." He glanced at the end table, where a phone was sitting. "She did *text* me tonight, though, agreeing to it."

"A text. Classy." He held his breath, waiting for his dad to get angry about the inappropriate amusement, but instead Dad snorted a laugh, although he sobered up within a half second.

Mom's the one who'd be angry. His dad seemed to be expecting more questions. "You've been waiting for an answer for six months?"

"Not really. For the first four I was going to counseling with her to try and work things out. Her idea." He blew out a long breath, letting it puff his cheeks. "That ended because our therapist said she couldn't work with us if Debra wasn't willing to make any compromises. The last two months, I've mostly been . . . persuading her to agree." He looked Seth in the eye and added softly, "I didn't want to force the issue because I had a feeling I was going to be fighting my brother at the same time."

Oh. *Oooh.* "So that's why you haven't opposed him over the house?" It made a weird sort of sense. Fighting a war on two fronts was tough, especially when your enemies were in cahoots. Except Seth had never expected him to oppose Kirk in the first place. Of course, before the house issue, Kirk had never made such a self-serving decision about Grandma's welfare. Not one that Seth knew about. *Yeah, all of his self-serving decision before then only affected my welfare.*

"I knew your mother would back him to the hilt." Dad sighed and ran his fingers through his hair in that gingerly way of men who didn't want to lose any more. Dad didn't have a comb-over, thank God, but as Seth sat there, he realized his dad must normally use as much product as he did—it was sleek and flat against his head. "You know, 'they' tell you to set an example for your kids, and tonight I was watching you protect Mom and . . ." He shook his head and played with the rim of his glass, circling it with a fingertip. "I didn't teach you to protect the people you love."

There's that protection thing again. Once more he shoved thoughts of Nate away for now and focused on what his father had said. "Grandma taught me." If the guy was going to be that honest, he probably wanted honesty in return. Plus, Seth had a few things to get off his chest. "Dad, what I learned from you was to not rock the boat." That was sugarcoating it a bit.

The look Dad gave him from under his brows made it clear he knew his son was being polite. "Believe it or not, I thought I was showing you how to get along. A lot of the world is run by assholes—"

"As we have daily proof in the form of your brother."

Dad grinned a second before continuing. "I wanted you to know that you shouldn't let it get to you. I think what my behavior modeling did was let the assholes *get* you."

"Dad . . ." He was pretty sure his father was saying his mother was an asshole. *She is, kind of.* Jesus, his life had a way of wandering into uncharted waters a lot, lately.

As if he could read Seth's mind, he continued explaining. "I *meant* to teach you that there are times when you have to tell the assholes to shut the fu—hell up." He muttered something under his breath, then repeated himself. Sort of. "Shut the fuck up. Turns out I wasn't even *doing* it, and in the end you're the one who taught *me*." He swallowed. "I'm sorry, Seth."

This had to be one of those times that straight guys could handle being touched in sympathy, didn't it? He stretched as far out of the chair as he could, just enough to wrap his fingers around his father's forearm and squeeze it. He would have hugged Grandma in the same circumstances, so hopefully that translated. "This—a divorce—is really what you want?"

"Hell yes," he responded immediately. "To tell you the truth, I've wanted one for years. You know I met her in college, and when I proposed I did it because . . ." He took a long, slow breath, then spit it out. "She seemed like a reasonable choice. I loved her, but not the way you're supposed to love someone you want to spend the rest of your life with." Ducking his head, Dad ran fingers through his hair harder, really messing it up this time before he clasped both his hands together and didn't quite meet Seth's eyes. "I waited so long to leave because I knew divorcing her would open a whole can of worms with my brother."

Of course it would. The issue none of them ever faced head-on. How much honesty was the man ready for? *What the hell.* "Why didn't she just marry Kirk in the first place?"

Dad laughed, eyes crinkling up, and fell back in the chair. He looked ten years younger in two seconds flat, even after he'd calmed enough to answer. "If she'd met him before I asked her, she probably would have. He went into the army after college, so he wasn't around when your mother and I were engaged. By the time Kirk came home for the wedding—" Dad shrugged. "Too late. For all of us. Don't ask me what makes a person—me—that clueless, but I kind of think . . ." He licked his lip thoughtfully. "When I was talking about what I was trying to teach you? I really did try. I watched how your brother and sister were turning out, and when you were born—I wanted things to be different for you."

Whoa. "So you were, like, what? Rebelling? Working the underground parenting resistance?" This conversation was going places he'd never imagined, and somehow it made him feel better than he had in days. He'd told Nate he'd decided he was happiest not meeting anyone else's expectations, but it still felt good to find out someone was happy with how he'd ended up . . . *Affirming.* "Maybe I did turn out the way someone wanted me to."

Dad's hand on his arm captured his attention. When he glanced over, his father was smiling. "I'm pretty damned proud of you."

Emotion prickled over his scalp, and Seth had to blink away the wetness in his eyes. "Thanks."

"Hey." Dad shoved up from his chair and stood, stretching. "I took the whole day off tomorrow. I know you have to work in the evening—"

He did?

"Wanna go out in the boat in the morning? I've got more confessions to make. And apologies." His ears went a little bit pink. *First the hair and now the blushing.* They were kind of alike, weren't they?

"Yeah, I'd like that." He stretched and then stood too, feeling bolstered enough now that he could face his place alone. Maybe because of the whiskey, but he believed it was because of his dad.

Smiling, Dad clapped him on the shoulder, then suddenly he yanked Seth toward him and gave him a hug, fisting his hand in the back of Seth's shirt for a second. When he let go, he cleared his throat, grabbed the pile of clothes Seth had brought him, and left the room.

The good feelings weren't total protection against reliving the bad parts of his day, but lying in bed, the television filling his room with flickering illumination, he was calmer about it than he'd been earlier. Able to look at things a little more objectively.

Not that his feelings weren't still kind of raw.

It chafed that Nate's bulldozer "fix" had worked.

They'd been making headway, but it would have taken them a lot longer without the mention of Finn Larson's existence—*Ugh, Finn Larson?* If Kirk *had* managed to get a majority of the local family on his side . . . Although Seth was pretty sure he could count on most of the female Larsons to support them—women's rights hadn't traditionally been recognized by the male members of Fennimore's descendants. Seth had seen resentments flare up over that more than once at family reunions. Great-aunt Beryl could really fling a pie in her day. Better than C work.

Fucking Nate. What kind of a jackass didn't give him a heads-up about something that monumental?

Maybe the kind of jackass that wanted to help someone he cared about deeply, even if it meant breaking things in the process. A sudden mental image of Nate blundering around inside a china shop nearly made him laugh. It was so easy to imagine the expression on his face—intent, determined and . . . protective.

That word again. Tonight, when Kirk had bordered on going too far with Grandma, Seth had completely understood that urge, to protect someone you loved.

Does he love me?

He wanted me to work on Wolf's Landing *because he assumed I'd go where he goes.* Assumed they'd be together, which was exactly what Seth wanted, and he knew he loved Nate, so . . .

God, Nate had even planned ways for them to be together, trying to find him a job . . . Oh no, he was back to the sweet thing, where his heart went a little gooey around the edges knowing that love *was* what motivated Nate. Probably.

God knew it motivated Seth in regard to Nate. Made him want to go to the guy right now and work things out.

Except he didn't want to be his parents. So he had to do what his father hadn't. Take the time to be certain before fully committing. He'd been the good-time guy for so long, if he was going to dive into becoming the commitment guy, he wanted to get it right the first time.

Figure out what he needed to be with someone, whether it was Nate or another guy down the road.

A *long* ways down the road. Because if he and Nate were incompatible, he couldn't imagine ever getting over him.

In the days since Seth had told him he needed more time, Nate must have checked his phone a minimum of once every three minutes. At work, Morgan had given him the side-eye, but hadn't confiscated it again. She'd also refrained from commenting—which must have meant his state of mind was obvious, and freaky enough that even

Morgan, who had no boundaries where Nate was concerned, wouldn't mention it.

This morning, the weather matched his temper: chill and gray and misty. Even Tarkus wasn't his usual exuberant self, slinking out to do his business before coming back inside to curl up on his bed with his back to Nate. No doubt he shared the opinion of everyone else in Bluewater Bay about Nate's screwups, as if he'd watched Nate crash and burn on some canine live-streaming site.

Great, now I'm anthropomorphizing my dog—and giving him an internet habit. On the other hand, dogs were pretty intuitive—maybe Nate should take lessons, since he seemed to be a total failure in that department.

He grabbed Tarkus's grooming brush and sat down cross-legged on the floor next to the dog bed, running the brush down Tarkus's spine and along his side, although it was tough to do with the dog curled up like a hedgehog.

"Hey, buddy. Sorry I'm such a stupid-ass bastard." Tarkus's ears twitched, but he didn't uncurl. Nate worked through the thick fur of Tark's ruff. "Maybe later today we can go—"

Nate's cell phone rang from where he'd left it on the counter. *Seth!* He dropped the brush, gave Tarkus a haphazard final pat, and heaved himself to his feet. As he rushed across the room, he caught his little toe on the leg of the coffee table and pain shot up his leg.

"Son of a *bitch*!" Gritting his teeth, he staggered the last two steps, scrabbling the phone off the counter. "Hello?"

"Nate?" The tentative voice on the line wasn't Seth, but despite the agony in his foot and over three years of distance, he recognized it immediately.

"Jorge." He didn't have it in him to put any welcome in his tone. The pain in his toe was negligible compared to his crashing disappointment.

"Are you—are you okay? You sound a little peculiar."

"I'm fine," he said between gritted teeth. "Why are you calling?" *Ow, damn it, ow.* He forced himself to look down at his bare feet— the little toe on his left foot was sticking out at an angle. *Just fucking fabulous.*

"I—I'm sorry. I shouldn't have bothered you. I—"

"No. Jorge, it's okay. I just . . . I was expecting someone else." *And I think I just broke my damn toe.* He couldn't complain about *that* to Jorge of all people. When they'd been together, before the accident when Jorge had still been dancing, his feet had been so beaten up sometimes they'd looked as if someone had taken a mallet to them.

"Oh. I won't keep you, then."

"No, wait." Nate took a deep breath and tried to compartmentalize the pain, his dejection over Seth, and the residual hurt from Jorge's abandonment—only to discover that the abandonment didn't need to be compartmentalized at all. He'd actually let it go. *Hunh. Who'd have thought?* "Don't hang up. I'd like to talk to you." He limped to the sofa and sat down sideways, propping his foot on a throw pillow. "How are you doing—and that's not a platitude. I really want to know."

"I was—" Jorge's deep breath was clearly audible "—worse for a while, but now I'm better. Getting better every day. This call is, well, a part of my therapy—facing the things in my life that I most regret. Franklin says—"

"Franklin. He's your husband, right?"

"Yes." How could one syllable convey so much contentment and joy? "He's a counselor—not mine, because that would be weird, but he's my support system. Anyway, I wanted to let you know that I'm sorry for how our relationship ended. I should have handled it better."

"Maybe, but I get it." Nate shifted his foot on the pillow, trying to get comfortable. "You weren't getting what you wanted from the relationship."

"It wasn't that. In a way, I was getting almost too much from you." *What the hell?* "Sorry, but that means . . . what exactly?"

Jorge heaved a giant sigh. "You may not realize it, Nate, but your expectations are pretty hard to live up to."

"My *expectations*?" Not this again. "But I didn't ask you to do anything you didn't want to do. Did I? I mean, I know I might not have initiated sex often—" *or at all* "—but did you think I wanted you to do more?"

"Not in bed, Nate, but out of it. After my—" his voice faltered, and he took another deep breath "—my accident, you kept bombarding me with options, things I could do since I could no longer dance, when dance was the one thing I was good at—the thing that attracted you to me to begin with."

"But—"

"I'm not a fool, Nate. I know how rare that attraction was for you. But I couldn't live with you for six years and not realize that you value competence—scratch that: excellence. I mean, your own mother can't even measure up, and she's world famous. How could I ever manage, once my claim to fame was gone?"

Nate's stomach plummeted. "I didn't care about that, I swear. But you were so happy when you were dancing. I wanted you to have that again—to find something else that would give you that spark."

"Exactly. I was happy when I was *dancing*, and I'd never be able to do it again. I was *mourning*. You, with your relentless efforts to find a replacement, didn't let me do that, and it made it worse."

Nate let his head fall back on the sofa cushion. God, he'd been an asshole, blaming Jorge for leaving when Nate had driven him right out the door and into Franklin's arms. "Sorry," he whispered. How many times could he say it—and it probably still wouldn't be enough.

But Jorge chuckled. "You know, that's the cliché—the one that women are always trotting out when they talk about communication problems with men. They just want to talk about their emotions, work them out so they can feel better; men wade in and try to fix things. You're a champion fixer. At the time, I didn't want to be fixed. I wanted someone who knew I was broken and *didn't care*."

"I . . . It didn't matter to me. That you couldn't dance."

"That's not how it seemed to me. What I got was you essentially saying, 'Right. Time to get back on another horse,' when all I wanted to do was recover from the shock."

"I'm sorry. That I didn't see that. I wish I had." At one point, the wish would have been for his own sake, since the breakdown of their relationship had led to years of isolation. But now, he wished he'd paid more attention for Jorge.

"I didn't call to force you to grovel, Nate, really. I just wanted to let you know that I've moved on." He chuckled again. "You'll never guess—I've got a part in a TV series."

It couldn't be. "Not . . . not *Wolf's Landing*?"

Jorge laughed outright this time. "Oh hell no. It's about a dance studio. I play—wait for it—a flamenco teacher."

This time, Nate joined the laughter. "Perfect casting. I truly mean that. You'll be great."

"In a way, I have you to thank—your dad got me the audition."

Nate clutched his phone tighter. "He did? He never said anything."

"I told him I wanted to tell you myself. He's a great guy, you know? He didn't have to go the distance for me, not after I treated you the way I did."

"Well, his heart attack gave him a different perspective." He'd sworn never to hold a grudge again—anger and resentment put too much strain on his heart. It was why he'd urged Nate to finally reach out to his mother.

"I'm glad he's on the mend. Franklin and I check in on him now and then. Invite him over for dinner—heart-healthy, I promise."

Tears prickled in Nate's eyes. His dad wasn't the only one who knew how to forgive. "Thanks. That means a lot to me."

"It's my pleasure. It was . . . good talking to you, Nate. Next time you're in LA—"

"I'd love to get together."

"Great. Take care."

"You too."

Nate lay back on the sofa for a moment, his phone on his chest. *Jorge.* He'd never expected to hear from him—and certainly had never expected the call to turn out this way. He lay there until the throb in his toe forced him upright to limp into the bathroom and dig out the first aid kit. After he taped up his toe, strapping it to its neighbor with a bit of cotton padding between, he wiggled it a bit. *Ow! Shit!*

Thank God it was autumn and he could wear boots with no comment. After icing it for a bit, and an Advil or two, he could disguise the limp and nobody would ever know he wasn't one hundred percent—as long as he didn't break out of a slow amble.

As he hobbled out to the living room, his thoughts returned to Jorge and his dad. They both had reasons for rage, and both had chosen to put them aside—far different from Nate's past behavior.

To spite his mother, he'd abandoned a career that he seriously loved—because it was something *she* wanted for him. Then, after

Jorge had left, he'd trashed ninety-nine percent of his industry connections when the rage bottled up inside him had popped. One public meltdown—okay, seven—and he'd been unemployable until Levi's call. Sure, he'd cleaned up his act, especially after his dad's heart attack, but the damage had been done in Hollywood. He'd needed a long stretch of drama-less dependability to rebuild his reputation, and he'd found it here.

In Bluewater Bay, he'd made a name for himself as the go-to guy. As long as he pretended he was okay, hid the pain, retreated to his self-imposed isolation, he'd be good.

Who the fuck are you kidding?

He was not good. He might be able to hide a fractured toe, but when it came to hiding a broken heart, he sucked.

I can't screw up this gig too. I can't depend on Levi or my dad or anyone else to pull my ass out of the fire. I'm thirty-seven fucking years old. It's time I learned to handle my own shit.

So what did that mean, and why did letting go of anger hurt more than its cause, like rebreaking a bone to set it properly? Maybe he needed some emotional ice packs to numb his feelings.

No. No more numbing. No more avoiding. *Just deal with it, because the world is not all about you.*

First step? Let go of his oldest grievance.

He sat on the floor next to Tarkus so he could take comfort from the dog's presence. Then he took a deep breath and sent a text.

Hey, Mom. I heard you'll be in town soon to meet with Levi. If you've got time, I'd like you to come over for dinner.

Less than ten seconds later, he got a return message: *I will always have time for you, my dear.*

Guess his mom didn't hold a grudge either, despite Nate behaving like a spoiled brat for fourteen years. God, he didn't deserve her. Didn't deserve any of them. But he'd damned well try—and the person he most wanted to deserve right at this moment was Seth.

But after Nate had poleaxed him not once, not twice, but three times, why would he bother to ever come back? It had taken a hospital-bed plea from his father before Nate had reached out to his mother that first time. What would it take for Seth to be willing to reach out to Nate—or to let Nate reach out to him?

Tarkus stood up in his bed, turned around three times, and settled again, his head on Nate's thigh. "What am I going to do, boy?" He scratched Tarkus's ears. "I don't want to be an island anymore." Tarkus whined and waved one paw feebly in the air. Nate caught it, chuckling. "I'm the one with the injured foot, not you, you faker. I should talk to Levi about putting you in his next show at the Playhouse. He could keep with the classics and stage *Lassie Come-Home*." He ruffled Tarkus's fur. "You wouldn't mind doing a little drag, would you? You could definitely pull it off. Look at the way you snowed Seth the other night. Maybe you should give me some pointers, because he sure wasn't buying what I . . ." Nate's hand stilled until Tarkus nudged his knee with an imperious nose to remind him of his petting duties.

Am I desperate enough to exploit my dog's charisma to rescue my romance? Why not? Against all the odds, Nate had found a third person who did it for him. He owed it to himself to give the relationship its best chance—and he owed it to Seth to prove he was more than enough for Nate, just as he was. To do that, he needed to stage the best effect of his life, but he couldn't do it alone. He needed sidekicks who loved Seth as much as Nate did.

"You'll help me, won't you, boy?" Tarkus just looked at Nate from under his ridiculously long doggy eyelashes. "But we need someone else. You're good, but you're distractible. Plus, I can't be anywhere near Seth's place or he'll smell a rat."

A rat. Like the one who'd started this whole thing—their adventures with the Cult of Fennimore; Shannon, Morgan, Pearl—

Pearl. She'd hugged him the other day—seemed like she approved of him. She was undoubtedly close to Seth—and more to the point for Nate's plan—she had Tarkus eating out of her hand . . . literally.

Now, the question was: did she think Nate was boyfriend material for her grandson? Because whatever the rest of the Larsons might think, Nate had no illusions about who had the most influence with Seth.

Only one way to find out. He had Pearl's number: she'd insisted on giving it to him when they'd been setting up the haunting—*"for emergencies,"* she'd said. If this wasn't an emergency, he didn't know what was.

She answered on the first ring. "Nate, it's about time you called. We have *got* to do something about my grandson. He's *miserable*."

Thank God. Well, not that he wanted Seth to be miserable, precisely—but still. "I'm with you, Pearl, one hundred percent. Here's my plan."

CHAPTER TWENTY-SEVEN

Seth woke up the morning after the big arguments—both of them—knowing immediately what he needed from Nate.

He's gotta take me the way I am.

It took him two more days for him to work up the courage to find out if Nate could do that. He had no doubt Nate would agree, but Seth needed to *believe*. Basically, he was going to ask Nate to prove it to him. It wasn't fair, but it turned out that was his hard limit for a relationship.

In the meantime, he suspected Grandma was piling more chores on him in his free time, not because they were actually getting the house ready to sell, but because she was trying to keep him distracted. He hadn't said much to her about what had happened, in spite of her many veiled—and later very unveiled—questions. Mostly he'd moped and shrugged, even when it wasn't a yes or no question.

That afternoon, when he came inside to fix an armoire, she waited until he was half-buried in it, about to tap some finish nails into the molding he was replacing, when she asked him, "Have you ever been in love with anyone? Other than Nate, I mean."

He couldn't answer—the way his throat seized up made it impossible. Crap, he couldn't even *be* here. Straightening up, he set the tack hammer down on the dining room buffet and walked out of the room. Then he kept going, through the kitchen, out the back door, past his place and down to the edge of the garden, to the rim of the West Twin River ravine. He hadn't been down there since he'd found the remains of the woodrat.

He'd left the house because he'd felt uncomfortably close to tears, but he didn't manage to escape them outside. He ended up sniffling over a rodent. The one that had brought him and Nate together.

Fuck. *Gotta do this, have to have the conversation with him. Except how do I start?*

He needed information from someone who'd done it. He called Lucas and arranged to meet him at Ma Cougar's.

Seth arrived first, at the beginning of happy hour, and ended up in nearly the same booth they'd had the night he'd met Nate.

Damn it. From here, he could see the exact spot it had happened. As he was scooting out of the booth to change sides, Lucas arrived.

"Hey there," he kissed Seth's cheek—*seriously universe, I could do without all the ironic reminders*—as Seth stood. "Are we changing spots?"

"No, I just want to sit on the other side."

Lucas shrugged and slid into the bench seat Seth had just vacated. Thank God for self-involved, unobservant people. Seth had already ordered them two beers, and they arrived immediately after Lucas did.

"So," Lucas began, lifting his glass in a toast. "Here's to revenging yourself on me. Gabe told me."

Oh. He'd forgotten all about that. "Sorry?" He tilted his head and studied Lucas's small, self-deprecating smile. "Yeah, I'm not really sorry."

"I wouldn't be. It was a good show. Nate appears to be *very* talented." He sipped at his beer, watching Seth attentively over the glass.

Sorry, man, no details forthcoming. At least not *his* details. "How did you and Gabe get back together?" he asked instead, tracing designs in the drink coaster with his fingernail. "After twelve years, how do you pick up where you left off?"

Lucas screwed up his brows. "We weren't really seeing each other twelve years ago. It was one night. When I got back, we didn't so much pick up where we left off as start a new relationship."

"Seriously?" He'd been certain they'd been in love before Lucas had left town at eighteen. "He was so hung up on you I thought it *had* to have been long-term and major." Every time Lucas's name had even been whispered within Gabe's hearing, the guy's expression would subtly change. He wasn't the most emotive person in the first place, but at the mention of Lucas Wilder, he'd blank out. "I can't believe it took that long for you guys to work things out."

"It didn't take us *that* long." Lucas flicked his fingers in the air. "We had it pretty much worked out in a weekend. What took twelve years was getting *to* that weekend."

Seth's stomach shriveled up into a solid ball of stress. *Okay, so, the lesson is you can't work things out if you aren't together.* The only thing he knew for sure was that if he never called Nate, he'd never be with him. Jesus, he needed to leave. Immediately.

But Lucas was still talking. "—mean, he was kind of an idiot a few times after that, so, like, everything wasn't worked out in those few days, but . . ." His eyes went a little foggy, trapped in misty memories. "Sometimes he's just an idiot. I can live with that as long as he can admit it later."

Chills erupted all over Seth, everywhere at once. *Yes, universe, I get it.* "Dude, I need to—"

His phone rang. His grandmother's tone. Shit, he had to answer. But if she had one more chore for him, she was out of luck. "Hi, Grandma?" He threw five bucks on the table and scooted out of the booth, leaving more than half of his beer. "Listen, I'm going to be—"

"Tarkus is here," she interrupted him. "He came scratching at the door, and he's limping, I think he might have a broken hind leg. You need to come home right now. Tell that Wilder boy your grandmother needs you."

He was already waggling his fingers at a strangely unconcerned Lucas and walking away. "I'm leaving now."

Tarkus limping, huh? A wounded animal had never made him so happy. Such an obvious ploy, it had to mean Nate was tired of waiting for him to think, didn't it? *He hasn't given up on me.*

He sent Tarkus because he knows I won't reject the dog.

Which means he's afraid I'm rejecting him.

"Grandma," he began as he ran through the kitchen door thirty seconds later, "he's probably faking it."

Two guilty, startled faces greeted him, both of them hovering over a bowl of doggie treats on the floor. Well, maybe only one guilty face—Tarkus probably couldn't make any faces while he was inhaling Grandma's biscuits like that.

"Really?" He gave her a look. "After he came to the door— obviously injured—you took the time to bake him treats before calling me?"

"What makes you think that?" She straightened and peered down her nose at him (which she had to lift her chin to do).

Seth gestured to the potholder still on her hand.

She yanked her arm behind her back. "He was hurt! He'd limped all the way down here from Nate's, I had to give him sustenance. Show him, Tark." Once she had the dog's attention, she twirled her finger in the air.

Tarkus immediately began to limp around his dish, head lowered, making pathetic eyes from under his doggy lashes. After he'd done a full circuit, he quirked his head questioningly at Grandma.

"Good boy," she gushed, petting him as he started wolfing down treats again.

Uh-huh. "I thought you said it was his hind leg."

Grandma didn't miss a beat. "I was mistaken."

"Oh my God," Seth groaned and hid his face in his hands a second. "This is so *him.*" A move born out of desperation, but as always, with that edge of mischief. Even when he was in pain. "Why didn't he just call and ask me to come over?"

"It's my understanding that you were supposed to tell him when *you* were ready to talk." Grandma sniffed and began straightening up her baking supplies. "Look at the extremes you drove him to. You should have gone to him already."

"I should have," Seth agreed, his heart perking up. Reminiscent of the piñata it became around Nate. "But I needed to . . . think."

Grandma set her mouth and returned his earlier exasperation with interest. "And how did that work for you?"

Gusting a laugh, Seth checked his coat pockets—he hadn't even taken it off after leaving Ma Cougar's—for his keys and wallet. "You," he said, squinting at her as if angry, "are the best grandmother."

"Well." She preened. "I think I know *that.*"

Crossing the kitchen, he pulled her into a brief hug and kissed her cheek. He could swear her skin felt less fragile lately. "I know we have a lot to do on the house, but I need a couple of days, at least—"

"Oh, no." Waving a dismissive hand in the air, she chuckled. "I've already got a buyer. Charley Sykes *is* going to turn it into a bed-and-breakfast. He's already talking to Nate about continuing to 'haunt' it."

Wait. "So, you *have* been giving me busywork?"

"I thought you'd get sick of it and it would speed up the process."

"Honestly, I think if you'd let me mope all alone it would have worked better."

"Next time," Grandma said breezily. "Now, *go*. Get your man." She shooed him all the way to the door, patting his back as he walked out of it.

He was halfway down the driveway path before he heard a dog barking. "Shit."

Grandma had it under control though. When Seth turned to go back, she already had the door open again and was now shooing Tarkus out. The dog came loping over to him, no evidence of any injury. Seth crouched so he could pet Tarkus—he *was* a good boy, wasn't he?—when the dog met him, but Tarkus galloped on past, not stopping until he got to Seth's car. *Smart, too.*

Tarkus barked, urging him on, and Seth broke into a trot, absolutely certain about what he was doing for the first time since he'd left Nate's.

If he wanted to be happy, he knew what he needed to do, and the things he needed to say. Yeah, he should have done this yesterday, or the day before. Then Nate wouldn't have had to mess around with the ruse.

Bet he had fun planning it, though. Or if he hadn't, Grandma definitely had.

"Let's have a little fun ourselves, Tark, should we?" he asked as they were pulling out of the driveway.

Pearl hadn't called him with any kind of heads-up on Seth's reaction, so when car wheels crunched in the gravel of his driveway, he didn't know who'd be there. Hell, without Tarkus's early-warning system, it could be the UPS for all he knew.

Tarkus's demanding yip at the door eliminated that option at least. Nate hobbled to the door, refusing to look out the window in case it wasn't Seth's Civic parked outside. He paused, hand on the doorknob, and took a deep breath. *If I don't look, then there's still a chance it'll be Seth.* Tarkus whined and pawed at the door. *Of course, if I never answer the damn thing, whoever's there might drive off in disgust.*

He eased the door open, and Tarkus wiggled through the gap, then dashed to his bed where he settled himself with the red Frisbee.

"Guess we know *his* priorities." *Seth's voice. Thank God.*

Nate let the door swing all the way open, and there he was. "You're here."

Seth shrugged. "Not like Tark could drive himself. I assumed that was why you sent him over. So . . . can I come in?"

"What? Oh. Sure." *Christ, Albano, get with the program.* "I wasn't sure if you'd bring him home or send him with your grandmother. I . . . ah . . . had contingency plans for both." He gestured to the bar, where he'd lined up the entire contents of his liquor cabinet like a derelict regiment on parade, along with a bucket with champagne on ice.

"Interesting." Seth strolled into the kitchen, hands in the pockets of his jacket. *No touching. Guess I'm not out of the woods yet.*

On the other hand, at least Seth hadn't driven off immediately. Nate closed the door but stayed next to it, to see what Seth would do next. And Seth . . .

Was absolutely still, clearly waiting for Nate to get his head out of his ass and do something romantic or meaningful or at least halfway intelligent. Unfortunately, he couldn't think of a damn thing.

Tarkus, however, leaped up, Frisbee in his jaws, and raced to the back door. Nate sighed and hobbled across the room before disaster struck. He didn't seem to be making any points with Seth so far, but the chances of any kind of romantic interlude were nil if he had to spend the first critical moments up to his elbows in dog pee.

"Why are you limping?" Did Seth sound concerned? *I can always hope.* "I thought Tarkus was the one with the allegedly injured paw. Please tell me you aren't faking it too." He compressed his lips, an expression Nate couldn't get a read on. But maybe that was the point.

Nate's first instinct was to deny it or blow it off—after all, that had made it possible for him to fly under the radar most of his life. But it wasn't as if Seth hadn't seen him at his worst. *Don't hide the pain. Treat it.*

"I kind of broke my toe."

Seth's eyebrows practically met his hairline. "'Kind of'? You either broke it or you didn't."

"Then, yeah. I broke it. I ran into the coffee table leg when I was trying to answer the phone."

"Must have been an important call if you were willing to risk maiming yourself for it."

"It wasn't." Nate dropped his gaze, opening the door for Tarkus. "But I thought it might be. I thought it might be you."

"Huh."

Outside, Tarkus had finished watering the bushes and was flinging the Frisbee up in the air. Naturally, on the second fling, it landed on the cabin roof, so he whined and launched into full hurt-puppy mode. Nate sighed. "I guess if I have to choke down some humble pie, I'd better get that or we'll never have a chance to talk." He glanced over his shoulder. Seth wasn't looking at him—he was studying the array of liquor bottles. "You do want to do that, right? Talk?"

"Yeah." He sighed. "It's why I'm here. Take your time."

Come on, Seth, give me something. I'm dying here. But his attention remained focused on the booze.

Nate closed the French doors behind him. Luckily, he'd had vast experience with Tarkus's Frisbee solitaire, so he retrieved the long-handled rake from the side of the cabin and dragged the Frisbee off the roof. Tarkus caught it before it hit the ground.

"No more of that. Come back inside now and I'll get you some chicken jerky." Tarkus trotted over, and Nate ran his fingers down the dog's spine until he wriggled in ecstasy. "Good boy. You deserve a special Rin Tin Tin medal for your performance today, but do you suppose you could give me a break now? I need to do a little tap-dancing if I want to keep Seth around, and that's not easy with a broken toe." *Or a broken heart.* "You want to keep Seth around, don't you?" Tarkus wagged his tail. "I'll take that as a yes."

He opened the door and followed Tarkus inside, but stalled, belly hollowing, when he saw Seth was pouring something into a highball glass. *He didn't pick the champagne. He's cutting me loose.*

Seth garnished the edge of the glass with a lemon round. "Don't stand there gawking. Get over here and take what's coming to you."

Nate paced across the room, slowly enough that his limp wasn't visible—much. The drink on the bar was layered—with a deep-orange bottom fading to cloudy pale at the top. Two bottles sat in front of Seth—the orange-flavored vodka and the Aperol.

"I thought you'd never seen Aperol before."

"I looked it up." He nudged the glass. "Come on. Try it."

Nate picked up the glass and peered at the swirling orange liquid. "What is this?"

"A Humble Pie." Then he grinned, and Nate's heart turned over in his chest, relief and hope clashing together inside him.

"Does . . . does that mean you're ready to listen to my apology?"

"*First* I have something to say to you. I want to work things out, Nate." He picked up the cap from the Aperol, then set it down and wiped his palms on his jeans. "But we can't unless you can promise me something. You have to accept me how I am, even if I'm a bartender forever."

"Seth, I'm so, so sorry. I—"

"Unh." He flung up a hand. "We're going to play a drinking game. Every time you want to tell me how sorry you are, or beg my forgiveness, or ask a question, you have to take a drink first. And maybe afterward too. Beginning now."

Nate blew out a breath. This glass wasn't that tall, but knowing Seth's skills, it could be lethal. How fast could he down this thing? He raised it to his lips, intending to chug it, but the first sip made him change his mind and savor it instead. He closed his eyes and took another sip, then a flat-out gulp. "It's like a high-octane Italian soda. It's delicious." He opened his eyes and gazed at Seth. "But shouldn't humble pie taste bitter?"

Seth waggled his palm back and forth. "Depends on how sincere you are, I reckon. The bartender's guide doesn't list an equivalent ingredient for regret." As he leaned forward and propped his forearms on the bar, batting the Aperol cap between his hands, Nate realized he'd taken off his jacket. *At least he's not planning to walk out immediately.* "Keep going. I love watching your face when you eat and drink."

Well, in that case . . . Keeping his gaze locked with Seth's, Nate took a sip. "I hope that means you'll be dining here with me."

"Of course I will." He made a shooing motion with his hands. "Two drinks this time—one because that was technically a question even if you didn't phrase it like one, and a penalty shot for trying to cheat."

Nate complied, uncertain whether the way his head was spinning was from the liquor or because the mischievous glint in Seth's eyes gave him hope. "You're enjoying this, aren't you?"

Seth drummed his fingers on the counter and raised an eyebrow. "Another question. Another drink."

Nate took a gulp this time, for courage. *Showtime.* Heart beating like a metronome, he extended his hand across the counter, palm up. Seth studied it, head tilted, but didn't take it. *Damn it.* "I'm so, so sorry for making it sound like I don't value you just as you are. That you need to do or be anything but what makes you happy. You're good at so many things—"

"Hold it right there." He nodded at the glass, and Nate quickly took another sip. "Say one word about my potential and I swear I'll—"

"No. God no. I've learned my lesson about that." He held up the glass in an air toast, then took a swig.

"All right, then." Seth laid his hand in Nate's. *Thank God.*

With their fingers interlaced—*touch, finally*—Nate tried to keep the desperation out of his tone. "Forget the P-word—you've already got a whole résumé of skills: boating, construction, bartending, *logging*, for Chrissake—"

"We're not going back to that whole tree-climbing thing again, are we?"

Nate smiled and tightened his grip. "Well, that was pretty impressive. And I believe that was a question, sir." He held out the glass. "Seems only fair that you pay the price."

Seth smirked, but took a tiny sip before handing it back, his fingers brushing Nate's. "You better make your point soon, because you're nearly done and I'm not making you another."

"My point is this: what bonehead would ever imagine all of that wasn't enough—that you'd need to do more? To *be* more?" He drank, ice chinking in the glass as he got near the dregs.

"So you admit you were wrong?" Seth let go of Nate's hand, but circled the bar to stand next to him. "You have one more tiny sip, then you can speak freely."

Nate put as much *intent* into that last swallow as he could, and by the time he was finished, Seth's pupils were huge and he'd leaned forward into near-kissing distance.

But Nate wasn't done with his confessions. "I meant it when I said that I'm in this for the long haul. I love you." Seth's eyes widened, his lips parting on a soundless *oh*. "Yeah, kinda forgot to mention that before, didn't I? But yes, I love you—you, whose anchors are all right here in Bluewater Bay."

"I love you too." Seth's voice was rough, as if his throat was tight. "And *damn*. We are *never* going out to dinner—or breakfast, lunch, or high fucking tea—because I don't want anyone else to see how hot you are when you eat."

"And once the show's canceled and I don't have a local job anymore? You've got a shitload of transferrable skills, but mine are pretty specialized. When it comes right down to it, *I'm* the one with the employment liability in this partnership."

"'Partnership'?" Seth's voice rose on the last syllable.

"Absolutely." He stood up and held out his arms, letting Seth decide when—*please when, not if*—to take the final step. "That is, if you'll have me."

Have him? Hell yeah, he would. And he should tell Nate immediately because he'd made the guy suffer a little too long. He hadn't been able to resist, though, once he'd seen the lost-puppy look on Nate's face as he'd opened the door. Like Tarkus knowing he'd done wrong and hoping you'd forgive him with a minimum of punishment.

"I'll have you." His voice thickened so much he barely got it out. Finally he pressed himself against Nate, completely in his arms, his heartbeat thundering. Partly at being this close to him again—yes, they needed to talk but he'd *missed* him. Physically—but also because he *believed* him. Nate truly wanted him the way he was. *Just a couple more items on the agenda.* "But I have to tell you a few things, first. And maybe make some demands."

Nate reared back, but he was careful not to pull out of Seth's hold, or even loosen his own embrace. "Demands? You mean this is *conditional?*" His voice almost cracked on that one, and Seth had to lower his chin to keep from smiling right in Nate's distressed face.

Once he could look serious again, he met his gaze. "Nothing too crazy, I promise." Nate kind of needed a trim, but that meant Seth could work his fingers into the waves of his hair, playing with it. "You already met one, and you didn't even know it."

"I did? What was that?" Nate's arms tightened around him, and he tilted his head forward, in that exact way he did when he was about to kiss him. Or wanted to be kissed.

To keep from jumping the gun, Seth slid his fingers over Nate's lips. "You admitted you were an idiot."

"That was easy," he murmured. Then he kissed the tips of Seth's fingers. "What else?"

He had such a beautiful mouth. Seth got so wrapped up in tracing the outline of it that he nearly forgot to answer. "Oh, um, you know you're a fixer, right? You fix things—"

"Yes." Nate cast his eyes heavenward, but they were sincere when they came back to meet Seth's. "You're not the first person to tell me that. In fact, you're not the first person in the last twelve hours. I'll ch—"

Seth pinched Nate's lips shut. "No. You can't change. Like, you can be a fixer, but if I tell you I don't want it fixed, you leave it. That's the owning-up-to-being-an-idiot part. But don't change. You're a *good* fixer, Nate, you fix things because you love people. But— Hey did I tell you my parents are getting divorced?"

"This is important *now*?" Nate's eyes nearly came out of their sockets.

"Sorry." God Nate was fun to tease, but Seth needed to focus. Make sure Nate understood what he was asking, here. "My dad and I talked a lot about it, we went out on the boat together, and he told me that when he married Mom, he thought she'd change. Mellow out. But people don't do that—they don't change, even for the people they love." According to every romantic comedy ever, as well as his dad. "I'll do the same, I promise." He dropped his hands from Nate's face and slid them around his body, bringing Nate's hard chest tight against his.

"You won't change, or you'll own up to being an idiot?"

"Both, probably." Pulling back without letting go, he forced Nate to come with him. Jockeying him toward the couch. Seth couldn't look where they were going—he was too busy watching Nate's face. It was true he loved watching him eat or drink something he enjoyed, but this was better. Watching Nate's face change as he listened to Seth. As he watched him. "One more thing, then we're done."

"Just one? Nothing else in your famous list of demands?" It was a good sign that Nate had relaxed enough to tease.

"Yeah, then you can kiss me." Before he realized what he was doing, he pulled his lower lip into his mouth and then let it slide out from under his teeth. "Or I could kiss you."

Nate swallowed, and his hands tightened on Seth's back. "Still waiting for that last condition."

Oh, yeah. That. He was having a hard time drawing enough breath to speak, either because Nate's hold was that tight or his heart was doing that thing, swelling up, and his lungs were getting crowded out.

"Don't make me wait anymore, Seth. Please," Nate whispered. His gaze flicked over Seth's shoulder, where the couch was. At least he hoped it was there, or they were about to land on the floor.

"About that thing you said the other morning, the good-time guy graffiti thing—"

"I really was trying to protect you. I don't care about your past."

"I know, I figured out it's maybe more my issue." At the confused scrunching of Nate's brow, Seth went on. "Okay, definitely more my issue. I'm sorry. I just, I was scared that you didn't really believe me when I said I was committed, because I've never been in a serious relationship. When that came up, I freaked out because I was so worried you didn't believe that you're the *only* guy I want to be with. Like . . ." Staring up into Nate's eyes, he swallowed, his throat so dry it clicked. "I don't ever want to be with anyone else."

Nate clasped Seth's wrist. "You don't? Ever?"

"Never." *Can we start the kissing now?* No, because he wasn't done. He couldn't stop himself from staring at Nate's lips, though. "So, can you forgive me?" he whispered, yanking his gaze up to meet Nate's. "For getting mad at you for trying to protect me?"

"I forgive you," Nate said immediately. "Even without a drinking game."

Thank God, the kissing could start. Seth tried to pull him down on the couch, but Nate resisted. "But I have demands too."

Seth's frustration over the lack of immediate lip lock must have been obvious, because Nate cupped his jaw and kissed him. Just lips, though, not enough to do anything other than make Seth ache for more.

"They had better be important demands," he warned. That wasn't really fair, though—he'd made Nate wait.

"They are. Both of them."

"Just two, huh? Seems reasonable. Let's hear them."

"Yeah. First, I need you to promise to give me the benefit of the doubt. I can't worry that you'll walk out on me because I suggest you might like to try something different—not because I think you need to improve yourself, but because I think you'll *like* it. Your curiosity was what attracted me to you in the first place. Don't make me afraid to spark it again."

Seth nodded, keeping his face somber. "I'll give you the benefit of the doubt, I promise. It's hand in hand with the protecting-me thing—you just want me to be happy. Is that the other demand? Wanna make me *happy*?" Forget avoiding the innuendoes, this was a perfect time for them. He let his hands creep south, looking for the waistband of Nate's jeans.

"In a minute. One more thing." Hands still cradling Seth's face, Nate traced Seth's lips with his thumbs. "Move in here with me."

He froze, letting the words sink in. He'd figured that was what Nate was getting at, but he wasn't prepared to actually hear the words.

Then he couldn't respond around the giant lump in his throat.

"When your grandmother sells the house, you'll have to go somewhere, right? Come here. You can have the second bedroom, if you, you know, need your space. But what I need—" he kissed Seth softly "—is you."

"I want you too," he croaked. Then they fell on the couch together, Seth unsure exactly who'd started them moving, but it was fine. Exactly what he wanted. And he wanted this too: Nate kissing him and pulling his shirt off while he teased under the waistband of Nate's jeans.

What he didn't want was Nate pulling away, breathless, to ask, "Is that a yes?"

"Of course it's a yes!" Jesus, how could that mean no? *He needs to hear it. I need to say it.* "Yes." He traced the line of Nate's cheekbone with his fingertips. "I'll live with you. Here and wherever else we end up."

A wicked grin spread across Nate's face. "Perfect. I have it on good authority that my liquor cabinet is pathetic. Who better than a professional bartender to save me from the endless shame?"

Seth laughed. "When you put it like that, it's a no-brainer." *No more teasing, though.* Cupping the back of Nate's skull, he pulled him closer to start on all the kisses he'd missed out on in the last two days. Plus the other stuff.

Just before Nate's lips touched his, he said, "Do I know how to show a guy a good time or what?"

Starruck
L.A. Witt

There's Something About Ari
L.B. Gregg

Hell on Wheels
Z.A. Maxfield

Lone Wolf
*Aleksandr Voinov and
L.A. Witt*

The Burnt Toast B&B
*Heidi Belleau and
Rachel Haimowitz*

Wedding Favors
Anne Tenino

The Deep of the Sound
Amy Lane

When to Hold Them
G.B. Gordon

Rain Shadow
L.A. Witt

Stuck Landing
Lauren Gallagher

How the Cookie Crumbles
Jaime Samms

Selfie
Amy Lane

All the Wrong Places
Ann Gallagher

Bluewater Blues
G.B. Gordon

No Small Parts
Ally Blue

Lights, Camera, Cupid!
*Valentine's Day collection, featuring: SE Jakes, Amy Lane,
Z.A. Maxfield, Anne Tenino, and L.A. Witt*

Dear Reader,

Thank you for reading Anne Tenino and E.J. Russell's *For a Good Time, Call . . .*!

We know your time is precious and you have many, many entertainment options, so it means a lot that you've chosen to spend your time reading. We really hope you enjoyed it.

We'd be honored if you'd consider posting a review—good or bad—on sites like **Amazon, Barnes & Noble, Kobo, Goodreads, Twitter, Facebook, Tumblr,** and your blog or website. We'd also be honored if you told your friends and family about this book. Word of mouth is a book's lifeblood!

For more information on upcoming releases, author interviews, blog tours, contests, giveaways, and more, please sign up for our weekly, spam-free newsletter and visit us around the web:

Newsletter: tinyurl.com/RiptideSignup
Twitter: twitter.com/RiptideBooks
Facebook: facebook.com/RiptidePublishing
Goodreads: tinyurl.com/RiptideOnGoodreads
Tumblr: riptidepublishing.tumblr.com

Thank you so much for Reading the Rainbow!

RiptidePublishing.com

Big thanks to the wonderful team at Riptide, including Sarah Lyons, Rachel Haimowitz, Alex Whitehall, L.C. Chase, Amelia Vaughn, and our fantabulous editor, May Peterson.

From E.J.:
Thank you, Anne, for inviting me to collaborate on this book and giving me a chance to be a part of the Bluewater Bay universe—even though your first response when I told you "Nate is ace" was "WTF?" Thanks to the other Bluewater Bay authors for creating characters that are such a hoot to riff off of. Also, my endless gratitude to C. Morgan Kennedy for lending me her name (and her hugs) for this story.

From Anne:
Special thanks go to E.J. for writing this with me, even when I was horribly slow. I'm also grateful for help from the real Adeline, and my bartender-on-call, Margaret Kranz (and Baby Kranz, who didn't know much about bartending, but was present and totally worth mentioning). I'll echo E.J.'s thanks to C. Morgan Kennedy, who's not only useful for naming characters after, but also makes a great friend and sounding board. Shannon Conley deserves a shout-out for legal information and just being generally fantastic.

Last, but certainly not least, I want to thank my crazy aunt for teaching me so much in such a short time about trusts, inheritance laws, the degrees of relationship between distant cousins, and, most of all, what constitutes C work.

Task Force Iota
18% Gray

Theta Alpha Gamma
Frat Boy and Toppy
Love, Hypothetically
Sweet Young Thang
Good Boy
Poster Boy

Romancelandia
Too Stupid to Live
Billionaire with Benefits

Helping Hand (in the Bluewater Bay *Lights, Camera, Cupid!*
anthology)
Wedding Favors (a Bluewater Bay novel)

Horny (in the *My Haunted Blender's Gay Love Affair* anthology)

Legend Tripping
Stumptown Spirits
Wolf's Clothing

Geeklandia
Lost in Geeklandia
Clickbait

Northern Light

Sun, Moon, and Stars (in *Magic and Mayhem: Fiction and Essays Celebrating LGBTQA Romance*)

Catalyzed by her discovery of LGBTQ romance, Anne Tenino left the lucrative fields of art history, nonprofit fundraising, and domestic engineering (in that order) to follow her dream of become a starving romance author. For good or ill, her snarky, silly, quasi-British sense of humor came along for the ride.

Anne applies her particular blend of romance, comedy, and gay protagonists to contemporary, sci-fi, and paranormal tales. Her works have won many awards; her novel, *Frat Boy and Toppy*, is frequently referred to as a gay romance classic; she's been featured in *RT Book Reviews* magazine; she holds the position of VP of Programming at her local RWA chapter; and she's achieved bestseller status on Amazon's gay romance list.

Born and raised in Oregon, Anne now lives in Portland with her family, who have all taken a sacred oath never to read her books. When not crocheting genitalia, growing tomatoes, driving teenagers around, or cooking something obscure, she can be found at her computer, procrastinating. Possibly while also lying on the couch, eating bon-bons.

Find her at:

Twitter: twitter.com/AnneTenino
G+: plus.google.com/u/0/115349772749167236252
Facebook: facebook.com/anne.tenino
Amazon: amazon.com/Anne-Tenino/e/B005FQZOHS
Goodreads: goodreads.com/annetenino

E.J. Russell holds a BA and an MFA in theater, so naturally she's spent the last three decades as a financial manager, database designer, and business intelligence consultant. Several years ago, she realized Darling Sons A and B would be heading off to college soon and she'd no longer need to spend half her waking hours ferrying them to dance class.

What to do with all that free time?

A lucky encounter with Jim Butcher's craft blog posts caused her to revisit her childhood dream of writing fiction, and now she wonders why she ever thought an empty nest meant leisure.

Her daily commute consists of walking from one side of her office to the other, from left-brain day job to right-brain writer's cave, where she's learned to type with a dog attached to her hip and a cat draped across her wrists.

E.J. is married to Curmudgeonly Husband, a man who cares even less about sports than she does. Luckily, C.H. also loves to cook, or all three of their children (Lovely Daughter and Darling Sons A and B) would have survived on nothing but Cheerios, beef jerky, and satsuma mandarins (the extent of E.J.'s culinary skill set).

E.J. lives in rural Oregon, enjoys visits from her wonderful adult children, and indulges in good books, red wine, and the occasional hyperbole.

Sign up for E.J.'s newsletter at ejrussell.com/newsletter or find her online at ejrussell.com, on Facebook at facebook.com/E.J.Russell. author, on Twitter at twitter.com/ej_russell, and on Goodreads at goodreads.com/ej_russell.

Enjoy more stories like
For a Good Time, Call...
at RiptidePublishing.com!

All the Wrong Places
ISBN: 978-1-62649-420-6

Blank Spaces
ISBN: 978-1-62649-484-8

Earn Bonus Bucks!

Earn 1 Bonus Buck for each dollar you spend. Find out how at
RiptidePublishing.com/news/bonus-bucks.

Win Free Ebooks for a Year!

Pre-order coming soon titles directly through our site and you'll
receive one entry into a drawing for a chance to win free books for
a year! Get the details at RiptidePublishing.com/contests.

www.ingramcontent.com/pod-product-compliance
Lightning Source LLC
Chambersburg PA
CBHW030644020726
47493CB00006B/1859